②9/98

The Roads from Bethlehem

Topographical map of Jerusalem (detail). (Eighteenth-century British)

The Roads from Bethlehem

*Christmas Literature from Writers
Ancient and Modern*

Pegram Johnson III
Edna M. Troiano
Editors

Westminster/John Knox Press
Louisville, Kentucky

Unless otherwise noted, scripture quotations are from the King James Version of the Bible.

Acknowledgment of copyrighted material is made on pp. xiii and xiv.

Book design by Drew Stevens

Cover art: *The Journey of the Magi* by Sassetta (Stefano di Giovanni), Italian (Sienese), active by 1423, d. 1450. Tempera and gold on wood. Courtesy of Superstock.

First edition

Published by Westminster/John Knox Press
Louisville, Kentucky

This book is printed on acid-free paper that meets the American National Standards Institute Z39.48 standard. ∞

PRINTED IN THE UNITED STATES OF AMERICA
9 8 7 6 5 4 3 2 1

Library of Congress Cataloging-in-Publication Data

The Roads from Bethlehem : Christmas literature from writers ancient
    and modern / edited by Pegram Johnson III and Edna M. Troiano.
            p.   cm.
        ISBN 0–664–22030–4

        1. Christmas—Literary collections.   I. Johnson, Pegram.
II. Troiano, Edna M.
PN6071.C6R58   1993
808.8'033—dc20   93-18699

Contents

v

Chapter 2 *The Middle Ages:*
From Liturgy to Literature

Chapter 4   *The Eighteenth and Nineteenth Centuries:*
The Age of Sentiment

Chapter 5   *The Twentieth Century:*
The Age of Anxiety

Index of Authors and Titles   *317*

Illustrations

Contemporary Holy Family, Sudanese, 1992. Courtesy of the Rev. Sylvester Thomas Kambaya of the Sudan. Photograph by Mark Borchelt.

Flight into Egypt by Lu Hung-Nien. Twentieth-century Chinese. Reprinted from *Each with His Own Brush: Contemporary Christian Art in Asia and Africa*, Daniel Johnson Fleming, copyright © 1938 by Friendship Press. Used by permission of Friendship Press. Photograph by Mark Borchelt.

Icon of the Theotokos: Virgin and Child. Seventeenth-century Russian. From the private collection of the Rev. Vienna Cobb Anderson. Photograph by Mark Borchelt.

The Nativity by Gustave Doré. Originally published in *Die Heilige Schrift Alten und Neuen Testaments verdeutscht von D. Martin Luther. Mit zweihundert und dreissig Bildern von Gustav Doré*, published in two volumes by Deutsche Verlags-Anstalt, in Stuttgart, Leipzig, Berlin, Vienna, about 1875.

Retablos of the Archangel San Raphael, Hispanic, circa 1920. From the private collection of the Rev. Pegram Johnson III. Photograph by John Kopp, Persimmon Bay Studio.

Topographical Map of Jerusalem (detail). Eighteenth-century British. From the private collection of the Rev. Pegram Johnson III. Photograph by John Kopp, Persimmon Bay Studio. (Frontispiece.)

World's Sunday Magazine, 1896. Facsimile version in the Virginia Historical Society Collections. Used by permission of the Virginia Historical Society. Photograph by Mark Borchelt.

Acknowledgments

"Anglo-Saxon Homily on Christmas," Aelfric of Cerne. Reprinted from *A Lectionary of Christian Prose from the 2nd to the 20th Century*, compiled by the Rev. A. C. Bouquet, copyright © 1939 by Longmans, Green, & Co. Used by permission of Random House/Alfred A. Knopf.

"Annunciation to Mary" reprinted from *Translations from the Poetry of Rainer Maria Rilke* by M. D. Herter Norton, by permission of W. W. Norton & Company, Inc. Copyright 1938 by W. W. Norton & Company, Inc. Copyright renewed 1966 by M. D. Herter Norton.

"Barrington Bunny," Martin Bell. Reprinted from *The Way of the Wolf* by Martin Bell, copyright © 1968, 1969, 1970 by Martin Bell. Used by permission of HarperCollins Publishers.

"Birth of Christ" reprinted from *Translations from the Poetry of Rainer Maria Rilke* by M. D. Herter Norton, by permission of W. W. Norton & Company, Inc. Copyright 1938 by W. W. Norton & Company, Inc. Copyright renewed 1966 by M. D. Herter Norton.

"The Blessed Virgin Mary," Jacopone da Todi. Reprinted from *Jacopone da Todi: The Lauds*, translated by Serge and Elizabeth Hughes, copyright © 1982 by The Missionary Society of St. Paul the Apostle in the State of New York. Used by permission of Paulist Press.

"Christ Climbed Down," by Lawrence Ferlinghetti: *A Coney Island of the Mind*. Copyright © 1958 by Lawrence Ferlinghetti. Reprinted by permission of New Directions Publishing Corporation.

"A Christmas Carol," ("The Christ-child lay on Mary's lap"), Gilbert Keith Chesterton. Reprinted from *The Collected Poems of G. K. Chesterton*, Methuen London. Used by permission of the Octopus Publishing Group Library.

"A Christmas Carol," ("God rest you merry gentlemen"), Gilbert Keith Chesterton. Reprinted from *The Collected Poems of G. K. Chesterton*, Methuen London. Used by permission of the Octopus Publishing Group Library.

"Christmas at Cold Comfort Farm," Stella Gibbons. Reprinted from *Christmas at Cold Comfort Farm and Other Stories*, copyright © 1940 by Stella Gibbons, published by Longman 1940. Used by permission of Curtis Brown Ltd., London.

"The Christmas Decorations," E. V. Lucas. Reprinted from *Character and Comedy* by E. V. Lucas. Published by Methuen London. Used by permission of the Octopus Publishing Group Library.

"Christmas 1924" reprinted with permission of Macmillan Publishing Company from *The Complete Poems of Thomas Hardy*, edited by James Gibson. Copyright 1928 by Florence E. Hardy and Sydney E. Cockerell, renewed 1956 by Lloyds Bank Ltd.

"Christmas 1945," James Agee. Reprinted from *The Collected Poems of James Agee*, copyright © 1969 by Yale University Press. Used by permission of Mary Newman, Trustee, James Agee Trust.

"Christmas Sermon," Adam of Dryburgh. Reprinted from *Analecta Cartusiana*, edited by Dr. James Hogg, as it appeared in *Adam of Dryburgh: Six Christmas Sermons*, pp. 197–198. Translated by M. J. Hamilton, copyright © 1974. Used by permission of the *Institut für Englische Sprache und Literatur*.

Fair and Tender Ladies, Lee Smith, pp. 25–31, copyright © 1988 by Lee Smith. Used by permission of the Putnam Publishing Group.

"Hostis Herodes impie," Sedulius. Reprinted from *The Hymn Book of the Anglican Church of Canada and the United Church of Canada*. Used by permission of the Anglican Book Center.

Preface

In a folktale from the Lowlands of Scotland entitled "The Yule Beggar," a young lad meets a beggar late on Christmas Eve. Unbeknownst to the boy, the beggar is really St. Ninian, called St. Ringan in the Lowlands, who according to local tradition returns to Kirkcudbrightshire every Christmas Eve to do a good deed. After the saint has helped the boy, he is offered a fireside for the evening:

"Thank you, laddie," the beggar replied. "It's a kind offer. But I must be on my way, or I'll be late."

"Late?" exclaimed the boy. "But where are you going at this time of night? It's nearly midnight."

"Where? Why, Bethlehem, of course! Where else would I be on Christmas night?"

On Christmas night all roads lead to Bethlehem. Those who cannot travel there physically can still travel there in their mind's eye and then back again to their own times and places with a new appreciation of the greatest story ever told. The human yearning for Bethlehem is expressed perceptively by the Japanese novelist Shusaku Endo in *A Life of Jesus*, when he explains that Bethlehem is revered in the human heart as "the purest and the most innocent place on God's earth."

At Christmas, Jesus himself is mystically experienced by the believers who in their minds and hearts go to Bethlehem to hear the original sacred story of a divine/human encounter. In the famous service of Lessons and Carols for Christmas presented each year at King's College, Cambridge, Christians are entreated to make this mystical journey:

> Beloved in Christ, in this Christmastide, let it be our care and delight to hear again the message of the angels, and in heart and mind to go even unto Bethlehem, and see this thing which is come to pass, and the babe lying in a manger.

This collection of Christmas literature is a selection of some of the best writings by authors of excellence from all times and places who in varying ways have been inspired by the Nativity. After reading the biblical prophecies, the reader will savor the original accounts of Jesus' birth and then travel some of the many roads along which the story has been taken for almost two thousand years. The roads from Bethlehem have led in many directions, to such far-flung places as China, Syria, Egypt, France, Spain, England, Mexico, Canada, and the United States. The universality of the story is further revealed in the accompanying artworks from the Far East, the Sudan, Russia, Hispanic America, and England. In following the roads from Bethlehem, the reader will witness both the impact of the story on diverse cultures and the reciprocal cultural adaptation of the story to new times and places.

The literary responses to the events of the Nativity—from the Annunciation to the coming of the Wise Men—have been arranged into chapters in a roughly chronological order. Within each chapter the works are divided into literary genres—liturgy, sermon or treatise, drama, fiction, poetry. Many of the earlier English works have been rendered into more accessible modern language by the editors. Several works in Latin, French, Spanish, and Arabic are presented here in previously unpublished translations.

We want to thank the following, who have rendered special service in the preparation of this anthology:

—The College of Preachers for Dr. Johnson's 1990 fellowship, especially Erica Wood, Director of Studies, and Linda Thomas, librarian

—Staff of the Virginia Theological Seminary, especially Richard Reid, dean; the staff of the Bishop Payne Library; Reginald H. Fuller, professor emeritus, who made invaluable corrections of the first draft; Raymond F. Glover, musicologist

—Vestry and Wardens of Christ Church, Accokeek, Maryland, who did not begrudge the time spent by their rector on this project

—Colleagues at Charles County Community College, especially Dean Josephine Williams, who offered continual encouragement; Martha Oberle, who offered her expertise in rendering medieval English into modern form

—Woodstock Library and the Society of Jesus, Georgetown University

—Translators who offered fresh renderings into English for this anthology: Elisa D'Avanzo and Jose Quesada-Embid for their translation of "Riu, riu, chiu" from Spanish; the Rev. Robert R. Smith for his translation of Coptic liturgy from Arabic; Vilma Smith for her translations of Sor Juana's poetry from Spanish; Peter Troiano for his translations of "Prose of the Ass," "*Officium Pastorum*," and "Sleep, my son, sleep!" from Latin

—Families and friends, especially Belva, Danielle, Julie, Leo, Matthew, Mildred, and Pete, for enduring Christmas literature all year round while the manuscript was in preparation

—Photographers of artwork: John Kopp of Persimmon Bay Studio; Mark Borchelt of Mark Borchelt, Photographer

—Those who lent art to be photographed: the Rev. Vienna Cobb Anderson of Washington; the Rev. Sylvester Thomas Kambaya of the Sudan; the Manuscripts Division of the Virginia Historical Society

—Our editor, Harold Twiss, for his invaluable advice and support.

Chapter 1

Scripture and
Early Traditions

Introduction

"In the beginning was the Word." From the beginning, the Christian proclamation involved finding the right words, the right verbal images, to express an experience. In the first millennium of the Christian era, writers expressed emerging Christian beliefs through a variety of literary genres: historical and miraculous narratives, letters, creeds, diatribes, poems, hymns. Some of the prose and poetry was sufficiently held in reverence as to be canonized by the early church and added to the Hebrew Scriptures; other writings that circulated freely retold the Nativity story in more elaborate form, spread or debated doctrine, or provided new hymns for public worship, in the tradition of the Hebrew psalms. These varied writings were often considered of great interest, but were not considered to be as inspired as those that came to be known as the New Testament.

The clear-cut literary genres of modern literature were more fluid in form in earlier centuries; for example, Luke's Gospel incorporates poetry with prose in ways difficult to separate into distinct modes. The Chinese Nestorian monument's inscription from the eighth century is at the same time history, creed, and poetry. Although genre distinctions of early literature are admittedly arbitrary, four general classifications can be constructed: canonical narratives, noncanonical narratives, miscellaneous prose (letters, meditations, debates), and lyrics (hymns).

In a sense, the Nativity story begins even earlier than the Gospels, for Christians from the beginning have understood portions of the ancient Hebrew Scriptures as foreshadowing Jesus' birth and confirming who they believe him to be. In this understanding, the prophecies point to the long-expected savior, who is identified with Jesus of Nazareth.

The way in which the early Christians adapted previously written texts for their own purposes can be seen in the following highly imagistic lines:

For while all things were in quiet silence,
And that night was in the midst of her swift course,
Thine Almighty word leaped down from heaven
  out of thy royal throne.
       (The Wisdom of Solomon, 18:14–15)

These isolated lines, probably used in Nativity celebrations as early as the fourth century, seem to evoke a touching picture of the night of Christ's birth. However, when read in its entirety, the original passage clearly refers not to the Nativity, but to the slaying of the first-born in Egypt, commemorated in the Passover. Even so, when read in the context of a Nativity celebration, the words resonate with new meaning, just as psalms in contemporary recitation may resonate with a meaning far different from that of their original utterance.

The most familiar Nativity stories are obviously those found in the Gospels. Christianity, like its sister religion, Judaism, has been marked by the dominance of auditory rather than visual images. The gospel was first of all something to be heard. Christianity found its origins in the telling and retelling of a story. The birth narratives of Matthew and Luke still have the power to move, whether read in solitude at fireside on a wintry evening or heard solemnly chanted at a communal midnight Christmas Eve celebration.

Matthew's birth narrative suggests the worldwide significance of the Nativity by telling of the travelers from afar who follow a new star to Bethlehem. An element of conflict quickly emerges with the intrusion of Herod into the sacred story, a reminder to the early believers immersed in a rapidly changing world order of the evil forces without and personal doubt within. In Luke's Gospel, the angelic messenger initiates the birth story, setting a mood of awe and wonder. Luke's elevated prose is subtly transformed into poetry, as is evident especially in the canticles of Mary, Zacharias, and Simeon.

The ancient world's literature made place for the esoteric, even the bizarre, as exemplified in the last book of the Christian Scriptures, The Revelation of St. John the Divine. Though not commonly read as a part of the Nativity story, the twelfth chapter of Revelation contains an archetypal narrative of a divine birth that may both illuminate and be illuminated by the Gospel birth narratives.

The writings of early Christians not included in the New Testament represent a wide spectrum, offering embellishment and simplification, discontinuity and continuity, obfuscation and clarification. Two nonbiblical narratives are included in this chapter, *The Protevangelium of James* and *The Arabic Gospel of the Infancy of the Saviour.* Both are highly imaginative, detailed accounts, stories that inevitably invite comparison with their sparer biblical counterparts. In the two selections the Nativity story is retold, each retelling taking on the coloration of its geographical and cultural context.

As Christianity developed and spread, the stories of and reflections on Jesus' birth also appeared in other prose forms. For example, in the second century, Ignatius spread doctrinal formulation in his polished, highly literary letters, and Tertullian wrote satiric diatribes against interpretations and beliefs he deemed unacceptable. In the fourth century, the "Rhythms" of St. Ephrem the Syrian reflected an ecstatically imaginative mind, a mind appreciatively rediscovered in our own time. And in the eighth century in China, a unique inscription on a monument revealed the early diffusion of Christianity to "the uttermost part of the earth" (Acts 1:8).

Although much of this early literature will be new to many readers, some of the hymns may be familiar because they are still being sung today. Many of the earliest Christian lyrics are thought to have arisen in a context of doctrinal conflict and typically represent what has been referred to as creedal liturgical hymnody, liturgical hymns that attempt to clarify Christian belief. The New Testament includes fragments of creedal liturgical hymns, such as the following lines from First Timothy (3:16):

> And without controversy great is the mystery of godliness:
> God was manifest in the flesh,
> justified in the Spirit,
> seen of angels,
> preached unto the Gentiles,
> believed on in the world,
> received up into glory.

Chants and songs were the means by which ordinary Christians expressed their faith long before the Holy Scriptures themselves were readily available for study and meditation in written form. The representative works of the early Christian hymn writers may be described as devotional, liturgical, and evangelical, repeating the basic Christian story in verse form for both personal and community use. Though there is undoubtedly truth to the statement that these early lyrics are more reflective of doctrine in formation than evocative of the tender human scene at Bethlehem often portrayed by later writers, this judgment need not denigrate the work of the early hymnodists, who had their own purposes in mind.

By the late eighth century, when the latest work in this chapter was written, the roads from Bethlehem had spread in many directions, and the birth of Christ had found literary expression in cultures as diverse as Syria, Ireland, Spain, and China. The Chinese text is especially interesting in that not only is the Christian gospel proclaimed in the radically different context of China's Middle Kingdom, but it is also in a form, Nestorianism, that was itself outside of what came to be the Christian mainstream. What makes the Chinese text not only interesting, but, indeed, remarkable, is the degree to which it succeeds in leaping a great wall of culture, custom, and language, and presenting a truly indigenous gospel—neither Hebrew, nor Greek, nor Latin, but Chinese.

Old Testament Prophecies

FROM THE BEGINNING, Christians interpreted the Hebrew Scriptures in the light of their own religious experience. The early Christians were less concerned with the original intentions of the writings than with finding evidence pointing toward Jesus' birth and divinity. Correlations between passages in the Hebrew Scriptures and Jesus' birth were read as more than coincidental and were seen as part of the eternal and mysterious purposes of God.

A virgin conceiving and bearing a son—Immanuel, "God with us" (Isa. 7:14–15)—was readily appropriated by the earliest Christians as a prefiguring of Mary's giving birth to Jesus. The description of the peaceable kingdom (Isa. 11:1–6, 10) led by a little child, an offspring of the family of Jesse, is often read as prophetic of Jesus' mission. This universal peace, as seemingly prophesied by Isaiah, became an integral part of the Nativity tradition. Isaiah's dramatic description of the inauguration of a golden age

The Nativity. Gustave Doré (1832–1883). Wood engraving.

(Isa. 40:1–11) in which the Lord shall reign as a good shepherd, having triumphed over every human iniquity, is frequently given a Christian frame of reference. Micah (5:2–4) gives Bethlehem as the specific place from which a Promised One would arise, and Matthew and Luke both identify Jesus' birthplace as Bethlehem.

Isaiah 7:14–15

Therefore the Lord himself shall give you a sign; Behold, a virgin shall conceive, and bear a son, and shall call his name Immanuel. Butter and honey shall he eat, that he may know to refuse the evil, and choose the good.

Isaiah 11:1–6, 10

And there shall come forth a rod out of the stem of Jesse, and a Branch shall grow out of his roots: And the spirit of the LORD shall rest upon him, the spirit of wisdom and understanding, the spirit of counsel and might, the spirit of knowledge and of the fear of the LORD; And shall make him of quick understanding in the fear of the LORD: and he shall not judge after the sight of his eyes, neither reprove after the hearing of his ears: But with righteousness shall he judge the poor, and reprove with equity for the meek of the earth: and he shall smite the earth: with the rod of his mouth, and with the breath of his lips shall he slay the wicked. And righteousness shall be the girdle of his loins, and faithfulness the girdle of his reins. The wolf also shall dwell with the lamb, and the leopard shall lie down with the kid; and the calf and the young lion and the fatling together; and a little child shall lead them. . . . And in that day there shall be a root of Jesse, which shall stand for an ensign of the people; to it shall the Gentiles seek: and his rest shall be glorious.

Isaiah 40:1–11

Comfort ye, comfort ye my people, saith your God. Speak ye comfortably to Jerusalem, and cry unto her, that her warfare is accomplished, that her iniquity is pardoned: for she hath received of the LORD's hand double for all her sins.

The voice of him that crieth in the wilderness, Prepare ye the way of the LORD, make straight in the desert a highway for our God. Every valley shall be exalted, and every mountain and hill shall be made low: and the crooked shall be made straight, and the rough places plain: And the glory of the LORD shall be revealed, and all flesh shall see it together: for the mouth of the LORD hath spoken it. The voice said, Cry. And he said, What shall I cry? All flesh is grass, and all the goodliness thereof is as the flower of the field: The grass withereth, the flower fadeth: because the spirit of the LORD bloweth upon it: surely the people is grass. The grass withereth, the flower fadeth: but the word of our God shall stand forever.

O Zion, that bringest good tidings, get thee up into the high mountain; O Jerusalem, that bringest good tidings, lift up thy voice with strength; lift it up, be not afraid; say unto the cities of Judah, Behold your God! Behold, the Lord GOD will come with strong hand, and his arm shall rule for him: behold, his reward is with him, and his work before him. He shall feed his flock like a shepherd: he shall gather the lambs with his arm, and carry them in his bosom, and shall gently lead those that are with young.

Micah 5:2–4

But thou, Bethlehem Ephratah, though thou be little among the thousands of Judah, yet out of thee shall he come forth unto me that is to be ruler in Israel; whose goings forth have been from of old, from everlasting. Therefore will he give them up, until the time that she which travaileth hath brought forth: then the remnant of his brethren shall return unto the children of Israel. And he shall stand and feed in the strength of the LORD, in the majesty of the name of the LORD his God; and they shall abide: for now shall he be great unto the ends of the earth.

The Gospel According to St. Matthew

OF THE TWENTY-SEVEN BOOKS that comprise the New Testament, only two, Matthew and Luke, contain narrative accounts of the birth of Christ. Although tradition ascribes the name *Matthew* to the opening book of the

New Testament, the authorship is speculative. This Gospel, like the other three, is believed to incorporate oral tradition and may also make use of earlier written accounts, now lost. Matthew's Gospel, written in Greek and generally dated after 70 C.E., is considered to have been written for Christians familiar with Jewish traditions. The portion of Matthew included here tells of the visit of the Wise Men to the Christ Child, an event that later found expression in the celebration variously known as the Feast of the Three Kings, Twelfth Night, or Epiphany.

Chapter 2:1–12

Now when Jesus was born in Bethlehem of Judaea in the days of Herod the king, behold, there came wise men from the east to Jerusalem, saying, Where is he that is born King of the Jews? for we have seen his star in the east, and are come to worship him. When Herod the king had heard these things, he was troubled, and all Jerusalem with him. And when he had gathered all the chief priests and scribes of the people together, he demanded of them where Christ should be born. And they said unto him, In Bethlehem of Judaea: for thus it is written by the prophet, And thou Bethlehem, in the land of Juda, art not the least among the princes of Juda: for out of thee shall come a Governor, that shall rule my people Israel. Then Herod, when he had privily called the wise men, enquired of them diligently what time the star appeared. And he sent them to Bethlehem, and said, Go and search diligently for the young child; and when ye have found him, bring me word again, that I may come and worship him also. When they had heard the king, they departed; and, lo, the star, which they saw in the east, went before them, till it came and stood over where the young child was. When they saw the star, they rejoiced with exceeding great joy.

And when they were come into the house, they saw the young child with Mary his mother, and fell down, and worshipped him: and when they had opened their treasures, they presented unto him gifts; gold, and frankincense, and myrrh. And being warned of God in a dream that they should not return to Herod, they departed into their own country another way.

The Gospel According to St. Luke

LUKE'S ACCOUNT OF THE BIRTH OF CHRIST, written in Greek, dates from
80–85 C.E. The authorship of Luke, like that of Matthew, is speculative.
Although the Gospel narratives have different origins and emphases, we
read them as parts of the same story. Luke anchors the divine birth in a
specific historical time and place, Roman-occupied Judea. The account
emphasizes the role of the angelic messenger who brings "good tidings of
great joy" to humankind. Luke's account provides a rich tapestry, depict-
ing an event of everlasting consequence. The narrative begins with the
announcement to Mary by the angel Gabriel that she will bear a child,
continues with Mary's visit to her cousin Elisabeth, the mother of John
the Baptist, and concludes with the visit of the shepherds to the manger.

Chapter 1:26–80

And in the sixth month the angel Gabriel was sent from God unto
a city of Galilee, named Nazareth, to a virgin espoused to a man
whose name was Joseph, of the house of David; and the virgin's
name was Mary. And the angel came in unto her, and said, Hail,
thou that art highly favoured, the Lord is with thee: blessed art
thou among women. And when she saw him, she was troubled at
his saying, and cast in her mind what manner of salutation this
should be. And the angel said unto her, Fear not, Mary: for thou
hast found favour with God. And, behold, thou shalt conceive in
thy womb, and bring forth a son, and shalt call his name JESUS.
He shall be great, and shall be called the Son of the Highest: and
the Lord God shall give unto him the throne of his father David:
and he shall reign over the house of Jacob for ever; and of his kingdom there shall be no end. Then said Mary unto the angel, How
shall this be, seeing I know not a man? And the angel answered and
said unto her, The Holy Ghost shall come upon thee, and the
power of the Highest shall overshadow thee: therefore also that
holy thing which shall be born of thee shall be called the Son of
God. And, behold, thy cousin Elisabeth, she hath also conceived a
son in her old age: and this is the sixth month with her, who was
called barren. For with God nothing shall be impossible. And
Mary said, Behold the handmaid of the Lord; be it unto me according to thy word. And the angel departed from her.

And Mary arose in those days, and went into the hill country with haste, into a city of Juda; and entered into the house of Zacharias, and saluted Elisabeth. And it came to pass, that, when Elisabeth heard the salutation of Mary, the babe leaped in her womb; and Elisabeth was filled with the Holy Ghost: and she spake out with a loud voice, and said, Blessed art thou among women, and blessed is the fruit of thy womb. And whence is this to me, that the mother of my Lord should come to me? For, lo, as soon as the voice of thy salutation sounded in mine ears, the babe leaped in my womb for joy. And blessed is she that believed: for there shall be a performance of those things which were told her from the Lord.

And Mary said,

My soul doth magnify the Lord,
And my spirit hath rejoiced in God my Saviour.
For he hath regarded the low estate of his handmaiden:
For, behold,from henceforth all generations shall call me blessed.
For he that is mighty hath done to me great things;
And holy is his name.
And his mercy is on them that fear him
From generation to generation.
He hath shewed strength with his arm;
He hath scattered the proud in the imagination of their hearts.
He hath put down the mighty from their seats,
And exalted them of low degree.
He hath filled the hungry with good things;
And the rich he hath sent empty away.
He hath holpen his servant Israel,
In remembrance of his mercy;
As he spake to our fathers,
To Abraham, and to his seed for ever.

And Mary abode with her about three months, and returned to her own house.

Now Elisabeth's full time came that she should be delivered; and she brought forth a son. And her neighbours and her cousins heard how the Lord had shewed great mercy upon her; and they rejoiced with her. And it came to pass, that on the eighth day they came to circumcise the child; and they called him Zacharias, after the name of his father. And his mother answered and said, Not so; but he shall be called John. And they said unto her, There is none of thy kindred that is called by this name. And they made signs to his father, how he would have him called. And he asked for a writing table, and wrote, saying, His name is John. And they marvelled all. And his mouth was opened immediately, and his tongue loosed, and he spake, and praised God. And fear came on all that dwelt round about them: and all these sayings were noised abroad throughout all the hill country of Judaea. And all they that heard them laid them up in their hearts, saying, What manner of child shall this be! And the hand of the Lord was with him.

And his father Zacharias was filled with the Holy Ghost, and prophesied, saying,

> Blessed be the Lord God of Israel;
> For he hath visited and redeemed his people,
> And hath raised up an horn of salvation for us
> In the house of his servant David;
> As he spake by the mouth of his holy prophets,
> Which have been since the world began:
> That we should be saved from our enemies,
> And from the hand of all that hate us;
> To perform the mercy promised to our fathers,
> And to remember his holy covenant;
> The oath which he sware to our father Abraham,
> That he would grant unto us, that we being delivered out of the
>   hand of our enemies
> Might serve him without fear,
> In holiness and righteousness before him,
> All the days of our life.
> And thou, child, shalt be called the prophet of the Highest:
> For thou shalt go before the face of the Lord
> To prepare his ways;
> To give knowledge of salvation unto his people
> By the remission of their sins,
> Through the tender mercy of our God;
> Whereby the dayspring from on high hath visited us,
> To give light to them that sit in darkness and in the
>   shadow of death,
> To guide our feet into the way of peace.

And the child grew, and waxed strong in spirit, and was in the deserts till the day of his shewing unto Israel.

Chapter 2:1–20

And it came to pass in those days, that there went out a decree from Caesar Augustus, that all the world should be taxed. (And this taxing was first made when Cyrenius was governor of Syria.) And all went to be taxed, every one into his own city. And Joseph also went up from Galilee, out of the city of Nazareth, into Judaea, unto the city of David, which is called Bethlehem; (because he was of the house and lineage of David:) to be taxed with Mary his espoused wife, being great with child. And so it was, that, while they were there, the days were accomplished that she should be delivered. And she brought forth her firstborn son, and wrapped him in swaddling clothes, and laid him in a manger; because there was no room for them in the inn.

And there were in the same country shepherds abiding in the field, keeping watch over their flock by night. And, lo, the angel of the Lord came upon them, and the glory of the Lord shone round about them: and they were sore afraid. And the angel said unto them, Fear not: for, behold, I bring you good tidings of great joy, which shall be to all people. For unto you is born this day in the city of David a Saviour, which is Christ the Lord. And this shall be a sign unto you; Ye shall find the babe wrapped in swaddling clothes, lying in a manger. And suddenly there was with the angel a multitude of the heavenly host praising God, and saying, Glory to God in the highest, and on earth peace, good will toward men. And it came to pass, as the angels were gone away from them into heaven, the shepherds said one to another, Let us now go even unto Bethlehem, and see this thing which is come to pass, which the Lord hath made known unto us. And they came with haste, and found Mary, and Joseph, and the babe lying in a manger. And when they had seen it, they made known abroad the saying which was told them concerning this child. And all they that heard it wondered at those things which were told them by the shepherds. But Mary kept all these things, and pondered them in her heart. And the shepherds returned, glorifying and praising God for all the things that they had heard and seen, as it was told unto them.

The Revelation of St. John the Divine

THE REVELATION OF ST. JOHN THE DIVINE includes a mystic, highly imaginative retelling of the Nativity story. The author, who refers to himself as John, wrote the Revelation while on the Greek Isle of Patmos, probably toward the end of the first century C.E. Unlike the more restrained narratives in Matthew and Luke, John's account is primarily mythological and archetypal, with cryptic symbols and images from Persian, Babylonian, Greek, and Egyptian religions. The woman referred to in the first instance in chapter 12 may be the Virgin Mary, and the later reference may be to the Christian church under persecution. Whereas the modern reader will find the symbolism obscure, the ancient reader would doubtlessly have been familiar with many of these symbols and images.

This account is part of a body of apocalyptic literature, works prophesying a cataclysmic destruction of evil. In the Revelation of St. John, the cosmic struggle in the heavens parallels the struggle the early Christians were beginning to experience. Sufferers on earth eventually triumph, just as Michael, one of the seven archangels of Judaism, eventually triumphs over Satan.

Chapter 12

And there appeared a great wonder in heaven; a woman clothed with the sun, and the moon under her feet, and upon her head a crown of twelve stars: And she being with child cried, travailing in birth, and pained to be delivered. And there appeared another wonder in heaven; and behold a great red dragon, having seven heads and ten horns, and seven crowns upon his heads. And his tail drew the third part of the stars of heaven, and did cast them to the earth: and the dragon stood before the woman which was ready to be delivered, for to devour her child as soon as it was born. And she brought forth a man child, who was to rule all nations with a rod of iron: and her child was caught up unto God, and to his throne. And the woman fled into the wilderness, where she hath a place prepared of God, that they should feed her there a thousand two hundred and threescore days. And there was war in heaven: Michael and his angels fought against the dragon; and the dragon fought and his angels, and prevailed not; neither was their place found any more in heaven. And the great dragon was cast out, that old serpent, called the Devil, and Satan, which deceiveth the whole world: he was cast out into the earth, and his angels were cast out with him. And I heard a loud voice saying in heaven, Now is come salvation, and strength, and the kingdom of our God, and the power of his Christ: for the accuser of our brethren is cast down, which accused them before our God day and night. And they overcame him by the blood of the Lamb, and by the word of their testimony; and they loved not their lives unto the death. Therefore rejoice, ye heavens, and ye that dwell in them. Woe to the inhabitants of the earth and of the sea! for the devil is come down unto you, having great wrath, because he knoweth that he hath but a short time. And when the dragon saw that he was cast unto the earth, he persecuted the woman which brought forth the man child. And to the woman were given two wings of a great eagle, that she might fly into the wilderness, into her place, where she is nourished for a time, and times, and half a time, from the face of the serpent. And the serpent cast out of his mouth water as a flood after the woman, that he might cause her to be carried away of the flood. And the earth helped the woman, and the earth opened her mouth, and swallowed up the flood which the dragon cast out of his mouth. And the dragon was wroth with the woman, and went to make war with the remnant of her seed, which keep the commandments of God, and have the testimony of Jesus Christ.

The Protevangelium of James

THE PROTEVANGELIUM OF JAMES, one of the earliest of the apocryphal infancy Gospels, was probably current in the second century. The last paragraph, which names the author, James, and the time, the death of Herod, may well have been appended to add authenticity. This excerpt from the *Protevangelium*, clearly an elaboration on the biblical narratives of the birth of Christ, heightens the elements of the miraculous and provides additional details and dialogue. The *Protevangelium* also introduces the character of Salome, who may have been intended to be the same woman who appears at the tomb in Mark's account of the resurrection.

The Protevangelium of James

(excerpt)

And there was an order from the Emperor Augustus, that all in Bethlehem of Judaea should be enrolled. And Joseph said: I shall enrol my sons, but what shall I do with this maiden? How shall I enrol her? As my wife? I am ashamed. As my daughter then? But all the sons of Israel know that she is not my daughter. The day of the Lord shall itself bring it to pass as the Lord will. And he saddled the ass, and set her upon it; and his son led it, and Joseph followed. And when they had come within three miles, Joseph turned and saw her sorrowful; and he said to himself: Likely that which is in her distresses her. And again Joseph turned and saw her laughing. And he said to her: Mary, how is it that I see in thy face at one time laughter, at another sorrow? And Mary said to Joseph: Because I see two peoples with my eyes; the one weeping and lamenting, and the other rejoicing and exulting. And they came into the middle of the road, and Mary said to him: Take me down from off the ass, for that which is in me presses to come forth. And he took her down from off the ass, and said to her: Whither shall I lead thee, and cover thy disgrace? for the place is desert.

And he found a cave there, and led her into it; and leaving his two sons beside her, he went out to seek a midwife in the district of Bethlehem.

And I Joseph was walking, and was not walking; and I looked up into the sky, and saw the sky astonished; and I looked up to the pole of the heavens, and saw it standing, and the birds of the air keeping still. And I looked down upon the earth, and saw a trough lying, and work-people reclining: and their hands were in the trough. And those that were eating did not eat, and those that were rising did not carry it up, and those that were conveying anything to their mouths did not convey it; but the faces of all were looking upwards. And I saw the sheep walking, and the sheep stood still; and the shepherd raised his hand to strike them, and his hand remained up. And I looked upon the current of the river, and I saw the mouths of the kids resting on the water and not drinking, and all things in a moment were driven from their course.

❦　❦　❦　❦

And the midwife went in, and said to Mary: Show thyself; for no small controversy has arisen about thee. And Salome put in her finger, and cried out, and said: Woe is me for mine iniquity and mine unbelief, because I have tempted the living God; and, behold, my hand is dropping off as if burned with fire. And she bent her knees before the Lord, saying: O God of my fathers, remember that I am the seed of Abraham, and Isaac, and Jacob; do not make a show of me to the sons of Israel, but restore me to the poor; for Thou knowest, O Lord, that in Thy name I have performed my services, and that I have received my reward at Thy hand. And, behold, an angel of the Lord stood by her, saying to her: Salome, Salome, the Lord hath heard thee. Put thy hand to the infant, and carry it, and thou wilt have safety and joy. And Salome went and carried it, saying: I will worship Him, because a great King has been born to Israel. And, behold, Salome was immediately cured, and she went forth out of the cave justified. And behold a voice saying: Salome, Salome, tell not the strange things thou hast seen, until the child has come into Jerusalem.

❦ ❦ ❦ ❦

And I James that wrote this history in Jerusalem, a commotion having arisen when Herod died, withdrew myself to the wilderness until the commotion in Jerusalem ceased, glorifying the Lord God, who had given me the gift and the wisdom to write this history. And grace shall be with them that fear our Lord Jesus Christ, to whom be glory to ages of ages. Amen.

The Arabic Gospel

THE ARABIC GOSPEL NARRATIVE, according to scholars, is based on the Gospel of Matthew, *The Protevangelium of James*, and the apocryphal Gospel of Thomas. Folkloric in nature, the Arabic Gospel has been compared to *The Arabian Nights* and *The Golden Ass* of Apuleius, and, like *The Protevangelium of James*, heightens the elements of the miraculous. The compilation was probably written in Syriac, but was not published until 1697 in a Latin version. Though obviously derivative, the work illuminates how traditions about Jesus were elaborated in the early church.

The Arabic Gospel

(excerpt)

In the name of the Father, and the Son, and the Holy Spirit, one God.

With the help and favour of the Most High we begin to write a book of the miracles of our Lord and Master and Saviour Jesus Christ, which is called the Gospel of the Infancy: in the peace of the Lord. Amen.

We find what follows in the book of Joseph the high priest, who lived in the time of Christ. Some say that he is Caiaphas. He has said that Jesus spoke, and, indeed, when He was lying in His cradle said to Mary His mother: I am Jesus, the Son of God, the Logos, whom thou hast brought forth, as the Angel Gabriel announced to thee; and my Father has sent me for the salvation of the world.

In the three hundred and ninth year of the era of Alexander, Augustus put forth an edict, that every man should be enrolled in his native place. Joseph therefore arose, and taking Mary his spouse, went away to Jerusalem, and came to Bethlehem, to be enrolled along with his family in his native city. And having come to a cave, Mary told Joseph that the time of the birth was at hand, and that she could not go into the city; but, said she, let us go into this cave. This took place at sunset. And Joseph went out in haste to go for a woman to be near her. When, therefore, he was busy about that, he saw an Hebrew old woman belonging to Jerusalem, and said: Come hither, my good woman, and go into this cave, in which there is a woman near her time.

Wherefore, after sunset, the old woman, and Joseph with her, came to the cave, and they both went in. And, behold, it was filled with lights more beautiful than the gleaming of lamps and candles, and more splendid than the light of the sun. The child, enwrapped in swaddling clothes, was sucking the breast of the Lady Mary His mother, being placed in a stall. And when both were wondering at this light, the old woman asks the Lady Mary: Art thou the mother of this child? And when the Lady Mary gave her assent, she says: Thou art not at all like the daughters of Eve. The Lady Mary said: As my son has no equal among children, so his mother has no equal among women. The old woman replied: my mistress, I came to get payment; I have been for a long time affected with palsy. Our mistress the Lady Mary said to her: Place thy hands upon the child. And the old woman did so, and was immediately cured. Then she went forth, saying: Henceforth I will be the attendant and servant of this child all the days of my life.

Then came shepherds; and when they had lighted a fire, and were rejoicing greatly, there appeared to them the hosts of heaven praising and celebrating God Most High. And while the shepherds were doing the same, the cave was at that time made like a temple of the upper world, since both heavenly and earthly voices glorified and magnified God on account of the birth of the Lord Christ.

❧   ❧   ❧   ❧

And it came to pass, when the Lord Jesus was born at Bethlehem of Judaea, in the time of King Herod, behold, magi came from the east to Jerusalem, as Zeraduscht [Zoroaster] had predicted; and there were with them gifts, gold, and frankincense, and myrrh. And they adored Him, and presented to Him their gifts. Then the Lady Mary took one of the swaddling-bands, and, on account of the smallness of her means, gave it to them; and they received it from her with the greatest marks of honour. And in the same hour there appeared to them an angel in the form of that star which had before guided them on their journey; and they went away, following the guidance of its light, until they arrived in their own country.

And their kings and chief men came together to them, asking what they had seen or done, how they had gone and come back, what they had brought with them. And they showed them that swathing-cloth which the Lady Mary had given them. Wherefore they celebrated a feast, and, according to their custom, lighted a fire and worshipped it, and threw that swathing-cloth into it; and the fire laid hold of it, and enveloped it. And when the fire had gone out, they took out the swathing-cloth exactly as it had been before, just as if the fire had not touched it. Wherefore they began to kiss it, and to put it on their heads and their eyes, saying: This verily is the truth without doubt. Assuredly it is a great thing that the fire was not able to burn or destroy it. They took it, and with the greatest honour laid it up among their treasures.

Tertullian

TERTULLIAN, A NORTH AFRICAN BORN AT CARTHAGE of wealthy pagan parents about 150, remains one of the most interesting individuals of the early church. A Roman lawyer, Tertullian converted to Christianity about 190. He was ordained a presbyter upon returning to Carthage, where he died about 225. During the latter part of his life, Tertullian became a bitter critic of the church, which considered his views unorthodox.

Though the early Christian doctrinal disputations for most modern readers are a wasteland best avoided, Tertullian's pungent Latin satire, as illustrated in the selection below, can still be enjoyed. Tertullian wrote to counter the Marcionite assertion that Jesus was not really a fully physical human being. If the Marcionites had won the day, the Nativity portion of the Gospel narratives might well have been forever suppressed.

On the Flesh of Christ

CHAP. II.—MARCION, WHO WOULD BLOT OUT THE RECORD OF
CHRIST'S NATIVITY, IS REBUKED FOR SO STARTLING A HERESY.

Clearly enough is the nativity announced by Gabriel. But what has he to do with the Creator's angel? The conception in the virgin's womb is also set plainly before us. But what concern has he with the Creator's prophet, Isaiah? He will not brook delay, since *suddenly* (without any prophetic announcement) did he bring down Christ from heaven. "Away," says he, "with that eternal plaguey taxing of Caesar, and the scanty inn, and the squalid swaddling-clothes, and the hard stable. We do not care a jot for that multitude of the heavenly host which praised their Lord at night. Let the shepherds take better care of their flock, and let the wise men spare their legs so long a journey; let them keep their gold to themselves. Let Herod, too, mend his manners, so that Jeremy may not glory over him. Spare also the babe from circumcision, that he may escape the pain thereof; nor let him be brought into the temple, lest he burden his parents with the expense of the offering; nor let him be handed to Simeon, lest the old man be saddened at the point of death. Let that old woman also hold her tongue, lest she should bewitch the child." After such a fashion as this, I suppose you have had, O Marcion, the hardihood of blotting out the original records (of the history) of Christ, that His flesh may lose the proofs of its reality. But, prithee, on what grounds (do you do this)? Show me your authority. If you are a prophet, foretell us a thing; if you are an apostle, open your message in public; if a follower of apostles, side with apostles in thought; if you are only a (private) Christian, believe what has been handed down to us: if, however, you are nothing of all this, then (as I have the best reason to say) cease to live. For indeed you are already dead, since you are no Christian, because you do not believe that which by being believed makes men Christian,—nay, you are the more dead, the more you are not a Christian; having fallen away, after you had been one, by rejecting what you formerly believed, even as you yourself acknowledge in a certain letter of yours, and as your followers do not deny, whilst our (brethren) can prove it. Rejecting, therefore, what you *once* believed, you have completed the act of rejection, by now no longer believing: the fact, however, of your having ceased to believe has not made your rejection of the faith right and proper; nay, rather, by your act of rejection you prove that what you believed previous to the said act was of a different character. What you believed to be of a different character, had been handed down just as *you believed it*. Now that which had been handed down was true, inasmuch as it had been transmitted by those whose duty it was to hand it down. Therefore, when rejecting that which had been handed down, you rejected that which was true. You had no authority for what you did. However, we have already in another treatise availed ourselves more fully of these prescriptive rules against all heresies. Our repetition of them here after that large (treatise) is superfluous, when we ask the reason why you have formed the opinion that Christ was not born.

Ignatius of Antioch

IGNATIUS WAS AN EARLY SECOND-CENTURY BISHOP of Antioch in Syria. Like Paul, Ignatius wrote highly personal letters that served to clarify his own beliefs as well as to instruct his recipients. Also like Paul, Ignatius was martyred. Like the Revelation of St. John the Divine, the Letter to the Ephesians offers a cosmic perspective. For Ignatius, the birth and death of Jesus are of heavenly as well as earthly consequence, as witnessed by the participation in the events of the sun, moon, and stars.

Letter to the Ephesians

Chapter 19:1–3

The virginity of Mary and her giving birth eluded the ruler of this age, likewise also the death of the Lord—three mysteries of a cry which were done in the stillness of God. How then was he revealed to the aeons?

> A star shone in heaven
> brighter than all the stars,
> and its light was ineffable,
> and its novelty caused astonishment;
> all the other stars
> together with sun and moon
> became a chorus for the star,
> and it outshone them all with its light;
> and there was perplexity (as to) whence (came)
>   this novelty (so) unlike them.
> Thence was destroyed all magic,
> and every bond vanished;
> evil's ignorance was abolished,
> the old kingdom perished,
> God being revealed as human
> to bring newness of eternal life,
> and what had been prepared by God
>   had its beginning;
> hence all things were disturbed
> because the destruction of death was being worked out.

Ephrem the Syrian

SAINT EPHREM, A PREACHER AND HYMN WRITER referred to by Basil the Great as the "professor of the desert," died at Edessa, in Macedonia, in 373. Syriac, the language in which Ephrem wrote, is a dialect of Aramaic, the same language Jesus spoke. Ephrem makes the celebration of the Nativity an event that transcends time. Just as for the Hebrews the Passover is an ancient event recalled and reexperienced in the present, so too, for Christians, the Nativity (like the Lord's Supper) can be reexperienced with the intensity of the original occasion.

The "Rhythms" are a kind of exuberant mystical reflection on the Scriptures. Ephrem finds foreshadowings of Christ's birth not only in Isaiah and Micah, but in many other places through his own imaginative reading of the Scriptures. Modern readers can read Ephrem's "Rhythms" only in a general impressionistic way because many of the specific references he makes are obscure.

The Rhythms of Saint Ephrem the Syrian on the Nativity

Rhythm the First (excerpt)

This is the day that gladdened them, the Prophets, Kings, and Priests, for in it were their words fulfilled, and thus were the whole of them indeed performed! For the Virgin did to-day bring forth Immanuel in Bethlehem. The voice that first Isaiah spake, to-day reality became. He was born there who in writing should the Gentiles' number tell! The Psalm that David once did sing, by its fulfilment came to-day! The word that Micah once did speak, to-day was actually done! For there came from Ephrata a Shepherd, and His staff swayed over souls. Lo! from Jacob shone the Star, and from Israel rose the Head. The prophecy that Balaam spake had its interpreting to-day! Down also came the hidden Light, and from the Body rose His beauty! The Light that spake in Zachary, to-day did gleam in Bethlehem!

Risen is the Light of the kingdom, in Ephrata the city of the King. The blessing wherewith Jacob blessed, to its fulfilment came to-day! That tree likewise, (the tree) of life bringeth hope to mortal men! Solomon his hidden proverb had to-day its explanation! To-day was born the Child, and His name was Wonder called! For a wonder 'tis that God as a Babe should shew Himself. By the word Worm [*Vermis*, a traditional reference to Jesus] did the Spirit Him in parable foreshew, because His generation was without marriage. The type the Holy Ghost did figure, to-day its meaning was (explained). He came up as a root before Him, as a root of parched ground. Aught that covertly was said, openly to-day was done! The King that was in Judah hidden, Thamar stole Him from his thigh; to-day arose His conquering beauty, which in hidden estate she loved. Ruth at Booz side fell down, because the Medicine of Life hidden in him she perceived. To-day fulfilled was her vow, since from her seed arose the Quickener of all. Travail Adam on the woman brought, that from him had come forth. She to-day her travail ransomed, who to her a Saviour bare! To Eve our mother birth a man gave, who had had no birth himself. How much more should Eve's daughter be believed to have borne a Child without a man! The virgin earth, she bare that Adam that was head over the earth! The Virgin bare to-day the Adam that was Head over the Heavens. The staff of Aaron, it budded, and the dry wood yielded fruit! Its mystery is cleared up to-day, for virgin womb a Child hath borne!

Shamed is that folk that holdeth the prophets as true; for unless our Saviour did come, falsified their words have been!

The Nestorian Monument of Hsî-an Fû in Shen-Hsî, China

IN CHINESE HISTORY THE WISE MAN OR SCHOLAR has always been especially venerated, so it is not surprising that the coming of the Wise Men to do homage has often captured the Chinese imagination. The earliest record of Christian activity in China is generally tied to the coming of a Nestorian Christian, A-lo-pen, in 635 Nestorian Christianity, flourishing for a time in Syria, Persia, and Southern India—and indeed still found in a few places in the Middle and Far East—issued out of a fifth-century dispute regarding the nature of Christ. Nestorius, patriarch of Constantinople, held that Christ had distinct human and divine persons.

"A virgin bore a Sage" is the Nestorian Chinese Christian view of the Nativity, this phrase being found on the famous Nestorian tablet erected in China in 781. The lengthy inscription, which blends Christianity and Chinese philosophy, summarizes the early history of Nestorian Christianity in China. In the inscription, Christianity is referred to as the illustrious or luminous religion of Tâ Ts`in (Ta-ch`in). At the heading of the text is a cross rising out of a cloud surrounded by a lotus bloom. Clouds are traditional Chinese symbols of wisdom, and the lotus is frequently depicted as the Throne of Buddha.

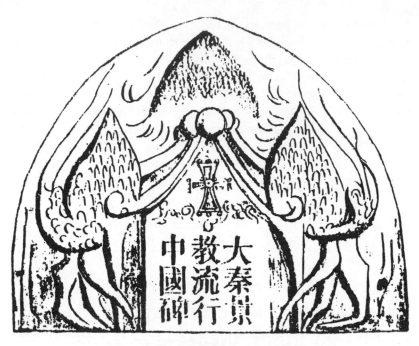

Head of the Monument

Monument (Commemorating)
the Diffusion of the Illustrious Religion
of Tâ Ts`in in the Middle Kingdom

(Inscription excerpt)

Some point to the creature,
to trust in it as the ultimate.
Some take things and nothingness,
and destroy the two.
Some pray and sacrifice to induce blessings.
Some set forth their own merit to deceive others.
Wise counsels were a-buzz.
Thoughts and feelings were a-toil.
Far and wide (they went) without achievement.
The dry hastened to turn to burning.
As darkness gathered they lost their way,
until confusion was beyond return.
Whereupon our Trinity became incarnate:
The Illustrious Honoured-One, Messiah,

hid away his true majesty,
and came into the world as a man.
An angel proclaimed the joy.
A virgin bore a Sage in Syria.
A bright star was the propitious portent.
Persians saw its glory and came to offer gifts.
He fulfilled the Old Law
of the Twenty-Four Sages' discourses,   [Old Testament]
governing tribes and nation . . .
He determined the salvation of the Eight Stages,   [Beatitudes]
refining the earthly and perfecting the heavenly.
He revealed the gate of the Three Constants,
unfolding life and destroying death.
He hung a brilliant sun
which scattered the regions of darkness.
The Devil's guile, lo, he has utterly cut off.

Ambrose of Milan

AMBROSE (340–397), A LEADING FOURTH-CENTURY CHRISTIAN who was
influential in the conversion of the great Augustine, is credited with establishing the tradition of Latin hymns. Ambrose introduced antiphonal
chanting and discovered the effectiveness of four-line verses in singing.
Hymns of the period, including those of Ambrose, emphasize emerging
Christian doctrine. This particular hymn, still sung today, is in a Victorian translation that reflects the meter of the Latin original.

Veni, redemptor gentium

O come, Redeemer of the earth,
Show to the world Thy virgin birth;
Let age to age the wonder tell;
Such birth, O God, beseems Thee well.

No earthly father Thou dost own;
By God's o'ershadowing alone
The Word made flesh to man is come,
The fair fruit of a mother's womb.

A maiden pure and undefiled
Is by the Spirit great with child;
Like standard fair, her virtues tell,
'Tis God within her deigns to dwell.

Forth from His chamber cometh He,
The court and bower of chastity;
Henceforth in two-fold substance one,
A giant glad His course to run.

From God the Father He proceeds,
To God the Father back He speeds;
Runs out His course to death and hell,
Returns on God's high throne to dwell.

O ancient as the Father Thou,
Gird on our flesh for victory now;
The weakness of our mortal state
With deathless might invigorate.

E'en now Thy manger glows; new light
Is borne upon the breath of night;
Let darkness ne'er eclipse the ray,
And faith make everlasting day.

All praise to God the Father be,
All praise, Eternal Son, to Thee,
Whom with the Spirit we adore,
For ever and for evermore.

Prudentius

MARCUS AURELIUS CLEMENS PRUDENTIUS (348–413), a Spaniard, was an eminent early Christian poet. A magistrate and author, Prudentius converted to Christianity late in life. His poems entered the liturgy through inclusion in the early Spanish Mozarabic Rite. Portions of two of his Nativity poems, which are still popularly sung as Christmas hymns, follow below.

Corde natus ex Parentis

Of the Father's love begotten
Ere the worlds began to be,
He is Alpha and Omega,
He the source, the ending He,
Of the things that are, that have been,
And that future years shall see,
Evermore and evermore.

O that Birth for ever blessèd!
When the Virgin, full of grace,
By the Holy Ghost conceiving,
Bare the Saviour of our race,
And the Babe, the world's Redeemer,
First reveal'd His sacred face,
Evermore and evermore.

Thee let old men, Thee let young men,
Thee let boys in chorus sing;
Matrons, virgins, little maidens,
With glad voices answering;
Let their guileless songs re-echo,
And the heart its music bring,
Evermore and evermore.

O sola magnarum urbium

Bethlehem, of noblest cities
    None can once with thee compare;
Thou alone the Lord from heaven
    Didst for us incarnate bear.

Fairer than the sun at morning
    Was the star that told his birth;
To the lands their God announcing,
    Hid beneath a form of earth.

By its lambent beauty guided
   See the eastern kings appear;
See them bend, their gifts to offer,
   Gifts of incense, gold, and myrrh.

Solemn things of mystic meaning:
   Incense doth the God disclose,
Gold a royal child proclaimeth,
   Myrrh a future tomb foreshows.

Holy Jesus, in thy brightness
   To the Gentile world displayed,
With the Father and the Spirit
   Endless praise to thee be paid.

Sedulius

COELIUS SEDULIUS, A FIFTH-CENTURY IRISHMAN, wrote secular poetry before turning to Christian themes. The portions of the two poems printed here, originally written in Latin, are from the *Paean Alphabeticus de Christo*, a twenty-three-quatrain hymn in which the verses begin with successive letters of the alphabet. Used in worship throughout much of Christian history, these two hymns illustrate the way in which Gospel narratives were rendered in an abbreviated, poetic form for both private and public devotion.

A solis ortus cardine

From east to west, from shore to shore,
Let ev'ry heart awake and sing
The holy Child whom Mary bore,
The Christ, the everlasting King.

Behold, the world's creator wears
The form and fashion of a slave;
Our very flesh our Maker shares,
His fallen creatures, all, to save.

All glory for this blessed morn
To God the Father ever be;
All praise to thee, O Virgin-born,
All praise, O Holy Ghost, to thee.

Hostis Herodes impie

When Christ's appearing was made known,
King Herod trembled for his throne;
But he who offers heavenly birth
Sought not the kingdoms of this earth.

The eastern sages saw from far
And followed on his guiding star;
By light their way to Light they trod,
And by their gifts confessed their God.

Within the Jordan's sacred flood,
The heavenly Lamb in meekness stood,
That he, to whom no sin was known,
Might cleanse his people from their own.

O what a miracle divine,
When water reddened into wine!
He spake the word, and forth it flowed
In streams that nature ne'er bestowed.

All glory, Jesus, be to thee
For this thy glad epiphany:
Whom with the Father we adore,
And Holy Ghost for ever more.

Chapter 2

The Middle Ages

*From
Liturgy
to
Literature*

Introduction

It used to be fashionable to refer to the Middle Ages as the Dark Ages, but today such a simplification and generalization is unacceptable. Christian culture, including literature, flowered during the Middle Ages in ways rarely equaled in subsequent centuries. The literature of the Nativity developed into set patterns or genres. By the end of the Middle Ages, the term *Christmas* had come into common usage for celebrations both sacred and secular.

Medieval Christian worship most typically took place within fully elaborated liturgies. These developed by geographical extension into variant liturgical traditions known by such names as the Gallican, the Roman, and the Mozarabic rites. The Roman rite came to dominate as the papacy increased in spiritual and political power in Western Europe, and liturgical motifs came to dominate much of the literature of Christmas.

The *"Laetabundus"* by Bernard of Clairvaux is an example of a seasonal insertion into the liturgy known as a trope, or in this case, a trope variation called a sequence. Such seasonal spinoffs typically elaborated some aspect of the liturgical observance of the feast or fast as a supplement to the nonvarying part of the liturgy. The *"Officium Pastorum,"* a Christmas trope, illustrates the connection between liturgy and the development of the Christmas portions of the great liturgical dramas. These dramas rank among the most remarkable works of medieval literature. The two specifically liturgical pieces included are both unusual. The "Prose of the Ass" is a liturgical farce from the Feast of Fools celebration in France, illustrating perhaps the most intriguing reach of the roads from Bethlehem. Closer geographically and spiritually to Bethlehem is the "Doxology" from the Entrance of the Lord into the Land of Egypt. This liturgical artifact is founded upon the biblical narrative of the Holy Family's flight into Egypt.

If predictable structure characterized Christian liturgy, homilies allowed for highly imaginative elaborations on the biblical and liturgical texts by the individual preacher. In this chapter, four excerpts—two anonymous, one by a Scot, and one attributed to Aelfric of Cerne—exemplify the preacher's art in the Middle Ages.

Medieval homilies were not the brief, seemingly spontaneous offerings to which modern ears are accustomed. They were often lengthy, intricate, and even poetic elaborations, matching in prose what the medieval worshiper would have seen in the cathedrals and churches or heard in the plainsong variations and descants of skilled choristers.

The Nativity clearly inspired the imaginations of medieval dramatists. The earliest Nativity plays centered on the manger, set up at Christmas as a visual symbol of the divine-human encounter. Such observances date back at least to eighth-century Rome. The hard life of the Middle Ages was considerably enlivened by drama. In England, four liturgical calendar cycles of vernacular plays exist in manuscript form. These dramatic cycles are connected with their supposed place of origin: Chester, Coventry (Hegge), York, and Townley Hall (Wakefield). When the plays moved from liturgical Latin to various vernacular languages, there was a greater reliance on poetic imagination to supplement the biblical accounts. For example, in *The Second Shepherds' Play*, excerpted in this chapter, the shepherds, minimally present in the Gospels, come alive as real people. Scriptural narrative is juxtaposed with daily life. The comic portrayal of jesting, complaining yeomen is reminiscent of the stock farcical elements of Roman comedy upon which the early church fathers had frowned.

A discussion of narrative texts—texts that tell a story—raises the issue of the relationship of new Christian and old pagan custom and story. In the Middle Ages, Christian and pagan practices were sometimes merged in ways that moderns find confusing. It was not accidental that December 25, a day connected in the Roman world with *Sol Invictus*, the Invincible Sun, was chosen as the symbolic birthday of Christ. In the excerpt from *Le Morte d'Arthur*, presumed to be by Sir Thomas Malory, a fifteenth-century knight of dubious character but obvious literary merit, pagan traditions are given only the faintest Christian overlay.

Local folk belief became inextricably intertwined with beliefs regarding the first Christmas night: bees sing, water turns into wine, hidden treasures are revealed during the singing of the Matthean genealogy at the midnight mass, and animals fall on their knees and speak. The short sketch of St. Francis by Bonaventure exemplifies a popular folk subcategory of medieval literature, the miracle story.

Icon of the Theotokos: Virgin and Child (Seventeenth-century Russian)

Indeed, sacred and profane intertwinings affected medieval drama, narrative, lyric, and hymnody, though the most peculiar intertwining was undoubtedly in the aforementioned Feast of Fools.

Seventeen examples of Nativity-inspired lyrics are included in this chapter, rendered into modern English by the editors, except for "In dulci jubilo," "A ship comes sailing," "St. Stephen and Herod," and "Lo, How a Rose." Today the term *Christmas carol* is applied to almost any Christmas song, though scholars of the Middle Ages would insist on a more limited and specific definition. Carols are sometimes associated with the *laude* of the Franciscans, songs in the vernacular on religious themes that parallel secular dance songs. Both sacred and secular carols were very popular in the fourteenth and fifteenth centuries. Carols typically added a more human dimension, both personal and tender, to theological reflections on Christ's birth, life, and death.

Hearers and singers could relate to the popular portrayal of the Franciscan mendicants and others who gave the baby Jesus a very human face, the face of one who was to know poverty and humiliation as they themselves had known poverty and humiliation. This human savior would go on to be, as the theologians said, "tempted in every way as we are." Indeed, the world into which Jesus had been born was similar in many ways to their own medieval world, just as both worlds are radically different from our own. Some scholars have suggested that vernacular carols and ballads began and came to be used in worship because the Latin office hymns were too severe and the plainsong tunes too lacking in liveliness and spontaneity to attain true popularity among the people. The lyrics in this chapter show a wide range from the folk oriented and the spontaneous to the more formal and liturgical. The ancient carols of Christmas continue today as an indelible part of the holiday celebration.

Bernard of Clairvaux

BERNARD OF CLAIRVAUX (1090–1153), A KNIGHT'S SON, became a monk at twenty-two. He entered the famous Cistercian monastery at Citeaux, in eastern France. The Cistercians, who followed the Rule of St. Benedict, were the dominant monastic order of the twelfth century. Bernard later founded the monastery at Clairvaux, in northeastern France, where he remained abbot for the rest of his life, rejecting higher ecclesiastical office.

A mystic of exemplary life, Bernard was devoted to the contemplation of Christ. Bernard, a popular preacher, traveled widely, took part in organizing the Second Crusade, and helped heal a papal schism. Perhaps the greatest ornament of the church of his time, Bernard was later admired even by such militant antipapists as Luther and Calvin.

A liturgical reformer, Bernard was instrumental in editing the monastic choir antiphons for his order. Perhaps the most famous seasonal insertion in the liturgy is the Christmas sequence known as the *"Laetabundus, exultet fidelis chorus, Alleluia"* written by Bernard. The *"Laetabundus,"* written in rhymed stanzas, is a theological exposition of human redemption through the Incarnation.

Laetabundus, exultet fidelis chorus, Alleluia

Come rejoicing,
Faithful men, with rapture singing
Alleluia!

Monarch's Monarch,
From a holy maiden springing,
Mighty wonder!

Angel of the Counsel here,
Sun from star, he doth appear,
Born of a maiden:

He a sun who knows no night,
She a star whose paler light
Fadeth never.

As a star its kindred ray,
Mary doth her Child display,
Like in nature;

Still undimmed the star shines on,
And the maiden bears a Son,
Pure as ever.

Lebanon his cedar tall
To the hyssop on the wall
Lowly bendeth;

From the highest, him we name
Word of God, to human frame
Now descendeth.

Yet the synagogue denied
What Esaias had descried:
Blindness fell upon the guide,
Proud, unheeding.

If her prophets speak in vain,
Let her heed a Gentile strain,
And, from mystic Sybil, gain
Light and leading.

No longer then delay,
Hear what the Scriptures say,
Why be cast away
A race forlorn?

Turn and this Child behold,
That very Son, of old
In God's writ foretold,
A maid hath borne.

A Christmas Trope

IRONICALLY, DRAMA, which the early church fathers fought so strenuously
to suppress as a pagan danger, was reborn within the church. The first
dramas of the Middle Ages were elaborated tropes, seasonal insertions
added to the mass. The first trope, the *Quem Quaeritis*, was used in the
Easter service and dramatized the resurrection of Christ. In that trope,
the Marys approach the tomb seeking the crucified Christ. Closely mod-
eled on its Easter prototype, the *Officium Pastorum* portrays the shepherds
arriving at the manger in search of the infant Christ. Despite its simplicity, this Christmas trope appealed to the imagination and developed into

more complex Christmas plays, including such fanciful later works as *The Second Shepherds' Play*. The version of the trope reprinted here is from an eleventh-century French manuscript.

Officium Pastorum

On the Nativity of the Lord, let two deacons dressed in dalmatics be prepared for Mass, speaking from behind the altar.

"You shepherds, who are you looking for in the crib, tell us?"
Let two cantors in the chorus answer:

"The Savior Christ the Lord, the infant wrapped in tatters, as the angel told us."
The deacons again:

"He is here with Mary, his mother about whom the prophet Isaiah foretold: 'Behold a virgin will conceive and give birth to a son.' And so you messengers speak out because he is born."
Then let a cantor sing in a high voice:

"Alleluia, Alleluia, For at last we know truly that Christ is born on earth, about whom let all of you sing out, saying with the prophet, exclaiming: A boy-child is born."
Then follows the Introit.

Feast of Fools

DURING THE MIDDLE AGES, boisterous liturgical revels known collectively as the Feast of Fools evolved during the Christmas season. These revels, which may have originated in the Roman Saturnalia, began as a festivity for lower clergy. During the twelfth century, subdeacons conducted services that sometimes included the election of a boy-bishop or pope of fools, dancing and singing lewd songs, and playing cards or dice in the church. Part of these revels included the introduction of an ass into the church, accompanied by the singing of the "Prose of the Ass." At the close of the mass, the priest, instead of saying "The mass is ended," would bray, and the people would respond by hee-hawing three times, instead of saying "Thanks be to God." Not surprisingly, serious attempts were made to eliminate the Feast of Fools; however, probably due to its popularity with the people and the lower clergy, the feast remained until the Renaissance.

Prose of the Ass

From points east
arrived a beautiful ass,
very strong and suitable for
the burden it was carrying.
    Hey! Sir Ass, for singing
    with your beautiful, balking mouth,
    you will have plenty of hay
    and enough oats to plant.

He was slow on his feet
unless there was a staff
and its sharp tip prodded
him in the rump.
    Hey! Sir Ass . . .

Here in the hills of Sichen
up to now nourished at the tribe of Ruben,
journeyed through Jordan
and showed up in Bethlehem.
    Hey! Sir Ass . . .

Behold the yoked son
fitted with large ears,
an extraordinary praiseworthy ass,
the lord of all asses.
    Hey! Sir Ass . . .

With his leap
he surpasses the young roebuck
as well as its dame and sire.
He is fleet as the Medians.
    Hey! Sir Ass . . .

Gold from Arabia,
incense and myrrh from Saba,
this excellent beast carries its
burden into the church.
    Hey! Sir Ass . . .

While he drags
a cart with many little bundles,
his jaws gnaw away at
the tough hay.
    Hey! Sir Ass . . .

He consumes thistle and barley
with their bristles: he separates
the wheat from the chaff on the
threshing floor.
    Hey! Sir Ass . . .

Oh, Ass, may you say amen,
now full from your meal.
Repeat it again, amen, amen,
and spurn the things of old.
    Hey! Sir Ass . . .

Entrance of the Lord into the Land of Egypt

THE FOLLOWING DOXOLOGY is from the Coptic Egyptian liturgy of the feast of the Entrance of the Lord into the Land of Egypt, celebrated on the twenty-fourth day of Bashons (June 1). This unique work is a liturgical remembering of the origins of the Egyptian church. Coptic Christian traditions go back to the earliest days of the church, though this specific feast-day text in the Coptic Bohairec dialect is presumed to be medieval. This doxology is a welcoming song, an exuberant burst of praise drawing on biblical imagery to suggest both the human and divine dimensions of the Nativity.

Doxology

God glorious in the renown of his saints,
    enthroned upon the cherubim,
      appeared in the land of Egypt.
We have seen him who created the heavens and the earth,

the Good One in the bosom of Mary,
the New Heaven,
together with the faithful Joseph the Righteous.
He who is of endless days,
praised of angels,
has come on this day to the Land of Egypt to save us,
for we are his people.
Rejoice and give praise, O Egypt,
together with her children and all her districts,
for unto you has come the Lover of Mankind,
he who is before all ages.
Isaiah the Great said,
'Behold the Lord comes into Egypt upon a swift cloud,
He who is king of heaven and earth.'
We praise him, we glorify him, and exalt him,
the Good One and Lover of Mankind;
have mercy upon us according to your great goodness.

Anonymous Christmas Sermons

IN THE MIDDLE AGES IN CHRISTIAN SOCIETIES, preaching held a prominent place. The homily provided not only edification but entertainment. The medieval preacher often accented and added to the realism of the Nativity scene. As in the first excerpt by an anonymous author, eloquent preachers loved to contrast Jesus' humble origins with the mightiness of earthly kings and kingdoms.

The aspect of marvel in the Nativity story, as illustrated in the second excerpt, also anonymous, often attracted the preacher's interest. The dramatic qualities of the story and the personality and motivation of the biblical characters appealed to the writers of the miracle and morality plays, drama and homily mutually influencing each other.

Excerpt 1

Here men may see, whoever looks carefully, great poverty in the array at this lord's birth. And both poor and rich must learn here a lesson, the poor to be glad in their poverty and bear meekly their estate, because their lord and their maker willfully gave them such example; the rich also to dread the misusing of their richness in lusts and likings out of measure, and little or nought to give of their riches to Christ's poor brethren.

Where were the great castles and their towers, with large halls and long chambers royally decked with hangings, tapestries and cushions, beds and curtains of gold and silk, appropriate to the birth of so high an emperor? Where were the royal ladies and worthy gentle women to be attendant to this worthy empress, and bear her company at that time? Where were the knights and squires to bring service to this lady of noble meats, costly arrays, with hot spices and useful drinks of divers sweet wines? Instead of a royal castle arrayed with rich cloths, they had a stinking stable in the highway. Instead of real beds and curtains, they had no other clothes but such as belonged to a poor carpenter's wife on pilgrimage. Instead of company of knights and ladies, she had but poor Joseph her husband and two dumb beasts.

Excerpt 2

Many marvels fell at this time of his coming, and divers miracles as witness Innocentius Quartus, that twelve years before Christ's birth there was a general peace throughout all the world. And therefore the Romans ordained a solemn and fair temple, and called it the temple of peace. Then they went to an idol that they had, that was called Appolyn, and asked him how long that the temple should last, and he answered them and said—"till a maid has born a child." And when they heard this, they said that the temple should last forever. Then they wrote above on the temple these words—"*Templum pacis est in eternum,*" for they believed that it might never be that a maiden should have conceived and born a child and after that birth to have been pure maiden. But that same night that Christ was born, the temple cleaved in two and fell to nothing, and then they believed the prophecy. The beasts also that know no reason fell on their knees and worshiped our savior. Truly this coming restored us to our heritage. For now we shall have the same joy in our souls as much as heart can think and tongue can tell.

Aelfric of Cerne

AELFRIC (955–1020), NOVICE-MASTER AT CERNE ABBEY in Winchester, England, from 987, wrote vernacular biblical translations as well as two series of sermons paralleling the events commemorated in the church calendar. He was a great interpreter for English-speaking peoples of the main stream of catholic Christendom as represented by Augustine of Hippo. In this excerpt from a homily attributed to Aelfric, the speaker narrates the events of the Nativity, providing contemporary correlations to the original events.

Anglo-Saxon Homily on Christmas

(excerpt)

My dearest brethren, our Saviour, the Son of God, co-eternal with and equal to His Father, who was ever with Him without beginning, vouchsafed that He would on this present day, for the redemption of the world, be corporally born of the Virgin Mary. He is Prince and Author of all things good and of peace, and He sent before His birth unwonted peace, for never was there such peace before that period in the world, as there was at the time of His birth; so that all the world was subjected to the empire of one man, and all mankind paid royal tribute to Him alone. Verily in such great peace was Christ born, who is our Peace, because He united angels and men to one family through His Incarnation. . . . All nations then went that each separately might declare concerning himself, in the city to which he belonged. As at that time, according to the emperor's proclamation, each once singly in their cities, declared concerning himself, so also now do our teachers make known to us Christ's proclamation, that we gather us to His holy congregation, and therein, with devout mind, pay to Him the tribute of our faith, that our names may be written in the book of life with His chosen.

The Lord was born in the city which is named Bethlehem, because it was so before prophesied in these words: "Thou Bethlehem, land of Judah, thou art not the meanest of cities among the Jewish princes, for of thee shall come the guide that shall govern the people of Israel." Christ would be born on journey, that He might be concealed from his persecutors. Bethlehem is interpreted "bread-house" and in it was Christ the True Bread brought forth, who saith of Himself, "I am the vital bread which descended from heaven, and he who eateth of this bread shall not die to eternity." This holy bread we taste where we with faith go to housel; because the holy communion spiritually is Christ's body; and through that we are redeemed from eternal death. Mary brought forth her first born son on this present day, and wrapped Him in swaddling clothes, and for want of room, laid Him in a bin. That child is not called her first born child because she afterwards brought forth another, but because Christ is the first-born of many spiritual brothers. All Christian men are His spiritual brothers, and He is the first-born, in grace and godliness only begotten of the Almighty Father. He was wrapped in mean swaddling clothes, that He might give us the immortal garment which we lost by the first created man's transgression. The Almighty Son of God whom the heavens could not contain, was laid in a narrow bin, that He might redeem us from the narrowness of hell. Mary was there a stranger, as the gospel tells us; and through the concourse of people the inn was greatly crowded. The son of God was crowded in this inn, that He might give us a spacious dwelling in the Kingdom of heaven, if we obey His will. He asks nothing of us as reward for His toil, except our soul's health, that we may prepare ourselves for Him pure and uncorrupted in bliss and everlasting joy. The shepherds that watched over their flock at Christ's birth, betokened the holy teachers in God's church, who are the spiritual shepherds of faithful souls: and the angel announced Christ's birth to the herdsmen, because to the spiritual shepherds, that is teachers, is chiefly revealed concerning Christ's humanity, through book-learning: and they shall sedulously preach to those placed under them, that which is manifested to them, as the shepherd proclaimed the heavenly vision. It beseemeth the teacher to be ever watchful over God's flock, that the invisible wolf scatter not the sheep.

Adam of Dryburgh

ADAM OF DRYBURGH (D. 1212), WAS A SCOTTISH PREACHER and Carthusian monk who lived in Anglo-Norman Britain, first in Scotland and later in England. Scotland in the twelfth century had a rich monastic tradition in such places as Melrose, Kelso, Jedburgh, and Dryburgh abbeys. Adam achieved enough fame as a preacher to be invited as far away as France to preach. A large number of his Scottish sermons remain today, six of which are Christmas sermons. The following excerpt is from the conclusion of his third Christmas sermon.

Christmas Sermon

(excerpt)

O child, Creator of All! how humbly You lie in the manger. You Who rule powerfully in heaven! There the heaven of heavens cannot contain you; here, however, You are held in the narrowest manger: there, in the beginning of the world you decorated the earth with green grasses that produced seed, with fruit-bearing trees that produced fruit, You ornamented the heavens with the sun, the moon, and the stars, the sky with winged birds, the waters with fish, You filled the land with reptiles, draft animals, and beasts; here, however, in the end of the world You are wrapped in swaddling clothes! O majesty! O lowness! O sublimity! O humility! O immense, eternal and Ancient of days! O small, temporal infant whose life is not yet one day upon the earth!

The Second Shepherds' Play

THE SECOND SHEPHERDS' PLAY, a fifteenth-century English pageant play, is the second play about the visitation of the shepherds by the author known only as the Wakefield Master. Pageant plays, also referred to as mystery and cycles plays, were short vernacular plays on biblical topics produced and performed outdoors by the trade guilds of a town, in this instance Wakefield, usually on Whitsunday or Corpus Christi Day. Pageant wagons, which progressed through the town from one station to another, were probably used in conjunction with stationary areas for performances. An entire cycle, which could take place in one or several days, might begin with the fall of Lucifer, move on to the creation, Noah's flood, and other Old Testament tales, continue with a Nativity play and several episodes from the life of Christ, include a resurrection play, and conclude with the last judgment.

Although *The Second Shepherds' Play* derives from Luke's Gospel and the *Officium Pastorum*, its brilliance lies in the freshness of the treatment. The author juxtaposes two Nativity scenes: a comic one in which the supposed newborn is the sheep stolen by Mak, and the traditional one in which the shepherds worship Christ, the Lamb of God. The author endows the traditionally anonymous shepherds with names—Gib, Coll, and Daw—and distinct, realistic personalities. They are simple men, rustic, driven by poverty, high-spirited yet devout. Anachronistically, the shepherds mention Christ, the cross, the Virgin, refer to the saints, and even misquote Latin bits of liturgy. Such anachronisms, common in medieval Christian drama, are not accidental, but presumably indicate the transcending of time.

The character of Mak, the sheep stealer, is probably taken from folklore. The magic charm Mak casts upon the shepherds to induce sleep while he steals the sheep, followed by their awakening, reflects the death and rebirth motif found in folk custom and literature; and the cherries presented to the baby are sometimes construed as a fertility symbol.

The portion of the play reprinted here begins when Mak's wife, Gill, devises the scheme to hide the stolen sheep in the cradle, and continues with the two Nativity scenes.

The Second Shepherds' Play

(excerpts)

WIFE:	A good trick have I spied, since you can do none:
	Here shall we hide him, till they be gone,
	In my cradle abide! Let me alone,
	And I shall lie beside in childbed and groan.

MAK:	Get ready,
	And I shall say you were delivered
	Of a boy-child this night.

WIFE:	Now well is my day bright
	That ever was I born!
	This is a good guise and a clever trick;
	Yet a woman's advice helps at the last.
	I never know who spies; return fast.

MAK: But I will come before they rise,
             Unless blows a cold blast!
             I will go sleep.
             Yet sleep all this company;
             And I shall go stalk privily,
             As if it had never been I
             That carried off their sheep.

[Mak returns to the shepherds upon whom he had cast a sleeping spell and feigns sleep. Upon awakening, the shepherds recount their dreams. Mak, claiming to have dreamed that his wife, Gill, has had a child, hurries home to her. Soon after, the shepherds discover a missing sheep and go immediately to Mak's cottage to confront the thief.]

MAK: As far as you may,
             Good men, speak softly,
             Over a sick woman's head, that is not at her ease;
             I had rather be dead than she had any disease.

WIFE: Go to another homestead! I can not well breathe;
             Each foot that you tread goes through my nose
             So high.

1 SHEPHERD: Tell us, Mak, if you may,
             How fare you, I say?

MAK: But are you in this town to-day?
             Now how fare you?
             You have run in the mire, and are wet yet;
             I shall make you a fire, if you will sit.
             A nurse would I hire.
             Think you on yet?
             Well ended is my hire—my dream, this is it—
             A season.
             I have children, as you know,
             Well more than enough;
             But we must drink what we brew,
             And that is but reason.
             I would you dined before you went. I think that you
             sweat.

2 SHEPHERD: Nay, neither mends our mood drink nor meat.

MAK: Why, sir, is anything wrong?

3 SHEPHERD:	Yes, our sheep that we tend Were stolen as they pastured. Our loss is great.
MAK:	Sirs, drink! Had I been there, Some should have paid for it.
1 SHEPHERD:	Marry, some men believe that you were, And that makes us think.
2 SHEPHERD:	Mak, some men believe that it must have been you.
3 SHEPHERD:	Either you or your spouse, so say we.
MAK:	Now if you suspect Gill or me, Come and search our house, and then may you see Who had the ewe. If I any sheep have got, Either ewe or ram—And Gill, my wife, rose not Here since she delivered— As I am true and loyal, to God here I pray That this be the first meal that I shall eat this day.
1 SHEPHERD:	Mak, as I have hope, I advise you, I say: He learned timely to steal that could not say nay.
WIFE:	I faint! Out, thieves, from my house! You come to rob us.
MAK:	Hear you not how she groans? Your hearts should melt.
WIFE:	Out, thieves, away from my child! Go not near.
MAK:	If you knew how she had labored, your hearts would be sore. You do wrong, I you warn, that thus come before. To a woman that has suffered; but I say no more.
WIFE:	Ah, my middle! I pray to God so mild, If ever I you beguiled, That I eat this child That lies in this cradle.

MAK:	Peace, woman, for God's pain, and cry not so!
	You spill your brain, and make me full of woe.
2 SHEPHERD:	I believe our sheep are slain. What find you two?
3 SHEPHERD:	We all work in vain; we may as well go.
	Nothing but clothes!
	I can find no flesh,
	Hard nor soft,
	Salt nor fresh,
	Only two empty platters.
	No livestock but this, tame or wild,
	None, as have I bliss, as strong as the sheep smelled.
WIFE:	No, God bless me, and give me joy of my child!
1 SHEPHERD:	We have marked amiss; I hold us beguiled.
2 SHEPHERD:	Sir, altogether.
	Sir—our Lady him save!—
	Is your child a boy?
MAK:	Any lord might him have,
	This child, as his son.
	When he wakens he grabs, that joy is to see.
3 SHEPHERD:	Good luck to him, and blessings.
	But who were his godparents, so soon ready?
MAK:	So good luck to them!
1 SHEPHERD:	[*Aside*] Hark now comes a lie!
MAK:	So God them thank,
	Parkins, and Gibbon Waller, I say,
	And gentle John Horne, in good faith—
	He, with his long shanks
	Made all the noise—
2 SHEPHERD:	Mak, friends will we be, for we are all one.
MAK:	We? Now I hold for me, for amends get I none.
	Farewell all three!—all glad were you gone.
3 SHEPHERD:	Fair words may there be, but love is there none
	This year.

[They leave the cottage.]

1 SHEPHERD: Gave you the child anything?

2 SHEPHERD: I think not one farthing.

3 SHEPHERD: Fast again will I fling;
Wait for you me here.

[He returns to the cottage.]

Mak, take it to no grief, if I come to your child.

MAK: May, you do me great wrong, and foully have you
behaved.

3 SHEPHERD: The child will it not grieve, that little day-star.
Mak, with your leave, let me give your child
But sixpence.

MAK: Nay, go way! He sleeps.

3 SHEPHERD: I think he peeps.

MAK: When he wakens he weeps.
I pray you go hence.

3 SHEPHERD: Give me leave to kiss him, and lift up the cloth.

[He glimpses the sheep.]

What the devil is this? He has a long snout!

1 SHEPHERD: He is ill-shaped. We wait ill about.

2 SHEPHERD: Ill-spun cloth, indeed, alway comes foul out.
Aye, so!
He is like to our sheep!

3 SHEPHERD: How, Gib, may I peep?

1 SHEPHERD: I believe nature will creep
Where it cannot walk.

2 SHEPHERD: This was a quaint disguise, a clever trick;
It was a high fraud.

3 SHEPHERD: Yes, sirs, it was.
Let burn this bawd and bind her fast.
A false scold hangs at the last;

So shall you.
Will you see how they swaddle
His four feet in the middle?
Saw I never in a cradle
A horned lad before now.

MAK: Peace, bid I. What, let be your fanfare!
I am he that him begot, and yonder woman him
bore.

1 SHEPHERD: What devil name shall he have, Mak?
Lo, God, Mak's heir!

2 SHEPHERD: Let be all that. Now God give him care, I say.

WIFE: A pretty child is he
As sits on a woman's knee;
A dillydown, by god,
To make a man laugh.

3 SHEPHERD: I know him by the ear-mark; that is a good token.

MAK: I tell you, sirs, hark! his nose was broken.
Since told me a cleric that he was bewitched.

1 SHEPHERD: This is a false work; I would willingly be avenged.
Get a weapon!

WIFE: He was bewitched by an elf,
I saw it myself;
When the clock struck twelve,
Was he misshapen.

2 SHEPHERD: You two are well matched.

1 SHEPHERD: Since they deny their theft, let's do them to death.

MAK: If I trespass again, strike off my head.
At your will I stay.

3 SHEPHERD: Sirs, listen to me:
For this trespass
We will neither curse nor quarrel,
Fight nor chide,
But have done at once,
And toss him in a blanket.

[They toss Mak in a blanket.]

1 SHEPHERD: Lord, but I am sore, ready to burst!
In faith, I may no more; therefore will I rest.

2 SHEPHERD: As a sheep of seven score he weighed in my fist.
To sleep anywhere, I think that I wish.

3 SHEPHERD: Now I pray you
Lie down on this green.

1 SHEPHERD: On these thieves yet I ponder.

3 SHEPHERD: Why should you trouble?
And do as I say to you.

[An angel sings 'Gloria in excelsis,' and then says:]

ANGEL: Rise, gentle shepherds, for now is he born
That shall take from the fiend whereof Adam
was forlorn;
That warlock to destroy, this night is he born.
God is made your friend now at this morn,
As He promised.
At Bethlelem go see
Where lies so free
In a crib full poorly,
Between two beasts.

1 SHEPHERD: This was as rare a voice as ever yet I heard.
It is a marvel to tell of, thus to be scared.

2 SHEPHERD: Of God's son of heaven he spoke from on high.
All the woodland lit by lightning he made appear.

3 SHEPHERD: He spoke of a child
In Bethlehem, I tell you.

1 SHEPHERD: That yonder star points;
Let us seek him there.

2 SHEPHERD: Say, what was his song?
Heard you not how he sang it,
Three short notes to a long?

3 SHEPHERD: Yes, indeed, he trilled it:
There was no note wrong, nor nothing that lacked it.

| 1 SHEPHERD: | For to sing among us, right as he performed it, |
| | I know how. |

| 2 SHEPHERD: | Let see how you croon. |
| | Can you bark at the moon? |

| 3 SHEPHERD: | Hold your tongues! Have done! |

| 1 SHEPHERD: | Listen to me, now. |

| 2 SHEPHERD: | To Bethlehem he bade that we should go; |
| | I am afraid that we tarry too long. |

3 SHEPHERD:	Be merry and not sad—of mirth is our song!
	Everlasting joy may we win
	Without trouble.

1 SHEPHERD:	Therefore, let us leave.
	If we be wet and weary,
	To that child and that lady;
	We have nothing to lose.

2 SHEPHERD:	We find by the prophecy—let be your din!—
	Of David and Isaiah, and more than I remember—
	They prophesied by clergy—that in a virgin
	Should be light and lie, to quench our sin,
	And relieve it,
	Our people, from woe;
	For Isaiah said so:
	Ecce virgo
	Concipiet a child that is naked.

3 SHEPHERD:	Very glad may we be, and await that day
	That lovely one to see, who is almighty.
	Lord, I would be happy for once and for all,
	If I could kneel on my knee, some word for to say
	To that child.
	But the angel said
	In a crib was he laid;
	He was poorly arrayed,
	Both meek and mild.

1 SHEPHERD:	Patriarchs that have been, and prophets before,
	They desired to have seen this child that is born.
	They are already gone; their chance have they lost.

We shall see him, I believe, before it be morn,
As a sign.
When I see him and feel,
Then know I full well
It is true as steel
What prophets have spoken:
To so poor as we are that he would appear,
First us find, and declare to us through his
messenger.

2 SHEPHERD: Go we now, let us fare; the place is us near.

3 SHEPHERD. I am ready and eager; go we together
To that bright one.
Lord, if thy will be—
We are simple all three—
Grant us some kind of joy
To comfort thy child.

[The stable in Bethlehem]

1 SHEPHERD: Hail, comely and pure; hail, young child!
Hail, Maker, as I mean, born of a maiden so mild!
Thou hast cursed, I believe, the devil so wild:
The false beguiler of evil, now he goes beguiled.
Lo, he is merry,
Lo, he laughs, my sweet one!
A very fine meeting!
I have hold my promise:
Have a bunch of cherries.

2 SHEPHERD: Hail, sovereign saviour, for you have us sought!
Hail, noble child and flower, that all things has
wrought!
Hail, full of favor, that made all of nought!
Hail! I kneel and I cower. A bird have I brought
To the child.
Hail, little tiny moppet!
Of our creed you are the head;
I would drink of your cup,
Little day-star.

3 SHEPHERD: Hail, darling dear, full of Godhead!
I pray you be near when I have need.

Hail, sweet is thy cheer! My heart would bleed
To see you sit here in so poor weed,
With no pennies.
Hail! Put forth your fist!
I bring thee but a ball:
Have and play you withal,
And go to the tennis.

MARY: The Father of heaven, God omnipotent,
That set all in order, his Son has he sent.
My name did he name, and alighted before he went.
I conceived him through God's might, as he meant;
And now is he born.
May He keep you from woe!—
I shall pray him so.
Tell forth as you go,
And treasure this morn.

1 SHEPHERD: Farewell, lady, so fair to behold,
With your child on your knee.

2 SHEPHERD: But he lies so cold.
Lord, well is me! Now we go, you behold.

3 SHEPHERD: Forsooth, already it seems to be told
Very often.

1 SHEPHERD: What grace we have found!

2 SHEPHERD: Come forth; now are we saved!

3 SHEPHERD: To sing are we bound:
Let us begin loudly.

St. Bonaventure

ST. BONAVENTURE (1221–1274) OF TUSCANY was a Franciscan who studied at the University of Paris. The Minister General of the Franciscan Order, Bonaventure quelled dissent within the order and provided a consistent theological framework for Franciscan teaching. Because of these achievements, he is called the "Second Founder" of the order.

Although the Christmas crèche is attributed to St. Francis and his Friars Minor at Grecchio, Italy, by St. Bonaventure in his medieval biography of

Francis, the actual origin of the custom is more obscure. It is clear, however, that the celebration of the Nativity was very important to Francis and the Franciscans. In Thomas of Celano's *First Life of St. Francis*, he describes the saint at the Christmas crèche as "overcome with tenderness and filled with wondrous joy. . . . Aglow with exceeding love he would call him the Child of Bethlehem, and uttering the word 'Bethlehem' in the manner of a sheep bleating, he filled his mouth with the sound." The excerpt below, from St. Bonaventure's biography of St. Francis, illustrates the belief, current until this century, that the Christmas crèche was originated by St. Francis.

Life of St. Francis of Assisi (1263)

(excerpt)

Now three years before his death it befell that he was minded, at the town of Greccio, to celebrate the memory of the Birth of the Child Jesus, with all the added solemnity that he might, for the kindling of devotion. That this might not seem an innovation, he sought and obtained license from the Supreme Pontiff, and then made ready a manger, and bade hay, together with an ox and an ass, be brought unto the place. The Brethren were called together, the folk assembled, the wood echoed with their voices, and that august night was made radiant and solemn with many bright lights, and with tuneful and sonorous praises. The man of God, filled with tender love, stood before the manger, bathed in tears, and overflowing with joy. Solemn Masses were celebrated over the manger, Francis, the Levite of Christ, chanting the Holy Gospel. Then he preached unto the folk standing round the Birth of the King in poverty, calling Him, when he wished to name Him, the Child of Bethlehem, by reason of his tender love for Him. A certain knight, valorous and true, Messer John of Greccio, who for the love of Christ had left the secular army, and was bound by closest friendship unto the man of God, declared that he beheld a little Child right fair to see sleeping in that manger, Who seemed to be awakened from sleep when the blessed Father Francis embraced him in both arms. This vision of the knight is rendered worthy of belief, not alone through the holiness of him that beheld it, but is also confirmed by the truth that it set forth, and withal proven by the miracles that followed it.

Sir Thomas Malory

SIR THOMAS MALORY (D. 1471) WAS A FIFTEENTH-CENTURY KNIGHT, traditionally but not definitively identified as from Newbold Revell in Warwickshire. Malory's profligate behavior landed him in prison on several occasions, and it was while imprisoned that he wrote a number of Arthurian stories based on earlier French sources. Malory's stories, published by William Caxton in 1485 and entitled *Le Morte d'Arthur*, comprise the best-known composite account of King Arthur and the Knights of the Round Table.

Le Morte d'Arthur offers a superb romantic version of life in the early Middle Ages. Religion and the chivalric tradition remained in a dynamic tension in the Middle Ages, with courtly love, heavenly love, and feudal loyalty all intertwined to form a romantic whole. In the excerpt below, the central action is placed within the twelve days between Christmas and Epiphany. In medieval Christian culture, with its elaborate intermingling of early Christian and pagan custom, Christmas is a magic time in which extraordinary, even miraculous things can be expected to happen, as in the incident of the sword related below.

Le Morte d'Arthur
Book I, Chapter 5

HOW ARTHUR WAS CHOSEN KING, AND OF WONDERS AND MARVELS OF A SWORD TAKEN OUT OF A STONE BY THE SAID ARTHUR

Then stood the realm in great jeopardy long while, for every lord that was mighty of men made him strong, and many weened to have been king. Then Merlin went to the Archbishop of Canterbury, and counselled him for to send for all the lords of the realm, and all the gentlemen of arms, that they should to London come by Christmas, upon pain of cursing; and for this cause, that Jesus, that was born on that night, that he would of his great mercy show some miracle, as he was come to be king of mankind, for to show some miracle who should be rightways king of this realm. So the Archbishop, by the advice of Merlin, sent for all the lords and gentlemen of arms that they should come by Christmas even unto London. And many of them made them clean of their life, that their prayer might be the more acceptable unto God. So in the greatest church of London, whether it were Paul's or not the French book maketh no mention, all the estates were long or day in the church for to pray. And when matins and the first mass was done, there was seen in the churchyard, against the high altar, a great stone four square, like unto a marble stone, and in the midst thereof was like an anvil of steel a foot on high, and therein stuck a fair sword naked by the point, and letters there were written in gold about the sword that said thus:—Whoso pulleth out this sword of this stone and anvil, is rightwise king born of all England. Then the people marvelled, and told it to the Archbishop. I command, said the Archbishop, that ye keep you within your church, and pray unto God still; that no man touch the sword till the high mass be all done. So when the masses were done all the lords went to behold the stone and the sword. And when they saw the scripture, some assayed; such as would have been king. But none might stir the sword nor move it. He is not here, said the Archbishop, that shall achieve the sword, but doubt not God will make him known. But this is my counsel, said the Archbishop, that we let purvey ten knights, men of good fame, and they to keep this sword. So it was ordained, and then there was made a cry, that every man should assay that would, for to win the sword. And upon New Year's Day the barons let make a jousts and a tournament, that all knights that would joust or tourney there might play, and all this was ordained for to keep the lords and the commons together, for the Archbishop trusted that God would make him known that should win the sword. So upon New Year's Day, when the service was done, the barons rode unto the field, some to joust and some to tourney, and so it happened that Sir Ector, that had great livelihood about London, rode unto the jousts, and with him rode Sir Kay his son, and young Arthur that was his nourished brother; and Sir Kay was made knight at All Hallowmass afore. So as they rode to the joustsward, Sir Kay had lost his sword, for he had left it at his father's lodging, and so he prayed young Arthur for to ride for his sword. I will well, said Arthur, and he rode fast after the sword, and when he came home, the lady and all were out to see the jousting. Then was Arthur wroth, and said to himself, I will ride to the churchyard, and take the sword with me that sticketh in the stone, for my brother Sir Kay shall not be without a sword this day. So when he came to the churchyard, Sir Arthur alit and tied his horse to the stile, and so he went to the tent, and found no knights there, for they were at jousting; and so he handled the sword by the handles, and lightly and fiercely pulled it out of the stone, and took his horse and rode his way until he came to his brother Sir Kay, and delivered him the sword. And as soon as Sir Kay saw the sword, he wist well it was the sword of the stone, and so he rode to his father Sir Ector, and said: Sir, lo here is the sword of the stone, wherefore I must be king of this land. When Sir Ector beheld the sword, he returned again and came to the church, and there they alit all three, and went into the church. And anon he made Sir Kay to swear upon a book how he came to that sword. Sir, said Sir Kay, by my brother Arthur, for he brought it to me. How gat ye this sword? said Sir Ector to Arthur. Sir, I will tell you. When I came home for my brother's sword, I found nobody at home to deliver me his sword, and so I thought my brother Sir Kay should not be swordless, and so I came hither eagerly and pulled it out of the stone without any pain. Found ye any knights about this sword? said Sir Ector. Nay, said Arthur. Now, said Sir Ector to Arthur, I understand ye must be king of this land. Wherefore I, said Arthur, and for what cause? Sir, said Ector, for God will have it so, for there should never man have drawn out this sword, but he that shall be rightways king of this land. Now let me see whether ye can put the sword there as it was, and pull it out again. That is no mastery, said Arthur, and so he put it in the stone, therewithal Sir Ector essayed to pull out the sword and failed.

Book I, Chapter 6

(excerpt)

How King Arthur Pulled Out the Sword Divers Times

Now assay, said Sir Ector unto Sir Kay. And anon he pulled at the sword with all his might, but it would not be. Now shall ye essay, said Sir Ector to Arthur. I will well, said Arthur, and pulled it out easily. And therewithal Sir Ector knelt down to the earth, and Sir Kay. Alas, said Arthur, my own dear father and brother, why kneel ye to me? Nay, nay, my lord Arthur, it is not so, I was never your father nor of your blood, but I wot well ye are of an higher blood than I weened ye were. And then Sir Ector told him all, how he was bitaken him for to nourish him, and by whose commandment, and by Merlin's deliverance.

❧　❧　❧　❧

Therewithal they went unto the Archbishop, and told him how the sword was achieved, and by whom; and on Twelfth-Day all the barons came thither, and to essay to take the sword, who that would essay. But there afore them all, there might none take it out but Arthur.

To bliss God bring us all in sum

"TO BLISS GOD BRING US ALL IN SUM" (all together) is one of many medieval English carols that use a Latin refrain for each stanza. The stanzas announce the birth of Christ and the slaughter of the Innocents, reflect on the miraculous nature of the virgin birth, and call the listener to celebrate. The Latin lines that conclude each stanza are drawn from liturgy and would doubtlessly have been familiar to educated listeners. The simile comparing Mary's conception to the sun's shining on glass, which it penetrates without harming, recurs in both carols and theological texts, including the writings of St. Augustine. Although the text printed below dates from the sixteenth century, other versions were current in the fifteenth century.

To bliss God bring us all in sum

To bliss God bring us all in sum,
Christe redemptor omnium.
["Christ, redeemer of all," Christmas Matins]

(1)
In Bethlehem, in that fair city,
A child was born of Our Lady,
Lord and Prince that he should be,
A solis ortus cardine.
["From the direction of the rising sun,"
Christmas Lauds]

(2)

Children were slain great plenty,
Jesus, for the love of thee;
Let us never damned be.
Hostes Herodes impie.
["Herod the Impious, our enemy,"
Vigil of Epiphany, Vespers]

(3)

He was born of Our Lady
Without womb of her body,
God's Son that sits on high,
Jesu salvator seculi.
["Jesus, savior of the world,"
First Sunday after Easter, Compline]

(4)

As the sun shines through the glass,
So Jesus in her body was;
To serve him he gave us grace,
O lux beata Trinitas.
["O blessed light of the Trinity,"
First Sunday after Trinity, I Vespers]

(5)

Now is born our Lord Jesus,
That made merry all us;
Be all merry in this house;
Exultet celum laudibus.
["Let heaven rejoice with praises,"
 Common of an Apostle]

Veni, redemptor gentium

IN THIS ANONYMOUS FIFTEENTH-CENTURY CAROL, each stanza concludes with the Latin refrain *Veni, redemptor gentium* (come, human redeemer). In stanza three, the author alludes to St. Ambrose's writings on the virgin birth. Although there are several passages where Ambrose refers to the virgin birth, one of the most famous is in the hymn by the same title in

Chapter 1. In stanza four, the reference to David is specifically to verse 12 of Psalm 84 of the Latin Vulgate Bible: *Veritas de terra orta est* (Truth is rising from the earth).

This carol is marked by simple rhymes and rhythms. The progression of ideas, however, is more sophisticated. The spirit of Advent is reflected in the opening plea, *Veni, redemptor gentium*. The opening stanza reveals a sense of wonder at a virgin bearing a king, but the next three stanzas reveal biblical and patristic authority for that miracle. In the final stanza, the correlation of Christ's birth and our death leads back to the refrain, *Veni, redemptor gentium*.

Veni, redemptor gentium

Veni, redemptor gentium;
Veni, redemptor gentium.

(1)
This world wonders of all things
How a maid conceived a king;
To give us all thereof showing,
Veni, redemptor gentium.

(2)
When Gabriel came with his greeting
To Mary mother, that sweet thing,
He granted and said with great liking,
Veni, redemptor gentium.

(3)
Ambrose said in his writing
Christ should be in a maid dwelling,
To make true all that singing:
Veni, redemptor gentium.

(4)
And David said in his speaking
That Truth should be on earth growing,
To you, bearer of all things.
Veni, redemptor gentium.

(5)
Christ, crowned at our beginning,
Be with us at our ending,
Us to thy joy for to bring;
Veni, redemptor gentium.

William Dunbar

SOME OF THE MOST MEMORABLE POETRY of the fifteenth century was composed in Scotland. Among the best of the Scottish poets was William Dunbar (c. 1460–c. 1530), who lived and wrote at the Scottish court of James IV. Of an aristocratic background, Dunbar received a B.A. at St. Andrews in 1477 and probably began his literary life when he was employed as court poet. Dunbar's work is extremely varied. Some of his poetry is written in ornate English, some in colloquial Scottish; some is devotional, some ceremonial, some allegorical, some satirical.

Like many devotional medieval poems, "On the Nativity of Christ" intersperses Latin with English. The poem opens with the Latin line *Rorate coeli desuper* (Let the dew of the heaven fall from above), and each stanza concludes with a variant of *Et nobis Puer natus est* (And for us a child is born). "On the Nativity" is an exuberant, celebratory hymn closely tied to two canticles, the *"Te Deum"* and the *"Benedicite,"* which invoke all creatures, powers, and hierarchies of the universe to worship the newborn Christ. The refrain, *Et nobis Puer natus est,* is from the introit for Christmas Day. Throughout the poem runs the metaphor of Jesus as light, the bright day-star, both Son and sun.

On the Nativity of Christ

Rorate coeli desuper!
Heavens, distill your balmy showers!
For now is risen the bright day-star,
From the rose Mary, flower of flowers:
The bright Son, whom no cloud devours,
Surmounting Phoebus in the East,
Is come from his heavenly tower:
Et nobis Puer natus est.

Archangels, angels, and dominions,
Principalities, powers, and martyrs many,
And all you heavenly forces,
Star, planet, firmament, and sphere,
Fire, earth, air, and water clear,
To Him give praise, most and least,
Who comes in with such meek manner;
Et nobis Puer natus est.

Sinners be glad, and penance do,
And thank your Maker heartfully;
For he, whom you may not come to,
Is come to you, full humbly
Your souls with his blood to buy
And free you of the fiend's arrest
And only of his own mercy;
Pro nobis Puer natus est.

All clergy should to him incline,
And bow unto that babe benign,
And do your observance divine
To him that is King of kings:
Incense his altar, read and sing
In holy church, with mind firm set
Him honoring above all things
Qui nobis Puer natus est.

Celestial fowls in the air,
Sing with your notes upon high,
In woods and in forests fair
Be mirthful now with all your might;
For past is your doleful night,
Aurora has the clouds pierced,
The Son is risen with gladsome light,
Et nobis Puer natus est.

Now spring up flowers from the root,
Turn you upward naturally,
In honor of the blessed fruit
That rose up from the rose Mary;

Unfurl your leaves joyfully,
From death take life now at the least
In worship of that Prince worthy
Qui nobis Puer natus est.

Sing, heaven imperial, highest of the high!
Regions of air make harmony!
All fish in flood and fowl of flight
Be mirthful and make melody!
All *Gloria in excelsis* cry!
Heaven, earth, sea, man, bird, and beast—
He that is crowned above the sky
Pro nobis Puer natus est!

Alleluia, alleluia

THIS LYRIC BEGINS with the paradox of the rose blossom issuing forth from a thorn tree, Christ being the blossom. The image originates in the Old Testament reference to the "root of Jesse," the family tree from which the Messiah would be born. The second and third stanzas evoke the image of a well of waters springing forth from the earth, an image associated here with the birth of Christ and the release of the Hebrews from captivity in Egypt. The next five stanzas concentrate on the coming of the three kings. In a seemingly unique characterization, the kings are described in terms of their ages, with the eldest coming first, then the "middlemost" king, and finally the youngest.

The Latin refrain is translated "Glory be to God the Father."

Alleluia, alleluia

Alleluia, alleluia,
Deo Patri sit gloria.

There is a blossom sprung of a thorn
To save mankind, that was forlorn,
As the prophets said before;
Deo Patri sit gloria.

There sprang a well at Mary's foot
That turned all this world to good;
Of her took Jesu flesh and blood;
   Deo Patri sit gloria.

From that well there struck a stream
Out of Egypt into Bethlehem;
God through his highness turned it again;
   Deo Patri sit gloria.

There were three kings of divers lands;
They thought a thought that was strong,
Him to seek and thank among;
   Deo Patri sit gloria.

They came richly with their presents,
With gold, myrrh, and frankincense,
As clergy read in their sequence;
   Deo Patri sit gloria.

The eldest king of them three,
He went foremost, for he would see
What royal judge that this should be;
   Deo Patri sit gloria.

The middlemost king, up he rose;
He saw a babe in arms close;
In middle age he thought he was;
   Deo Patri sit gloria.

The youngest king, up he stood;
He made his offering rich and good
To Jesu Christ, that shed his blood;
   Deo Patri sit gloria.

There shone a star out of heaven bright,
That men of earth should deem aright
That this was Jesu full of might;
   Deo Patri sit gloria.

Heinrich Suso

HEINRICH SUSO (1300–1366), A DOMINICAN MONK from the age of thirteen, served as prior in the order before becoming an itinerant preacher and pastor. Suso was not anti-women, as were Jacopone and many other medieval monastics who tended to see women as temptresses sent by the devil. Suso's imagery for the quest for Eternal Wisdom/God has feminine as well as masculine components and is typically personal, even autobiographical.

According to tradition, this hymn interweaving German and Latin was given by an angel to Suso. In his vision, Suso was invited into a divine dance by "a radiant youth of noblest bearing." The hymn has maintained its popularity over the span of centuries. For example, it is recorded that in 1745 at the Moravian mission in Bethlehem, Pennsylvania, the hymn was sung in thirteen European and Native American languages at the same time. The modern Christmas carol "Good Christian men, rejoice," which first appeared in English in a collection of the well-known Victorian hymnodist John Mason Neale in 1853, is based roughly on the old German/Latin carol.

In dulci jubilo

In dulci jubilo   [In a sweet song of joy]
Sing ye, and gladness show!
See our bliss reclining
In praesepio,   [In the manger]
The very sun outshining
Matris in gremio   [In his mother's lap]
Qui Alpha es et O,   [Who is Alpha and Omega]
Qui Alpha es et O!

O Jesu parvule,   [O little Jesus]
I yearn for thee alway:
Grant my heart may hold Thee,
O puer optime!   [O best of children]
Through her that did enfold Thee,
Princeps gloriae   [Of highest renown]
Trahe me post te,   [Draw me after you]
Trahe me post te!

Ubi sent gaudia?   [Where are the joys?]
If not in Heaven afar,
There where birds go singing
Nova cantica,   [A new song]
And there where bells go ringing
In regis curia   [In the king's palace]
Eia qualia,   [Oh, what nobility!]
Eia qualia!

Mater et filia   [Mother and son]
Is maiden Maria
Doomed were we sore stained
Per nostra crimina   [For our sins]
Till she for us regained
Coelorum gaudia   [The joys of heaven]
O quanta gratia,   [Oh, such great joy!]
O quanta gratia!

Make we mirth

IN THE FIFTEENTH-CENTURY ENGLISH CAROL "Make we mirth," the anonymous poet calls for jubilation throughout the Christmas season until Candlemas, the February 2 church festival that commemorates the purification rite of the Virgin Mary and the presentation of the Christ Child in the Temple. The poem used the popular device of cataloguing, in this instance using each stanza for an event or a saint associated with the Christmas season. The poem starts with the birth of Christ on the first day of the Yule season, lists the subsequent days of Christmas honoring St. Stephen, St. John, the slaughter of the Innocents, St. Thomas à Becket, the presentation in the Temple, the visit by the Magi, and concludes with Candlemas. The somewhat didactic tone of the stanzas suggests that the carol may have been intended as educational as well as celebratory. A similar form of catalog carol exists in secular folksongs, the best known undoubtedly being "The Twelve Days of Christmas."

Make we mirth

Make we mirth
For Christ's birth,
   And sing we Yule till Candlemas.

(1)
The first day of Yule have we in mind
How God was man born of our kind
For he the bonds would unbind
   Of all our sins and wickedness.

(2)
The second day we sing of Stephen,
That stoned was and ascended even
To God, who saw him stoned from heaven,
   And crowned was for his prowess.

(3)
The third day belongs to Saint John,
Who was Christ's darling, dearer none,
To whom he gave when he should be gone,
   His mother dear for her innocence.

(4)
The fourth day of the children young
That Herod had put to death with wrong,
And Christ they could not tell with tongue
   But with their blood bore him witness.

(5)
The fifth day belongs to Saint Thomas,
That as a strong pillar of brass
Held up the Church, and slain he was,
   For he stood with righteousness.

(6)

The eighth day took Jesus his name,
That saved mankind from sin and shame,
And circumcised was for no blame
But for example of meekness.

(7)

The twelfth day offered to him kings three,
Gold, myrrh, and incense, these gifts free,
For God, and man, and king was he:
Thus worshipped they his worthiness.

(8)

On the fortieth day came Mary mild
Unto the temple with her child
To show her clean that never was fouled,
And therewith ends Christmas.

John Audelay

JOHN AUDELAY, WHO SIGNED HIMSELF "JOHN THE BLIND AWDLAY," was a chantry priest in the vicinity of Haghmond Abbey in Shropshire. His writings are found in the mutilated manuscript known as MS. Douce 302, now in the Bodleian Library at Oxford. At the close of the twenty-seventh of his poems, he wrote, "As I lay sick in my langor . . . this book I made with great sorrow," thereby telling us something of his situation. In the first part of the manuscript, finished in 1426, he refers to his earlier sinful life, and it is speculated that he may even have been a Goliard, one of the wandering musicians popular in his day. Indeed, his "caroles in cristemas," with their repetitive structure, probably reflect the medieval usage of the term "carol" as a dance song.

The first carol, *"In die Natalis domini"* (on the day of our Lord's birth), incorporates two familiar motifs, the catalog of saints' days and the festival welcoming song. In the second Christmas lyric, *"In die sanctorum Innocencium"* (on Holy Innocents' Day), the term "Childermas" in the opening refrain is a fitting medieval term for what is more commonly called the Feast of the Holy Innocents (December 28). Childermas is indeed the "mass of the children," just as Christmas is the "mass of Christ." Herod's order to kill all male children of two and under is explained by the tradition that

Herod was summoned to Rome immediately after his encounter with the Magi. His journey lasted two years, and he gave an order to execute the children upon his return. The 140,000 innocents in stanza three are identified with the 144,000 referred to in the Revelation of St. John. The "chrisomed children" in stanza four are children in the baptismal gowns that also became their shrouds, symbolically anointed and baptized through martyrdom.

In die Natalis domini

Welcome Yule in glad array
In worship of the holy day

welcome be you heaven's king
welcome born in this morning
welcome to you now will we sing
welcome Yule for ever and aye

welcome be you Mary mild
welcome be you and the child
welcome, from the fiend you us shield
welcome Yule for ever and aye

welcome be you Stephen and John
welcome children every one
welcome Thomas, martyrs everyone
welcome Yule for ever and aye

welcome be you good new year
welcome you twelve days efere   [together]
welcome you all that be here
welcome Yule for ever and aye

welcome be you lord and lady
welcome be you all this company
for Yule's love now makes merry
welcome Yule for ever and aye

In die sanctorum Innocencium

With all the reverence that we may
Worship we Childermas Day.

(1)

Christ cried in cradle, "Mother, ba ba!"
The children of Israel cried, "Wa wa!"
For here mirth it was gone
    When Herod fiercely did kill them.

(2)

All male children with two years
Of age in Bethlehem far or near,
They shed their blood with sword and spear;
    Alas, there was an awful array!

(3)

A hundred and forty thousand there were;
Christ them christened altogether
In their blood, and were martyred,
    All pure virgins, it is no nay:

(4)

The chrisomed children to Christ can cry:
"We are slain for great envy;
Lord, revenge our blood for thy mercy,
    And take our souls to thee, we pray."

(5)

A heavenly voice answered again,
"Abide a while, and suffer your pain;
Until the number be slain
    Of your brothers, as I tell you."

(6)

"For you have suffered martyrdom
For Christ's sake, all and some,
He will you crown in his kingdom,
    And follow the Lamb in joy for aye."

John Tauler

JOHN TAULER (C. 1300–1361) OF STRASSBURG was influenced by mystics Meister Eckhart and Heinrich Suso and, like them, was a Dominican friar. A great preacher, contemplative, and spiritual director, Tauler became known as "the Illuminated Doctor." His use of the simple, direct style of German popular songs, or *Volkslieder*, associated with secular topics such as love, dancing, and drinking, shows Tauler's ability, like Luther's, to communicate Christian doctrine in everyday language to a wide German audience. For example, in "A ship comes sailing onwards" Christ is the "precious freight" borne to us by a ship whose sails are powered by the Holy Spirit.

German hymnody later became a primary mode for the spread of Reformation ideas throughout Europe. These German carols are not esoteric, but rather express the central themes of the great church festivals. The Incarnation was a central doctrine to the mystics, who taught that the Lord Jesus must be reborn in the soul of the individual believer.

A ship comes sailing onwards

A ship comes sailing onwards,
　　With a precious freight on board;
It bears the only Son of God,
　　It bears the Eternal Word.

A precious freight it brings us,
　　Glides gently on, yet fast;
Its sails are filled with Holy Love,
　　The Spirit is its mast.

And now it casteth anchor,
　　The ship hath touched the land;
God's Word hath taken flesh, the Son
　　Among us men doth stand.

At Bethlehem, in the manger,
　　He lies, a babe of days;
For us He gives Himself to death,
　　O give Him thanks and praise.

Whoe'er would hope in gladness
   To kiss this Holy Child,
Must suffer many a pain and woe
   Patient like Him and mild;

Must die with Him to evil
   And rise to righteousness,
That so with Christ he too may share
   Eternal life and bliss.

St. Stephen and Herod

THIS BALLAD FROM THE MID-FIFTEENTH CENTURY depicts an imaginary conversation between Stephen, the first Christian martyr, and King Herod. Stephen meets his death because of his desire to leave Herod's service and serve the Babe of Bethlehem. The cock who speaks Latin, "*Christus natus est,*" gives a miraculous element that modern readers might find humorous. Rhyming couplets conjure up a vivid scene in which the medieval world and biblical characters interact dramatically and pointedly.

St. Stephen and Herod

Saint Stephen was a clerk in King Herod's hall,
And served him with bread and cloth, as every king doth befall.

Stephen out of kitchen came with boar's head in hand;
He saw a star was fair and bright over Bethlehem stand.

He cast adown the boar's head and went into the hall.
"I forsake thee, King Herod, and thy workes all."

"I forsake thee, King Herod, and thy workes all;
There is a child born in Bethlehem is better than we all."

"What aileth thee, Stephen? what is thee befall?
Lacketh thee either meat or drink in King Herod's hall?"

"Lacketh me neither meat nor drink in King Herod's hall;
There is a child born in Bethlehem is better than we all."

"What aileth thee, Stephen? art thou mad or raving indeed?
Lacketh thee either gold or fee or any rich weed?"

"Lacketh me neither gold nor fee nor any rich weed;
There is a child born in Bethlehem shall help us in our need."

"That is as sooth, Stephen, all as sooth, ywis,
As this capon shall crow that lieth here in my dish."

That word was no sooner said, that word in that hall,
That capon crew *"Christus natus est!"* among the lords all.

"Rise up, my tormenters, by two and by one,
And lead Stephen out of this town and stone him with stone!"

Then took they Stephen and stoned him in the way,
And therefore is his eve on Christ's own day.

I sing of a maiden

THIS CAROL IS ONE OF A NUMBER OF HYMNS TO THE VIRGIN that were
popular throughout the Middle Ages, though it is less complex in its imagery than many. The carol is familiar through its inclusion in Benjamin
Britten's *A Ceremony of Carols*, a popular modern choral anthology of medieval carols and chants. Simple repetition of the simile "He came also
still . . . as dew in April" gives a certain gentleness to the divine Incarnation, and the gradual extension of the objects upon which the dew falls is a
pretty poetic device consistent with folk lyric technique. In the original,
the second line ends with the term "makeles," a purposeful ambiguity
meaning both mateless and matchless.

I sing of a maiden

I sing of a maiden,
    That is matchless,
King of all kings
    For her son she chose.
He came also still
    Where his mother was

As dew in April
 That falls on the grass.
He came also still
 To his mother's bower,
As dew in April
 That falls on the flower.
He came also still
 Where his mother lay,
As dew in April
 That falls on the spray.
Mother and maiden
 Was never none but she;
Well may such a lady
 God's mother be.

Lo, how a Rose e'er blooming

THOUGH FIRST PUBLISHED IN COLOGNE IN 1599, this German carol may
have originated in the fourteenth century. The original text had twenty-
two stanzas and included lyrical versions of the birth narratives found in
Matthew and Luke. A number of different translations have been made,
including "A spotless rose is blowing," "I know a rose tree springing," and
"Behold, a branch is growing." The melody popularly associated with this
carol was arranged by Michael Praetorius in 1609, who based it on a sixteenth-century folk melody.

In German horticulture, tree roses are greatly cherished, the tree rose in
the cathedral garden at Hildesheim being over a thousand years old. Rose
symbolism is pervasive in Christian art and literature in a variety of forms
and contexts, the rose being commonly associated with the Virgin Mary
or, as in this carol, with Christ.

Lo, how a Rose e'er blooming

Lo, how a Rose e'er blooming
 From tender stem hath sprung!
Of Jesse's lineage coming
 As men of old have sung.

It came, a floweret bright,
    Amid the cold of winter,
When half spent was the night.

Isaiah hath foretold it
    In words of promise sure,
And Mary's arms enfold it,
    A virgin meek and pure.
Through God's eternal will
    This child to her is given,
At midnight calm and still.

The shepherds heard the story
    Proclaimed by angels bright,
How Christ, the Lord of glory
    Was born on earth this night.
To Bethlehem they sped,
    and in the manger found Him,
As angel-heralds said.

This Flower, whose fragrance tender
    With sweetness fills the air,
Dispels with glorious splendor
    The darkness everywhere.
True Man, yet very God,
    From sin and death He saves us
And lightens every load.

O Saviour, Child of Mary,
    Who felt our human woe,
O Saviour, King of glory,
    Who dost our weakness know,
Bring us at length we pray
    To the bright courts of heaven,
And to the endless day.

This ender night I saw a sight

ALTHOUGH THIS VERSION OF "THIS ENDER NIGHT" is from a sixteenth-century manuscript, the lullaby exists in widely differing versions, some of which date from the previous century. The poem recounts a dream the narrator had recently ("this ender night"). In the dream, he envisions a dialogue by the Holy Family in which Mary and Joseph lament the poverty of their Son's surroundings, but the infant Christ reminds his parents that both his humble origins and his crucifixion are to be accepted as God's will.

This ender night I saw a sight

"Ah, my dear, ah, my dear Son,"
   Said Mary, "Ah, my dear;
Ah, my dear, ah, my dear son,"
   Said Mary, "Ah, my dear;
Kiss thy mother, Jesus,
Kiss thy mother, Jesus,
   With a laughing cheer."

This ender night
I saw a sight
   All in my sleep:
Mary, that maid,
She sang lullay
   And sore did weep;
To keep she sought
Full fast about
   Her Son from cold.

Joseph said, "Wife,
My joy, my life,
   Say what you would."
"Nothing, my spouse,
Is in this house
   Unto my pay;
My Son, a King
That made all thing,
   Lies in hay."

"My mother dear,
Amend your cheer,
   And now be still;
Thus for to lie,
It is truly
   My Father's will.
Derision,
Great passion,
   Infinitely, infinitely,
As it is found,
Many a wound
   Suffer shall I.
On Calvary,
That is so high,
   There shall I be,
Man to restore,
Nailed full sore
   Upon a tree."

Latin lullaby

THIS LULLABY, ORIGINALLY IN LATIN, is a folksong of unknown origin, although the form suggests a date no earlier than the twelfth century. The speaker is the Virgin Mary, singing to the Christ Child. In earlier times, attributing such lullabies to the Virgin was common practice. Like most lullabies, the rhythm of the original is simple and singsong, the words repetitive. The content is reminiscent of the modern folk lullaby "Hush, little baby," in which the mother promises a sequence of gifts to her child.

Sleep, my son, sleep!

Sleep, my son, sleep! Your mother
   is singing to her only child.
Sleep, little boy, sleep! Your father
   exclaims to his little newborn.
We sing you sweet praises,
   over and over again, countless times.

I have made up a bed for you alone.
   Sleep, my pretty son!
I have made up a bed of soft hay.
   Sleep my dear, love of my soul.
We sing you sweet praises,
   over and over again, countless times.

Sleep, my pride and garland!
   Sleep, you who are God's milk to mankind.
I, your mother, will give you gifts;
   I will give you a honeycomb.
We sing you sweet praises,
   over and over again, countless times.

Sleep, my honey!
   Sleep, my little one filled with sweetness.
Sleep, life of my life,
   Born from a pure womb.
We sing you sweet praises,
   over and over again, countless times.

Whatever you might want I will give you.
   Sleep, my little boy.
Sleep, my son; sleep, you
   priceless darling of your mother.
We sing you sweet praises,
   over and over again, countless times.

Sleep, you who are the seat of my love and my honor.
   Sleep, joy of your mother.
Oh, heavenly sound and delightful
   melody to my ears!
We sing you sweet praises,
   over and over again, countless times.

Sleep, my son! Sweetly will
   your mother join in your delightful sounds.
Sleep, my baby, sweetly. Father
   will sing you a song.
We sing you sweet praises,
   over and over again, countless times.

So that nothing will go wrong, I will scatter roses;
      I will cover your hay with violets.
I will strew hyacinths on the ground, and
      I will line your crib with lilies.
We sing you sweet praises,
      over and over again, countless times.

If you want music, I will summon
      shepherds at this very moment!
Nothing is more important to them, and
      no one sings more purely.
We sing you sweet praises,
      over and over again, countless times.

Jacopone da Todi

JACOPONE DA TODI (c. 1230–December 25, 1306), a well-born lawyer/accountant, underwent religious conversion at the time of the accidental death of his wife at a wedding, according to a fifteenth-century legend, *La Franceschina*. When her clothes were removed, she was discovered to be wearing a hair shirt. Jacopone, according to the legend, was so affected as to himself become an ascetic. A pious, rustic mystic given to extreme penance, he was reckoned a "holy madman." An ardent admirer of St. Francis, Jacopone was eventually accepted into the Franciscan lay brotherhood. During the time when the Franciscan movement was trying to define itself, Jacopone was among those who stressed always the physical and spiritual rigors of the Christian life, as opposed to those who sought a more moderate path. For Jacopone, awe and wonder were of more value in the religious life than logic and intellect.

Jacopone wrote wide-ranging devotional and dramatic verse for the ordinary Christian. His imagery is often realistic, highly emotional, and lacking in restraint—even rapturous. Though Jacopone frequently speaks of the Christ Child sweetly as "Bambolino" and "Jesulino," as one might speak endearingly to any baby, he also conveys the central Christian paradox of the Christ Child as God-Man.

The selection below, from "The Lauds," reflects the developing doctrine of the immaculate conception of the Virgin Mary, promoted by the Franciscans but opposed by the Dominicans.

The Blessed Virgin Mary

Hail, Virgin, more than woman, holy, blessed Mary!
More than woman, I say: For humankind,
As Scripture teaches us, is born in sin;
In you, holiness preceded birth.
Womb-hidden, a mighty presence enfolded you
And shielded you from all contagion.

The sin that Adam sowed did not take root in you;
No sin, great or small, has place in you.
High above all others is your virginity and your consecration.
Your secret virgin vow leads you,
All unaware of charity's intent,
To a wedding feast, to your spouse.

The high-born messenger's annunciation strikes fear in your heart:
"If you accept the counsel I bring, you will conceive a son without
    peer."
"O Virgin, assent, assent!" the multitude cries out,
"If aid does not come quickly, we shall hurtle to our doom."
You consented, and so conceived the loving Christ,
And gave Him to those who had lost their way.

Conception by a word stuns worldly wisdom—
To conceive without corruption, untouched, intact!
Reason and experience know nothing of such a possibility;
Never was a woman made pregnant without seed. You alone,
Mary Immaculate, you alone; in you the Word, *creans omnia*,
Residing in majesty, becomes flesh, God Incarnate.

You carry God within you, God and man,
And the weight does not crush you.
Unheard-of birth, the child issuing from the sealed womb!
The infant joyously leaving the castle, through locked gates,
For it would not be fitting for God to do violence
To the womb that sheltered Him.

O Mary, what did you feel when you first saw Him?
Did love nearly destroy you?

As you gazed upon Him, how could you sustain such love?
When you gave Him suck, how could you bear such excess of joy?
When He turned to you and called you Mother,
How could you bear being called the Mother of God?

O Lady, I am struck mute
When I think of how you looked on Him,
As you fondled Him and ministered to His needs.
What did you feel then
When you held Him at your breast?
The love that bound you makes me weep!

O salamander-heart, living in flame,
How is it that love did not consume you utterly?
Fortitude sustained you, and steadied the burning heart.
Yet the humility of the child dwarfed yours:
With your acceptance you ascended in glory;
He, instead, abased Himself, descended to wretched state.

Compared to His humility in becoming man,
All other humility is nothing but pride.
Come one and all, come running!
Come see Eternal Life in swaddling clothes!
Take Him in your arms; He cannot run away;
He has come to redeem those who have lost all hope.

Clement Marot

CLEMENT MAROT (1495–1544), SON OF THE POET JEAN MAROT, succeeded his father as the valet to King Francis I in 1526. Although best
known for his courtly verses and witty, frequently ironic epistles, Marot,
encouraged by Calvin, also translated fifty psalms into French, creating
the Huguenot Psalter. Frequently in exile or prison for indiscretions,
Marot died in exile, possibly in Turin.

The poem below is a pastoral, named for the Latin word for shepherd,
pastor. Common pastoral themes are shepherds' laments for an unrequited
love, elegies for the death of a friend, or homages to a personage. Although pastorals are traditionally written in artificial, elevated language,

Marot's poem is simpler and more rustic. Because the refrain in the first verse is a simple, singsong, nonsense rhyme the shepherds chant while playing ball, it has been left untranslated.

Pastoral

A pleasant pastoral
And shepherds in an orchard
The other day, while playing ball,
were talking to each other, to pass the time:
> Roger
> Bergier
> Legiere
> Bergiere

That's too much playing ball:
Let us sing Noel, Noel, Noel.

Do you still remember the prophets
Who told us with such high authority
That a flawless Virgin
Would give birth to a flawless Child?
> The deed
> Is done
> The beautiful
> Virgin
Had the Son promised by heaven:
Let us sing Noel, Noel, Noel.

Jolly Wat the Shepherd

"JOLLY WAT THE SHEPHERD" is prized for its lively, joyful tone and for its realistic depiction of the simple, devout shepherd who hears the angel and travels to Bethlehem to see the newborn Christ. The dialogue within the stanzas, the gaiety, the psychological realism, and the humble gifts offered by Jolly Wat have parallels in *The Second Shepherds' Play*. The giving of gifts by the shepherds, found in many French and English lyrics, doubtlessly developed as a parallel to the gifts of the Magi.

Although this version has been modernized, the refrain "Ut hoy" remains: "Hoy" is a sound used to drive animals in herding, and "ut" is the term for the musical tone "do." Mall and Will appear to be two of Wat's flock, Mall being a common name for a ewe, and Will apparently being the bell-wether.

Jolly Wat the Shepherd

Can I not sing, "Ut hoy,"
When the jolly shepherd made so much joy?

The shepherd upon a hill he sat;
He had on him his tabard and his hat,   [loose garment]
His tarbox, his pipe, and his flagat;   [salve box; flask]
His name was called Jolly, Jolly Wat,
For he was a good herd-boy,
    Ut hoy!
For in his pipe he made so much joy.

The shepherd upon a hill was laid;
His dog unto his girdle was tied;
He had not slept but a little time,
But "Gloria in excelsis" was to him said.
    Ut hoy!
For in his pipe he made so much joy.

The shepherd on a hill he stood;
Round about him his sheep they went;
He put his hand under his hood;
He saw a star as red as blood.
    Ut hoy!
For in his pipe he made so much joy.

The shepherd said straight away,
"I will go see yon wondrous sight,
Where the angel sings on high,
And the star shines so bright!"
    Ut hoy!
For in his pipe he made so much joy.

"Now farewell, Mall, and also Will!
For my love goes to you all still
Until I come again to you,
And evermore, Will, ring well thy bell."
    Ut hoy!
For in his pipe he made so much joy.

"Now must I go where Christ was born;
Farewell! I come again at morn.
Dog, keep well my sheep from the corn,
And warn well, lad, when I blow my horn!"
    Ut hoy!
For in his pipe he made so much joy.

When Wat to Bethlehem was come,
He sweat; he had gone faster than apace;
He found Jesus in a simple place,
Between an ox and an ass.
    Ut hoy!
For in his pipe he made so much joy.

"Jesus, I offer to Thee, here my pipe,
My skirt, my tarbox, and my scripe;   [satchel]
Home to my fellows now will I skip,
And also look unto my sheep!"
    Ut hoy!
For in his pipe he made so much joy.

"Now farewell, mine own herdsman Wat!"—
"Yes, for God, lady, even so am I;
Sleep well, Jesus, in thy lap,
And farewell, Joseph, with thy round cap!"
    Ut hoy!
For in his pipe he made so much joy.

"Now may I well both hope and sing,
For I have been at Christ's bearing;
Home to my fellows now will I fling.
Christ of heaven to His bliss us bring!"
    Ut hoy!
For in his pipe he made so much joy.

Chapter 3

The Renaissance

Visions
Individual
and
Communal

Introduction

Almyghtye God, whiche haste geuen us thy onlye begotten sonne
to take our nature upon hym, and this daye to bee borne of a pure
Vyrgyn; Graunte that we beyng regenerate, and made thy children
by adoption and grace, maye dailye be renued by thy holy spirite,
through the same our Lorde Jesus Christe who lyueth and
reygneth &c

First Prayer-Book of Edward VI, 1549

The period of history generally known as the Renaissance in Europe was marked by both continuities and discontinuities. In England, as in Germany, language "understanded of the people"
replaced the Latin Scriptures, just as the 1549 and 1552 Book of
Common Prayer replaced the Latin Mass in the Church of England. Literary historians, like historians in general, will often accent either avenues of continuity with the Middle Ages or delineate
a new spirit of the age. The literature inspired by the Nativity is illustrative of both continuity and the new spirit. Some of the writing is reminiscent of the literature of the Middle Ages and of
earlier Christian literary traditions. In terms of theme and style,
the Irish poem by Aodh Mac Cathmhaoil could have been placed
in the medieval chapter, save for its later date of composition. The
ornate poems of Robert Southwell and Richard Crashaw are certainly in the tradition of the medieval ecclesiastical poets and are
also reminiscent of the spiritual and emotional elevations of St.
Ephrem in the fourth century. Ben Jonson's masques also trade on
dramatic traditions medieval and earlier.

In the sermons of Lancelot Andrewes and John Donne, we find el-
egant English rhetoric that is new in form and spirit. The English
language in the Renaissance experienced a flowering, and the individual craftsman of genius was able to bend and twist vocabulary,
syntax, and figurative speech into literary works of art. The linguistic roots of English melded into a rich interweaving that was
no longer primarily Anglo-Saxon, or Latinate, or Norman French,

but uniquely English. Regional linguistic tributaries were replaced in large measure by a broad English mainstream. Indeed, it can be argued that the English language reached its pinnacle in the King James Version of the Bible, the sermons of Donne and Andrewes, *The Book of Common Prayer*, the poetry of Donne, Herbert, and Milton, and the plays and sonnets of Shakespeare.

A distinction to be found in the Christmas literature of the Renaissance is that, unlike in previous centuries, the writings usually can be associated with particular authors. Exceptions to known authorship in this chapter are the Spanish and French-Canadian folksongs. The Scottish tale is also anonymous, having been passed down by word of mouth for many succeeding generations until finally transcribed in modern times.

The flowering of the seventeenth-century metaphysical poets represents a notable occurrence in the development of English literature. A rich assortment of writings from this tradition is offered in this chapter. John Donne is the best-known writer of metaphysical verse, with George Herbert as a worthy though less well-known successor in the next generation. Henry Vaughan continued the mystical literary tradition of Suso, Jacopone, and Ephrem.

A different style is represented by Robert Herrick, who reflects a more secularized Christmas celebration, though he himself was a cleric. Shakespeare is included here for his brief, though memorable, description in *Hamlet* of the Christmas folk beliefs. The Ben Jonson masque represents the extreme of an entirely secularized Christmas observance, such as will become common in succeeding centuries where connections with the initiating events of the Nativity become tenuous. Writing representing a return to classicism is found in John Dryden's work. His translation of Vergil is often associated with the Christmas season, though the connection, like that of the Old Testament prophecies, is a matter of interpretation.

The New World, which was of such interest to Renaissance Europeans, is also represented in this chapter. The French-Canadian experience is glimpsed in both "Where are you coming from, Shepherdess?" and in the Huron Carol, a northern Native-American song of somewhat obscure origin, which has found its way into numerous anthologies and contemporary collections of Christmas

Flight into Egypt *by Lu Hung-Nien (Twentieth-century Chinese)*

carols. Edward Taylor represents the English metaphysical poetry tradition carried to the American side of the Atlantic, a tradition somewhat surprisingly reborn in Puritan New England.

A unique literary artist from this time period is Sor Juana Inés, the seventeenth-century Mexican nun and poet. The reader has a surprise in store if the selection here represents a first reading of the work of this most remarkable woman. In some ways, she blends all of the traditions together—metaphysical, baroque, folk, ecclesiastical.

Lancelot Andrewes

LANCELOT ANDREWES (1555–1626), AN ELOQUENT BIBLICAL PREACHER, served both Elizabeth I and James I of England. A prominent Anglican bishop noted for his erudition, Andrewes was one of the translators of the King James version of the Scriptures. As headmaster of Westminster School, Andrewes influenced young George Herbert. Another student, John Hacket, described him as "of a most venerable Gravity, and yet most sweet in all Commerce; the most Devout that I ever saw." Andrewes' *Preces Privatae*, a devotional manual, is still read and admired.

Bishop Andrewes loved to preach on the Nativity. His rational and scholarly style requires perseverance by the reader unfamiliar with seventeenth-century oratory, of which Andrewes may have been the greatest practitioner. Rarely do literary art and devotion so perfectly find single expression as in the writings of Lancelot Andrewes. In the opening of his famous poem "The Journey of the Magi," twentieth-century poet T. S. Eliot, obviously influenced by the sermon printed below, quotes Andrewes: "A cold coming they had of it . . . just the worst time of the year. . . . The ways deep . . . the weather sharp . . . 'the very dead of winter.'"

A Sermon Preached
Before the King's Majesty, at Whitehall, on Wednesday, the twenty-fifth of December, A.D. MDCXXII., being Christmas-Day.

(excerpt)

Behold there came wise men from the East to Jerusalem,
Saying, Where is the King of the Jews that is born? For we have
seen His star in the East, and are come to worship Him.

Matthew ii.1, 2

Ecce magi ab Oriente venerunt Jerosolymam,
Dicentes, Ubi est Qui natus est Rex Judaeorum? vidimus enim stellam
Ejus in Oriente, et venimus adorare Eum.

Latin Vulgate

There be in these two verses two principal points, as was observed
when time was; 1. The persons that arrived at Jerusalem, 2. and
their errand. The persons in the former verse, whereof hath been
treated heretofore. Their errand in the latter, whereof we are now
to deal.

❦   ❦   ❦   ❦

The text is of a star, and we may make all run on a star, that so the
text and day may be suitable, and Heaven and earth hold a correspondence. St. Peter calls faith "the day-star rising in our hearts,"
(2. Peter i.19), which sorts well with the star in the text rising in
the sky. That in the sky manifesting itself from above to them; this
in their hearts manifesting itself from below to Him, to Christ.

❦   ❦   ❦   ❦

We have now got us a star on earth for that in Heaven, and these
both lead us to a third. So as upon the matter three stars we have,
and each his proper manifestation. 1. The first in the firmament;
that appeared unto them, and in them to us—a figure of St. Paul's
epiphane charis, "the grace of God appearing, and bringing salvation
to all men," (Tit.ii.11), Jews and Gentiles and all. 2. The second

here on earth is St. Peter's *Lucifer in cordibus;* and this appeared in them, and so must in us. Appeared 1. in their eyes—*vidimus;* 2. in their feet—*venimus;* 3. in their lips—*dicentes ubi est;* 4. in their knees—*procidentes,* "falling down"; 5. in their hands—*obtulerunt,* "by offering." These five every one a beam of that star. 3. The third in Christ Himself. St. John's star. "The generation and root of David, the bright morning Star, Christ." And He, His double appearing. 1. One at this time now, when He appeared in great humility; and we see and come to Him by faith. 2. The other, which we wait for, even "the blessed hope, and appearing of the great God and our Saviour" (Tit.ii.13) in the majesty of His glory.

These three: 1. The first that manifested Christ to them; 2. The second that manifested them to Christ; 3. The third Christ Himself, in Whom both these were as it were in conjunction. Christ "the bright morning Star" of that day which shall have no night; the *beatifica visio,* 'the blessed sight' of which day is the *consummatum est* of our hope and happiness for ever.

Of these three stars the first is gone, the third yet to come, the second only is present.

❧   ❧   ❧   ❧

Last we consider the time of their coming, the season of the year. It was no summer progress. A cold coming they had of it at this time of the year, just the worst time of the year to take a journey, and specially a long journey in. The ways deep, the weather sharp, the days short, the sun farthest off, in *solstitio brumali,* "the very dead of winter." *Venimus,* "we are come," if that be one, *venimus,* "we are now come," come at this time, that sure is another.

And these difficulties they overcame, of a wearisome, irksome, troublesome, dangerous, unseasonable journey; and for all this they came. And came it cheerfully and quickly, as appeareth by the speed they made. It was but *vidimus, venimus,* with them; "they saw," and "they came"; no sooner saw, but they set out presently. So as upon the first appearing of the star, as it might be last night, they knew it was Balaam's star; it called them away, they made ready straight to begin their journey this morning. A sign they were highly conceited of His birth, believed some great matter of it, that they took all these pains, made all this haste that they might be there to worship Him with all the possible speed they could. Sorry for nothing so much as that they could not be there soon enough, with the very first, to do it even this day, the day of His birth.

John Donne

OF ALL THE AUTHORS INCLUDED IN THIS ANTHOLOGY, John Donne (1572–1631) is the only one for whom works from two different genres, poetry and homily, are included. Raised a Roman Catholic, John Donne took Holy Orders in the Church of England in 1615, and from 1621 until his death held the prominent position of Dean of St. Pauls Cathedral in London. Donne was the most popular preacher of his day, preaching to large numbers at both the cathedral and Paul's Cross, an outdoor preaching station nearby. Preaching in his shroud as a sign of his own mortality, John Donne is at the same time one of the most human and spiritual of preachers. Donne is what would today be called a contextualist, one passionately concerned with the specific world context in which he lived. However, like Lancelot Andrewes, Donne was always able to move from the very particular to the universal.

Though clearly a seventeenth-century figure, Donne is strangely modern. Generations of English students who can find little in other Renaissance writers with which to relate typically appreciate John Donne the poet; however, Donne the preacher is also accessible to moderns, as the following sermon will show.

Number 11.
Preached at S. Pauls
upon Christmas-day. 1626.

(excerpt)

Luke 2.29 and 30. Lord now lettest thou thy servant depart in peace, according to thy word: for mine eyes have seen thy salvation.

The whole life of Christ was a continuall Passion; others die Martyrs, but Christ was born a Martyr. He found a *Golgotha*, (where he was crucified) even in Bethlem, where he was born; For, to his tendernesse then, the strawes were almost as sharp as the thornes after; and the Manger as uneasie at first, as his Crosse at last. His birth and his death were but one continuall act, and his Christmasday and his Good Friday, are but the evening and morning of one and the same day. And as even his birth, is his death, so every action and passage that manifests Christ to us, is his birth; for, *Epiphany* is *manifestation;* And therefore, though the Church doe now call Twelf-day Epiphany, because upon that day Christ was manifested to the Gentiles, in those Wise men who came then to worship him, yet the Ancient Church called this day, (the day of Christs birth) the Epiphany, because this day Christ was manifested to the world, by being born this day. Every manifestation of Christ to the world, to the Church, to a particular soule, is an Epiphany, a Christmas-day. Now there is no where a more evident manifestation of Christ, then in that which induced this text, *Lord now lettest thou thy servant, &c.*

It had been revealed to *Simeon* (whose words these are) that he should see Christ before he dyed; And actually, and really, substantially, essentially, bodily, presentially, personally he does see him; so it is *Simeons* Epiphany, *Simeons* Christmas-day. So also this day, in which we commemorate and celebrate the generall Epiphany, the manifestation of Christ to the whole world in his birth, all we, we, who besides our interest in the universall Epiphany and manifestation implyed in the very day, have this day received the Body and Blood of Christ in his holy and blessed Sacrament, have had another Epiphany, another Christmas-day, another manifestation and application of Christ to our selves; And as the Church prepares our devotion before Christmas-day, with foure Sundayes in Advent, which brings Christ nearer and nearer unto us, and remembers us that he is comming, and then continues that remembrance again, with the celebration of other festivals with it, and after it, as *S. Stephen, S. Iohn,* and the rest that follow; so for this birth of Christ, in your particular soules, for this Epiphany, this Christmas-day, this manifestation of Christ which you have had in the most blessed Sacrament this day, as you were prepared before by that which was said before, so it belongs to the through celebration of the day, and to the dignity of that mysterious act, and to the blessednesse of worthy, and the danger of unworthy Receivers, to presse that evidence in your behalf, and to enable you by a farther examination of your selves, to *depart in peace,* because your *eyes have seen his salvation.*

To be able to conclude to your selves, that because you have had a Christmas-day, a manifestation of Christs birth in your soules, by the Sacrament, you shall have a whole Good-Friday, a crucifying, and a *consummatum est*, a measure of corrections, and joy in those corrections, tentations, and the issue with the tentation; And that you shall have a Resurrection, and an Ascension, an inchoation, and an unremoveable possession of heaven it self in this world; Make good your Christmas-day, that Christ by a worthy receiving of the Sacrament, be born in you, and he that dyed for you, will live with you all the yeare, and all the yeares of your lives, and inspire into you, and receive from you at the last gasp, this blessed acclamation, *Lord now lettest thou thy servant, &c.*

William Shakespeare

WILLIAM SHAKESPEARE (1564–1616), Elizabethan poet and playwright, needs no extended introduction. However, two of his works refer to Christmas observances, one a play title and the other a speech from a play. The play title *Twelfth Night* reflects seasonal and cultural associations with Epiphany and the traditional round of liturgical dramas still being written and performed in Shakespeare's day. The plot of the play itself, however, lacks any obvious connection with the religious dimension of the feast.

Contrariwise, the well-known speech from *Hamlet* is quite explicit and indeed memorable in its depiction of the mood of the season. In the scene from Act I, the ghost of Prince Hamlet's father has just disappeared at the cock crow. This marvel is being discussed by a soldier, Marcellus, and Horatio, Prince Hamlet's friend.

MARCELLUS: It faded on the crowing of the cock.
Some say that ever 'gainst that season comes
Wherein our Saviour's birth is celebrated,
The bird of dawning singeth all night long:
And then, they say, no spirit dare stir abroad;
The nights are wholesome; then no planets strike,
No fairy takes, nor witch hath power to charm,
So hallow'd and so gracious is the time.

Ben Jonson

BEN JONSON (1572–1637), A CONTEMPORARY OF SHAKESPEARE, was in effect England's first poet laureate by virtue of a pension granted him in 1616 by King James I. Jonson's interest in the theater began in his mid-twenties when he joined the company of Philip Henslowe as both a writer and player. Beginning in 1605, he devoted much of his time and energy to the writing of a series of court masques. Masques, characterized by a procession of masked figures known as mummings, date back to the Middle Ages and are related to primitive seasonal rituals (see first printed mummers' play in Chapter 4). Masques developed into elaborate spectacles commonly performed at celebrations such as weddings, coronations, or court balls.

Ben Jonson was a man of difficult temperament, as instanced by his killing of a fellow actor in a duel in 1598. Nonetheless, he was admired for his talent and is the bearer of the wonderfully simple epitaph in Westminster Abbey, "O rare Ben Jonson." His Christmas Masque is illustrative of the secular side of Christmas. In an age in which continuing medieval custom was increasingly challenged, much that was ancient was for a time swept away by the triumph of Oliver Cromwell's Puritans in 1642.

The Masque of Christmas,
As it was Presented at Court, 1616.

The court being seated,

Enter CHRISTMAS, *with two or three of the guard, attired in round hose, long stockings, a close doublet, a high-crowned hat, with a brooch, a long thin beard, a truncheon, little ruffs, white shoes, his scarfs and garters tied cross, and his drum beaten before him.*

CHRISTMAS: Why, gentlemen, do you know what you do? ha! would you have kept me out? Christmas, old Christmas, Christmas of London, and captain Christmas? Pray you, let me be brought before my lord chamberlain, I'll not be answered else: *'Tis merry in hall, when beards wag all:* I have seen the time you have wish'd for me, for a merry Christmas; and now you have me, they would not let me in: *I must come another time!* a good jest, as if I could come more than once a year: Why I am no dangerous person, and so I told my friends of the guard. I am old Gregory Christmas still, and though I come out of Pope's-head alley, as good a Protestant as any in my parish. The truth is, I have brought a Masque here, out o' the city, of my own making, and do present it by a set of my sons, that come out of the lanes of London, good dancing boys all. It was intended, I confess, for Curriers-Hall; but because the weather has been open, and the Livery were not at leisure to see it till a frost came, that they cannot work, I thought it convenient, with some little alterations, and the groom of the revels' hand to't, to fit it for a higher place; which I have done, and though I say it, another manner of device than your New-year's-night. Bones o' bread, the King! *(seeing James)* Son Rowland! son Clem! be ready there in a trice: quick, boys!

Enter his SONS *and* DAUGHTERS, *(ten in number,) led in, in a string, by* CUPID, *who is attired in a flat cap, and a prentice's coat, with wings at his shoulders.*

MISRULE, *in a velvet cap, with a sprig, a short cloak, great yellow ruff, like a reveller, his torch-bearer bearing a rope, a cheese, and a basket.*

CAROL, *a long tawney coat, with a red cap, and a flute at his girdle, his torch-bearer carrying a song-book open.*

MINCED-PIE, *like a fine cook's wife, drest neat; her man carrying a pie, dish and spoons.*

GAMBOL, *like a tumbler, with a hoop and bells; his torch-bearer arm'd with a colt-staff, and a binding cloth.*

POST AND PAIR, *with a pair-royal of aces in his hat; his garment all done over with pairs and purs; his squire carrying a box, cards, and counters.*

NEW-YEAR'S GIFT, *in a blue coat, serving-man like, with an orange, and a sprig of rosemary gilt on his head, his hat full of brooches, with a collar of ginger-bread, his torch-bearer carrying a march-pane with a bottle of wine on either arm.*

MUMMING, *in a masquing pied suit, with a vizard, his torch-bearer carrying the box, and ringing it.*

WASSEL, *like a neat sempster and songster; her page bearing a brown bowl, drest with ribands, and rosemary before her.*

OFFERING, *in a short gown, with a porter's staff in his hand, a wyth born before him, and a bason, by his torch-bearer.*

BABY-CAKE, *drest like a boy, in a fine long coat, biggin-bib, muckender, and a little dagger; his usher bearing a great cake, with a bean and a pease.*

They enter singing.

> Now God preserve, as you well do deserve,
>   Your majesties all, two there;
> Your highness small, with my good lords all,
>   And ladies, how do you do there?
>
> Give me leave to ask, for I bring you a masque
>   From little, little, little London;
> Which say the king likes, I have passed the pikes,
>   If not, old Christmas is undone.   *[Noise without.]*

CHRISTMAS: Ha, peace! what's the matter there?

GAMBOL: Here's one o' Friday-street would come in.

CHRISTMAS: By no means, nor out of neither of the Fish-streets, admit not a man; they are not Christmas creatures: fish and fasting days, foh! Sons, said I well? look to't.

GAMBOL: No body out o' Friday-street, nor the two Fish-streets there, do you hear?

CAROL: Shall John Butter o' Milk street come in? ask him.

GAMBOL: Yes, he may slip in for a torch-bearer, so he melt not too fast, that he will last till the masque be done.

CHRISTMAS: Right, son.

> Our dance's freight is a matter of eight,
>   And two, the which are wenches:
> In all they be ten, four cocks to a hen,
>   And will swim to the tune like tenches.   [fish]

> Each hath his knight for to carry his light,
>   Which some would say are torches;
> To bring them here, and to lead them there,
>   And home again to their own porches.

Now their intent—

Enter VENUS, *a deaf tire-woman.*

VENUS: Now, all the lords bless me! where am I, trow? where is Cupid? "Serve the king!" they may serve the cobler well enough, some of 'em, for any courtesy they have, I wisse; they have need o' mending: unrude people they are, your courtiers; here was thrust upon thrust indeed! was it ever so hard to get in before, trow?

CHRISTMAS: How now? what's the matter?

VENUS: A place, forsooth, I do want a place: I would have a good place, to see my child act in before the king and queen's majesties, God bless 'em! to-night.

CHRISTMAS: Why, here is no place for you.

VENUS: Right, forsooth, I am Cupid's mother, Cupid's own mother, forsooth; yes, forsooth: I dwell in Pudding-lane:—ay, forsooth, he is prentice in Love-lane, with a bugle maker, that makes of your bobs, and bird-bolts for ladies.

CHRISTMAS: Good lady Venus of Pudding-lane, you must go out for all this.

VENUS: Yes, forsooth, I can sit any where, so I may see Cupid act: he is a pretty child, though I say it, that perhaps should not, you will say. I had him by my first husband, he was a smith, forsooth, we dwelt in Do-little-lane then: he came a month before his time, and that may make him somewhat imperfect; but I was a fishmonger's daughter.

CHRISTMAS: No matter for your pedigree, your house: good Venus, will you depart?

VENUS: Ay, forsooth, he'll say his part, I warrant him, as well as e'er a play-boy of 'em all: I could have had money enough for him, an I would have been tempted, and have let him out by the week to the king's players. Master Burbage has been about and about with me, and so has old master Hemings too, they have need of him: where is he, now, ha! I would fain see him—pray God they have given him some drink since he came.

CHRISTMAS: Are you ready, boys! Strike up, nothing will drown this noise but a drum: a' peace, yet! I have not done. Sing—

Now their intent is above to present—

CAROL: Why, here be half of the properties forgotten, father.

OFFERING: Post and Pair wants his pur-chops, and his pur-dogs.

CAROL: Have you ne'er a son at the groom porter's, to beg or borrow a pair of cards quickly?

GAMBOL:	It shall not need, here's your son Cheater without, has cards in his pocket.
OFFERING:	Ods so! speak to the guards to let him in, under the name of a property.
GAMBOL:	And here's New-year's-gift has an orange and rosemary, but not a clove to stick in't.
NEW-YEAR:	Why let one go to the spicery.
CHRISTMAS:	Fy, fy, fy! it's naught, it's naught, boys!
VENUS:	Why, I have cloves, if it be cloves you want, I have cloves in my purse, I never go without one in my mouth.
CAROL:	And Mumming has not his vizard neither.
CHRISTMAS:	No matter! his own face shall serve, for a punishment, and 'tis bad enough; has Wassel her bowl, and Minced-pie her spoons?
OFFERING:	Ay, ay: but Misrule doth not like his suit: he says, the players have lent him one too little, on purpose to disgrace him.
CHRISTMAS:	Let him hold his peace, and his disgrace will be the less: what! shall we proclaim where we were furnish'd? Mum! Mum! a' peace! be ready, good boys.

Now their intent, is above to present,
    With all the appurtenances,
A right Christmàs, as of old it was,
    To be gathered out of the dances.

Which they do bring, and afore the king,
    The queen, and prince, as it were now
Drawn here by love; who over and above,
    Doth draw himself in the geer too.   [gyre]

Here the drum, and fife sounds, and they march about once. In the second coming up, CHRISTMAS *proceeds in his Song.*

Hum drum, sauce for a coney;   [rabbit]
    No more of your martial music;
Even for the sake o' the next new stake,
    For there I do mean to use it.

And now to ye, who in place are to see
    With roll and farthingale hooped: [hoopskirt]
I pray you know, though he want his bow,
    By the wings, that this is Cupid.

He might go back, for to cry *What you lack?*
    But that were not so witty:
His cap and coat are enough to note,
    That he is the Love o' the city.

And he leads on, though he now be gone,
    For that was only his-rule:
But now comes in, Tom of Bosoms-inn,
    And he presenteth Mis-rule.

Which you may know, by the very show,
    Albeit you never ask it:
For there you may see, what his ensigns be,
    The rope, the cheese, and the basket.

This Carol plays, and has been in his days
    A chirping boy, and a kill-pot:
Kit cobler it is, I'm a father of his,
    And he dwells in the lane called Fill-pot.

But who is this? O, my daughter Cis,
    Minced-pie; with her do not dally
On pain o' your life: she's an honest cook's wife,
    And comes out of Scalding-alley.

Next in the trace, comes Gambol in place;
    And, to make my tale the shorter,
My son Hercules, tane out of Distaff-lane,
    But an active man, and a porter.

Now Post and Pair, old Christmas's heir,
    Doth make and a gingling sally;   [jingling excursion]
And wot you who, 'tis one of my two
    Sons, card-makers in Pur-alley.

Next in a trice, with his box and his dice,
    Mac'-pipin my son, but younger,
Brings Mumming in; and the knave will win,
    For he is a costermonger.   [fruiterer]

But New-year's-gift, of himself makes shift,
    To tell you what his name is;
With orange on head, and his ginger-bread,
    Clem Waspe of Honey-lane 'tis.

This, I you tell, is our jolly Wassel,
    And for Twelfth-night more meet too:
She works by the ell, and her name is Nell,
    And she dwells in Threadneedle-street too.

Then Offering, he, with his dish and his tree,
    That in every great house keepeth,
Is by my son, young Little-worth, done,
    And in Penny-rich street he sleepeth.

Last, Baby-cake, that an end doth make
    Of Christmas' merry, merry vein-a,
Is child Rowlan, and a straight young man,
    Though he come out of Crooked-lane-a.

There should have been, and a dozen I ween,
    But I could find but one more
Child of Christmas, and a Log it was,
    When I them all had gone o'er.

I prayed him, in a time so trim,
    That he would make one to prance it:
And I myself would have been the twelfth,
    O' but Log was too heavy to dance it.

Now, Cupid, come you on.

CUPID: You worthy wights, king, lords, and knights,
     Or queen and ladies bright:
    Cupid invites you to the sights
     He shall present to-night.

VENUS: 'Tis a good child, speak out; hold up your head, Love.

CUPID: And which Cupid—and which Cupid—

VENUS: Do not shake so, Robin; if thou be'st a-cold, I have some warm waters for thee here.

CHRISTMAS: Come, you put Robin Cupid out with your waters, and your fisling; will you be gone?   [fussing]

VENUS: Ay, forsooth, he's a child, you must conceive, and must be used tenderly; he was never in such an assembly before, forsooth, but once at the Warmoll Quest, forsooth, where he said grace as prettily as any of the sheriff's hinch-boys, forsooth.

CHRISTMAS: Will you peace, forsooth?

CUPID: And which Cupid—and which Cupid,—

VENUS: Ay, that's a good boy, speak plain, Robin: how does his majesty like him, I pray? will he give eight-pence a day, think you? Speak out, Robin.

CHRISTMAS: Nay, he is out enough, you may take him away, and begin your dance: this it is to have speeches.

VENUS: You wrong the child, you do wrong the infant; I 'peal to his majesty.

Here they dance.

CHRISTMAS: Well done, boys, my fine boys, my bully boys!

THE EPILOGUE

Sings.

Nor do you think that their legs is all
    The commendation of my sons,
For at the Artillery garden they shall
    As well forsooth use their guns,

And march as fine, as the Muses nine,
    Along the streets of London:
And in their brave tires, to give their false fires
    Especially Tom my son.

Now if the lanes and the allies afford
    Such an ac-ativity as this;
At Christmas next, if they keep their word,
    Can the children of Cheapside miss?

Though, put the case, when they come in place,
    They should not dance, but hop:
Their very gold lace, with their silk, would 'em grace,
    Having so many knights o' the shop.

But were I so wise, I might seem to advise
    So great a potentate as yourself:
They should, sir, I tell ye, spare't out of their belly,
    And this way spend some of their pelf.   [money]

Ay, and come to the court, for to make you some sport,
    At the least once every year:
As Christmas hath done, with his seventh or eighth son,
    And his couple of daughters dear.

AND THUS IT ENDED.

The Yule Beggar

THIS STORY WAS PASSED DOWN IN SCOTLAND for some two and a half centuries, the events supposedly having taken place in the late sixteenth century in the area of Castle Douglas in the Kirkcudbrightshire (Galloway) section of the Lowlands. Like all good folktales, there is a universal quality that this story shares with many more familiar Christmas legends, making time and place, in a sense, irrelevant. On Christmas Eve, all roads do indeed lead to Bethlehem, even from the far-off Lowlands of Scotland.

The Yule Beggar

There is a tradition that St. Ninian, in the name of [St.] Ringan, returns to Galloway every Christmas Eve. He reveals himself, however, only to simple, God-fearing shepherds, as the shepherds in the gospels, and as he himself sought to follow in the footsteps of Jesus.

It was Christmas Eve. The shepherd of a flock in a rural wilderness had gone away to a yule fair and left a young herd-boy in charge of the ewes. Alone in a wattled clay hut the boy looked out from the fire and saw that the short afternoon light was already fading. His master had left strict instructions that all the sheep must be in before dusk, for in those days they easily got lost, and wild animals sometimes killed them in the darkness. Also it was wintry weather and the snow might come. Pulling on a ragged jacket the boy went out into the cold afternoon to bring in the flock.

Soon he had them rounded up and safely penned for the night—all but one ewe. He searched and searched, remembering the shepherd's parting words, but he could not find the animal anywhere. The light faded, the last dark fires sank in the west. In the faint light that fell from the evening sky through gaps in the cloud he searched on, fearing to let down his master.

At length, after hours of wandering in the darkness, filling his boots with icy bog water, scratching his face and hands on briars and the twigs of thickets, he stood once more by the little clay hut. Dejectedly he went in and sat by the side of the dying fire. His little crusie lamp flickered in the draught, throwing shadows on the rough walls.

After a while he stirred the embers into life and threw on a few twigs and some broken ends of peat. Smoke rose and filtered in the air before finding its way through the chimney and chinks in the roof. He pushed off the hard, broken boots and nursed his bare feet in the warmth. Soon the moon would rise. He would wait until then and go out again, but he had little hope of finding the lost sheep.

Then suddenly he thought of St. Ringan's Well, which lay a little distance away. People often went there in time of trouble to enlist the saint's aid—sometimes people who had lost things. More than that, it was Christmas Eve: everyone said that Saint Ringan came back to Galloway every Christmas Eve. He paused—but a saint only helped proper folk, he wouldn't be interested in a ragged herd-boy like himself. And they always took him a gift. The boy looked around. He had nothing. All he possessed in the world were his few poor clothes and the bowl of kail brose he was to eat for his supper. It was hardly enough to offer a saint. Besides, he was hungry. Regretfully he realized that hungry or not, he must offer the brose to Saint Ringan. He just had to find the ewe, and he needed help.

The herd-boy warmed the bowl of brose at the fire, and carried it carefully through the darkness to the well. He set it down on the stone edge. Then he knelt, and fervently, though with an eye half open in case anything creepy happened, he begged Saint Ringan to help him find the lost sheep. When he had finished he stood up. Nothing had changed. He waited, looking around into the dark bushes. No bleat came to his ears. Through clear, widening gaps between the clouds, like tracks of water, the stars glittered frostily. A bitter breeze chilled his face and felt through his jacket. With a last, longing look at the dish of brose, the boy turned away and began to walk back to the hut.

He had not gone very far when he heard a little noise behind him. Turning, he saw a thin, ragged man sitting on the edge of the well, supping at his brose. The herd boy began to protest—he had left his supper for a saint, not this tattered beggar. Then charitably he thought that since Saint Ringan had not turned up, the poor hungry man might as well have it.

The beggar waved his spoon at the boy. "It's a grand night, laddie," he called cheerfully.

"I wish it was," the herd-boy replied dejectedly, coming back. "I've lost one of my master's ewes. Some wild animal will kill it during the night, or it will stray so that I'll never find it."

"Don't worry yourself," the beggar cried. "It's not so far away. You'll find it caught in a bramble bush—in the deep ditch beneath yon saugh trees that always bloom first in the spring."

The boy shook his head. "I won't. I've been along that ditch a dozen times, and it's not there."

"Well, that's where you'll find her."

The boy sighed. He could have done with more helpful advice than that.

In a while the beggar finished the dish of brose, and together they walked to the place he had described.

To the shepherd boy's astonishment there was the ewe, caught in the thorns near the bottom of the ditch, its wool screwed up so tightly in the brambles that it could not move. He scrambled down through the tangled vegetation until the verge was high above his head. His boots went through the cat-ice into the water and mud. But no matter how he tugged and tore his fingers on the thorns, the boy could not release it.

The thin beggar joined him deep down in the cold ditch, and somehow together they pulled the wool apart, broke off the bramble stems, and hauled the animal up to the grassy brink. But the sheep was so far gone with exhaustion and cold that it could not stand, and slumped to the ground when they released it.

The boy was not yet strong enough to carry it, and looked down at the forlorn beast. "I doubt it will die here, anyway," he said, not far from tears. "I don't know how to get it home."

For answer the beggar bent, and catching the sheep by the legs slung it around his shoulders. Side by side they returned to the little clay hut and set the tattered animal down by the still glowing fire.

"Will you not stay here the night?" the boy said. "It's cold outside. I have nothing more to eat, but you're welcome to the fire."

"Thank you, laddie," the beggar replied. "It's a kind offer. But I must be on my way, or I'll be late."

"Late?" exclaimed the boy. "But where are you going at this time of night? It's nearly midnight."

"Where! Why, Bethlehem, of course! Where else would I be on Christmas night?"

The herd-boy was bending for a handful of sticks for the fire. When he looked up in surprise at the words, the beggar was nowhere to be seen. Quickly he crossed to the entrance and stared out into the cold night. The beggar had gone. But there, by the rising moon, was a glittering pathway that led from the poor doorway of the little clay hut, straight to the east.

Robert Southwell

ROBERT SOUTHWELL (1561–1595), BORN IN NORFOLK, was educated on the continent and thereafter returned to England in 1586. A Jesuit priest during the time of intense religious-political conflict, Southwell was arrested in 1592 and martyred in 1595. His poems, written mostly in prison, were published shortly after his death. A spiritual writer of vivid imagination and passion, his poem "The Burning Babe" remains one of the most remarkable of Christmas poems; it is a curious, extended metaphor in which the baby Jesus is likened to a smelting furnace. In "New Heaven, New War," after calling on the archangels to stand guard over the divine infant, the poet recounts the many remarkable feats this singular infant will accomplish before his life is done. "New Prince, New Pomp" reflects on the poverty of Jesus' birth.

The Burning Babe

As I in hoary Winter's night stood shivering in the snow,
Surprised I was with sudden heat, which made my heart to glow;
And lifting up a fearful eye, to view what fire was near,
A pretty Babe all burning bright did in the air appear;
Who scorched with excessive heat, such floods of tears did shed,
As though his floods should quench his flames, which with his tears
    were bred:
Alas (quoth he) but newly born, in fiery heats I fry,
Yet none approach to warm their hearts or feel my fire, but I;

My faultless breast the furnace is, the fuel wounding thorns:
Love is the fire, and sighs the smoke, the ashes, shames and scorns;
The fuel Justice layeth on, and Mercy blows the coals,
The metal in this furnace wrought, are men's defiled souls:
For which, as now on fire I am to work them to their good,
So will I melt into a bath, to wash them in my blood.
With this he vanished out of sight, and swiftly shrunk away,
And straight I called unto mind, that it was Christmas day.

New Heaven, New War

Come to your heaven you heavenly choirs,
Earth hath the heaven of your desires;
Remove your dwelling to your God,
A stall is now his best abode;
Since men their homage do deny,
Come Angels all their fault supply.

His chilling cold doth heat require,
Come Seraphins in lieu of fire;
This little Ark no cover hath,
Let Cherubs' wings his body swath.
Come Raphael, this Babe must eat,
Provide our little Tobie meat.

Let Gabriel be now his groom,
That first took up his earthly room;
Let Michael stand in his defense,
Whom love hath linked to feeble sense,
Let Graces rock when he doth cry,
Let Angels sing his lullaby.

The same you saw in heavenly seat,
Is he that now sucks Mary's teat;
Agnize your King a mortal wight,   [recognize] [creature]
His borrowed weed lets not your sight;
Come kiss the manger where he lies,
That is your bliss above the skies.

This little Babe so few days old,
Is come to rifle Satan's fold;   [plunder]
All hell doth at his presence quake,
Though he himself for cold do shake:
For in this weak unarmed wise,
The gates of hell he will surprise.

With tears he fights and wins the field,
His naked breast stands for a shield;
His battering shot are babish cries,
His Arrows looks of weeping eyes,
His Martial ensigns cold and need,
And feeble flesh his warrior's steed.

His Camp is pitched in a stall,
His bulwark but a broken wall:
The Crib his trench, hay stalks his stakes,
Of Shepherds he his Muster makes;
And thus as sure his foe to wound,
The Angel's trumps alarum sound.

My soul with Christ join thou in fight,
Stick to the tents that he hath dight;   [pitched]
Within his crib is surest ward,
This little Babe will be thy guard:
If thou wilt foil thy foes with joy,
Then flit not from the heavenly boy.

New Prince, New Pomp

Behold a silly, tender babe
   In freezing winter night
In homely manger trembling lies—
   Alas, a piteous sight.
The inns are full; no man will yield
   This little pilgrim bed,
But forced he is with silly beasts
   In crib to shroud his head.

Despise him not for lying there
    First what he is inquire;
An orient pearl is often found
    In depth of dirty mire.
Weigh not his crib, his wooden dish
    Nor beasts that by him feed;
Weigh not his mother's poor attire
    Nor Joseph's simple weed
This stable is a prince's court.
    The crib his chair of state;

The beasts are parcel of his pomp,
    The wooden dish his plate.
The persons in that poor attire
    His royal liveries wear;
The prince himself is come from heaven,
    This pomp is prized there.
With joy approach, O Christian wight!
    Do homage to thy king,
And highly praise his humble pomp
    Which he from heaven doth bring.

William Alabaster

WILLIAM ALABASTER (1568–1640), AN ANGLICAN CHAPLAIN with the earl of Essex in 1596 on the Cadiz Expedition, became a Roman Catholic intending to join the Society of Jesus. Later he converted back to the Anglican Church. Alabaster married the mother of the noted physician and alchemist Robert Fludd, became a royal chaplain, and finally settled down as a country parson. His Petrarchan sonnets, only one of which was printed in his lifetime, apparently date from the period of his first conversion (1597–98), when he practiced the meditation techniques of Ignatius Loyola.

A Latinist and Hebraist, Alabaster achieved some reputation as a theologian. He became interested in cabalism, a Jewish mystical tradition, which he applied to the Revelation of St. John. In both poems below, Alabaster meditates on the paradoxes of the Incarnation, using the Nicene Creed's image of Jesus as light of light.

Incarnatio est maximum donum Dei
[becoming flesh, God's greatest gift]

Like as the fountain of all light created
Doth pour out streams of brightness undefined
Through all the conduits of transparent kind
That heaven and air are both illuminated,
And yet his light is not thereby abated;
So God's eternal bounty ever shined
The beams of being, moving, life, sense, mind,
And to all things himself communicated.
But see the violent diffusive pleasure
Of goodness, that left not, till God had spent
Himself by giving us himself his treasure
In making man a God omnipotent.
How might this goodness draw our souls above
Which drew down God with such attractive Love.

#37 To the Blessed Virgin

Hail graceful morning of eternal Day,
the period of Juda's throned right
and latest minute of the Legal night,   [Hebrew Law]
whom wakeful Prophets spied, far away,
chasing the night from the world's Eastern bay;
within whose pudent lap and rosal plight   [modest womb]
conceived was the Son of unborn light
whose light gave being to the world's array,
unspotted morning whom no mist of Sin
nor cloud of human mixture did obscure,
strange morning that, since day hath entered in
before and after doth alike endure;
and well it seems a Day that never wasteth
should have a morning that for ever lasteth.

Aodh Mac Cathmhaoil

A Franciscan monastic and priest, Aodh Mac Cathmhaoil (1571–1626) was born in Downpatrick, County Down, Ireland. Given the nickname Aodh Mac Aingil, which translates as "Hugo Angelicus," this saintly priest was involved in the founding of Irish colleges in Louvain and Rome. He died before he could assume the archbishopric of Armagh, to which he was appointed in 1626. He was the author of philosophical and devotional work, mostly prose, in Irish and Latin.

The excerpt below, originally in Irish, has an appealing homely quality in which the speaker has an almost desperate desire to be of humble service to the newborn king, even to the point of offering to "chase the hill-boys' dogs / away from this helpless Prince." References to Patrick and Bridget make this devotional poem unmistakably Irish.

The Sacred Child
(excerpt)

God greet You, sacred Child,
    poor in the manger there,
yet happy and rich tonight
    in your own stronghold in glory.

Motherless once in Heaven,
    Fatherless now in our world,
true God at all times You are,
    but tonight You are human first.

Grant room in Your cave, O King,
    (though not of right) to this third brute
among the mountain dogs
    —for my nature was ever like theirs.

Mary, Virgin and Mother,
    open the stable door
till I worship the King of Creation.
    Why not I more than the ox?

I will do God's service here,
    watchful early and late.
I will chase the hill-boys' dogs
    away from this helpless Prince.

The ass and the ox, likewise,
    I will not let near my King;
I will take their place beside Him,
    ass and cow of the living God!

In the morning I'll bring him water.
    I'll sweep God's Son's poor floor.
I'll light a fire in my cold soul
    and curb with zeal my wicked body.

I'll wash his poor garments for Him
    and, Virgin, if you let me,
I'll shed these rags of mine
    as a covering for your Son.

And I'll be the cook for His food.
    I'll be doorman for the God of Creation!
On behalf of all three I'll beg,
    since they need my help to speak.

No silver or gold I'll ask
    but a daily kiss for my King.
I will give my heart in return
    and He'll take it from all three.

Patrick, who through this Child
    by grace got Jesus' crozier
—O born without body's bile—
    and Bridget . . . be with us always.

Patron of the Isle of Saints,
    obtain God's graces for us.
Receive a poor friar from Dún
    as a worm in God's cave tonight.

A thousand greetings in body tonight
     from my heart to my generous King.
In that He assumed two natures
     here's a kiss and a greeting to God!

John Donne

JOHN DONNE (1572–1631) RANKS AMONG the foremost of the seventeenth-
century metaphysical poets and rhetoricians (see Donne's Christmas sermon). In T. S. Eliot's view, John Donne and his metaphysical kinsmen
succeeded in overcoming in their writing what Eliot called "dissociation
of sensibility," a separation of intellect and emotion. In the writing of
John Donne we find passionate feeling and intellect combining, so that
his work might be equally well described as illustrative of passionate intellect or intellectual passion. Few other writers are remembered for both
physical love songs that often make use of religious imagery ("For Godsake
hold your tongue, and let me love") and for divine poems and sermons in
which human passion is an integral part of a theological perspective ("Bat-
ter my heart, three person'd God").

The two Donne poems below are from *La Corona*, a sequence of seven
sonnets intended to be an endless wreath of praise, similar to traditional
meditations on the Virgin Mary. The individual poems are really a seven-
part whole, held together by repetition and paradox. In "The Annunciation," the paradox is that Mary is now "Thy maker's maker, and thy
Father's mother . . . *Immensity cloistered in thy dear womb.*" In "Nativity"
the paradox is in "how he / Which fills all place, yet none holds him, doth
lie" in Mary's womb.

2
Annunciation

Salvation to all that will is nigh;
That All, which always is All every where,
Which cannot sin, and yet all sins must bear,
Which cannot die, yet cannot choose but die,
Lo, faithful Virgin, yields himself to lie
In prison, in thy womb; and though he there
Can take no sin, nor thou give, yet he will wear

Taken from thence, flesh, which death's force may try.
Ere by the spheres time was created, thou
Wast in his mind, who is thy Son, and Brother;
Whom thou conceiv'st, conceiv'd; yea thou art now
Thy Maker's maker, and thy Father's mother;
Thou hast light in dark; and shutst in little room,
Immensity cloistered in thy dear womb.

3
Nativity

Immensity cloistered in thy dear womb,
Now leaves his well-beloved imprisonment,
There he hath made himself to his intent
Weak enough, now into our world to come;
But Oh, for thee, for him, hath the Inn no room?
Yet lay him in this stall, and from the Orient,
Stars, and wisemen will travel to prevent
The effect of Herod's jealous general doom.
Seest thou, my Soul, with thy faith's eyes, how he
Which fills all place, yet none holds him, doth lie?
Was not his pity towards thee wondrous high,
That would have need to be pitied by thee?
Kiss him, and with him into Egypt go,
With his kind mother, who partakes thy woe.

George Wither

GEORGE WITHER (1588–1667), author of pastoral and satirical works, is perhaps best remembered for his emblem poetry, poetry in which quaint pictures were used with texts, each medium illustrative of its companion piece. Sometimes these became shape poems, such as Herbert's famous altar and angel wings poems or Wither's own dirge in the rhomboid shape of a coffin. Wither's satires sometimes got him into trouble: he endured several brief imprisonments, though his attacks on the deadly sins and such habits as fox hunting seem mild enough today. A Puritan, Wither served with Cromwell in the English Civil War. The amusing story is told that he was saved from hanging by Sir John Denham, who said that as long as Wither lived, he (Denham) would not be considered the worst living English poet!

In "A Christmas Carol" the reader is seduced into a lovely sounding description of the customs of Christmas observance reminiscent of Herrick; however, on reflection the reader recognizes that the theme is different than first appears, for there is a strongly implied indictment of the everyday sorry state of folks who have to drown their sorrows annually in one day of frenetic merriment, Christmas day.

A Christmas Carol

So now is come our joyful'st feast,
    Let every man be jolly;
Each room with ivy leaves is dressed,
    And every post with holly.
        Though some churls at our mirth repine,
        Round your foreheads garlands twine,
        Drown sorrow in a cup of wine,
And let us all be merry.

Now all our neighbors' chimneys smoke,
    And Christmas blocks are burning;
Their ovens they with baked meats choke,
    And all their spits are turning.
        Without the door let sorrow lie,
        And if for cold it hap to die,
        We'll bury it in a Christmas pie,
And evermore be merry.

Now every lad is wondrous trim,
    And no man mind his labor;
Our lasses have provided them
    A bagpipe and a tabor.
        Young men and maids, and girls and boys
        Give life to one another's joys;
        And you anon shall by their noise
Perceive that they are merry.

Rank misers now do sparing shun,
   Their hall of music soundeth;
And dogs thence with whole shoulders run,
   So all things there aboundeth.
      The country-folk themselves advance,
      For Crowdy-Mutton's come out of France,
      And Jack shall pipe and Jill shall dance,
And all the town be merry.

Ned Swash hath fetched his bands from pawn,   [ruffs]
   And all his best apparel;
Brisk Nell hath bought a ruff of lawn
   With droppings of the barrel.
      And those that hardly all the year
      Had bread to eat or rags to wear,
      Will have both clothes and dainty fare,
And all the day be merry.

Now poor men to the justices
   With capons make their arrants,   [errands]
And if they hap to fail of these,
   They plague them with their warrants.
      But now they feed them with good cheer,
      And what they want they take in beer,
      For Christmas comes but once a year,
And then they shall be merry.

Good farmers in the country nurse
   The poor, that else were undone;
Some landlords spend their money worse,
   On lust and pride at London.
      There the roisters they do play,
      Drab and dice their land away,
      Which may be ours another day;
And therefore let's be merry.

The client now his suit forbears,
   The prisoner's heart is easèd;
The debtor drinks away his cares,
   And for the time is pleasèd.

Though others' purses be more fat,
    Why should we pine and grieve at that?
    Hang sorrow, care will kill a cat,
And therefore let's be merry.

Hark how the wags abroad do call
    Each other forth to rambling;
Anon you'll see them in the hall,
    For nuts and apples scrambling.
        Hark how the roofs with laughters sound!
        Anon they'll think the house goes round;
        For they the cellar's depths have found,
And there they will be merry.

The wenches with their wassail bowls
    About the streets are singing;
The boys are come to catch the owls,   [a game]
    The wild mare in is bringing.   [seesaw]
        Our kitchen boy hath broke his box,   [Christmas box]
        And to the dealing of the ox   [dividing]
        Our honest neighbors come by flocks,
And here they will be merry.

Now kings and queens poor sheep-cotes have,
    And mate with everybody;
The honest now may play the knave,
    And wise men play at noddy.
        Some youths will now a-mumming go,
        Some others play at rowland-hoe,
        And twenty other gameboys more;
Because they will be merry.

Then wherefore in these merry days
    Should we, I pray, be duller?
No, let us sing some roundelays
    To make our mirth the fuller.
        And while we thus inspirèd sing,
        Let all the streets with echoes ring;
        Woods and hills and everything
Bear witness we are merry.

Robert Herrick

IT IS TO ROBERT HERRICK (1591–1674) THAT WE ARE INDEBTED for the poetic accounting of so many seventeenth-century folk customs, sacred and secular:

> Thy Morris-dance; thy Whitsun-ale;
> Thy Shearing-feast, which never fail.
> Thy Harvest home; thy Wassail bowl,
> That's tossed up after Fox i'th'Hole.
> Thy Mummeries; thy Twelve-tide Kings
> And Queens; thy Christmas revellings.
> ("The Country Life")

Herrick was a country parson who obviously denied himself few of the pleasures of life; it is not surprising that for fifteen years he was deprived of his living in Devonshire by the dour Puritans for whom the life and attitudes of such a "sporting parson" were sacrilege. A classicist reminiscent of such Roman poets as Catullus, Herrick's religious lyrics tend toward graceful simplicity, lacking the metaphysical surprises of a Donne or Herbert.

"A Christmas Carol" reflects Herrick's love of nature. Trading on the familiar Christmas images of others, Herrick's holiday celebration is familiar, comfortable, even homely. The divine Incarnation that inspires awe in other parson-poets is for Herrick simply an occasion for "public mirth." To compare Herrick's poem on the subject of the Incarnation with, for example, Søren Kierkegaard's meditation on the same subject in the nineteenth century (see Chapter 4) is to experience something of the range of literary and theological responses to the Nativity.

A Christmas Carol, sung to the King in the Presence at White-Hall.

> What sweeter music can we bring,
> Than a Carol, for to sing
> The Birth of this our heavenly King?
> Awake the Voice! Awake the String!
> Heart, Ear, and Eye, and every thing
> Awake! the while the active Finger
> Runs division with the Singer.

Dark and dull night, fly hence away,
And give the honor to this Day,
That sees *December* turned to *May*.

If we may ask the reason, say;
The why, and wherefore all things here
Seem like the Spring-time of the year?

Why does the chilling Winter's morn
Smile, like a field beset with corn?
Or smell, like to a Meade new-shorn,
Thus, on the sudden?

Come and see
The cause, why things thus fragrant be:
'Tis He is born, whose quickening Birth
Gives life and luster, public mirth,
To Heaven, and the under-Earth.

We see Him come, and know him ours,
Who, with His Sun-shine, and His showers,
Turns all the patient ground to flowers.

The Darling of the world is come,
And fit it is, we find a room
To welcome Him. The nobler part
Of all the house here, is the heart,

Which we will give Him; and bequeath
This Holly, and this Ivy Wreath,
To do Him honor; who's our King,
And Lord of all this Revelling.

George Herbert

GEORGE HERBERT (1593–1633), the seventeenth-century Anglican divine and poet, has sometimes been viewed as a quaint provincial, a clerical versifier of marginal interest; however, the critical attention given him by prominent twentieth-century critics such as T. S. Eliot has elevated Herbert's reputation to that of the first rank of metaphysical poets. Herbert's poems, most of which are to be found in the collection known as *The Temple*, have been aptly described as "love lyrics to God."

The remarkable thing about Herbert's art is the degree to which the reader is drawn into feeling actually present at the dialogue between the poet and his God. Indeed, the fine construction of the poems fades from consciousness as Herbert takes us into the very experience of divine-human encounter. Herbert the poetic craftsman is seen in the simple conceit of the two-line anagram on the Incarnation, reproduced below.

"Christmas" may be read as two separate reflections printed under one title. The opening verses use the image of the wayfarer seeking accommodation in an inn, intentionally bringing to mind Jesus' birth under similar circumstances. A fine example of the richness of the metaphysical poet's imagination is found in lines 9–10: "O Thou, whose glorious, yet contracted light, / Wrapt in night's mantle, stole into a manger." In the second part of the poem, the poet plays with the images of shepherds, flocks, and suns, the Lord's birth requiring an eternal paean of praise.

$$\text{Ana-} \begin{Bmatrix} \text{Mary} \\ \text{Army} \end{Bmatrix} \text{gram.}$$

How well her name an *Army* doth present,
  In whom the *Lord of Hosts* did pitch his tent!

Christmas.

All after pleasures as I rid one day,
  My horse and I, both tired, body and mind,
  With full cry of affections, quite astray,
I took up in the next inn I could find.
There when I came, whom found I but my dear,
  My dearest Lord, expecting till the grief
  Of pleasures brought me to him, ready there
To be all passengers' most sweet relief?
O Thou, whose glorious, yet contracted light,
  Wrapt in night's mantle, stole into a manger;
  Since my dark soul and brutish is thy right,
To Man of all beasts be not thou a stranger:
  Furnish and deck my soul, that thou mayst have
  A better lodging then a rack or grave.

The shepherds sing; and shall I silent be?
    My God, no hymn for thee?
My soul's a shepherd too; a flock it feeds
    Of thoughts, and words, and deeds.
The pasture is thy word: the streams, thy grace
    Enriching all the place.
Shepherd and flock shall sing, and all my powers
    Out-sing the day-light hours.
Then we will chide the sun for letting night
    Take up his place and right:
We sing one common Lord; wherefore he should
    Himself the candle hold.
I will go searching, till I find a sun
    Shall stay, till we have done;
A willing shiner, that shall shine as gladly,
    As frost-nipt suns look sadly.
Then we will sing, and shine all our own day,
    And one another pay:
His beams shall cheer my breast, and both so twine,
Till ev'n his beams sing, and my music shine.

Riu, riu, chiu

AN ANONYMOUS SIXTEENTH-CENTURY Spanish folk song, "Riu, riu, chiu" accents the elevated estate of the Virgin Mary in Latin Catholicism. In this tradition, the high regard for Jesus is matched by the high regard for his mother; and in some instances, Marian devotions even eclipse those offered to her Son. The role of Mary in theology and devotion became a debated issue in this era, which included the religious wars of the Reformation and Counter-Reformation.

The opening lines of the folk song are a bit obscure. Frequently Jesus is described as the lamb who is at risk because of the threats of Herod, referred to in Scripture as "that fox." However, in this song Mary, rather than Jesus, is the lamb, and the identity of the wolf who tries to harm Mary is unclear.

Riu, riu, chiu

Riu, riu, chiu, the safe riverbank:
God kept the wolf away from our lamb.

The fierce wolf wanted to bite her
But almighty God knew how to defend her
He wanted to make her incapable of sin
Not even original sin did this Virgin have

Riu, riu, chiu . . .

The one born is the great king
Christ, patriarch in the flesh
He has redeemed us by becoming a child
Although He was immortal, He became mortal

Riu, riu, chiu . . .

Many prophecies have foretold Him
Already in our time we have known Him
A human God we have seen on earth
So that humans can ascend to heaven

Riu, riu, chiu . . .

I saw a thousand herons who came here singing
Flying, making a thousand sounds
Saying to the shepherds: Glory be to heaven
And peace on earth for Jesus has been born

Riu, riu, chiu . . .

Huron Carol

THIS CAROL HAS A CURIOUS AND OBSCURE HISTORY. The purported author, Jean de Brébeuf, was a French Jesuit who in 1625 began four years on Georgian Bay, Ontario, among the Huron Native Americans. Brébeuf returned to France for his final vows and then came back to New France in 1633, dying tragically in 1649 during a massacre involving Hurons and Iroquois.

Though this carol is often attributed to Brébeuf, some claim another Jesuit, Paul Ragueneau, to have been the true author. Passed down orally, the words and music were supposedly later transcribed by another Jesuit, Étienne-Thomas Girault de Villeneuse. The sixteenth-century carol tune "Une jeune pucelle" may have been originally associated with the hymn. The Huron is attributed to Paul Picard Tsa8enhohi. The text below is our translation of the French version found in Ernest Myrand's *Noels Anciens de la Nouvelle France*. Different versions are popularly sung today, some of which bear little resemblance to the supposed original.

Huron Carol

Men, take heart, for Jesus is born.
Now that the reign of the devil is destroyed,
No longer listen to what he says to your spirits,
      Jesus is born.

Listen to the angels in heaven.
Do not reject what they told you:
Mary has given birth to the Great Spirit.
      Jesus is born.

Three chiefs spoke among themselves,
Seeing the star in the firmament,
And they then agreed to follow the star,
      Jesus is born.

Thus Jesus gave them, the idea to come see him,
That the star would guide them, they said to each other:
Towards the star we shall go.
      Jesus is born.

These chiefs brought him offerings.
Happy were they, seeing Jesus.
Wondrous things they told him, bending low.
      Jesus is born.

Now come you all, pray and adore Him,
Listen to Him, who has granted your prayers:
He calls you to glory.
        Jesus is born.

John Milton

JOHN MILTON (1608–1674) IS PROBABLY THE MOST HIGHLY RATED, least-read poet in the English language, which is a great pity. Deeply educated in the classics, Milton settled into life as a tutor after a period of time spent traveling. An ardent pamphleteer, Milton became involved in attacks on episcopacy. His fortunes rose and fell with the Cromwellian commonwealth, for which he was a chief apologist while serving as Latin secretary to the Council of State. Even his blindness did not stop his prolific output of literature.

"On the Morning of Christ's Nativity" was written when Milton was only twenty-one and a student at Cambridge University. Uniquely appealing among the poet's works, the poem was apparently intended as one of a series on the events in the life of Christ. The poem is both highly visual and highly auditory. It has been described as "a combination of deliberate quaintness in imagery and conceits and a studied simplicity of feeling," with classical references abounding, as is appropriate to his theme of the overthrow of the pagan world at the Nativity.

On the Morning of Christ's Nativity

(1)
This is the month, and this the happy morn,
Wherein the Son of Heaven's Eternal King,
Of wedded maid and virgin mother born,
Our great redemption from above did bring;
For so the holy sages once did sing,
    That he our deadly forfeit should release,
And with his Father work us a perpetual peace.

(2)
That glorious form, that light unsufferable,
And that far-beaming blaze of majesty,

Wherewith he wont at Heaven's high council-table
To sit the midst of Trinal Unity,
He laid aside, and, here with us to be,
　　Forsook the courts of everlasting day,
And chose with us a darksome house of mortal clay.

(3)

Say, Heavenly Muse, shall not thy sacred vein
Afford a present to the Infant God?
Hast thou no verse, no hymn, or solemn strain,
To welcome him to this his new abode,
Now while the heaven, by the Sun's team untrod,
　　Hath took no print of the approaching light,
And all the spangled host keep watch in squadrons bright?

(4)

See how from far upon the eastern road
The star-led wizards haste with odors sweet!
Oh run, prevent them with thy humble ode,
And lay it lowly at his blessed feet;
Have thou the honor first thy Lord to greet,
　　And join thy voice unto the angel choir
From out his secret altar touched with hallowed fire.

The Hymn
(1)

It was the winter wild,
While the heaven-born child
　　All meanly wrapt in the rude manger lies;
Nature, in awe to him,
Had doffed her gaudy trim,
　　With her great Master so to sympathize:
It was no season then for her
To wanton with the Sun, her lusty paramour.

(2)

Only with speeches fair
She woos the gentle air
　　To hide her guilty front with innocent snow,
And on her naked shame,

Pollute with sinful blame,
   The saintly veil of maiden white to throw;
Confounded, that her Maker's eyes
Should look so near upon her foul deformities.

(3)

But he, her fears to cease,
Sent down the meek-eyed Peace:
   She, crowned with olive green, came softly sliding
Down through the turning sphere,
His ready harbinger,
   With turtle wing the amorous clouds dividing;
And, waving wide her myrtle wand,
She strikes a universal peace through sea and land.

(4)

No war, or battle's sound,
Was heard the world around;
   The idle spear and shield were high uphung;
The hookèd chariot stood,
Unstained with hostile blood;
   The trumpet spake not to the armèd throng;
And kings sat still with awful eye,
As if they surely knew their sovran Lord was by.

(5)

But peaceful was the night
Wherein the Prince of Light
   His reign of peace upon the earth began.
The winds, with wonder whist,
Smoothly the waters kissed,
   Whispering new joys to the mild Ocean,
Who now hath quite forgot to rave,
While birds of calm sit brooding on the charmèd wave.

(6)

The stars, with deep amaze,
Stand fixed in steadfast gaze,
   Bending one way their precious influence,
And will not take their flight,

For all the morning light,
    Or Lucifer that often warned them thence;
But in their glimmering orbs did glow,
Until their Lord himself bespake, and bid them go.

(7)

And, though the shady gloom
Had given day her room,
    The Sun himself withheld his wonted speed,
And hid his head for shame,
As his inferior flame
    The new-enlightened world no more should need:
He saw a greater Sun appear
Than his bright throne or burning axletree could bear.

(8)

The shepherds on the lawn,
Or ere the point of dawn,
    Sat simply chatting in a rustic row;
Full little thought they than
That the mighty Pan
    Was kindly come to live with them below:
Perhaps their loves, or else their sheep,
Was all that did their silly thoughts so busy keep.

(9)

When such music sweet
Their hearts and ears did greet
    As never was by mortal finger strook,
Divinely-warbled voice
Answering the stringèd noise,
    As all their souls in blissful rapture took:
The air, such pleasure loth to lose,
With thousand echoes still prolongs each heavenly close.

(10)

Nature, that heard such sound
Beneath the hollow round
    Of Cynthia's seat the airy region thrilling,
Now was almost won

To think her part was done,
    And that her reign had here its last fulfilling:
She knew such harmony alone
Could hold all Heaven and Earth in happier uniön.

(11)
At last surrounds their sight
A globe of circular light,
    That with long beams the shamefaced Night arrayed;
The helmèd cherubim
And sworded seraphim
    Are seen in glittering ranks with wings displayed,
Harping loud and solemn quire,
With unexpressive notes, to Heaven's new-born Heir.

(12)
Such music (as 'tis said)
Before was never made,
    But when of old the sons of morning sung,
While the Creator great
His constellations set,
    And the well-balanced world on hinges hung,
And cast the dark foundations deep,
And bid the weltering waves their oozy channel keep.

(13)
Ring out, ye crystal spheres,
Once bless our human ears,
    If ye have power to touch our senses so;
And let your silver chime
Move in melodious time;
    And let the bass of heaven's deep organ blow;
And with your ninefold harmony
Make up full consort to th' angelic symphony.

(14)
For, if such holy song
Enwrap our fancy long,
    Time will run back and fetch the age of gold;
And speckled vanity

Will sicken soon and die;
   And leprous sin will melt from earthly mold;
And Hell itself will pass away,
And leave her dolorous mansions to the peering day.

(15)

Yea, Truth and Justice then
Will down return to men,
   Orbed in a rainbow; and, like glories wearing,
Mercy will sit between,
Throned in celestial sheen,
   With radiant feet the tissued clouds down steering;
And Heaven, as at some festival,
Will open wide the gates of her high palace-hall.

(16)

But wisest Fate says no,
This must not yet be so;
   The Babe lies yet in smiling infancy
That on the bitter cross
Must redeem our loss,
   So both himself and us to glorify:
Yet first, to those ychained in sleep,
The wakeful trump of doom must thunder through the deep,

(17)

With such a horrid clang
As on Mount Sinai rang,
   While the red fire and smoldering clouds outbrake:
The aged Earth, aghast,
With terror of that blast,
   Shall from the surface to the center shake,
When, at the world's last sessiön,
The dreadful Judge in middle air shall spread his throne.

(18)

And then at last our bliss
Full and perfect is,
   But now begins; for from this happy day
Th' old Dragon under ground,

In straiter limits bound,
    Not half so far casts his usurpèd sway,
And, wroth to see his kingdom fail,
Swinges the scaly horror of his folded tail.

(19)

The Oracles are dumb;
No voice or hideous hum
    Runs through the archèd roof in words deceiving.
Apollo from his shrine
Can no more divine,
    With hollow shriek the steep of Delphos leaving.
No nightly trance, or breathèd spell,
Inspires the pale-eyed priest from the prophetic cell.

(20)

The lonely mountains o'er,
And the resounding shore,
    A voice of weeping heard and loud lament;
From haunted spring, and dale
Edged with poplar pale,
    The parting genius is with sighing sent;
With flower-inwoven tresses torn
The Nymphs in twilight shade of tangled thickets mourn.

(21)

In consecrated earth,
And on the holy hearth,
    The Lars and Lemures moan with midnight plaint;
In urns and altars round,
A drear and dying sound
    Affrights the flamens at their service quaint;
And the chill marble seems to sweat,
While each peculiar power forgoes his wonted seat.

(22)

Peor and Baälim
Forsake their temples dim,
    With that twice-battered God of Palestine;
And moonèd Ashtaroth,

Heaven's queen and mother both,
  Now sits not girt with tapers' holy shine:
The Libyc Hammon shrinks his horn;
In vain the Tyrian maids their wounded Thammuz mourn.

(23)

And sullen Moloch, fled,
Hath left in shadows dread
  His burning idol all of blackest hue;
In vain with cymbals' ring
They call the grisly king,
  In dismal dance about the furnace blue;
The brutish gods of Nile as fast,
Isis, and Orus, and the dog Anubis, haste.

(24)

Nor is Osiris seen
In Memphian grove or green,
  Trampling the unshowered grass with lowings loud;
Nor can he be at rest
Within his sacred chest;
  Nought but profoundest Hell can be his shroud;
In vain, with timbreled anthems dark,
The sable-stolèd sorcerers bear his worshiped ark.

(25)

He feels from Juda's land
The dreaded Infant's hand;
  The rays of Bethlehem blind his dusky eyn;
Nor all the gods beside
Longer dare abide,
  Not Typhon huge ending in snaky twine:
Our Babe, to show his Godhead true,
Can in his swaddling bands control the damnèd crew.

(26)

So, when the sun in bed,
Curtained with cloudy red,
  Pillows his chin upon an orient wave,
The flocking shadows pale

Troop to th' infernal jail;
   Each fettered ghost slips to his several grave,
And the yellow-skirted fays
Fly after the night-steeds, leaving their moon-loved maze.

(27)

But see! the Virgin blest
Hath laid her Babe to rest.
   Time is our tedious song should here have ending:
Heaven's youngest-teemèd star
Hath fixed her polished car,
   Her sleeping Lord with handmaid lamp attending;
And all about the courtly stable
Bright-harnessed angels sit in order serviceable.

Sidney Godolphin

SIDNEY GODOLPHIN (1610–1643), A NATIVE OF CORNWALL, was a minor Cavalier poet whose work was first collected and published in the twentieth century. Godolphin lost his life during the English Civil War. A man of delicate physical constitution, Godolphin was described by Edward Hyde, Earl of Clarendon, as so sensitive that "when he rid abroad with those in whose company he most delighted, if the wind chanced to be in his face, he would (after a little pleasant murmuring) suddenly turn his horse, and go home."

Although generally classified as a metaphysical poet, in the poem below the poet makes a straightforward comparison between the journeys of wise men and shepherds. He concludes that though there are different kinds of knowledge as represented by the different approaches of wise men and shepherds, it is knowledge of self that "best pleases his creator so."

Hymn

Lord when the wise men came from far,
Led to thy Cradle by a Star,
Then did the shepherds too rejoice,
Instructed by thy Angel's voice:

Blest were the wisemen in their skill,
And shepherds in their harmless will.

Wisemen in tracing Nature's laws
Ascend unto the highest cause,
Shepherds with humble fearfulness
Walk safely, though their light be less:
Though wisemen better know the way
It seems no honest heart can stray.

There is no merit in the wise
But love, (the shepherds' sacrifice).
Wisemen all ways of knowledge past,
To the shepherds wonder come at last:
To know, can only wonder breed,
And not to know, is wonder's seed.

A wiseman at the Altar bows
And offers up his studied vows
And is received; may not the tears,
Which spring too from a shepherd's fears,
And sighs upon his frailty spent,
Though not distinct, be eloquent?

'Tis true, the object sanctifies
All passions which within us rise,
But since no creature comprehends
The cause of causes, end of ends,
He who himself vouchsafes to know
Best pleases his creator so.

When then our sorrows we apply
To our own wants and poverty,
When we look up in all distress
And our own misery confess,
Sending both thanks and prayers above,
Then though we do not know, we love.

Richard Crashaw

RICHARD CRASHAW (1612–1649), SON OF A PURITAN CLERGYMAN, came under the influence of Archbishop Laud's high churchmanship at Peterhouse, Cambridge, where he was a fellow for eight years. With the rise of Puritanism, Crashaw left the Church of England and became a Roman Catholic, living his final years in Europe. Crashaw was one of many combatants in the tug of war between traditionalist and reforming elements within the established Church of England itself, another notable combatant two centuries later being the poet Gerard Manley Hopkins.

Crashaw's poetry is often fulsome and marked by the baroque excesses that sometimes characterized the Counter-Reformation in Roman Catholicism. "In the Holy Nativity of Our Lord God: A Hymn Sung as by the Shepherds" is written in a classical pastoral mode. Less well known, though perhaps the more original and finely crafted, are stanzas from "Satan's Sight of the Nativity," a section of *Sospetto d'Herode*. Herein is found one of the most memorable of Renaissance images of the Nativity: "That the great angel-blinding Light should shrink / His blaze, to shine in a poor shepherd's eye."

In the Holy Nativity of Our Lord God: A Hymn Sung as by the Shepherds.

The Hymn.

CHORUS.
Come, we shepherds, whose blest sight
Hath met Love's noon in Nature's night;
Come, lift we up our loftier song
And wake the sun that lies too long.

To all our world of well-stolen joy
He slept; and dreamt of no such thing.
    While we found out Heaven's fairer eye
And kissed the cradle of our King.
    Tell him He rises now, too late
To show us ought worth looking at.

Tell him we now can show him more
Than he e're showed to mortal sight;
  Than he himself e're saw before,
Which to be seen needs not his light.
  Tell him, Tityrus, where th' hast been,
Tell him, Thyrsis, what th' hast seen.

TITYRUS.
  Gloomy night embraced the place
Where the noble Infant lay.
  The Babe looked up and showed His face;
In spite of darkness, it was day.
  It was Thy day, Sweet! and did rise
Not from the East, but from Thine eyes.

CHORUS.
It was Thy day, Sweet . . .

THYRSIS.
  Winter chid aloud, and sent
The angry North to wage his wars.
  The North forgot his fierce intent,
And left perfumes instead of scars.
  By those sweet eyes' persuasive powers
Where he meant frost, he scattered flowers.

CHORUS.
By those sweet eyes . . .

BOTH.
  We saw Thee in Thy balmy-nest,
Young dawn of our eternal Day!
  We saw Thine eyes break from their East
And chase the trembling shades away.
  We saw Thee; and we blest the sight,
We saw Thee by Thine Own sweet light.

TITYRUS.
  Poor world (said I), what wilt thou do
To entertain this starry Stranger?

Is this the best thou canst bestow?
A cold, and not too cleanly, manger?
    Contend, the powers of Heaven and Earth,
To fit a bed for this huge birth?

CHORUS.
Contend, the powers . . .

THYRSIS.
Proud world, said I, cease your contest
And let the mighty Babe alone.
    The phoenix builds the phoenix's nest,
Love's architecture is his own.
    The Babe whose birth embraves this morn,
Made His Own bed e're He was born.

CHORUS.
The Babe whose . . .

TITYRUS.
I saw the curled drops, soft and slow,
Come hovering o'er the place's head;
    Offring their whitest sheets of snow
To furnish the fair Infant's bed:
    Forbear, said I; be not too bold,
Your fleece is white but 'tis too cold.

CHORUS.
Forbear, said I . . .

THRYSIS.
I saw the obsequious Seraphims
Their rosy fleece of fire bestow.
    For well they now can spare their wing,
Since Heaven itself lies here below.
    Well done, said I; but are you sure
Your down so warm, will pass for pure?

CHORUS.
Well done, said I . . .

TITYRUS.

No, no! your King's not yet to seek
Where to repose His royal head;
    See, see! how soon His new-bloomed cheek
Twixt's mother's breasts is gone to bed.
    Sweet choice, said we! no way but so
Not to lie cold, yet sleep in snow.

CHORUS.

Sweet choice, said we . . .

BOTH.

We saw Thee in Thy balmy nest,
Bright dawn of our eternal Day!
    We saw Thine eyes break from their East
And chase the trembling shades away.
    We saw Thee: and we blest the sight,
We saw Thee, by Thine Own sweet light.

CHORUS.

We saw Thee, . . .

FULL CHORUS.

Welcome, all wonders in one sight!
Eternity shut in a span!
    Summer in Winter, Day in Night!
Heaven in Earth, and God in man!
    Great, little One! Whose all-embracing birth
Lifts Earth to Heaven, stoops Heaven to Earth.

Welcome, though not to gold nor silk,
To more than Caesar's birth-right is;
    Two sister-seas of virgin-milk,
With many a rarely-tempered kiss,
    That breathes at once both maid and mother,
Warms in the one, cools in the other.
    She sings Thy tears asleep, and dips
Her kisses in Thy weeping eye;
    She spreads the red leaves of Thy lips,

That in their buds yet blushing lie:
    She 'gainst those mother-diamonds, tries
The points of her young eagle's eyes.
    Welcome, though not to those gay flies,
Gilded in the beams of earthly kings;
    Slippery souls in smiling eyes:
But to poor shepherds' home-spun things;
    Whose wealth's their flock; whose wit, to be
Well-read in their simplicity.
    Yet when young April's husband-showers
Shall bless the fruitful Maja's bed,
    We'll bring the first-born of her flowers
To kiss Thy feet, and crown Thy head.
    To Thee, dread Lamb! Whose love must keep
The shepherds, more than they the sheep.
    To Thee, meek Majesty! soft King
Of simple Graces and sweet Loves:
    Each of us his lamb will bring,
Each his pair of silver doves:
    Till burnt at last in fire of Thy fair eyes,
Ourselves become our own best sacrifice.

Satan's Sight of the Nativity
Sospetto d'Herode, stanzas xiii–xvii; xxii–xxiv

Heaven's golden-wingèd herald, late he saw
To a poor Galilean virgin sent:
How low the bright youth bowed, and with what awe
Immortal flowers to her fair hand present.
He saw th' old Hebrew's womb, neglect the law
Of age and barrenness, and her babe prevent   [anticipate]
   His birth by his devotion, who began
   Betimes to be a saint, before a man.

He saw rich nectar-thaws, release the rigour
Of th' icy North; from frost-bound Atlas hands,
His adamantine fetters fall: green vigour
Gladding the Scythian rocks and Libyan sands.
He saw a vernal smile, sweetly disfigure

Winter's sad face, and through the flowery lands
    Of fair Engaddi, honey-sweating fountains
    With manna, milk, and balm, new-broach the mountains.

He saw how in that blest Day-bearing Night,
The Heaven-rebukèd shades made haste away;
How bright a dawn of angels with new light
Amazed the midnight world, and made a Day
Of which the Morning knew not. Mad with spite
He marked how the poor shepherds ran to pay
    Their simple tribute to the Babe, Whose birth
    Was the great business both of Heaven and Earth.

He saw a threefold Sun, with rich increase
Make proud the ruby portals of the East.
He saw the Temple sacred to sweet Peace,
Adore her Prince's birth, flat on her breast.
He saw the falling idols, all confess
A coming Deity: He saw the nest
    Of poisonous and unnatural loves, Earth-nursed,
    Touched with the World's true antidote, to burst.

He saw Heaven blossom with a new-born light,
On which, as on a glorious stranger gazed
The golden eyes of Night: whose beam made bright
The way to Beth'lem, and as boldly blazed,
(Nor asked leave of the sun) by day as night.
By whom (as Heaven's illustrious hand-maid) raised,
    Three kings (or what is more) three wise men went
    Westward to find the World's true orient.

❦   ❦   ❦   ❦

That the great angel-blinding Light should shrink
His blaze, to shine in a poor shepherd's eye:
That the unmeasured God so low should sink,
As prisoner in a few poor rags to lie:
That from His mother's breast He milk should drink,
Who feeds with nectar Heaven's fair family:
    That a vile manger His low bed should prove,
    Who in a throne of stars thunders above.

That He Whom the sun serves, should faintly peep
Through clouds of infant flesh: that He the old
Eternal Word should be a child, and weep:
That He who made the fire, should fear the cold:
That Heaven's high majesty His court should keep
In a clay-cottage, by each blast controlled:
    That Glory's self should serve our griefs and fears,
    And free Eternity, submit to years.

And further, that the Law's eternal Giver
Should bleed in His Own Law's obedience:
And to the circumcising knife deliver
Himself, the forfeit of His slave's offence:
That the unblemish'd Lamb, blessèd for ever,
Should take the mark of sin, and pain of sense.
    These are the knotty riddles, whose dark doubt
    Entangles his lost thoughts, past getting out.

Henry Vaughan

THE RELATIONSHIP BETWEEN HENRY VAUGHAN'S LIFE (1621–1695) and
his work remains something of an enigma, with little evidence in his writings of the dramatic times through which he lived: British civil war, commonwealth, and royal restoration. Born into an aristocratic Welsh family, Vaughan had a dramatic religious conversion in 1648 or 1649. It was his gift to be able to express that which is often considered humanly inexpressible, the experience of the divine. What theologians call the *numinous* is a Vaughan familiar: "I saw Eternity the other night / Like a great *Ring* of pure and endless light."

For Henry Vaughan, reality is intricately tied up with his peculiar mystical way of knowing, a way of perceiving which the modern rationalistic mind has great difficulty accepting. Vaughan can be read as illustrative of a special connection between mystic experience and poetry, a kind of poetry that trades in paradoxes: "There is in God (some say) / A deep and dazzling darkness."

Although Vaughan's Christmas poems are not his most memorable, the two below may serve as a point of entry into a body of work well worth discovery. Both poems, reminiscent of Vaughan's mentor, George Herbert, accent the paradox of the self-emptying of the divine in becoming human, and the unworthiness of physical matter "that could have / A God Enclosed within your Cell."

The Incarnation, and Passion

Lord! when thou didst thy self undress
Laying by thy robes of glory,
To make us more, thou wouldst be less,
And becamest a woeful story.

To put on Clouds instead of light,
And clothe the morning-star with dust,
Was a translation of such height
As, but in thee, was ne'r expressed;

Brave worms, and Earth! that thus could have
A God Enclosed within your Cell,
Your maker pent up in a grave,
Life locked in death, heaven in a shell;

Ah, my dear Lord! what couldst thou spy
In this impure, rebellious clay,
That made thee thus resolve to die
For those that kill thee every day?

O what strange wonders could thee move
To slight thy precious blood, and breath!
Sure it was *Love*, my Lord; for *Love*
Is only stronger far than death.

Christ's Nativity

Awake, glad heart! get up, and Sing,
It is the Birth-day of thy King,
    Awake! awake!
    The Sun doth shake
Light from his locks, and all the way
Breathing Perfumes, doth spice the day.

Awake, awake! hark, how the *wood* rings,
Winds whisper, and the busy *springs*
    A concert make;
    Awake, awake!
Man is their high-priest, and should rise
To offer up the sacrifice.

I would I were some *Bird*, or Star,
Fluttering in woods, or lifted far
    Above this *Inn*
    And Road of sin!
Then either Star, or *Bird*, should be
Shining, or singing still to thee.

I would I had in my best part
Fit Rooms for thee! or that my heart
    Were so clean as
    Thy manger was!
But I am all filth, and obscene,
Yet, if thou wilt, thou canst make clean.

Sweet *Jesu!* will then; Let no more
This Leper haunt, and soil thy door,
    Cure him, Ease him
    O release him!
And let once more by mystic birth
The Lord of life be born on Earth.

Edward Taylor

EDWARD TAYLOR (1642?–1729) EMIGRATED FROM ENGLAND to the Massachusetts Bay Colony in 1668. A Puritan minister, Taylor lived as a pastor for almost sixty years in Westfield, Massachusetts. His work is reminiscent of that of John Donne, George Herbert, Richard Crashaw, and Henry Vaughan. Thematically, we find the familiar seventeenth-century sense of personal unworthiness coupled with an ardent love of Christ. Taylor brought the practice of metaphysical poetry from England to New England after that tradition had already run its course in England. If his poetry is little known, this is largely because he forbade publication, and his work was not known until a manuscript surfaced in 1937 in the Yale library.

Taylor was particularly adept at typology, a technique in which Old Testament figures and scenes are taken as prefiguring a New Testament figure or scene. For example, a typology found in the New Testament is John 3:14: "And as Moses lifted up the serpent in the wilderness, even so must the Son of man be lifted up." In the poem below, a typology is made between Samson and Jesus. Christian writers from earlier centuries were often ingenious in establishing such typological correlations.

Meditation Eleven (Second Series)
Judges XIII:3: And the angel of the Lord appeared unto the woman.

Eternall Love, burnisht in Glory thick,
    Doth but[t] and Center in thee, Lord, my joy.
Thou portrai'd art in Colours bright, that stick
    Their Glory on the Choicest Saints, whereby
    They are thy Pictures made. Samson exceld
    Herein thy Type, as he thy foes once queld.

An Angell tells his mother of his birth.
    An Angell telleth thine of thine. Ye two
Both Males that ope the Womb in Wedlock Kerfe;   [cut]
    Both Nazarited from the Womb up grow.
    He after pitchy night a Sunshine grows,
    And thou the Sun of Righteousness up rose.

His Love did Court a Gentile spouse; and thine
    Espous'd a Gentile to bebride thyselfe.
His Gentile Bride apostatizd betime:
    Apostasy in thine grew full of Wealth.
    He sindgd the Authours of 't with Foxes tails;
    And foxy men by thee on thine prevail.

The Fret now rose. Thousands upon him pour.
    An asses Jaw his javling is, whereby

He slew a Thousand, heap by heap that hour.
    Thou by weak means mak'st many thousands fly.
    Thou ribbon-like wast platted in his Locks,
    And hence he thus his Enemies did box.

He's by his Friend betray'd, for money sold,
    Took, bound, blindfolded, made a May game Flout;
Dies freely with great sinners, when they hold
    A Sacred Feast: with arms stretcht greatly out:
    Slew more by death, than in his Life he slew.
    And all such things, my Lord, in thee are true.

Samson at Gaza went to bed to sleep.
    The Gazites watch him, and the Soldiers thee.
He Champion stout at midnight rose full deep,
    Took Gaza's Gate on's back: away went hee.
    Thou rose didst from thy Grave, and also tookst
    Deaths Doore away, throwing it off o' th' hooks.

Thus all the shine that Samson wore is thine,
    Thine in the Type. Oh, Glorious One, Rich glee!
God's Love hath made thee thus. Hence thy bright shine
    Commands our Love to bow thereto the Knee.
    Thy Glory chargeth us in Sacrifice
    To make our Hearts and Love to thee to rise.

But woe is me! my heart doth run out to
    Poor bits of Clay, or dirty Gayes embrace: [things ornamental]
Doth leave thy Lovely Selfe for loveless shows;
    For lumps of Lust, nay, sorrow and disgrace.
    Alas, poore Soule! a Pardon, Lord, I crave.
    I have dishonourd thee and all I have.

Be thou my Samson, Lord, a Rising Sun
    Of Righteousness unto my Soule I pray.
Conquour my Foes. Let Graces Spouts all run
    Upon my Soule, o're which thy sunshine lay.
    And set me in thy Sunshine, make each flower
    Of Grace in me, thy Praise perfum'd out poure.

Sor Juana Inés de la Cruz

A REMARKABLE DISCOVERY AWAITS the first-time reader of Sor (sister) Juana Inés de la Cruz (1648?–1695), Mexican nun, precursor of feminism, intellectual, and poet. An illegitimate child, she was sent to the capital to live at an early age. Her prodigious learning was soon noticed, even in a society in which women were allowed few freedoms. She was taken into the household of the newly arrived viceroy and vicereine in 1664 as a maid-in-waiting, where her beauty, wit, and charm were much admired.

Sor Juana became a novice in the Discalced Carmelite order in 1667. Finding the order too strict, in 1669 she entered the Convent of Santa Paula (Hieronymite). This order allowed nuns a great deal of freedom, including rather elaborate private living quarters and personal servants. There Sor Juana continued her learning, writing, and significant correspondence and also was the center of an intellectual salon. She was criticized by the envious for her intellect and worldliness, but her friends in high places protected her until near the end of her life. She died of plague while nursing her fellow nuns in 1695.

Sor Juana's style is baroque, like the famous highly elaborated sixteenth- and seventeenth-century churches of Mexico. Her classical learning, buttressed by ingenious wit, is worthy of comparison with the best European metaphysical poets. At the same time, Sor Juana also writes with compelling simplicity. Examples of both styles are found in the selections below. The second poem reflects the Mexican custom of the *posada* in which bands of people go from door to door at the Feast of the Three Kings searching for the Christ Child.

Christmas Day, 1678

Carols for the Nativity of Our Lord Christ, that were sung in the Cathedral of Puebla de los Angeles the year 1678, when they were printed.

First Nocturnal: Carol #1

Among floods of love
melted in tears,
crying the Sun is born,
pouring fire on crystals;
It wants, with such floods,

to inflame the frozen earth
and deluge the blinded world.
Fire of God in the fire,
that is not put out with water!

Refrain: *1.* Fire, fire, the world is in flames!
                 2. Ring fire with all the bells!
                 3. Ding, dang, water, water;
                     dong, dong, dong, water, water!

When we see the burning water
so against its ancient form,
to throw water is to throw kindling
and extinguish it we cannot;
the more water that we throw,
will in it be ablaze
and burn more fiercely later.
Fire of God in the fire,
that is not put out with water!

Refrain: *1.* Tear down the house, water, water!
                 2. Don't throw water, anymore,
                     that the water is now the fire,
                     and in it the fire is ablaze!
                 3. If it's a flood, let's run away!

It is in vain to try
its live fire to extinguish,
that until it stops its love
it cannot stop the burning;
and since it cannot be
unloving while being human,
it cries and burns restlessly.

Refrain: *1.* Fire of God in the fire
                     that is not put out with water!
                 2. Is it St. Anselm's fire?
                 3. No, it isn't, but God's fire,
                     that blazes the souls
                     and burns with love.

Carol #3

1. Where are you going, children?
2. To Bethlehem,
   to see wonders,
   that are to be seen.
1. Tell us, children,
   how do you know this?
2. In the air it is sung by Angels
   with loud voices. Listen, heed!

Verses
Today you see in a stable
the Word speechless,
Greatness in smallness,
Immensity in blankets.

All.   Such wonders!

From a Star the Sun is born,
the Ocean reaches a shore,
and a Flower blooms,
infant Fruit awakens.

All.   Such wonders!

The Immutable is in pain,
the burning Fire cools down,
Divinity becomes human,
and Rectitude inclines.

All.   Such wonders!

The One before all tremble, trembles;
Sovereignty steps down,
Courage diminishes
and Laughter itself cries.

All.   Such wonders!

The earth is Heaven now
in this Night that is Dawn;
Eternity is temporary,
and death is what Life was.

All.   Such wonders!

Truth is today disguised,
Strength weakens,
Omnipotence shrinks
and clear Light is now eclipsed.

All.   Such wonders!

Now Royalty is humble,
now Happiness is tears,
now hardships are tenderness
and Justice is now Mercy.

All.   Such wonders!

Now Wealth is poverty,
and the Powerful a beggar,
and the Lion, always victor,
is now Lamb for sacrifice.

All.   Such wonders!

He who had no beginning,
his being of Time begins;
the Creator, as a creature,
is now subject to our griefs.

All.   Such wonders!

Men: Hear these wonders
that are more than human joys:
God is Man, Man is God,
and among them they are in touch.

All. Such wonders!

Christmas Day, 1680

Carols sung in the Cathedral of the City of Los Angeles, in the
Nativity of Our Lord Jesus Christ, the year of 1680, when they
were printed.

First Nocturnal: Carol #3

Some little Shepherds
to the Stable came,
they talked to the Child
very much in love:

Where do you come from,
beautiful Boy,
that none such as You
has ever come here?

Without going to school yet,
you are already trembling;
what else could you do
sitting on hard wood?

Like a little Lamb
you are born in the fields:
for sure it will mean
you'll one day be branded.

In the House of Bread,
like flowering Wheat
you are amidst the hay:
You will be harvested.

Child, don't cry;
sleep for a while
since that Heart
stayed up all night.

You are coming to pay
the debts of a bankruptcy;
because of this bond
on a tree you'll be hung.

Rockabye, Baby,
rockabye, sleep,
before you're awakened
by so many enemies.

The snow that surrounds you,
as a relic's framing
of a Baby Jesus,
will safely keep you.

Take Him, He's sleeping
to the gentle humming
that his Dawn, his Mother,
in her arms is holding:

Refrain: Hold back, hold back, hold back
the breezes of frozen winter!
Don't make noise in the hay;
hold on, hold on to the palm fronds.

Christmas Day, 1689

Carols sung in the Cathedral of Puebla de los Angeles, in the
solemn Matins of the Birth Day of our Lord Jesus Christ, this year
of 1689.

First Night: Carol #1

Introduction
To celebrate the Child's
timely Birth,
the four elements arrive:
Water, Earth, and Air and Fire.

With good reason, since is made
the humanity of his Body
of Water, Fire, Earth and Air,
clean, pure, fragile, fresh.

In the Child the elements improve
their qualities and inner beings,
since they are given better berth
in Eyes, Breast, Flesh, Breath.

To such great favors rendered,
in loving giftgivings
they search, serve, love, adore,
promptly, delicately, purely, tenderly.

Refrain: And all joined together
go to my Lord,
that Humanized is served
by the four elements:
Water serves his Eyes,
Air, his Breath,
Earth, his Soles,
Fire, his Breast;
that from them all, by the Child
a Whole today is made.

"Where are you coming from, Shepherdess?"

THIS BALLAD COMES FROM SIXTEENTH-CENTURY "NEW FRANCE." As such, it bears comparison with the other French-Canadian piece in this chapter, the "Huron Carol," and the Spanish folk song "Riu, riu, chiu." All three conjure up for the reader domestic scenes of the Nativity. All three come out of Catholic cultures; all three focus on the Virgin Mary. In this ballad, Mary and Joseph, a shepherdess, and three angels replace the three kings of the "Huron Carol" and the thousand singing herons of the Spanish folk song. The question-and-answer motif, with an increment of information added with each question and answer, is typical of the ballad form. In both works from French Canada, there is little added to the basic biblical scene. By comparison, the Spanish folk song is more theological and more imaginative. The "Huron Carol" is more indigenous in its imagery, whereas this ballad is easily imagined as originating in France itself.

"Where are you coming from, shepherdess?"

"Where are you coming from, shepherdess?
Where are you coming from?"
"I'm coming from the stable, where I was walking.
I saw a miracle occur this evening."

"What did you see, shepherdess?
What did you see?"
"I saw in the manger a little child
tenderly laid on the cool straw."

"Nothing more, shepherdess, nothing more?
Nothing more, shepherdess, nothing more?"
"Saint Mary, His Mother, giving Him milk to drink,
Saint Joseph, His father, trembling from the cold."

"Nothing more, shepherdess, nothing more?
Nothing more, shepherdess, nothing more?"
"The ox and the ass, who leaned over Him,
Warming him with their breath."

"Nothing more, shepherdess, nothing more?
Nothing more, shepherdess, nothing more?"
"Three little angels came down from the sky,
Singing the praises of the eternal God."

John Dryden

JOHN DRYDEN (1631–1700) WROTE POETRY, drama, criticism, and satire;
he also translated, among others, Ovid, Horace, and Vergil. He and Milton are considered the greatest poets of the late seventeenth century. A
classicist, Dryden influenced literature and literary criticism throughout
the eighteenth century.

Vergil's *Eclogues* introduced the Greek pastoral poem into Roman literature. The "Fourth Eclogue," sometimes referred to as the "Messianic,"
was considered prophetic because it foretells the coming of a new era and
mentions a virgin and a child. Vergil's new world, however, was Stoic, not
Christian. Stoics believed that the world was periodically destroyed by fire
and re-created; in each re-creation, human history repeated itself. Vergil
hopes the new era will be a golden age of peace and innocence and that
Pollio, Vergil's patron, will live to see it. Because the poem seems so appropriate to the birth of Christ and the dawn of Christianity, Dryden's
translation is often included in collections of Christmas literature.

Vergil's Eclogue IV

Sicilian Muse, begin a loftier strain!
Though lowly shrubs, and trees that shade the Plain,
Delight not all; Sicilian Muse, prepare
To make the vocal Woods deserve a Consul's care.
The last great Age, foretold by sacred Rimes,
Renews its finish'd course: Saturnian times
Roll round again; and mighty years, begun
From their first Orb, in radiant circles run.
The base degenerate iron Offspring ends;
A golden Progeny from Heaven descends.
O Chaste Lucina! speed the Mother's pains,
And hast the glorious Birth! thy own Apollo reigns!

The lovely Boy, with his auspicious face,
Shall Pollio's consulship and triumph grace.
Majestick months set out with him to their appointed Race.
The Father banish'd virtue shall restore,
And crimes shall threat the guilty World no more.
The Son shall lead the life of Gods, and be
By Gods and Heroes seen, and Gods and Heroes see.
The jarring Nations he in peace shall bind,
And with paternal Virtues rule Mankind.
Unbidden Earth shall wreathing Ivy bring
And fragrant Herbs (the promises of Spring)
As her first offerings to her infant King

Chapter 4

The Eighteenth and Nineteenth Centuries

The

Age

of

Sentiment

Introduction

Sweeping changes in society, religion, literature, and philosophy marked eighteenth- and nineteenth-century life in Europe, Britain, and North America. Among the watershed events of the age were the Industrial Revolution, the American War of Independence, and the French Revolution. Change occurred with a rapidity unknown in previous centuries.

The Renaissance burst of scientific discovery and hypothesis dramatically affected religious belief in subsequent centuries. Ordinary believers were left confused, while philosophers and theologians sought to reconcile reason and faith. Scepticism became increasingly common. Moribund established churches were challenged by the new waves of pietism, evangelicalism, and ecstatic religious practices. Wesleyan Methodism and other personalistic, revivalistic movements resulted eventually in the so-called Great Awakening in its several phases, which swept through the developing United States like a prairie fire. New Protestant denominations laid stress on personal belief, emotion, and spontaneity as opposed to the formal incorporation of the established churches, where to be born in a particular place meant automatically to be a member of the church. John Wesley's statement "The world is my parish" is illustrative of the breaking down of old boundaries and customs.

The multiple changes in society also affected literature. The movement known as romanticism came to dominate as the eighteenth century merged into the nineteenth. Romantic literature accented the simple country life and values of the pre–Industrial Revolution period, as instanced in the writings of William Wordsworth. At the same time there was a fascination with the exotic and the far away, as instanced in the writings of Samuel Taylor Coleridge.

The accents of Christmas literature reflected those of literature in general. For example, many of the Victorian hymnodists wrote pieces of intense personal piety, hymns fondly remembered if not so often sung today. Of a very different sort is the work of Søren Kierkegaard, Danish existentialist philosopher and theologian, who struggled with the alternate claims of reason and revelation. In the parable in this chapter, Kierkegaard examines the Incarnation and attempts to reconcile the seemingly illogical through logic. However, for Kierkegaard it is the unique existing individual who must ultimately make the leap of faith into belief, when all logical constructs are left behind.

This period also saw the rise of sophisticated dramatic genres—witty Restoration comedies, comedies of manners, bourgeois theater, and both classical and romantic tragedies. Of a very different order is the first printed mummers' play. This anachronistic form, with its stock characters and plot, swordplay and blatant symbolism, reflects a long popular folk tradition.

The growth of journalism in the eighteenth century profoundly affected fiction. Newspapers proliferated, and the novel in serialized form became popular middle-class entertainment. Christmas stories found their way into newspapers and journals with increasing frequency. Less formal language began to replace the ornate rhetoric that sometimes marked previous centuries.

In theme, the literature of Christmas paralleled the rise of secularism, moving further away from viewing the Nativity as an occasion of devotion and closer to the secular holiday mode of seasonal celebration. The focal point of fiction writers became the human family rather than the Holy Family. Interest lay primarily in the foibles of individuals—sentimental or humorous—as illustrated in all four pieces of short fiction in this chapter.

Although key events do indeed occur at Christmas in Anthony Trollope's story, one cannot help but imagine that the motive for the writing was financial rather than devotional. Special Christmas issues sold very well, as all nineteenth-century writers were aware. In fact, almost every major writer wrote at least one Christmas story. Humor finds its way into the Christmas canon in the wonderfully funny E. V. Lucas piece "The Christmas Decorations" and in H. H. Munro's "Reginald's Christmas Revel." Indeed, the comic vision—looking at our customs and foibles with something less than dreadful seriousness—is not contrary to the religious vision, but sometimes a necessary counterpoint to it.

The Sarah Orne Jewett story, "Mrs. Parkins's Christmas Eve," uses the love and charity associated with the season to transform the main character from a parsimonious, lonely widow into a charitable

Retablos of the Archangel San Raphael (Hispanic, circa 1920)

member of the community. Such is the prototypical Victorian Christmas story, with Ebenezer Scrooge being the prototypical Victorian Christmas story character. To the degree that readers are moved or unmoved by stories that are heartwarming, they will love or dislike Victorian Christmas stories.

The range of literature of the eighteenth and nineteenth centuries is even more evident in poetry than in fiction. Poets who felt at home in neither established nor "free" churches sometimes turned to mysticism, as in the cases of Christopher Smart and William Blake. Others turned to a romanticized past, as did the Rosettis, Gerard Hopkins, and many another Victorian. Kipling's "Eddi's Service" may be read as a fond looking back at the early Middle Ages. Finally, folk songs such as the American "Jesus, Jesus, rest your head" and the Sacred Harp text "The Babe of Bethlehem" represent continuations of the folk religion and devotion inherited from previous centuries.

Søren Kierkegaard

SøREN KIERKEGAARD (1813–1855), DANISH PHILOSOPHER, psychologist, and theologian of the inner life, published his first work, *Either/Or*, in 1843. A literary critic and controversialist, Kierkegaard produced a remarkable series of philosophical and theological works. The first and perhaps the greatest of the existential philosophers, Kierkegaard referred to himself as a poet, not an apostle. In the parables, which appear scattered throughout his work, Kierkegaard also displays his considerable talent as a storyteller. The parable printed here, "The King and the Maiden," excerpted from *Philosophical Fragments*, illustrates how, through the Incarnation, God bridges the infinite chasm between the human and the divine.

The King and the Maiden

(excerpt)

To what shall we compare the divine love
that overcomes the infinite distance between human
sin and the holiness of God?

Suppose there was a king who loved a humble maiden. But the reader has perhaps already lost his patience, seeing that our beginning sounds like a fairy tale, and is not in the least systematic. So the very learned Polos found it tiresome that Socrates always talked about meat and drink and doctors, and similar unworthy trifles, which Polos deemed beneath him *(Gorgias)*. But did not the Socratic manner of speech have at least one advantage, in that he himself and all others were from childhood equipped with the necessary prerequisites for understanding it? And would it not be desirable if I could confine the terms of my argument to meat and drink, and did not need to bring in kings, whose thoughts are not always like those of other men, if they are indeed kingly. But perhaps I may be pardoned the extravagance, seeing that I am only a poet, proceeding now to unfold the carpet of my discourse (recalling the beautiful saying of Themistocles), lest its workmanship be concealed by the compactness of its folding.

Suppose then a king who loved a humble maiden. The heart of the king was not polluted by the wisdom that is loudly enough proclaimed; he knew nothing of the difficulties that the understanding discovers in order to ensnare the heart, which keep the poets so busy, and make their magic formulas necessary. It was easy to realize his purpose. Every statesman feared his wrath and dared not breathe a word of displeasure; every foreign state trembled before his power, and dared not omit sending ambassadors with congratulations for the nuptials; no courtier grovelling in the dust dared wound him, lest his own head be crushed. Then let the harp be tuned, let the songs of the poets begin to sound, and let all be festive while love celebrates its triumph. For love is exultant when it unites equals, but it is triumphant when it makes that which was unequal equal in love.—Then there awoke in the heart of the king an anxious thought; who but a king who thinks kingly thoughts would have dreamed of it! He spoke to no one about his anxiety; for if he had, each courtier would doubtless have said: "Your majesty is about to confer a favor upon the maiden, for which she can never be sufficiently grateful her whole life long." This speech would have moved the king to wrath, so that he would have commanded the execution of the courtier for high treason against the beloved, and thus he would in still another way have found his grief increased. So he wrestled with his troubled thoughts alone. Would she be happy in the life at his side? Would she be able to summon confidence enough never to remember what the king wished only to forget, that he was king and she had been a humble maiden? For if this memory were to waken in her soul, and like a favored lover sometimes steal her thoughts away from the king, luring her reflections into the seclusion of a secret grief; or if this memory sometimes passed through her soul like the shadow of death over the grave: where would then be the glory of their love? Then she would have been happier had she remained in her obscurity, loved by an equal, content in her humble cottage; but confident in her love, and cheerful early and late. What a rich abundance of grief is here laid bare, like ripened grain bent under the weight of its fruitfulness, merely awaiting the time of the harvest, when the thought of the king will thresh out all its seed of sorrow! For even if the maiden would be content to become as nothing, this could not satisfy the king, precisely because he loved her, and because it was harder for him to be her benefactor than to lose her. And suppose she could not even understand him? For while we are thus speaking foolishly of human relationships, we may suppose a difference of mind between them such as to render an understanding impossible. What a depth of grief slumbers not in this unhappy love, who dares to rouse it! . . .

Moved by love, the God is thus eternally resolved to reveal himself. But as love is the motive so love must also be the end; for it would be a contradiction for the God to have a motive and an end which did not correspond. His love is a love of the learner, and his aim is to win him. For it is only in love that the unequal can be made equal, and it is only in equality or unity that an understanding can be effected. . . .

But this love is through and through unhappy, for how great is the difference between them! It may seem a small matter for the God to make himself understood, but this is not so easy of accomplishment if he is to refrain from annihilating the unlikeness that exists between them.

Let us not jump too quickly to a conclusion at this point. . . . Much is heard in the world about unhappy love, and we all know what this means: the lovers are prevented from realizing their union, the causes being many and various. There exists another kind of unhappy love, the theme of our present discourse, for which there is no perfect earthly parallel, though by dint of speaking foolishly a little while we may make shift to conceive it through an earthly figure. The unhappiness of this love does not come from the inability of the lovers to realize their union, but from their inability to understand one another. This grief is infinitely more profound than that of which men commonly speak, since it strikes at the very heart of love, and wounds for an eternity; not like that other misfortune which touches only the temporal and the external, and which for the magnanimous is as a sort of jest over the inability of the lovers to realize their union here in time. This infinitely deeper grief is essentially the prerogative of the superior, since only he likewise understands the misunderstanding. . . .

Our problem is now before us, and we invite the poet, unless he is already engaged elsewhere, or belongs to the number of those who must be driven out from the house of mourning, together with the flute-players and the other noise-makers, before gladness can enter in. The poet's task will be to find a solution, some point of union, where love's understanding may be realized in truth, the God's anxiety be set at rest, his sorrow banished. For the divine love is that unfathomable love which cannot rest content with that which the beloved might in his folly prize as happiness.

A

The union might be brought about by an elevation of the learner. The God would then take him up unto himself, transfigure him, fill his cup with millennial joys (for a thousand years are as one day in his sight), and let the learner forget the misunderstanding in tumultuous joy. Alas, the learner might perhaps be greatly inclined to prize such happiness as this. How wonderful suddenly to find his fortune made, like the humble maiden, because the eye of the God happened to rest upon him! And how wonderful also to be his helper in taking all this in vain, deceived by his own heart! Even the noble king could perceive the difficulty of such a method, for he was not without insight into the human heart, and understood that the maiden was at bottom deceived; and no one is so terribly deceived as he who does not himself suspect it, but is as if enchanted by a change in the outward habiliments of his existence.

The union might be brought about by the God's showing himself to the learner and receiving his worship, causing him to forget himself over the divine apparition. Thus the king might have shown himself to the humble maiden in all the pomp of his power, causing the sun of his presence to rise over her cottage, shedding a glory over the scene, and making her forget herself in worshipful admiration. Alas, and this might have satisfied the maiden, but it could not satisfy the king, who desired not his own glorification but hers. It was this that made his grief so hard to bear, his grief that she could not understand him; but it would have been still harder for him to deceive her. And merely to give his love for her an imperfect expression was in his eyes a deception, even though no one understood him and reproaches sought to mortify his soul.

Not in this manner then can their love be made happy, except perhaps in appearance, namely the learner's and the maiden's, but not the Teacher's and the king's, whom no delusion can satisfy. . . .

B

The union must therefore be brought about in some other way. Let us here again recall Socrates, for what was the Socratic ignorance if not an expression for his love of the learner, and for his sense of equality with him? . . . In the Socratic conception the teacher's love would be merely that of a deceiver if he permitted the disciple to rest in the belief that he really owed him anything, instead of fulfilling the function of the teacher to help the learner become sufficient to himself. But when the God becomes a Teacher, his love cannot be merely seconding and assisting, but is creative, giving a new being to the learner, or as we have called him, the man born anew; by which designation we signify the transition from nonbeing to being. The truth then is that the learner owes the Teacher everything. But this is what makes it so difficult to effect an understanding: that the learner becomes as nothing and yet is not destroyed; that he comes to owe everything to the Teacher and yet retains his confidence. . . .

Since we found that the union could not be brought about by an elevation it must be attempted by a descent. Let the learner be x. In this x we must include the lowliest; for if even Socrates refused to establish a false fellowship with the clever, how can we suppose that the God would make a distinction! In order that the union may be brought about, the God must therefore become the equal of such an one, and so he will appear in the likeness of the humblest. But the humblest is one who must serve others, and the God will therefore appear in the form of a *servant*. But this servant-form is no mere outer garment, like the king's beggar-cloak, which therefore flutters loosely about him and betrays the king; it is not like the filmy summer-cloak of Socrates, which though woven of nothing yet both conceals and reveals. It is his true form and figure. For this is the unfathomable nature of love, that it desires equality with the beloved, not in jest merely, but in earnest and truth. And it is the omnipotence of the love which is so resolved that it is able to accomplish its purpose, which neither Socrates nor the king could do, whence their assumed figures constituted after all a kind of deceit. . . .

But the servant-form was no mere outer garment, and therefore the God must suffer all things, endure all things, make experience of all things. He must suffer hunger in the desert, he must thirst in the time of his agony, he must be forsaken in death, absolutely like the humblest—behold the man! . . .

Every other form of revelation would be a deception in the eyes of love, for either the learner would first have to be changed, and the fact concealed from him that this was necessary (but love does not alter the beloved, it alters itself); or there would be permitted to prevail a frivolous ignorance of the fact that the entire relationship was a delusion. . . .

Now if someone were to say: "This poem of yours is the most wretched piece of plagiarism ever perpetrated, for it is neither more nor less than what every child knows," I suppose I must blush with shame to hear myself called a liar. But why the most wretched? Every poet who steals, steals from some other poet, and in so far as we are all equally wretched; indeed, my own theft is perhaps less harmful since it is more readily discovered.

Mummers' Plays

THROUGHOUT THE MIDDLE AGES, MUMMERS' PLAYS, simple dramas characterized by a procession of masked figures, were popular entertainment throughout England and Europe. These plays were associated with the revels of Christmas. Their origins, however, were pagan ceremonies marking the change of the seasons. The earth's death in winter and revitalization in spring, symbolically dramatized in the death and resurrection of a character, is undoubtedly the original focus of the ceremony.

Most mummers' plays include the characters of the King of Egypt, George, and a doctor. The plots include a sword fight, a resuscitation, and actors begging alms from the audience at the end of the play. Earlier forms of the play focused on the struggles between Christianity and Islam; however, in the following version, the only remnants of this theme are in the characters of the King of Egypt and his son George, Prince of Morocco, and in the reference to Alexander as a "cursed Christian."

Despite their popularity as a type of folk performance, mummers' plays were not written down until the eighteenth century. However, surviving texts in English are so similar as to argue a common, no longer extant, chapbook source. One of the most famous mummers' plays is the version created by Thomas Hardy and included in his novel *Return of the Native*. The interest in folk literature that arose in the nineteenth century was accompanied by a correspondent resurgence in interest in mummers' plays.

The Alexander Text printed here, from a 1771 English chapbook, is the oldest complete extant mummers' play.

Alexander, and the King of Egypt. A Mock Play

As it is Acted by
The MUMMERS every CHRISTMAS.
NEWCASTLE: Printed in the Year 1788.

A MOCK PLAY
ACT I. SCENE I.

Enter ALEXANDER.
ALEXANDER *speaks.*

SILENCE, Brave Gentlemen; if you will give an
Eye
Alexander is my Name, I'll sing the Tragedy;
A Ramble here I took, the Country for to see,
Three Actors here I've brought so far from Italy;
The first I do present, he is a noble King,
He's just come from the Wars, good Tidings he
doth bring.

The next that doth come in, he is a Doctor good,
Had it not been for him, I'd surely lost my Blood.
Old Dives is the next, a Miser, you may see,
Who, by lending of his Gold, is come to Poverty.
So, Gentlemen, you see four Actors will go round,
Stand off a little While, more Pastime shall be
found.

Exeunt.

ACT I. SCENE II.
Enter Actors.

ROOM, Room, brave Gallants, give us Room to
Sport,
For in this Room we have a mind to resort,
Resort, and to repeat to you our merry Rhyme,
For remember, good Sirs, this is Christmas Time;
The Time to cut up Goose Pies now doth appear,
So we are come to act our merry Mirth here:
At the sounding of the Trumpet, and beating of the
Drum,
Make room, brave Gentlemen, and let our Actors
come.
We are the merry Actors that traverses the Street;
We are the merry Actors that fight for our Meat;
We are the merry Actors that shew the pleasant
Play,
Step in, thou King of Egypt, and clear the Way.

KING OF   I am the King of Egypt, as plainly doth appear
EGYPT: And Prince George he is my only Son and Heir:
          Step in therefore, my Son, and act thy part with me,
          And shew forth thy Praise before the Company.

PRINCE   I am Prince George, a Champion brave and bold
GEORGE: For with my Spear I've won three Crowns of Gold;
          'Twas I that brought the Dragon to the Slaughter,
          And I that gain'd the Egyptian Monarch's Daughter,
          In Egypt's Fields I Prisoner long was kept,
          But by my Valour I from them soon 'scaped:
          I sounded at the Gates of a Divine,

And out came a Giant of no good Design,
He gave me a blow, which almost struck me dead,
But I up with my Sword and did cut off his Head.

ALEXANDER: Hold, Slacker, hold, pray do not be so hot,
For on this Spot thou knowest not who thou's got;
'Tis I that's to hash thee and smash thee, as small as
Flies,
And send thee to Satan to make minch Pies:
Minch Pies hot, minch Pies cold,
I'll send thee to Satan e'er thou be three Days old.
But hold, Prince George, before thou go away,
Either thou or I must die this bloody Day;
Some mortal Wounds thou shalt receive by me,
So let us fight it out most manfully.

Exeunt.

ACT II. SCENE I.

ALEXANDER *and* PRINCE GEORGE *fight, the latter is wounded and falls.*
KING OF EGYPT *speaks.*

Curs'd Christian, what is this thou hast done?
Thou hast ruin'd me by killing my best Son.

ALEXANDER: He gave me a Challenge, why should I him deny,
How high he was but see how low he lies.

KING OF
EGYPT: O Sambo! Sambo! help me now,
For I never was in more Need;
For thou to stand with Sword in hand,
And to fight at my Command.

DOCTOR: Yes, my Liege, I will thee obey,
And by my Sword I hope to win the Day;
Yonder stands he who has kill'd my Master's Son,
I'll try if he be sprung from Royal Blood,
And through his Body make an Ocean Flood.
Gentlemen, you see my Sword Point is broke,
Or else I'd run it down that Villain's Throat.

KING OF
EGYPT: Is there never a Doctor to be found,
That can cure my Son of his deadly Wound.

DOCTOR:	Yes, there is a Doctor to be found,
	That can cure your Son of his deadly wound.
KING OF EGYPT:	What Diseases can he cure?
DOCTOR:	All Diseases both within and without,

DOCTOR: Yes, there is a Doctor to be found,
That can cure your Son of his deadly wound.

KING OF
EGYPT: What Diseases can he cure?

DOCTOR: All Diseases both within and without,
Especially the Itch, Pox, Palsy, and the Gout:
Come in you ugly, nasty, dirty, Whore,
Whose age is threescore Years or more,
Whose Nose and Face stands all awry,
I'll make her very fitting to pass by.
I'll give a Coward a Heart, if he be willing,
Will make him stand without Fear of killing;
And any Man that's got a scolding Spouse,
That wearies him with living in his House;
I'll ease him of his Complaint, and make her civil,
Or else will send her headlong to the Devil.
Ribs, Legs, or arms, when any's broke, I'm sure I
presently of them will make a Cure;
Nay, more than this by far, I will maintain,
If you should break your Neck, I'll cur't again.
So here's a Doctor rare, who travels much at Home,
Here take my Pills, I cure all Ills, past, present, and
to come.
I in my Time have many Thousands directed,
And likewise have as many more dissected,
To cure the Love-sick Maid, like me there's none,
For with two of my Pills the Job I've done;
I take her Home, and rubs her o'er and o'er,
Then if she dies ne'er believe me more.
To cure your Son, good Sir, I do fear not,
With this small Bottle, which by me I've got;
The Balsam is the best which it contains,
Rise up, my good Prince George, and fight again.

Exeunt.

ACT II. SCENE II.

PRINCE GEORGE *arises*.
PRINCE GEORGE *speaks*.

O Horrible! terrible! the like was never seen,
A man drove out of seven Senses into fifteen;
And out of fifteen into fourscore,
O horrible! terrible! the like was ne'er before.

ALEXANDER: Thou silly Ass that lives by Grass, dost thou abuse a
Stranger
I live in hopes to buy new Ropes, and tie thy Nose
to the Manger.

PRINCE
GEORGE: Sir unto you I bend.

ALEXANDER: Stand off, thou Slave, I think thee not my Friend.

PRINCE A Slave, Sir! that is for me by far too base a Name,
GEORGE: That Word deserves to stab thy Honour's Fame.

ALEXANDER: To be stab'd, Sir, is the least of all my Care,
Appoint your Time and Place, I'll meet you there.

PRINCE
GEORGE: I'll cross the Water at the Hour of Five.

ALEXANDER: I'll meet you there, Sir, if I be alive.

PRINCE But stop, Sir—I'd wish you to a Wife, both lusty and
GEORGE: young,
She can talk both Dutch, French, and the Italian,
Tongue.

ALEXANDER: I'll have none such.

PRINCE
GEORGE: Why, don't you love your Learning?

ALEXANDER: Yes, I love my Learning as I do my Life,
I love a learned Scholar, but not a learned Wife,
Stand off, had I as many Hussians, Shusians, Chairs
and Stools,
As you have had Sweet-hearts, Boys, Girls, and
Fools;

I love a Woman, and a Woman loves me,
And when I want a Fool I'll send for thee.

KING OF   Sir, to express thy Beauty, I am not able,
EGYPT: For thy Face shines like the very Kitchen Table;
Thy Teeth are no whiter than the Charcoal,
And thy Breath stinks like the Devil's A-se H-le.

ALEXANDER: Stand off, thou dirty Dog, for by my Sword thou's die.
I'll make thy Body full of Holes, and cause thy But-
tons flie.

Exeunt.

ACT III. SCENE I.

KING OF EGYPT *fights and is killed.*
Enter PRINCE GEORGE.

OH! what is here? Oh! what is to be done?
Our King is slain, the Crown is likewise gone:
Take up the Body, bear it hence away,
For in this Place no longer shall it stay.

The CONCLUSION.

Bouncer Buckler, Velvet's dear,
And Christmas comes but once a Year;
Though when it comes, it brings good Cheer,
But farewel Christmas once a Year.

Farewel, farewel, adieu! Friendship and Unity.
I hope we have made Sport, and pleas'd the Company;
But, Gentleman, you see we're but young actors
four,
We've done the best we can, and the best can do no
more.

FINIS.

Anthony Trollope

ANTHONY TROLLOPE (1815–1882), A PROLIFIC NOVELIST best known for his six novels of clergy life, the Barchester novels, also wrote political novels, novels of manners, social satires, travel books, and short stories. According to novelist Henry James, the "inestimable merit" of Trollope is his "complete appreciation of the usual." Trollope's focus is on the ordinary, and his observations of people are generally indulgent. His typical method, exemplified in "The Two Generals," is to describe a group of characters, their interrelationship, and their circumstance; the plot then evolves almost inevitably from the interplay of character and circumstance. "The Two Generals," written during the Civil War, presents a view of the American conflict by a Britisher known for his shrewd observations of human foibles.

The Two Generals:
A Christmas Story of
the War in Kentucky

Christmas of 1860 is now three years past, and the civil war which was then being commenced in America is still raging without any apparent sign of an end. The prophets of that time who prophesied the worst never foretold anything so black as this. On that Christmas day Major Anderson, who then held the command of the forts in Charleston harbour on the part of the United States Government, removed his men and stores from Fort Moultrie to Fort Sumter, thinking that he might hold the one though not both against any attack from the people of Charleston, whose State, that of South Carolina, had seceded five days previously. That was in truth the beginning of the war, though at that time Mr. Lincoln was not yet President. He became so on the 4th March, 1861, and on the 15th of April following Fort Sumter was evacuated by Major Anderson, on the part of the United States Government, under fire from the people of Charleston. So little bloody, however, was that affair that no one was killed in the assault;—though one poor fellow perished in the saluting fire with which the retreating officer was complimented as he retired with the so-called honours of war. During the three years that have since passed, the combatants have better learned the use of their weapons of war. No one can now laugh at them for bloodless battles. Never have the sides of any stream been so bathed in blood as have the shores of those Virginian rivers whose names have lately become familiar to us. None of those old death-dooming generals of Europe whom we have learned to hate for the cold-blooded energy of their trade,—Tilly, Gustavus Adolphus, Frederic, or Napoleon;—none of these ever left so many carcases to the kites as have the Johnsons, Jacksons, and Hookers of the American armies, who come and go so fast, that they are almost forgotten before the armies they have led have melted into clay.

Of all the states of the old union, Virginia has probably suffered the most, but Kentucky has least deserved the suffering which has fallen to her lot. In Kentucky the war has raged hither and thither, every town having been subject to inroads from either army. But she would have been loyal to the Union if she could;—nay, on the whole she has been loyal. She would have thrown off the plague chain of slavery if the prurient virtue of New England would have allowed her to do so by her own means. But virtuous New England was too proud of her own virtue to be content that the work of abolition should thus pass from her hands. Kentucky, when the war was beginning, desired nothing but to go on in her own course. She wished for no sudden change. She grew no cotton. She produced corn and meat, and was a land flowing with milk and honey. Her slaves were not as the slaves of the Southern States. They were few in number; tolerated for a time because their manumission was understood to be of all questions the most difficult;—rarely or never sold from the estates to which they belonged. When the war broke out Kentucky said that she would be neutral. Neutral,—and she lying on the front lines of the contest! Such neutrality was impossible to her,—impossible to any of her children!

Near to the little State capital of Frankfort there lived at that Christmas time of 1860 an old man, Major Reckenthorpe by name, whose life had been marked by many circumstances which had made him well known throughout Kentucky. He had sat for nearly thirty years in the Congress of the United States at Washington, representing his own State sometimes as senator, and sometimes in the lower house. Though called a major he was by profession a lawyer, and as such had lived successfully. Time had been when friends had thought it possible that he might fill the President's chair; but his name had been too much and too long in men's mouths for that. Who had heard of Lincoln, Pierce, or Polk, two years before they were named as candidates for the Presidency? But Major Reckenthorpe had been known and talked of in Washington longer perhaps than any other living politician.

Upon the whole he had been a good man, serving his country as best he knew how, and adhering honestly to his own political convictions. He had been and now was a slaveowner, but had voted in the Congress of his own State for the abolition of slavery in Kentucky. He had been a passionate man, and had lived not without the stain of blood on his hands, for duels had been familiar to him. But he had lived in a time and in a country in which it had been hardly possible for a leading public man not to be familiar with a pistol. He had been known as one whom no man could attack with impunity; but he had also been known as one who would not willingly attack anyone. Now at the time of which I am writing, he was old,—almost on the shelf,—past his duellings and his strong short invectives on the floors of Congress; but he was a man whom no age could tame, and still he was ever talking, thinking, and planning for the political well-being of his State.

In person he was tall, still upright, stiff and almost ungainly in his gait, with eager grey eyes which the waters of age could not dim, with short, thick, grizzled hair which age had hardly thinned, but which ever looked rough and uncombed, with large hands, which he stretched out with extended fingers when he spoke vehemently;—and of the Major it may be said that he always spoke with vehemence. But now he was slow in his steps, and infirm on his legs. He suffered from rheumatism, sciatica, and other maladies of the old, which no energy of his own could repress. In these days he was a stern, unhappy, all but broken-hearted old man; for he saw that the work of his life had been wasted.

And he had another grief which at this Christmas of 1860 had already become terrible to him, and which afterwards bowed him with sorrow to the ground. He had two sons, both of whom were then at home with him, having come together under the family roof tree that they might discuss with their father the political position of their country, and especially the position of Kentucky. South Carolina had already seceded, and other Slave States were talking of secession. What should Kentucky do? So the Major's sons, young men of eight-and-twenty and five-and-twenty, met together at their father's house;—they met and quarrelled deeply, as their father had well known would be the case.

The eldest of these sons was at that time the owner of the slaves and land which his father had formerly possessed and farmed. He was a Southern gentleman, living on the produce of slave labour, and as such had learned to vindicate, if not love, that social system which has produced as its result the war which is still raging at this Christmas of 1863. To him this matter of secession or non-secession was of vital import. He was prepared to declare that the wealth of the South was derived from its agriculture, and that its agriculture could only be supported by its slaves. He went further than this, and declared also that no further league was possible between a Southern gentleman and a Puritan from New England. His father, he said, was an old man, and might be excused by reason of his age from any active part in the contest that was coming. But for himself there could be but one duty;—that of supporting the new Confederacy, to which he would belong, with all his strength and with whatever wealth was his own.

The second son had been educated at Westpoint, the great military school of the old United States, and was now an officer in the National Army. Not on that account need it be supposed that he would, as a matter of course, join himself to the Northern side in the war,—to the side which, as being in possession of the capital and the old Government establishments, might claim to possess a right to his military services. A large proportion of the officers in the pay of the United States leagued themselves with Secession,— and it is difficult to see why such an act would be more disgraceful in them than in others. But with Frank Reckenthorpe such was not the case. He declared that he would be loyal to the Government which he served; and in saying so, seemed to imply that the want of such loyalty in any other person, soldier or non-soldier, would be disgraceful, as in his opinion it would have been disgraceful in himself.

"I can understand your feeling," said his brother, who was known as Tom Reckenthorpe, "on the assumption that you think more of being a soldier than of being a man; but not otherwise."

"Even if I were no soldier, I would not be a rebel," said Frank.

"How a man can be a rebel for sticking to his own country, I cannot understand," said Tom.

"Your own country!" said Frank. "Is it to be Kentucky or South Carolina? And is it to be a republic or a monarchy;—or shall we hear of Emperor Davis? You already belong to the greatest nation on earth, and you are preparing yourself to belong to the least;—that is, if you should be successful. Luckily for yourself, you have no chance of success."

"At any rate I will do my best to fight for it."

"Nonsense, Tom," said the old man, who was sitting by.

"It is no nonsense, sir. A man can fight without having been at Westpoint. Whether he can do so after having his spirit drilled and drummed out of him there, I don't know."

"Tom!" said the old man.

"Don't mind him, father," said the younger. "His appetite for fighting will soon be over. Even yet I doubt whether we shall ever see a regiment in arms sent from the Southern States against the Union."

"Do you?" said Tom. "If you stick to your colours, as you say you will, your doubts will soon be set at rest. And I'll tell you what, if your regiment is brought into the field, I trust that I may find myself opposite to it. You have chosen to forget that we are brothers, and you shall find that I can forget it also."

"Tom!" said the father, "you should not say such words as that; at any rate, in my presence."

"It is true, sir," said he. "A man who speaks as he speaks does not belong to Kentucky, and can be no brother of mine. If I were to meet him face to face, I would as soon shoot him as another;—sooner, because he is a renegade."

"You are very wicked,—very wicked," said the old man, rising from his chair,—"very wicked." And then, leaning on his stick, he left the room.

"Indeed, what he says is true," said a sweet, soft voice from a sofa in the far corner of the room. "Tom, you are very wicked to speak to your brother thus. Would you take on yourself the part of Cain?"

"He is more silly than wicked, Ada," said the soldier. "He will have no chance of shooting me, or of seeing me shot. He may succeed in getting himself locked up as a rebel; but I doubt whether he'll ever go beyond that."

"If I ever find myself opposite to you with a pistol in my grasp," said the elder brother, "may my right hand—"

But his voice was stopped, and the imprecation remained unuttered. The girl who had spoken rushed from her seat and put her hand before his mouth. "Tom," she said, "I will never speak to you again if you utter such an oath,—never." And her eyes flashed fire at his and made him dumb.

Ada Forster called Mrs. Reckenthorpe her aunt, but the connection between them was not so near as that of aunt and niece. Ada nevertheless lived with the Reckenthorpes, and had done so for the last two years. She was an orphan, and on the death of her father had followed her father's sister-in-law from Maine down to Kentucky;—for Mrs. Reckenthorpe had come from that farthest and most straitlaced State of the Union, in which people bind themselves by law to drink neither beer, wine, nor spirits, and all go to bed at nine o'clock. But Ada Forster was an heiress, and therefore it was thought well by the elder Reckenthorpes that she should marry one of their sons. Ada Forster was also a beauty, with slim, tall form, very pleasant to the eye; with bright, speaking eyes and glossy hair; with ivory teeth of the whitest,—only to be seen now and then when a smile could be won from her; and therefore such a match was thought desirable also by the younger Reckenthorpes. But unfortunately it had been thought desirable by each of them, whereas the father and mother had intended Ada for the soldier.

I have not space in this short story to tell how progress had been made in the troubles of this love affair. So it was now, that Ada had consented to become the wife of the elder brother,—of Tom Reckenthorpe, with his home among the slaves,—although she, with all her New England feelings strong about her, hated slavery and all its adjuncts. But when has Love stayed to be guided by any such consideration as that? Tom Reckenthorpe was a handsome, high-spirited, intelligent man. So was his brother Frank. But Tom

Reckenthorpe could be soft to a woman, and in that, I think, had he found the means of his success. Frank Reckenthorpe was never soft.

Frank had gone angrily from home when, some three months since, Ada had told him her determination. His brother had been then absent, and they had not met till this their Christmas meeting. Now it had been understood between them, by the intervention of their mother, that they would say nothing to each other as to Ada Forster. The elder had, of course, no cause for saying aught, and Frank was too proud to wish to speak on such a matter before his successful rival. But Frank had not given up the battle. When Ada had made her speech to him, he had told her that he would not take it as conclusive. "The whole tenor of Tom's life," he had said to her, "must be distasteful to you. It is impossible that you should live as the wife of a slaveowner."

"In a few years there will be no slaves in Kentucky," she had answered.

"Wait till then," he had answered; "and I also will wait." And so he had left her, resolving that he would bide his time. He thought that the right still remained to him of seeking Ada's hand, although she had told him that she loved his brother. "I know that such a marriage would make each of them miserable," he said to himself over and over again. And now that these terrible times had come upon them, and that he was going one way with the Union, while his brother was going the other way with Secession, he felt more strongly than ever that he might still be successful. The political predilections of American women are as strong as those of American men. And Frank Reckenthorpe knew that all Ada's feelings were as strongly in favour of the Union as his own. Had not she been born and bred in Maine? Was she not ever keen for total abolition, till even the old Major, with all his gallantry for womanhood and all his love for the young girl who had come to his house in his old age, would be driven occasionally by stress of feeling to rebuke her? Frank Reckenthorpe was patient, hopeful, and firm. The time must come when Ada would learn that she could not be a fit wife for his brother. The time had, he thought, perhaps come already; and so he spoke to her a word or two on the evening of that day on which she had laid her hand upon his brother's mouth.

"Ada," he had said, "there are bad times coming to us."

"Good times, I hope," she had answered. "No one could expect that the thing could be done without some struggle. When the struggle has passed we shall say that good times have come." The thing of which she spoke was that little thing of which she was ever thinking, the enfranchisement of four millions of slaves.

"I fear that there will be bad times first. Of course I am thinking of you now."

"Bad or good they will not be worse to me than to others."

"They would be very bad to you if this State were to secede, and if you were to join your lot to my brother's. In the first place, all your fortune would be lost to him and to you."

"I do not see that; but of course I will caution him that it may be so. If it alters his views, I shall hold him free to act as he chooses."

"But Ada, should it not alter yours?"

"What,—because of my money?—or because Tom could not afford to marry a girl without a fortune?"

"I did not mean that. He might decide that for himself. But your marriage with him under such circumstances as those which he now contemplates, would be as though you married a Spaniard or a Greek adventurer. You would be without country, without home, without fortune, and without standing-ground in the world. Look you, Ada, before you answer. I frankly own that I tell you this because I want you to be my wife, and not his."

"Never, Frank; I shall never be your wife,—whether I marry him or no."

"All I ask of you now is to pause. This is no time for marrying or for giving in marriage."

"There I agree with you; but as my word is pledged to him, I shall let him be my adviser in that."

Late on that same night Ada saw her betrothed and bade him adieu. She bade him adieu with many tears, for he came to tell her that he intended to leave Frankfort very early on the following morning. "My staying here now is out of the question," said he. "I am resolved to secede, whatever the State may do. My father is resolved against secession. It is necessary, therefore, that we should part. I have already left my father and mother, and now I have come to say good-bye to you."

"And your brother, Tom?"

"I shall not see my brother again."

"And is that well after such words as you have spoken to each other? Perhaps it may be that you will never see him again. Do you remember what you threatened?"

"I do remember what I threatened."

"And did you mean it?"

"No; of course I did not mean it. You, Ada have heard me speak many angry words, but I do not think that you have known me do many angry things."

"Never one, Tom:—never. See him then before you go, and tell him so."

"No,—he is hard as iron, and would take any such telling from me amiss. He must go his way, and I mine."

"But though you differ as men, Tom, you need not hate each other as brothers."

"It will be better that we should not meet again. The truth is, Ada, that he always despises anyone who does not think as he thinks. If I offered him my hand he would take it, but while doing so he would let me know that he thought me a fool. Then I should be angry, and threaten him again, and things would be worse. You must not quarrel with me, Ada, if I say that he has all the faults of a Yankee."

"And the virtues too, sir, while you have all the faults of a Southern—. But, Tom, as you are going from us, I will not scold you. I have, too, a word of business to say to you."

"And what's the word of business, dear?" said Tom, getting nearer to her as a lover should do, and taking her hand in his.

"It is this. You and those who think like you are dividing yourselves from your country. As to whether that be right or wrong, I will say nothing now,—nor will I say anything as to your chance of success. But I am told that those who go with the South will not be able to hold property in the North."

"Did Frank tell you that?"

"Never mind who told me, Tom."

"And is that to make a difference between you and me?"

"That is just the question that I am asking you. Only you ask me with a reproach in your tone, and I ask you with none in mine. Till we have mutually agreed to break our engagement you shall be my adviser. If you think it better that it should be broken,—better for your own interests, be man enough to say so."

But Tom Reckenthorpe either did not think so, or else he was not man enough to speak his thoughts. Instead of doing so he took the girl in his arms and kissed her, and swore that whether with fortune or no fortune she should be his, and his only. But still he had to go,—to go now, within an hour or two of the very moment at which they were speaking. They must part, and before parting must make some mutual promise as to their future meeting. Marriage now, as things stood at this Christmas time, could not be thought of even by Tom Reckenthorpe. At last he promised that if he were then alive he would be with her again, at the old family house in Frankfort, on the next coming Christmas day. So he went, and as he let himself out of the old house, Ada, with her eyes full of tears, took herself up to her bedroom.

During the year that followed—the year 1861—the American war progressed only as a school for fighting. The most memorable action was that of Bull's Run, in which both sides ran away, not from individual cowardice in either set of men, but from that feeling of panic which is engendered by ignorance and inexperience. Men saw waggons rushing hither and thither, and thought that all was lost. After that the year was passed in drilling and in camp-making,—in the making of soldiers, of gunpowder, and of cannons. But of all the articles of war made in that year, the article that seemed easiest of fabrication was a general officer. Generals were made with the greatest rapidity, owing their promotion much more frequently to local interest than to military success. Such a State sent such and such regiments, and therefore must be rewarded by having such and such generals nominated from among its citizens. The wonder perhaps is that with armies so formed battles should have been fought so well.

Before the end of 1861 both Major Reckenthorpe's sons had become general officers. That Frank, the soldier, should have been so promoted was, at such a period as this, nothing strange. Though a young man he had been soldier, or learning the trade of a soldier, for more than ten years, and such service as that might well be counted for much in the sudden construction of an army intended to number seven hundred thousand troops, and which at one time did contain all those soldiers. Frank too was a clever fellow, who knew his business, and there were many generals made in those days who understood less of their work than he did. As much could not be said for Tom's quick military advancement. But this could be said for them in the South,—that unless they did make their generals in this way, they would hardly have any generals at all, and General Reckenthorpe, as he so quickly became,—General Tom as they used to call him in Kentucky,—recommended himself specially to the Confederate leaders by the warmth and eagerness with which he had come among them. The name of the old man so well known throughout the Union, who had ever loved the South without hating the North, would have been a tower of strength to them. Having him they would have thought that they might have carried the State of Kentucky into open secession. He was now worn out and old, and could not be expected to take upon his shoulders the crushing burden of a new contest. But his eldest son had come among them, eagerly, with his whole heart; and so they made him a general.

The poor old man was in part proud of this and in part grieved. "I have a son a general in each army," he said to a stranger who came to his house in those days; "but what strength is there in a fagot when it is separated? of what use is a house that is divided against itself? The boys would kill each other if they met."

"It is very sad," said the stranger.

"Sad?" said the old man. "It is as though the Devil were let loose upon the earth;—and so he is; so he is."

The family came to understand that General Tom was with the Confederate army which was confronting the Federal army of the Potomac and defending Richmond; whereas it was well known that Frank was in Kentucky with the army on the Green River, which was hoping to make its way into Tennessee, and which did so early in the following year. It must be understood that Kentucky, though a slave state, had never seceded, and that therefore it was divided off from the Southern States, such as Tennessee and that part of Virginia which had seceded, by a cordon of pickets; so that there was no coming up from the Confederate army to Frankfort in Kentucky. There could, at any rate, be no easy or safe coming up for such a one as General Tom, seeing that being a soldier he would be regarded as a spy, and certainly treated as a prisoner if found within the Northern lines. Nevertheless, General as he was, he kept his engagement with Ada, and made his way into the gardens of his father's house on the night of Christmas-eve. And Ada was the first who knew that he was there. Her ear first caught the sound of his footsteps, and her hand raised for him the latch of the garden door.

"Oh, Tom, it is not you?"

"But it is though, Ada, my darling!" Then there was a little pause in his speech. "Did I not tell you that I should see you to-day?"

"Hush. Do you know who is here? Your brother came across to us from the Green River yesterday."

"The mischief he did. Then I shall never find my way back again. If you knew what I have gone through for this!"

Ada immediately stepped out through the door and on to the snow, standing close up against him as she whispered to him, "I don't think Frank would betray you," she said. "I don't think he would."

"I doubt him,—doubt him hugely. But I suppose I must trust him. I got through the pickets close to Cumberland Gap, and I left my horse at Stoneley's, half way between this and Lexington. I cannot go back to-night now that I have come so far!"

"Wait, Tom; wait a minute, and I will go in and tell your mother. But you must be hungry. Shall I bring you food?"

"Hungry enough, but I will not eat my father's victuals out here in the snow."

"Wait a moment, dearest, till I speak to my aunt." Then Ada slipped back into the house and soon managed to get Mrs. Reckenthorpe away from the room in which the Major and his second son were sitting. "Tom is here," she said, "in the garden. He has encountered all this danger to pay us a visit because it is Christmas.

Oh, aunt, what are we to do? He says that Frank would certainly give him up!"

Mrs. Reckenthorpe was nearly twenty years younger than her husband, but even with this advantage on her side Ada's tidings were almost too much for her. She, however, at last managed to consult the Major, and he resolved upon appealing to the generosity of his younger son. By this time the Confederate General was warming himself in the kitchen, having declared that his brother might do as he pleased;—he would not skulk away from his father's house in the night.

"Frank," said the father, as his younger son sat silently thinking of what had been told him, "it cannot be your duty to be false to your father in his own house."

"It is not always easy, sir, for a man to see what is his duty. I wish that either he or I had not come here."

"But he is here; and you, his brother, would not take advantage of his coming to his father's house?" said the old man.

"Do you remember, sir, how he told me last year that if ever he met me on the field he would shoot me like a dog?"

"But, Frank, you know that he is the last man in the world to carry out such a threat. Now he has come here with great danger."

"And I have come with none; but I do not see that that makes any difference."

"He has put up with it all that he may see the girl he loves."

"Psha!" said Frank, rising up from his chair. "When a man has work to do, he is a fool to give way to play. The girl he loves! Does he not know that it is impossible that she should ever marry him? Father, I ought to insist that he should leave this house as a prisoner. I know that that would be my duty."

"You would have, sir, to bear my curse."

"I should not the less have done my duty. But, father, independently of your threat, I will neglect that duty. I cannot bring myself to break your heart and my mother's. But I will not see him. Good-bye, sir. I will go up to the hotel, and will leave the place before daybreak to-morrow."

After some few further words Frank Reckenthorpe left the house without encountering his brother. He also had not seen Ada Forster since that former Christmas when they had all been together, and he had now left his camp and come across from the army much more with the view of inducing her to acknowledge the hopelessness of her engagement with his brother, than from any domestic idea of passing his Christmas at home. He was a man who would not have interfered with his brother's prospects, as regarded either love or money, if he had thought that in doing so he would in truth have injured his brother. He was a hard man, but one not wilfully unjust. He had satisfied himself that a marriage between Ada and his brother must, if it were practicable, be ruinous to both of them. If this were so, would not it be better for all parties that there should be another arrangement made? North and South were as far divided now as the two poles. All Ada's hopes and feelings were with the North. Could he allow her to be taken as a bride among perishing slaves and ruined whites?

But when the moment for his sudden departure came he knew that it would be better that he should go without seeing her. His brother Tom had made his way to her through cold, and wet, and hunger, and through infinite perils of a kind sterner even than these. Her heart now would be full of softness towards him. So Frank Reckenthorpe left the house without seeing any one but his mother. Ada, as the front door closed behind him, was still standing close by her lover over the kitchen fire, while the slaves of the family, with whom Master Tom had always been the favourite, were administering to his little comforts.

Of course General Tom was a hero in the house for the few days that he remained there, and of course the step he had taken was the very one to strengthen for him the affection of the girl whom he had come to see. North and South were even more bitterly divided now than they had been when the former parting had taken place. There were fewer hopes of reconciliation; more positive certainty of war to the knife; and they who adhered strongly to either side, and those who did not adhere strongly to either side were very few,—held their opinions now with more acrimony than they had then done. The peculiar bitterness of civil war, which adds personal hatred to national enmity, had come upon the minds of the people. And here, in Kentucky, on the borders of the contest, members of the same household were in many cases, at war with each other. Ada Forster and her aunt were passionately Northern, while the feelings of the old man had gradually turned themselves to that division in the nation to which he naturally belonged. For months past the matter on which they were all thinking,—the subject which filled their minds morning, noon, and night,—was banished from their lips because it could not be discussed without the bitterness of hostility. But, nevertheless, there was no word of bitterness between Tom Reckenthorpe and Ada Forster. While these few short days lasted it was all love. Where is the woman whom one touch of romance will not soften, though she be ever so impervious to argument? Tom could sit up-stairs with his mother and his betrothed, and tell them stories of the gallantry of the South,—of the sacrifices women were making, and of the deeds men were doing,—and they would listen and smile and caress his hand, and all for a while would be pleasant; while the old Major did not dare to speak before them of his Southern hopes. But down in the parlour, during the two or three long nights which General Tom passed in Frankfort, open secession was discussed between the two men. The old man now had given away altogether. The Yankees, he said, were too bitter for him. "I wish I had died first; that is all," he said. "I wish I had died first. Life is wretched now to a man who can do nothing." His son tried to comfort him, saying that secession would certainly be accomplished in twelve months, and that every Slave State would certainly be included in the Southern Confederacy. But the Major shook his head. Though he hated the political bitterness of the men whom he called Puritans and Yankees, he knew their strength and acknowledged their power. "Nothing good can come in my time," he said; "not in my time,—not in my time."

In the middle of the fourth night General Tom took his departure. An old slave arrived with his horse a little before midnight, and he started on his journey. "Whatever turns up, Ada," he said, "you will be true to me."

"I will; though you are a rebel, all the same for that."

"So was Washington."

"Washington made a nation;—you are destroying one."

"We are making another, dear; that's all. But I won't talk secesh to you out here in the cold. Go in, and be good to my father; and remember this, Ada, I'll be here again next Christmas-eve, if I'm alive."

So he went, and made his journey back to his camp in safety. He slept at a friend's house during the following day, and on the next night again made his way through the Northern lines back into Virginia. Even at that time there was considerable danger in doing this, although the frontier to be guarded was so extensive. This arose chiefly from the paucity of roads, and the impossibility of getting across the country where no roads existed. But General Tom got safely back to Richmond, and no doubt found that the tedium of his military life had been greatly relieved by his excursion.

Then, after that, came a year of fighting,—and there has since come another year of fighting; of such fighting that we, hearing the accounts from day to day, have hitherto failed to recognise its extent and import. Every now and then we have even spoken of the inaction of this side or of that, as though the drawn battles which have lasted for days, in which men have perished by tens of thousands, could be renewed as might the old German battles, in which an Austrian general would be ever retreating with infinite skill and military efficacy. For constancy, for blood, for hard determination to win at any cost of life or material, history has known no such battles as these. That the South has fought the best as regards skill no man can doubt. As regards pluck and resolution there has not been a pin's choice between them. They have both fought as Englishmen fight when they are equally in earnest. As regards result, it has been almost altogether in favour of the North, because they have so vast a superiority in numbers and material.

General Tom Reckenthorpe remained during the year in Virginia, and was attached to that corps of General Lee's army which was commanded by Stonewall Jackson. It was not probable, therefore, that he would be left without active employment. During the whole year he was fighting, assisting in the wonderful raids that were made by that man whose loss was worse to the Confederates than the loss of Vicksburg or of New Orleans. And General Tom gained for himself mark, name, and glory, —but it was the glory of a soldier rather than of a general. No one looked upon him as the future commander of an army; but men said that if there was a rapid stroke to be stricken, under orders from some more thought-ful head, General Tom was the hand to strike it. Thus he went on making wonderful rides by night, appearing like a warrior ghost leading warrior ghosts in some quiet valley of the Federals, seizing supplies and cutting off cattle, till his name came to be great in the State of Kentucky, and Ada Forster, Yankee though she was, was proud of her rebel lover.

And Frank Reckenthorpe, the other general, made progress also, though it was progress of a different kind. Men did not talk of him so much as they did of Tom; but the War Office at Washington knew that he was useful,—and used him. He remained for a long time attached to the western army, having been removed from Kentucky to St. Louis, in Missouri, and was there when his brother last heard of him. "I am fighting day and night," he once said to one who was with him from his own State, "and, as far as I can learn, Frank is writing day and night. Upon my word, I think that I have the best of it."

It was but a couple of days after this, the time then being about the latter end of September, that he found himself on horseback at the head of three regiments of cavalry near the foot of one of those valleys which lead up into the Blue Mountain ridge of Virginia. He was about six miles in advance of Jackson's army, and had pushed forward with the view of intercepting certain Federal supplies which he and others had hoped might be within his reach. He had expected that there would be fighting, but had hardly expected so much fighting as came that day in his way. He got no supplies. In-deed, he got nothing but blows, and though on that day the Con-federates would not admit that they had been worsted, neither could they claim to have done more than hold their own. But Gen-eral Tom's fighting was in that day brought to an end.

It must be understood that there was no great battle fought on this occasion. General Reckenthorpe, with about 1500 troopers, had found himself suddenly compelled to attack about double that number of Federal infantry. He did so once, and then a second time, but on each occasion without breaking the lines to which he was opposed; and towards the close of the day he found himself unhorsed, but still unwounded, with no weapon in his hand but his pistol, immediately surrounded by about a dozen of his own men, but so far in advance of the body of his troops as to make it almost impossible that he should find his way back to them. As the smoke cleared away and he could look about him, he saw that he was close to an uneven, irregular line of Federal soldiers. But there was still a chance, and he had turned for a rush, with his pistol ready for use in his hand, when he found himself confronted by a Federal officer. The pistol was already raised, and his finger was on the trigger, when he saw that the man before him was his brother.

"Your time has come," said Frank, standing his ground very calmly. He was quite unarmed, and had been separated from his men and ridden over; but hitherto he had not been hurt.

"Frank!" said Tom, dropping his pistol arm, "is that you?"

"And you are not going to do it, then?" said Frank.

"Do what?" said Tom, whose calmness was altogether gone. But he had forgotten that threat as soon as it had been uttered, and did not even know to what his brother was alluding.

But Tom Reckenthorpe, in his confusion at meeting his brother, had lost whatever chance there remained to him of escaping. He stood for a moment or two, looking at Frank, and wondering at the coincidence which had brought them together, before he turned to run. Then it was too late. In the hurry and scurry of the affair all but two of his own men had left him, and he saw that a rush of Federal soldiers was coming up around him. Nevertheless he resolved to start for a run. "Give me a chance, Frank," he said, and prepared to run. But as he went,—or rather before he had left the ground on which he was standing before his brother, a shot struck him, and he was disabled. In a minute he was as though he were stunned; then he smiled faintly, and slowly sunk upon the ground. "It's all up, Frank," he said, "and you are in at the death."

Frank Reckenthorpe was soon kneeling beside his brother amidst a crowd of his own men. "Spurrell," he said to a young officer who was close to him, "it is my own brother." —"What, General Tom?" said Spurrell. "Not dangerously, I hope?"

By this time the wounded man had been able, as it were, to feel himself and to ascertain the amount of the damage done him. "It's my right leg," he said; "just on the knee. If you'll believe me, Frank, I thought it was my heart at first. I don't think much of the wound, but I suppose you won't let me go?"

Of course they wouldn't let him go, and indeed if they had been minded so to do, he could not have gone. The wound was not fatal, as he had at first thought; but neither was it a matter of little consequence as he afterwards asserted. His fighting was over, unless he could fight with a leg amputated between the knee and the hip.

Before nightfall General Tom found himself in his brother's quarters, a prisoner on parole, with his leg all but condemned by the surgeon. The third day after that saw the leg amputated. For three weeks the two brothers remained together, and after that the elder was taken to Washington,—or rather to Alexandria, on the other side of the Potomac, as a prisoner, there to wait his chance of exchange. At first the intercourse between the two brothers was cold, guarded, and uncomfortable; but after a while it became more kindly than it had been for many a day. Whether it were cold or kindly, its nature, we may be sure, was such as the younger brother made it. Tom was ready enough to forget all personal animosity as soon as his brother would himself be willing to do so; though he was willing enough also to quarrel,—to quarrel bitterly as ever,—if Frank should give him occasion. As to that threat of the pistol, it had passed away from Tom Reckenthorpe, as all his angry words passed from him. It was clean forgotten. It was not simply that he had not wished to kill his brother, but that such a deed was impossible to him. The threat had been like a curse that means nothing,—which is used by passion as its readiest weapon when passion is impotent. But with Frank Reckenthorpe words meant what they were intended to mean. The threat had rankled in his bosom from the time of its utterance, to that moment when a strange coincidence had given the threatener the power of executing it. The remembrance of it was then strong upon him, and he had expected that his brother would have been as bad as his word. But his brother had spared him; and now, slowly, by degrees, he began to remember that also.

"What are your plans, Tom?" he said, as he sat one day by his brother's bed before the removal of the prisoner to Alexandria.

"Plans," said Tom. "How should a poor fellow like me have plans? To eat bread and water in prison at Alexandria, I suppose."

"They'll let you up to Washington on your parole, I should think. Of course I can say a word for you."

"Well, then, do say it. I'd have done as much for you, though I don't like your Yankee politics."

"Never mind my politics now, Tom."

"I never did mind them. But at any rate, you see I can't run away."

It should have been mentioned a little way back in this story that the poor old Major had been gathered to his fathers during the past year. As he had said to himself, it would be better for him that he should die. He had lived to see the glory of his country, and had gloried in it. If further glory or even further gain were to come out of this terrible war,—as great gains to men and nations do come from contests which are very terrible while they last,—he at least would not live to see it. So when he was left by his sons, he turned his face to the wall and died. There had of course been much said on this subject between the two brothers when they were together, and Frank had declared how special orders had been given to protect the house of the widow if the waves of the war in Kentucky should surge up around Frankfort. Land very near to Frankfort had become debatable between the two armies, and the question of flying from their house had more than once been mooted between the aunt and her niece; but, so far, that evil day had been staved off, and as yet Frankfort, the little capital of the State, was Northern territory.

"I suppose you will get home?" said Frank, after musing awhile, "and look after my mother and Ada?"

"If I can I shall, of course. What else can I do with one leg?"

"Nothing in this war, Tom, of course." Then there was another pause between them. "And what will Ada do?" said Frank.

"What will Ada do? Stay at home with my mother."

"Ah,—yes. But she will not remain always as Ada Forster."

"Do you mean to ask whether I shall marry her;—because of my one leg? If she will have me, I certainly shall."

"And will she? Ought you to ask her?"

"If I found her seamed all over with small-pox, with her limbs broken, blind, disfigured by any misfortune which could have visited her, I would take her as my wife all the same. If she were pennyless it would make no difference. She shall judge for herself; but I shall expect her to act by me, as I would have acted by her." Then there was another pause. "Look here, Frank," continued General Tom; "if you mean that I am to give her up as a reward to you for being sent home, I will have nothing to do with the bargain."

"I had intended no such bargain," said Frank, gloomily.

"Very well; then you can do as you please. If Ada will take me, I shall marry her as soon as she will let me. If my being sent home depends upon that, you will know how to act now."

Nevertheless he was sent home. There was not another word spoken between the two brothers about Ada Forster. Whether Frank thought that he might still have a chance through want of firmness on the part of the girl; or whether he considered that in keeping his brother away from home he could at least do himself no good; or whether, again, he resolved that he would act by his brother as a brother should act, without reference to Ada Forster, I will not attempt to say. For a day or two after the above conversation he was somewhat sullen, and did not talk freely with his brother. After that he brightened up once more, and before long the two parted on friendly terms. General Frank remained with his command, and General Tom was sent to the hospital at Alexandria,—or to such hospitalities as he might be able to enjoy at Washington in his mutilated state,—till that affair of his exchange had been arranged.

In spite of his brother's influence at headquarters this could not be done in a day; nor could permission be obtained for him to go home to Kentucky till such exchange had been effected. In this way he was kept in terrible suspense for something over two months, and mid-winter was upon him before the joyful news arrived that he was free to go where he liked. The officials in Washington would have sent him back to Richmond had he so pleased, seeing that a Federal general officer, supposed to be of equal weight with himself, had been sent back from some Southern prison in his place; but he declined any such favour, declaring his intention of going home to Kentucky. He was simply warned that no pass South could after this be granted to him, and then he went his way.

Disturbed as was the state of the country, nevertheless railways ran from Washington to Baltimore, from Baltimore to Pittsburgh, from Pittsburgh to Cincinnati, and from Cincinnati to Frankfort. So that General Tom's journey home, though with but one leg, was made much faster, and with less difficulty, than that last journey by which he reached the old family house. And again he presented himself on Christmas-eve. Ada declared that he remained purposely at Washington, so that he might make good his last promise to the letter; but I am inclined to think that he allowed no such romantic idea as that to detain him among the amenities of Washington.

He arrived again after dark, but on this occasion did not come knocking at the back door. He had fought his fight, had done his share of the battle, and now had reason to be afraid of no one. But again it was Ada who opened the door for him, "Oh, Tom; oh, my own one." There never was a word of question between them as to whether that unseemly crutch and still unhealed wound was to make any difference between them. General Tom found before three hours were over that he lacked the courage to suggest that he might not be acceptable to her as a lover with one leg. There are times in which girls throw off all their coyness, and are as bold in their loves as men. Such a time was this with Ada Forster. In the course of another month the elder General simply sent word to the younger that they intended to be married in May, if the war did not prevent them; and the younger General simply sent back word that his duties at headquarters would prevent his being present at the ceremony.

And they were married in May, though the din of war was going on around them on every side. And from that time to this the din of war is still going on, and they are in the thick of it. The carnage of their battles, the hatreds of their civil contests, are terrible to us when we think of them; but may it not be that the beneficient power of Heaven, which they acknowledge as we do, is thus cleansing their land from that stain of slavery, to abolish which no human power seemed to be sufficient?

Sarah Orne Jewett

AMERICAN AUTHOR SARAH ORNE JEWETT (1849–1909), the daughter of a Maine physician, is a regional writer adept at capturing the New England countryside and people she encountered on her travels alongside her father. Her strength, like Trollope's, lies in finding significance within the seemingly mundane and trivial. American writer Willa Cather reported that Jewett once told her that "her head was full of dear old houses and dear old women, and that when an old house and an old woman came together in her brain with a click, she knew that a story was under way."

She might well have been describing "Mrs. Parkins's Christmas Eve," which appeared in two installments in *Ladies' Home Journal* (December 1890/January 1891). Christmas stories, including the preceding story by Anthony Trollope, were published in the Christmas issues of numerous magazines, such as the *World's Sunday Magazine*. These Christmas issues were very popular with Victorian readers.

Mrs. Parkins's Christmas Eve

One wintry-looking afternoon the sun was getting low, but still shone with cheerful radiance into Mrs. Lydia Parkins' sitting-room. To point out a likeness between the bareness of the room and the appearance of the outside world on that twenty-first of December might seem ungracious; but there was a certain leaflessness and inhospitality common to both.

The cold, gray wall-paper, and dull, thin furniture; the indescribable poverty and lack of comfort of the room were exactly like the leaflessness and sharpness and coldness of that early winter day—unless the sun shone out with a golden glow as it had done in the latter part of the afternoon; then both the room and the long hillside and frozen road and distant western hills were quite transfigured.

Mrs. Parkins sat upright in one of the six decorous wooden chairs with cane seats; she was trimming a dismal gray-and-black winter bonnet and her work-basket was on the end of the table in front of her, between the windows, with a row of spools on the window-sill at her left. The only luxury she permitted herself was a cricket, a little bench such as one sees in a church pew, with a bit of carpet to

World's Sunday Magazine, *1896*
(Facsimile version in Virginia Historical Society Collections)

cover its top. Mrs. Parkins was so short that she would have been quite off-roundings otherwise in her cane-seated chair; but she had a great horror of persons who put their feet on chair rungs and wore the paint off. She was always on the watch to break the young of this bad habit. She cast a suspicious glance now and then at little Lucy Deems, who sat in another cane-seated chair opposite. The child had called upon Mrs. Parkins before, and was now trying so hard to be good that both her feet had gone to sleep and had come to the prickling stage of that misery. She wondered if her mother were not almost ready to go home.

Mrs. Deems sat in the rocking-chair, full in the sunlight and faced the sun itself, unflinchingly. She was a broad-faced gay-hearted, little woman, and her face was almost as bright as the winter sun itself. One might fancy that they were having a match at trying to outshine one another, but so far it was not Mrs. Deems who blinked and withdrew from the contest. She was just now conscious of little Lucy's depression and anxious looks, and bade her go out to run about a little while and see if there were some of Mrs. Parkins' butternuts left under the big tree.

The door closed, and Mrs. Parkins snapped her thread and said that there was no butternuts out there; perhaps Lucy should have a few in a basket when she was going home.

"Oh, 'taint no matter," said Mrs. Deems, easily. "She was kind of distressed sittin' so quiet; they like to rove about, children does."

"She won't do no mischief?" asked the hostess, timidly.

"Lucy?" laughed the mother. "Why you ought to be better acquainted with Lucy than that, I'm sure. I catch myself wishing she wa'n't quite so still; she takes after her father's folks, all quiet and dutiful, and ain't got the least idea how to enjoy themselves; we was all kind of noisy to our house when I was grown up, and I can't seem to sense the Deems."

"I often wish I had just such a little girl as your Lucy," said Mrs. Parkins, with a sigh. She held her gray-and-black bonnet off with her left hand and looked at it without approval.

"I shall always continue to wear black for Mr. Parkins," she said, "but I had this piece of dark-gray ribbon and I thought I had better use it on my black felt; the felt is sort of rusty, now, and black silk trimmings increase the rusty appearance."

"They do so," frankly acknowledged Mrs. Deems. "Why don't you go an' get you a new one for meetin', Mrs. Parkins? Felts ain't high this season, an' you've got this for second wear."

"I've got one that's plenty good for best," replied Mrs. Parkins, without any change of expression. "It seems best to make this do one more winter." She began to rearrange the gray ribbon, and Mrs. Deems watched her with a twinkle in her eyes; she had something to say, and did not know exactly how to begin, and Mrs. Parkins knew it as well as she did, and was holding her back which made the occasion more and more difficult.

"There!" she exclaimed at last, boldly, "I expect you know what I've come to see you for, an' I can't set here and make talk no longer. May's well ask if you can do anything about the minister's present."

Mrs. Parkins' mouth was full of pins, and she removed them all, slowly, before she spoke. The sun went behind a low snow cloud along the horizon, and Mrs. Deems shone on alone. It was not very warm in the room, and she gathered her woolen shawl closer about her shoulders as if she were getting ready to go home.

"I don't know's I feel to give you anything to-day, Mrs. Deems," said Mrs. Parkins in a resolved tone. "I don't feel much acquainted with the minister's folks. I must say *she* takes a good deal upon herself; I don't like so much of a ma'am."

"She's one of the pleasantest, best women we ever had in town, *I* think," replied Mrs. Deems. "I was tellin' 'em the other day that I always felt as if she brought a pleasant feelin' wherever she came, so sisterly and own-folks-like. They've seen a sight o' trouble and must feel pinched at times, but she finds ways to do plenty o' kindnesses. I never see a mite of behavior in 'em as if we couldn't do enough for 'em because they was ministers. Some minister's folks has such expectin' ways, and the more you do the more you may; but it ain't so with the Lanes. They are always a thinkin' what they can do for other people, an' they do it, too. You never liked 'em, but I can't see why."

"He ain't the ablest preacher that ever was," said Mrs. Parkins.

"I don't care if he ain't; words is words, but a man that lives as Mr. Lane does, is the best o' ministers," answered Mrs. Deems.

"Well, I don't owe 'em nothin' to-day," said the hostess, looking up. "I haven't got it in mind to do for the minister's folks any more than I have; but I may send 'em some apples or somethin', by'n-bye."

"Jest as you feel," said Mrs. Deems, rising quickly and looking provoked. "I didn't know but what 'twould be a pleasure to you, same's 'tis to the rest of us."

"They ain't been here very long, and I pay my part to the salary, an' 'taint no use to overdo in such cases."

"They've been put to extra expense this fall, and have been very feeling and kind; real interested in all of us, and such a help to the parish as we ain't had for a good while before. Havin' to send their boy to the hospital, has made it hard for 'em."

"Well, folks has to have their hard times, and minister's families can't escape. I am sorry about the boy, I'm sure," said Mrs. Parkins, generously. "Don't you go, Mrs. Deems; you ain't been to see me for a good while. I want you to see my bonnet in jest a minute."

"I've got to go way over to the Dilby's, and it's goin' to be dark early. I should be pleased to have you come an' see me. I've got to find Lucy and trudge along."

"I believe I won't rise to see you out o' the door, my lap's so full," said Mrs. Parkins politely, and so they parted. Lucy was hopping up and down by the front fence to keep herself warm and occupied.

"She didn't say anything about the butternuts, did she mother?" the child asked; and Mrs. Deems laughed and shook her head. Then they walked away down the road together, the big-mittened hand holding fast the little one, and the hooded heads bobbing toward each other now and then, as if they were holding a lively conversation. Mrs. Parkins looked after them two or three times, suspiciously at first, as if she thought they might be talking about her; then a little wistfully. She had come of a saving family and had married a saving man.

"Isn't Mrs. Parkins real poor, mother?" little Lucy inquired in a compassionate voice.

Mrs. Deems smiled, and assured the child that there was nobody so well off in town except Colonel Drummond, so far as money went; but Mrs. Parkins took care neither to enjoy her means herself, nor to let anybody else. Lucy pondered this strange answer for awhile and then began to hop and skip along the rough road, still holding fast her mother's warm hand.

This was the twenty-first of December, and the day of the week was Monday. On Tuesday Mrs. Parkins did her frugal ironing, and on Wednesday she meant to go over to Haybury to put some money into the bank and to do a little shopping. Goods were cheaper in Haybury in some of the large stores, than they were at the corner store at home, and she had the horse and could always get dinner at her cousin's. To be sure, the cousin was always hinting for presents for herself or her children, but Mrs. Parkins could bear that, and always cleared her conscience by asking the boys over in haying-time, though their help cost more than it came to with their growing appetites and the wear and tear of the house. Their mother came for a day's visit now and then, but everything at home depended upon her hard-working hands, as she had been early left a widow with little else to depend upon, until now, when the boys were out of school. One was doing well in the shoe factory and one in a store. Mrs. Parkins was really much attached to her cousin, but she thought if she once began to give, they would always be expecting something.

As has been said, Wednesday was the day set for the visit, but when Wednesday came it was a hard winter day, cold and windy, with an occasional flurry of snow, and Mrs. Parkins being neuralgic, gave up going until Thursday. She was pleased when she waked Thursday morning to find the weather warmer and the wind stilled. She was weather-wise enough to see snow in the clouds, but it was only eight miles to Haybury and she could start early and come home again as soon as she got her dinner. So the boy who came every morning to take care of her horse and bring in wood, was hurried and urged until he nearly lost his breath, and the horse was put into the wagon and, with rare forethought, a piece of salt-pork was wrapped up and put under the wagon-seat; then with a cloud over the re-trimmed bonnet, and a shawl over her Sunday cloak, and mittens over her woolen gloves Mrs. Parkins drove away. All her neighbors knew that she was going to Haybury to put eighty-seven dollars into the bank that the Dilby brothers had paid her for some rye planted and harvested on the halves. Very likely she had a good deal of money beside, that day; she had the best farm in that sterile neighborhood and was a famous manager.

The cousin was a hospitable, kindly soul, very loyal to her relations and always ready with a welcome. Beside, though the ears of Lydia Parkins were deaf to hints of present need and desire, it was more than likely that she would leave her farm and savings to the boys; she was not a person to speak roughly to, or one whom it was possible to disdain. More than this, no truly compassionate heart could fail to pity the thin, anxious, forbidding little woman, who behaved as if she must always be on the defensive against a plundering and begging world.

Cousin Mary Faber, as usual, begged Mrs. Parkins to spend the night; she seemed to take so little pleasure in life that the change might do her good. There would be no expense except for the horse's stabling, Mrs. Faber urged openly, and nobody would be expecting her at home. But Mrs. Parkins, as usual refused, and feared that the cellar would freeze. It had not been banked up as she liked to have it that autumn, but as for paying the Dilbys a dollar and a quarter for doing it, she didn't mean to please them so much.

"Land sakes! Why don't you feel as rich as you be, an' not mind them little expenses?" said cousin Faber, daringly. "I do declare I don't see how you can make out to grow richer an' poorer at the same time." The good-natured soul could not help laughing as she spoke, and Mrs. Parkins herself really could not help smiling.

"I'm much obliged to you for the pleasure of your company," said cousin Faber, "and it was very considerate of you to bring me that nice piece o' pork." If she had only known what an effort her guest had made to carry it into the house after she had brought it! Twice Mrs. Parkins had pushed it back under the wagon-seat with lingering indecision, and only taken it out at last because she feared that one of those prowling boys might discover it in the wagon and tell his mother. How often she had taken something into her hand to give away and then put it back and taken it again half a dozen times, irresolutely. There were still blind movements of the heart toward generosity, but she had grown more and more skillful at soothing her conscience and finding excuses for not giving.

The Christmas preparations in the busy little town made her uncomfortable, and cheerful cousin Faber's happiness in her own pinched housekeeping was a rebuke. The boys' salaries were very small indeed, this first year or two; but their mother was proud of their steadiness, and still sewed and let rooms to lodgers and did everything she could to earn money. She looked tired and old before her time, and acknowledged to Mrs. Parkins that she should like to have a good, long visit at the farm the next summer and let the boys take their meals with a neighbor. "I never spared myself one step until they were through with their schooling; but now it will be so I can take things a little easier," said the good soul with a wistful tone that was unusual.

Mrs. Parkins felt impatient as she listened; she knew that a small present of money now and then would have been a great help, but she never could make up her mind to begin what promised to be the squandering of her carefully saved fortune. It would be the ruin of the boys, too, if they thought she could be appealed to in every emergency. She would make it up to them in the long run; she could not take her money with her to the next world, and she would make a virtue of necessity.

The afternoon was closing in cold and dark, and the snow came sifting down slowly before Mrs. Parkins was out of the street of Haybury. She had lived too long on a hill not to be weatherwise and for a moment, as the wind buffeted her face and she saw the sky and the horizon line all dulled by the coming storm, she had a great mind to go back to cousin Faber's. If it had been any other time in the year but Christmas eve! The old horse gathered his forces and hurried along as if he had sense enough to be anxious about the weather; but presently the road turned so that the wind was not so chilling and they were quickly out of sight of the town, crossing the level land which lay between Haybury and the hills of Holton. Mrs. Parkins was persuaded that she should get home by dark, and the old horse did his very best. The road was rough and frozen and the wagon rattled and pitched along; it was like a race between Mrs. Parkins and the storm, and for a time it seemed certain that she would be the winner.

The gathering forces of the wind did not assert themselves fully until nearly half the eight miles had been passed, and the snow which had only clung to Mrs. Parkins' blanket-shawl like a white veil at first, and sifted white across the frozen grass of the lowlands, lay at last like a drift on the worn buffalo-robe, and was so deep in the road that it began to clog the wheels. It was a most surprising snow in the thickness of the flakes and the rapidity with which it gathered; it was no use to try to keep the white-knitted cloud over her face, for it became so thick with snow that it blinded and half-stifled her. The darkness began to fall, the snow came thicker and faster, and the horse climbing the drifted hills with the snow-clogged wagon, had to stop again and again. The awful thought suddenly came to Mrs. Parkins' mind that she could not reach home that night, and the next moment she had to acknowledge that she did not know exactly where she was. The thick flakes blinded her; she turned to look behind to see if any one were coming; but she might have been in the middle of an Arctic waste. She felt benumbed and stupid, and again tried to urge the tired horse, and the good creature toiled on desperately. It seemed as if they must have left the lowland far enough behind to be near some houses, but it grew still darker and snowier as they dragged slowly for another mile until it was impossible to get any further, and the horse stopped still and then gave a shake to rid himself of the drift on his back, and turned his head to look inquiringly at his mistress.

Mrs. Parkins began to cry with cold, and fear and misery. She had read accounts of such terrible, sudden storms in the west, and here she was in the night, foodless, and shelterless, and helpless.

"Oh! I'd give a thousand dollars to be safe under cover!" groaned the poor soul. "Oh, how poor I be this minute, and I come right away from that warm house!"

A strange dazzle of light troubled her eyes, and a vision of the brightly-lighted Haybury shops, and the merry customers that were hurrying in and out, and the gayety and contagious generosity of Christmas eve mocked at the stingy, little lost woman as she sat there half bewildered. The heavy flakes of snow caught her eyelashes and chilled her cheeks and melted inside the gray bonnet-strings; they heaped themselves on the top of the bonnet into a high crown that toppled into her lap as she moved. If she tried to brush the snow away, her clogged mitten only gathered more and grew more and more clumsy. It was a horrible, persistent storm; at this rate the horse and driver both would soon be covered and frozen in the road. The gathering flakes were malicious and mysterious; they were so large and flaked so fast down out of the sky.

"My goodness! How numb I be this minute," whispered Mrs. Parkins. And then she remembered that the cashier of the bank had told her that morning when she made her deposit, that everybody else was taking out their money that day; she was the only one who had come to put any in.

"I'd pay every cent of it willin' to anybody that would come along and help me get to shelter," said the poor soul. "Oh, I don't know as I've hoed so's to be worth savin'"; and a miserable sense of shame and defeat beat down whatever hope tried to rise in her heart. What had she tried to do for God and man that gave her a right to think of love and succor now?

Yet it seemed every moment as if help must come and as if this great emergency could not be so serious. Life had been so monotonous to Mrs. Parkins, so destitute of excitement and tragic situations that she could hardly understand, even now, that she was in such great danger. Again she called as loud as she could for help, and the horse whinnied louder still. The only hope was that two men who had passed her some miles back would remember that they had advised her to hurry, and would come back to look for her. The poor, old horse had dragged himself and the wagon to the side of the road under the shelter of some evergreens; Mrs. Parkins slipped down under the buffalo into the bottom of her cold, old wagon, and covered herself as well as she could. There was more than a chance that she might be found frozen under a snow-drift in the morning.

The morning! Christmas morning!

What did the advent of Christmas day hold out for her—buried in the snow-drifts of a December storm!

Anything? Yes, but she knew it not. Little did she dream what this Christmas eve was to bring into her life!

II

Lydia Parkins was a small woman of no great vigor, but as she grew a little warmer under her bed of blankets in the bottom of the old wagon, she came to her senses. She must get out and try to walk on through the snow as far as she could; it was no use to die there in this fearful storm like a rabbit. Yes, and she must unharness the horse and let him find his way; so she climbed boldly down into the knee-deep snow where a drift had blown already. She would not admit the thought that perhaps she might be lost in the snow and frozen to death that very night. It did not seem in character with Mrs. Nathan Parkins, who was the owner of plenty of money in Haybury Bank, and a good farm well divided into tillage and woodland, who had plenty of blankets and comforters at home, and firewood enough, and suitable winter clothes to protect her from the weather. The wind was rising more and more, it made the wet gray-and-black bonnet feel very limp and cold about her head, and her poor head itself felt duller and heavier than ever. She lost one glove and mitten in the snow as she tried to unharness the old horse, and her bare fingers were very clumsy, but she managed to get the good old creature clear, hoping that he would plod on and be known farther along the road and get help for her; but instead of that he only went round and round her and the wagon, floundering and whinnying, and refusing to be driven away. "What kind of a storm is this going to be?" groaned Mrs. Parkins, wading along the road and falling over her dress helplessly. The old horse meekly followed and when she gave a weak, shrill, womanish shout, old Major neighed and shook the snow off his back. Mrs. Parkins knew in her inmost heart, that with such a wind and through such drifts she could not get very far, and at last she lost her breath and sank down at the roadside and the horse went on alone. It was horribly dark and the cold pierced her through and through. In a few minutes she staggered to her feet and went on; she could have cried because the horse was out of sight, but she found it easier following in his tracks.

Suddenly there was a faint twinkle of light on the left, and what a welcome sight it was! The poor wayfarer hastened, but the wind behaved as if it were trying to blow her back. The horse had reached shelter first and somebody had heard him outside and came out and shut the house door with a loud bang that reached Mrs. Parkins' ears. She tried to shout again but she could hardly make a sound. The light still looked a good way off, but presently she could hear voices and see another light moving. She was so tired that she must wait until they came to help her. Who lived in the first house on the left after you passed oak ridge? Why, it couldn't be the Donnells, for they were all away in Haybury, and the house was shut up; this must be the parsonage, and she was off the straight road home. The bewildered horse had taken the left-hand road. "Well," thought Mrs. Parkins, "I'd rather be most any-where else, but I don't care where 'tis so long as I get under cover. I'm all spent and wore out."

The lantern came bobbing along quickly as if somebody were hur-rying, and wavered from side to side as if it were in a fishing boat on a rough sea. Mrs. Parkins started to meet it, and made herself known to her rescuer.

"I declare, if 'taint the minister," she exclaimed. "I'm Mrs. Parkins, or what's left of her. I've come near bein' froze to death along back here a-piece. I never saw such a storm in all my life."

She sank down in the snow and could not get to her feet again. The minister was a strong man; he stooped and lifted her like a child and carried her along the road with the lantern hung on his arm. She was a little woman and she was not a person given to sentiment, but she had been dreadfully cold and frightened, and now at last she was safe. It was like the good shepherd in the Bible, and Lydia Parkins was past crying; but it seemed as if she could never speak again and as if her heart were going to break. It seemed inevitable that the minister should have come to find her and carry her to the fold; no, to the parsonage; but she felt dizzy and strange again, and the second-best gray-and-black bonnet slipped its knot and tumbled off into the snow without her knowing it.

When Mrs. Parkins opened her eyes a bright light made them shut again directly; then she discovered, a moment afterward, that she was in the parsonage sitting-room and the minister's wife was kneeling beside her with an anxious face, and there was a Christmas tree at the other side of the room, with all its pretty, shining things and gay little candles on the boughs. She was comfortably wrapped in warm blankets, but she felt very tired and weak. The minister's wife smiled with delight: "Now you'll feel all right in a few minutes," she exclaimed. "Think of your being out in this awful storm! Don't try to talk to us yet, dear," she added kindly, "I'm going to bring you a cup of good hot tea. Are you all right? Don't try to tell anything about the storm. Mr. Lane has seen to the horse. Here, I'll put my little red shawl over you, it looks prettier than the blankets, and I'm drying your clothes in the kitchen."

The minister's wife had a sweet face, and she stood for a minute looking down at her unexpected guest; then something in the thin, appealing face on the sofa seemed to touch her heart, and she stooped over and kissed Mrs. Parkins. It happened that nobody had kissed Mrs. Parkins for years, and the tears stole down her cheeks as Mrs. Lane turned away.

As for the minister's wife, she had often thought that Mrs. Parkins had a most disagreeable hard face; she liked her less than any one in the parish, but now as she brightened the kitchen fire, she began to wonder what she could find to put on the Christmas tree for her, and wondered why she never had noticed a frightened, timid look in the poor woman's eyes. "It is so forlorn for her to live all alone on that big farm," said Mrs. Lane to herself, mindful of her own happy home and the children. All three of them came close about their mother at that moment, lame-footed John with his manly pale face, and smiling little Bell and Mary, the girls.

The minister came in from the barn and blew his lantern out and hung it away. The old horse was blanketed as warm as his mistress, and there was a good supper in his crib. It was a very happy household at the parsonage, and Mrs. Parkins could hear their whispers and smothered laughter in the kitchen. It was only eight o'clock after all, and it was evident that the children longed to begin their delayed festivities. The little girls came and stood in the doorway and looked first at the stranger guest and then at their Christmas tree, and after a while their mother came with them to ask whether Mrs. Parkins felt equal to looking on at the pleasuring or whether she would rather go to bed and rest, and sleep away her fatigue.

Mrs. Parkins wished to look on; she was beginning to feel well again, but she dreaded being alone, she could not tell exactly why.

"Come right into the bedroom with me then," said Mrs. Lane, "and put on a nice warm, double gown of mine; 'twill be large enough for you, that's certain, and then if you do wish to move about by-and-by, you will be better able than in the blankets."

Mrs. Parkins felt dazed by this little excitement, yet she was strangely in the mood for it. The reaction of being in this safe and pleasant place, after the recent cold and danger, excited her, and gave her an unwonted power of enjoyment and sympathy. She felt pleased and young, and she wondered what was going to happen. She stood still and let Mrs. Lane brush her gray hair, all tangled with the snow damp, as if she were no older than the little girls themselves; then they went out again to the sitting-room. There was a great fire blazing in the Franklin stove; the minister had cleared a rough bit of the parsonage land the summer before and shown good spirit about it, and these, as Mrs. Parkins saw at once, were some of the pitch-pine roots. She had said when she heard of his hard work, that he had better put the time into his sermons, and she remembered that now with a pang at her heart, and confessed inwardly that she had been mean spirited sometimes toward the Lanes, and it was a good lesson to her to be put at their mercy now. As she sat in her corner by the old sofa in the warm double gown and watched their kindly faces, a new sense of friendliness and hopefulness stole into her heart. "I'm just as warm now as I was cold a while ago," she assured the minister.

The children sat side by side, the lame boy and the two little sisters before the fire, and Mrs. Lane sat on the sofa by Mrs. Parkins, and the minister turned over the leaves of a Bible that lay on the table. It did not seem like a stiff and formal meeting held half from superstition and only half from reverence, but it was as if the good man were telling his household news of some one they all loved and held close to their hearts. He said a few words about the birth of Christ, and of there being no room that night in the inn. Room enough for the Roman soldier and the priest and the tax-gatherer, but no room for Christ; and how we all blame that innkeeper, and then are like him too often in the busy inn of our hearts. "Room for our friends and our pleasures and our gains, and no room for Christ," said the minister sadly, as the children looked soberly into the fire and tried to understand. Then they heard again the story of the shepherds and the star, and it was a more beautiful story than ever, and seemed quite new and wonderful; and then the minister prayed, and gave special thanks for the friend who made one of their household that night, because she had come through such great danger. Afterward the Lanes sang their Christmas hymn, standing about a little old organ which the mother played: "While shepherds watched their flocks by night—"

They sang it all together as if they loved the hymn, and when they stopped and the room was still again, Mrs. Parkins could hear the wind blow outside and the great elm branches sway and creak above the little house, and the snow clicked busily against the windows. There was a curious warmth at her heart, she did not feel frightened or lonely, or cold, or even selfish any more.

They lighted the candles on the Christmas tree, and the young people capered about and were brimming over with secrets and shouted with delight, and the tree shown and glistened brave in its gay trimming of walnuts covered with gold and silver paper, and little bags sewed with bright worsteds, and all sorts of pretty home-made trifles. But when the real presents were discovered, the presents that meant no end of thought and management and secret self-denial, the brightest part of the household love and happiness shone out. One after another they came to bring Mrs. Parkins her share of the little tree's fruit until her lap was full as she sat on the sofa. One little girl brought a bag of candy, though there wasn't much candy on the tree; and the other gave her a book-mark, and the lame boy had a pretty geranium, grown by himself, with a flower on it, and came limping to put it in her hands; and Mrs.

Lane brought a pretty hood that her sister had made for her a few weeks before, but her old one was still good and she did not need two. The minister had found a little book of hymns which a friend had given him at the autumn conference, and as Mrs. Parkins opened it, she happened to see these words: "Room to deny ourselves." She didn't know why the tears rushed to her eyes: "I've got to learn to deny myself of being mean," she thought, almost angrily. It was the least she could do, to do something friendly for these kind people; they had taken her in out of the storm with such loving warmth of sympathy; they did not show the least consciousness that she had never spoken a kind word about them since they came to town; that she alone had held aloof when this dear boy, their only son, had fought through an illness which might leave him a cripple for life. She had heard that there was a hope of his being cured if by-and-by his father could carry him to New York to a famous surgeon there. But all the expense of the long journey and many weeks of treatment, had seemed impossible. They were so thankful to have him still alive and with them that Christmas night. Mrs. Parkins could see the mother's eyes shine with tears as she looked at him, and the father put out a loving hand to steady him as he limped across the room.

"I wish little Lucy Deems, that lives next neighbor to me, was here to help your girls keep Christmas," said Mrs. Parkins, speaking half unconsciously. "Her mother has had it very hard; I mean to bring her over some day when the traveling gets good."

"We know Lucy Deems," said the children with satisfaction. Then Mrs. Parkins thought with regret of cousin Faber and her two boys, and was sorry that they were not all at the minister's too. She seemed to have entered upon a new life; she even thought of her dreary home with disapproval, and of its comfortable provisioning in cellar and garret, and of her money in the Haybury bank, with secret shame. Here she was with Mrs. Lane's double gown on, as poor a woman as there was in the world; she had come like a beggar to the Lanes' door that Christmas eve, and they were eagerly giving her house-room and gifts great and small; where were her independence and her riches now? She was a stranger and they had taken her in, and they did it for Christ's sake, and he would bless them, but what was there to say for herself? "Lord, how poor I be!" faltered Lydia Parkins for the second time that night.

There had not been such a storm for years. It was days before people could hear from each other along the blockaded country roads. Men were frozen to death, and cattle; and the telegraph wires were down and the safe and comfortable country side felt as if it had been in the power of some merciless and furious force of nature from which it could never again feel secure. But the sun came out and the blue-jays came back, and the crows, and the white snow melted, and the farmers went to and fro again along the highways. A new peace and good-will showed itself between the neighbors after their separation, but Mrs. Parkins' good-will outshown the rest. She went to Haybury as soon as the roads were well broken, and brought cousin Faber back with her for a visit, and sent her home again with a loaded wagon of supplies. She called in Lucy Deems and gave her a peck basketful of butternuts on New Year's Day, and told her to come for more when these were gone; and, more than all, one Sunday soon afterward, the minister told his people that he should be away for the next two Sundays. The kindness of a friend was going to put a great blessing within his reach, and he added simply, in a faltering voice, that he hoped all his friends would pray for the restoration to health of his dear boy.

Mrs. Parkins sat in her pew; she had not worn so grim an expression since before Christmas. Nobody could tell what secret pangs these gifts and others like them had cost her, yet she knew that only a right way of living would give her peace of mind. She could no longer live in a mean, narrow world of her own making; she must try to take the world as it is, and make the most of her life.

There were those who laughed and said that her stingy ways were frightened out of her on the night of the storm; but sometimes one is taught and led slowly to a higher level of existence unconsciously and irresistibly, and the decisive upward step once taken is seldom retraced. It was not long before Mrs. Deems said to a neighbor cheerfully: "Why, I always knew Mrs. Parkins meant well enough, but she *didn't know how* to do for other folks; she seemed kind of scared to use her own money, as if she didn't have any right to it. Now she is kind of persuaded that she's got the whole responsibility, and just you see how pleased she behaves. She's just a beginnin' to live; she never heard one word o' the first prayer yesterday mornin'; I see her beamin' an' smilin' at the minister's boy from the minute she see him walk up the aisle straight an' well as anybody."

"She goin' to have one of her cousin Faber's sons come over and stop awhile, I hear. He got run down workin' in the shoe factory to Haybury. Perhaps he may take hold and she'll let him take the farm by-an'-by. There, we musn't expect too much of her," said the other woman compassionately. "I'm sure 'tis a blessed change as far as she's got a'ready. Habits'll live sometimes after they're dead. Folks don't find it so easy to go free of ways they've settled into; life's truly a warfare, ain't it?"

"It is, so," answered Mrs. Deems, soberly. "There comes Mrs. Parkins this minute, in the old wagon, and my Lucy settin' up 'long side of her as pert as Nathan! Now ain't Mrs. Parkins' countenance got a pleasanter look than it used to wear? Well, the more she does for others, and the poorer she gets, the richer she seems to feel."

"It's a very unusual circumstance for a woman o' her age to turn right about in her tracks. It makes us believe that Heaven takes hold and helps folks," said the neighbor; and they watched the thin, little woman out of sight along the hilly road with a look of pleased wonder on their own faces. It was mid-spring, but Mrs. Parkins still wore her best winter bonnet; as for the old rusty one trimmed with gray, the minister's little girls found it when the snow drifts melted, and carefully hid it away to deck the parsonage scarecrow in the time of corn-planting.

E. V. Lucas

E. V. Lucas (1868–1938), a prolific British writer, unfortunately is rarely read today. His forte is short comic pieces—essays, sketches, letters. Lucas is a master of character depiction, revealing in brief passages the foibles of characters who, although often both highly individualistic and eccentric, are yet instantly recognizable. "The Christmas Decorations," from a collection of short pieces titled *Character and Comedy*, is vintage Lucas: clever, charming, and funny. Members of any church community will undoubtedly also perceive the psychological realism underlying the comic characters.

The Christmas Decorations

I

The Rev. Lawrence Lidbetter to his curate,
the Rev. Arthur Starling

Dear Starling,—I am sorry to appear to be running away at this busy season, but a sudden call to London on business leaves me no alternative. I shall be back on Christmas Eve for certain, perhaps before. You must keep an eye on the decorations, and see that none of our helpers get out of hand. I have serious doubts as to Miss Green.—Yours,

L.L.

II

Mrs. Clibborn to the Rev. Lawrence Lidbetter

Dear Rector,—I think we have got over the difficulty which we were talking of—Mr. Lulham's red hair and the discord it would make with the crimson decorations. Maggie and Popsy and I have been working like slaves, and have put up a beautiful and effectual screen of evergreen which completely obliterates the keyboard and organist. I think you will be delighted. Mr. Starling approves most cordially.—Yours sincerely,

Mary Clibborn

III

Miss Pitt to the Rev. Lawrence Lidbetter

My Dear Mr. Lidbetter,—We are all so sorry you have been called away, a strong guiding hand being never more needed. You will remember that it was arranged that I should have sole charge of the memorial window to Colonel Soper—we settled it just outside the Post Office on the morning that poor Blades was kicked by the Doctor's pony. Well, Miss Lockie now says that Colonel Soper's window belongs to her, and she makes it impossible for me to do anything. I must implore you to write to her putting it right, or the decorations will be ruined. Mr. Starling is kind, but quite useless. —Yours sincerely,

Virginia Pitt

IV

Miss Lockie to the Rev. Lawrence Lidbetter

My Dear Mr. Lidbetter,—I am sorry to have to trouble you in your enforced rest, but the interests of the church must not be neglected, and you ought to know that Miss Pitt not only insists that the decoration of Colonel Soper's window was entrusted to her, but prevents me carrying it out. If you recollect, it was during tea at Mrs. Millstone's that it was arranged that I should be responsible for this window. A telegram to Miss Pitt would put the matter right at once. Dear Mr. Starling is always so nice, but he does so lack firmness.—Yours sincerely,

Mabel Lockie

V

Mrs. St. John to the Rev. Lawrence Lidbetter

Dear Rector,—I wish you would let Miss Green have a line about the decoration of the pulpit. It is no use any of us saying anything to her since she went to the Slade School and acquired artistic notions, but a word from you would work wonders. What we all feel is that the pulpit should be bright and gay, with some cheerful texts on it, a suitable setting for you and your helpful Christmas sermon, but Miss Green's idea is to drape it entirely in black muslin and purple, like a lying in state. One can do wonders with a little cotton-wool and a few yards of Turkey twill, but she will not understand this. How with all her *nouveau art* ideas she got permission to decorate the pulpit at all I cannot think, but there it is, and the sooner she is stopped the better. Poor Mr. Starling drops all the hints he can, but she disregards them all.—Yours sincerely,

Charlotte St. John

VI

Miss Olive Green to the Rev. Lawrence Lidbetter

Dear Mr. Lidbetter,—I am sure you will like the pulpit. I am giving it the most careful thought, and there is every promise of a scheme of austere beauty, grave and solemn and yet just touched with a note of happier fulfilment. For the most part you will find the decorations quite conventional—holly and evergreens, the old terrible cotton-wool snow on crimson background. But I am certain that you will experience a thrill of satisfied surprise when your eyes alight upon the simple gravity of the pulpit's drapery and its flowing sensuous lines. It is so kind of you to give me this opportunity to realise some of my artistic self. Poor Mr. Starling, who is entirely Victorian in his views of art, has been talking to me about gay colours, but my work is done for *you* and the few who can *understand.*—Yours sincerely,

Olive Green

VII

Mrs. Millstone to the Rev. Lawrence Lidbetter

Dear Rector,—Just a line to tell you of a delightful device I have hit upon for the decorations. Cotton-wool, of course, makes excellent snow, and rice is sometimes used, on gum, to suggest winter too. But I have discovered that the most perfect illusion of a white rime can be obtained by wetting the leaves and then sprinkling flour on them. I am going to get all the others to let me finish off everything like that on Christmas Eve (like varnishing-day at the Academy, my husband says), when it will be all fresh for Sunday. Mr. Starling, who is proving himself such a dear, is delighted with the scheme. I hope you are well in that dreadful foggy city.—Yours sincerely,

Ada Millstone

VIII

Mrs. Hobbs, charwoman, to the Rev. Lawrence Lidbetter

Honoured Sir,—I am writing to you because Hobbs and me dispare of getting any justice from the so called ladies who have been turning the holy church of St. Michael and all Angels into a Covent Garden market. To sweep up holly and other green stuff I don't mind, because I have heard you say year after year that we should all do our best at Christmas to help each other. I always hold that charity and kindness are more than rubys, but when it comes to flour I say no. If you would believe it, Mrs. Millstone is first watering the holly and the lorrel to make it wet, and then sprinkling flour on it to look like hore frost, and the mess is something dreadful, all over the cushions and carpet. To sweep up ordinery dust I don't mind, more particulerly as it is my paid work and bounden duty; but unless it is made worth my while Hobbs says I must say no. We draw the line at sweeping up dough. Mr. Starling is very kind, but as Hobbs says you are the founting head.—Awaiting a reply, I am, your humble servant,

Martha Hobbs

IX

Mrs. Vansittart to the Rev. Lawrence Lidbetter

Dear Rector,—If I am late with the north windows you must understand that it is not my fault, but Pedder's. He has suddenly and most mysteriously adopted an attitude of hostility to his employers (quite in the way one has heard of gardeners doing), and nothing will induce him to cut me any evergreens, which he says he cannot spare. The result is that poor Horace and Mr. Starling have to go out with lanterns after Pedder has left the garden, and cut what they can and convey it to the church by stealth. I think we shall manage fairly well, but thought you had better know in case the result is not equal to your anticipation.—Yours sincerely,

Grace Vansittart

X

Mr. Lulham, organist, to the Rev. Lawrence Lidbetter

Dear Sir,—I shall be glad to have a line from you authorising me to insist upon the removal of a large screen of evergreens which Mrs. Clibborn and her daughters have erected by the organ. There seems to be an idea that the organ is unsightly, although we have had no complaints hitherto, and the effect of this barrier will be to interfere very seriously with the choral part of the service. Mr. Starling sympathises with me, but has not taken any steps. Believe me, yours faithfully,

Walter Lulham

XI

The Rev. Lawrence Lidbetter to Mrs. Lidbetter

My Dearest Harriet,—I am having, as I expected, an awful time with the decorations, and I send you a batch of letters and leave the situation to you. Miss Pitt had better keep the Soper window. Give the Lockie girl one of the autograph copies of my *Narrow Path*, with a reference underneath my name to the chapter on self-sacrifice, and tell her how sorry I am that there has been a misunderstanding. Mrs. Hobbs must have an extra half-a-crown, and the flouring must be discreetly discouraged—on the ground of waste of food material. Assure Lulham that there shall be no barrier, and then tell Mrs. Clibborn that the organist has been given a pledge that nothing should intervene between his music and the congregation. I am dining with the Lawsons to-night, and we go afterwards to the *Tempest*, I think.—Your devoted

L.

H. H. Munro

H. H. MUNRO (1870–1916) IS BETTER KNOWN AS SAKI—a pseudonym taken from the cup-bearer in a favorite poem of his, the "Rubaiyat" of Omar Khayyam. Although he worked as a journalist and foreign correspondent, Saki is best known for his short fiction. The sparkling wit, charm, and whimsy that characterize his stories make them delightful reading; they also mark a lighthearted, effervescent style infrequently found after the trauma of World War I.

"Reginald's Christmas Revel" is one of a series of sketches that originally appeared in the *Westminster Gazette;* these sketches were published in 1904 with the title *Reginald.* The stories all have an anonymous narrator who describes the reactions, insights, and antics of his friend Reginald, a character Saki described as a composite of many young men about town he had encountered.

Reginald's Christmas Revel

They say (said Reginald) that there's nothing sadder than victory except defeat. If you've ever stayed with dull people during what is alleged to be the festive season, you can probably revise that saying. I shall never forget putting in a Christmas at the Babwolds'. Mrs. Babwold is some relation of my father's—a sort of to-be-left-till-called-for cousin—and that was considered sufficient reason for my having to accept her invitation at about the sixth time of asking; though why the sins of the father should be visited by the children—you won't find any notepaper in that drawer; that's where I keep old menus and first-night programmes.

Mrs. Babwold wears a rather solemn personality, and has never been known to smile, even when saying disagreeable things to her friends or making out the Stores list. She takes her pleasures sadly. A state elephant at a Durbar gives one a very similar impression. Her husband gardens in all weathers. When a man goes out in the pouring rain to brush caterpillars off rose trees, I generally imagine his life indoors leaves something to be desired; anyway, it must be very unsettling for the caterpillars.

Of course there were other people there. There was a Major Somebody who had shot things in Lapland, or somewhere of that sort; I forget what they were, but it wasn't for want of reminding. We had them cold with every meal almost, and he was continually giving us details of what they measured from tip to tip, as though he thought we were going to make them warm underthings for the winter. I used to listen to him with a rapt attention that I thought rather suited me, and then one day I quite modestly gave the dimensions of an okapi I had shot in the Lincolnshire fens. The Major turned a beautiful Tyrian scarlet (I remember thinking at the time that I should like my bathroom hung in that colour), and I think that at that moment he almost found it in his heart to dislike me. Mrs. Babwold put on a first-aid-to-the-injured expression, and asked him why he didn't publish a book of his sporting reminiscences; it would be *so* interesting. She didn't remember till afterwards that he had given her two fat volumes on the subject, with his portrait and autograph as a frontispiece and an appendix on the habits of the Arctic mussel.

It was in the evening that we cast aside the cares and distractions of the day and really lived. Cards were thought to be too frivolous and empty a way of passing the time, so most of them played what they called a book game. You went out into the hall—to get an inspiration, I suppose—then you came in again with a muffler tied round your neck and looked silly, and the others were supposed to guess that you were *Wee MacGreegor*. I held out against the inanity as long as I decently could, but at last, in a lapse of good-nature, I consented to masquerade as a book, only I warned them that it would take some time to carry out. They waited for the best part of forty minutes while I went and played wineglass skittles with the page-boy in the pantry; you play it with a champagne cork, you know, and the one who knocks down the most glasses without breaking them wins. I won, with four unbroken out of seven; I think William suffered from over-anxiousness. They were rather mad in the drawing-room at my not having come back, and they weren't a bit pacified when I told them afterwards that I was *At the end of the passage.*

"I never did like Kipling," was Mrs. Babwold's comment, when the situation dawned upon her. "I couldn't see anything clever in *Earthworms out of Tuscany*—or is that by Darwin?"

Of course these games are very educational, but, personally, I prefer bridge.

On Christmas evening we were supposed to be specially festive in the Old English fashion. The hall was horribly draughty, but it seemed to be the proper place to revel in, and it was decorated with Japanese fans and Chinese lanterns, which gave it a very Old English effect. A young lady with a confidential voice favoured us with a long recitation about a little girl who died or did something equally hackneyed, and then the Major gave us a graphic account of a struggle he had with a wounded bear. I privately wished that the bears would win sometimes on these occasions; at least they wouldn't go vapouring about it afterwards. Before we had time to recover our spirits, we were indulged with some thought-reading by a young man whom one knew instinctively had a good mother and an indifferent tailor—the sort of young man who talks unflaggingly through the thickest soup, and smooths his hair dubiously as though he thought it might hit back. The thought-reading was rather a success; he announced that the hostess was thinking about poetry, and she admitted that her mind was dwelling on one of Austin's odes. Which was near enough. I fancy she had been really wondering whether a scrag-end of mutton and some cold plum-pudding would do for the kitchen dinner next day. As a crowning dissipation, they all sat down to play progressive halma, with milk-chocolate for prizes. I've been very carefully brought up, and I don't like to play games of skill for milk-chocolate, so I invented a headache and retired from the scene. I had been preceded a few minutes earlier by Miss Langshan-Smith, a rather formidable lady, who always got up at some uncomfortable hour in the morning, and gave you the impression that she had been in communication with most of the European Governments before breakfast. There was a paper pinned on her door with a signed request that she might be called particularly early on the morrow. Such an opportunity does not come twice in a lifetime. I covered up everything except the signature with another notice, to the effect that before these words should meet the eye she would have ended a misspent life, was sorry for the trouble she was giving, and would like a military funeral. A few minutes later I violently exploded an air-filled paper bag on the landing, and gave a stage moan that could have been heard in the cellars. Then I pursued my original intention and went to bed. The noise those people made in forcing open the good lady's door was positively indecorous; she resisted gallantly, but I believe they searched her for bullets for about a quarter of an hour, as if she had been a historic battlefield.

I hate travelling on Boxing Day, but one must occasionally do things that one dislikes.

Christopher Smart

CHRISTOPHER SMART (1722–1771), A BRITISH POET, was dismissed for years as a madman and is only recently being recognized for his poetic genius. Smart, whose insanity was primarily a religious mania, was confined to an asylum for seven years. Obsessed by the Pauline injunction to "pray without ceasing," Smart would impulsively drop to his knees regardless of his surroundings, for example, while crossing busy intersections. During his confinement, he created a verse translation of the Psalms and wrote his great works, *Jubilate Agno, A Song to David,* and *Hymns and Spiritual Songs for the Fasts and Festivals of the Church of England.* Unfortunately, his works were either ignored or condemned as the work of a madman, and Smart died in prison, where he had been jailed for debt. The following hymn is from the collection of *Hymns and Spiritual Songs.*

Hymn XXXII
The Nativity of Our Lord
and Saviour Jesus Christ

Where is this stupendous stranger?
   Swains of Solyma, advise.
Lead me to my Master's manger,
   Shew me where my Saviour lies.

O Most Mighty! O MOST HOLY!
   Far beyond the seraph's thought,
Art thou then so mean and lowly
   As unheeded prophets taught?

O the magnitude of meekness!
   Worth from worth immortal sprung;
O the strength of infant weakness,
   If eternal is so young!

If so young and thus eternal,
   Michael tune the shepherd's reed,
Where the scenes are ever vernal,
   And the loves be love indeed!

See the God blasphem'd and doubted
   In the schools of Greece and Rome;
See the pow'rs of darkness routed,
   Taken at their utmost gloom.

Nature's decorations glisten
   Far above their usual trim;
Birds on box and laurel listen,
   As so near the cherubs hymn.

Boreas now no longer winters
   On the desolated coast;
Oaks no more are riv'n in splinters
   By the whirlwind and his host.

Spinks and ouzles sing sublimely,   [finches and thrushes]
　'We too have a Saviour born,'
Whiter blossoms burst untimely
　On the blest Mosaic thorn.

God all bounteous, all creative,
　Whom no ills from good dissuade,
Is incarnate, and a native
　Of the very world he made.

William Blake

ARTIST AND POET WILLIAM BLAKE (1757–1827), who in his childhood
saw a vision of the prophet Ezekiel under a tree, was a visionary and mystic throughout his life. Blake created engravings to illustrate his poems,
intending the verbal and visual elements together to embody his highly
individualistic vision. Best known for his *Songs of Innocence* (1789) and
Songs of Experience (1794), Blake saw human progression as a journey
through joyous childlike innocence to the sadder adult world; salvation lay
in passing beyond these stages to a spiritual world of imagination. "The
Cradle Song," from the *Songs of Innocence*, shares with the other poems in
that collection the qualities of simplicity and spontaneity. In this tender
lullaby, Blake draws parallels between the human child and the Holy
Child.

A Cradle Song

Sweet dreams, form a shade
O'er my lovely infant's head;
Sweet dreams of pleasant streams
By happy, silent, moony beams.

Sweet sleep, with soft down
Weave thy brows an infant crown.
Sweet sleep, Angel mild,
Hover o'er my happy child.

Sweet smiles, in the night
Hover over my delight;

Sweet smiles, Mother's smiles,
All the livelong night beguiles.

Sweet moans, dovelike sighs,
Chase not slumber from thy eyes.
Sweet moans, sweeter smiles,
All the dovelike moans beguiles.

Sleep, sleep, happy child,
All creation slept and smil'd;
Sleep, sleep, happy sleep,
While o'er thee thy mother weep.

Sweet babe, in thy face
Holy image I can trace.
Sweet babe, once like thee,
Thy maker lay and wept for me,

Wept for me, for thee, for all,
When he was an infant small
Thou his image ever see,
Heavenly face that smiles on thee,

Smiles on thee, on me, on all;
Who became an infant small.
Infant smiles are his own smiles;
Heaven and earth to peace beguiles.

Alfred, Lord Tennyson

ALFRED TENNYSON (1809–1892) was arguably the greatest Victorian
poet. A prolific author, Tennyson wrote many works familiar to most
English-speaking readers: *The Idylls of the King*, "The Charge of the Light
Brigade," "The Lady of Shallot," "Crossing the Bar," and "In Memoriam." Like many Victorians, Tennyson wrestled with optimism and despair, reason and religion, faith and science.

Over a seventeen-year period, Tennyson wrote "In Memoriam A.H.H."
for his friend Arthur Henry Hallam. The five sections below reflect Tennyson's evocation of three Christmases and a New Year's. The first re-

flects his sense of loss, and the last, "Ring out wild bells," reflects the sense of optimism evoked by the coming year. In his *Memoir*, Tennyson said the poem depicted "the different moods of sorrow" and revealed his "conviction that fears, doubts, and suffering will find answer and relief only through Faith in a God of Love."

In Memoriam

28

The time draws near the birth of Christ.
    The moon is hid; the night is still;
    The Christmas bells from hill to hill
Answer each other in the mist.

Four voices of four hamlets round,
    From far and near, on mead and moor,
    Swell out and fail, as if a door
Were shut between me and the sound;

Each voice four changes on the wind,
    That now dilate, and now decrease,
    Peace and goodwill, goodwill and peace,
Peace and goodwill, to all mankind.

This year I slept and woke with pain,
    I almost wished no more to wake,
    And that my hold on life would break
Before I heard those bells again.

But they my troubled spirit rule,
    For they controlled me when a boy;
    They bring me sorrow touched with joy,
The merry merry bells of Yule.

78

Again at Christmas did we weave
    The holly round the Christmas hearth;
    The silent snow possessed the earth;
And calmly fell our Christmas Eve.

The yule-log sparkled keen with frost,
    No wing of wind the region swept,
    But over all things brooding slept
The quiet sense of something lost.

As in the winters left behind,
    Again our ancient games had place,
    The mimic picture's breathing grace,
And dance and song and hoodman-blind.

Who showed a token of distress?
    No single tear, no mark of pain:
    O sorrow, then can sorrow wane?
O grief, can grief be changed to less?

O last regret, regret can die!
    No—mixed with all this mystic frame,
    Her deep relations are the same,
But with long use her tears are dry.

104

The time draws near the birth of Christ;
    The moon is hid, the night is still;
    A single church below the hill
Is pealing, folded in the mist.

A single peal of bells below,
    That wakens at this hour of rest
    A single murmur in the breast,
That these are not the bells I know.

Like strangers' voices here they sound,
    In lands where not a memory strays,
    Nor landmark breathes of other days,
But all is new unhallowed ground.

105

Tonight ungathered let us leave
   This laurel, let this holly stand;
   We live within the stranger's land,
And strangely falls our Christmas Eve.

Our father's dust is left alone
   And silent under other snows;
   There in due time the woodbine blows,
The violet comes, but we are gone.

No more shall wayward grief abuse
   The genial hour with mask and mime;
   For change of place, like growth of time,
Has broke the bond of dying use.

Let cares that petty shadows cast,
   By which our lives are chiefly proved,
   A little spare the night I loved,
And hold it solemn to the past.

But let no footstep beat the floor,
   Nor bowl of wassail mantle warm;
   For who would keep an ancient form
Through which the spirit breathes no more?

Be neither song, nor game, nor feast;
   Nor harp be touched, nor flute be blown;
   No dance, no motion, save alone
What lightens in the lucid East.

Of rising worlds by yonder wood.
   Long sleeps the summer in the seed;
   Run out your measured arcs, and lead
The closing cycle rich in good.

Ring out, wild bells, to the wild sky,
   The flying cloud, the frosty light;
   The year is dying in the night;
Ring out, wild bells, and let him die.

Ring out the old, ring in the new,
   Ring, happy bells, across the snow;
   The year is going, let him go;
Ring out the false, ring in the true.

Ring out the grief that saps the mind,
   For those that here we see no more;
   Ring out the feud of rich and poor,
Ring in redress to all mankind.

Ring out a slowly dying cause,
   And ancient forms of party strife;
   Ring in the nobler modes of life,
With sweeter manners, purer laws.

Ring out the want, the care, the sin,
   The faithless coldness of the times;
   Ring out, ring out my mournful rimes,
But ring the fuller minstrel in.

Ring out false pride in place and blood,
   The civic slander and the spite;
   Ring in the love of truth and right,
Ring in the common love of good.

Ring out old shapes of foul disease;
   Ring out the narrowing lust of gold;
   Ring out the thousand wars of old,
Ring in the thousand years of peace.

Ring in the valiant man and free,
   The larger heart, the kindlier hand;
   Ring out the darkness of the land,
Ring in the Christ that is to be.

Theophile Gautier

THE FRENCH WRITER THEOPHILE GAUTIER (1811–1872) was a painter before he turned to literature, writing novels, poetry, criticism, and travel books. The chief proponent of the art for art's sake movement, Gautier claimed that "as soon as art becomes useful, it ceases to be beautiful." The poem below, "Noel," is from his major volume of poetry, *Emaux and Camees* (enamels and cameos). As the title suggests, these poems are small, precise evocations, detached and unemotional. "Noel," like many other poems in the collection, focuses on the appearance of the setting and not on the psychology of the characters.

Noel

The heavens are black, the earth is white;
—Bells, ring out merrily—
Jesus is born: the Virgin bends
Her charming face over Him.

No draped curtains
Guard the child from the cold,
Only the spider webs
Which hang from the roof beams.

He shivers on the chilly straw,
This dear little infant Jesus,
While to warm Him in the manger,
The ass and the ox breathe on Him.

The snow on the thatch weaves its fringes,
But above the roof the sky opens,
And, all in white, the choir of angels
Sings to the shepherds: Noel! Noel!

Christina Georgina Rossetti

CHRISTINA ROSSETTI (1830–1894) WAS THE YOUNGER SISTER of Dante Gabriel Rossetti, the noted Pre-Raphaelite painter and poet. Like Gerard Manley Hopkins, she was influenced by the Oxford Movement, which attempted to restore the Catholic heritage of the Church of England. Although her work often has the "holy gloom" typical of much Victorian religious poetry, occasional flights of fancy led her in different directions, such as her fascinating children's poem "Goblin Market."

Her religious poems often center on liturgical observances, the carols of Christmas being among her best work. The two below are typical in their spontaneity, their disarming tenderness, and their literal descriptions. In the first poem, Rossetti deftly moves the reader back and forth between the original Christmas scene, the present, and the future return of Christ the Lord. Deceptively simple, the second carol contains a Christ who is paradoxically born a stranger into the world he created in which he is both lamb and shepherd; at the same time the scene includes the usual tableau set pieces—stable, manger, angel, ox, ass.

A Christmas Carol

In the bleak mid-winter
    Frosty wind made moan,
Earth stood hard as iron,
    Water like a stone;
Snow had fallen, snow on snow,
    Snow on snow,
In the bleak mid-winter
    Long ago.

Our God, Heaven cannot hold Him
    Nor earth sustain;
Heaven and earth shall flee away
    When He comes to reign:

In the bleak mid-winter
    A stable-place sufficed
The Lord God Almighty
    Jesus Christ.

Enough for Him, whom cherubim
    Worship night and day,
A breastful of milk
    And a mangerful of hay;
Enough for Him, whom angels
    Fall down before,
The ox and ass and camel
    Which adore.

Angels and archangels
    May have gathered there,
Cherubim and seraphim
    Thronged the air;
But only His mother
    In her maiden bliss
Worshipped the Beloved
    With a kiss.

What can I give Him,
    Poor as I am?
If I were a shepherd
    I would bring a lamb,
If I were a Wise Man
    I would do my part,—
Yet what I can I give Him,
    Give my heart.

A Christmas Carol

Before the paling of the stars,
    Before the winter morn,
    Before the earliest cock-crow
Jesus Christ was born:
    Born in a stable
Cradled in a manger,

In the world His hands had made
    Born a stranger.

Priest and King lay fast asleep
    In Jerusalem,
Young and old lay fast asleep
    In crowded Bethlehem:
Saint and Angel, ox and ass,
    Kept a watch together,
    Before the Christmas daybreak
    In the winter weather.

Jesus on his Mother's breast
    In the stable cold,
Spotless Lamb of God was He,
    Shepherd of the fold:
Let us kneel with Mary Maid,
    With Joseph bent and hoary,
With Saint and Angel, ox and ass,
    To hail the King of Glory.

Gerard Manley Hopkins

GERARD MANLEY HOPKINS (1844–1880) wrote poetry from childhood. Sensitive to the religious conflict that marked nineteenth-century English life, Hopkins converted to Catholicism and joined the Jesuit Order in 1868. His internal struggles are reflected in the so-called terrible sonnets, which reveal his soul's private agonizing over faith and despair. In 1875, when Hopkins became a teacher at the University of Dublin, he resumed writing poetry. None of his works had been published when he died suddenly; in fact, his poems did not appear until 1918, when they were published by physician/poet Robert Bridges.

Hopkins's poetry stands well outside the Victorian tradition. Hopkins was fascinated by what he termed "inscape," those aspects of an object that constitute its essence and its individuality, and therefore its beauty. His images are frequently obscure, his language dense, his syntax difficult. Still, his poetry is marked by a keen observation of nature, fresh perceptions, a stylistic beauty. The two poems below are meditations on the Virgin Mary. The first, "The Blessed Virgin Compared to the Air We

Breathe," is a complex work illustrative of his mingling of theology and a fascination with the natural world. The second poem, a portion of "The Wreck of the Deutchland," reflects on the Incarnation—the mystery of grace in a world that is simultaneously broken and beautiful.

The Blessed Virgin Compared to the Air We Breathe

Wild air, world-mothering air,
Nestling me everywhere,
That each eyelash or hair
Girdles; goes home betwixt
The fleeciest, frailest-flixed
Snowflake; that's fairly mixed
With, riddles, and is rife
In every least thing's life;
This needful, never spent,
And nursing element;
My more than meat and drink,
My meal at every wink;
This air, which, by life's law,
My lung must draw and draw
Now but to breathe its praise,
Minds me in many ways
Of her who not only
Gave God's infinity
Dwindled to infancy
Welcome in womb and breast,
Birth, milk, and all the rest
But mothers each new grace
That does now reach our race—
Mary Immaculate,
Merely a woman, yet
Whose presence, power is
Great as no goddess's
Was deemèd, dreamèd; who
This one work has to do—
Let all God's glory through,
God's glory which would go
Through her and from her flow

Off, and no way but so.
    I say that we are wound
With mercy round and round
As if with air: the same
Is Mary, more by name.
She, wild web, wondrous robe,
Mantles the guilty globe,
Since God has let dispense
Her prayers his providence:
Nay, more than almoner,
The sweet alms' self is her
And men are meant to share
Her life as life does air.
    If I have understood,
She holds high motherhood
Towards all our ghostly good
And plays in grace her part
About man's beating heart,
Laying, like air's fine flood,
The deathdance in his blood;
Yet no part but what will
Be Christ our Saviour still.
Of her flesh he took flesh:
He does take fresh and fresh,
Though much the mystery how,
Not flesh but spirit now
And makes, O marvellous!
New Nazareths in us,
Where she shall yet conceive
Him, morning, noon, and eve;
New Bethlems, and he born
There, evening, noon, and morn—
Bethlem or Nazareth,
Men here may draw like breath
More Christ and baffle death;
Who, born so, comes to be
New self and nobler me
In each one and each one
More makes, when all is done,
Both God's and Mary's Son.

Again, look overhead
How air is azurèd;
O how! Nay do but stand
Where you can lift your hand
Skywards: rich, rich it laps
Round the four fingergaps.
Yet such a sapphire-shot,
Charged, steepèd sky will not
Stain light. Yea, mark you this:
It does no prejudice.
The glass-blue days are those
When every colour glows,
Each shape and shadow shows.
Blue be it: this blue heaven
The seven or seven times seven
Hued sunbeam will transmit
Perfect, not alter it.
Or if there does some soft,
On things aloof, aloft,
Bloom breathe, that one breath more
Earth is the fairer for.
Whereas did air not make
This bath of blue and slake
His fire, the sun would shake,
A blear and blinding ball
With blackness bound, and all
The thick stars round him roll
Flashing like flecks of coal,
Quartz-fret, or sparks of salt,
In grimy vasty vault.
So God was god of old:
A mother came to mould
Those limbs like ours which are
What must make our daystar
Much dearer to mankind;
Whose glory bare would blind
Or less would win man's mind.
Through her we may see him
Made sweeter, not made dim,
And her hand leaves his light

Sifted to suit our sight.
   Be thou then, O thou dear
Mother, my atmosphere;
My happier world, wherein
To wend and meet no sin;
Above me, round me lie
Fronting my froward eye
With sweet and scarless sky;
Stir in my ears, speak there
Of God's love, O live air,
Of patience, penance, prayer:
Worldmothering air, air wild,
Wound with thee, in thee isled,
Fold home, fast fold thy child.

The Wreck of the Deutchland
Part the First
Stanzas 4–10

I am soft sift
In an hourglass—at the wall
Fast, but mined with a motion, a drift,
And it crowds and it combs to the fall;
I steady as a water in a well, to a poise, to a pane,
But roped with, always, all the way down from the tall
Fells or flanks of the voel, a vein   [bare hill]
Of the gospel proffer, a pressure, a principle, Christ's gift.

I kiss my hand
To the stars, lovely-asunder
Starlight, wafting him out of it; and
Glow, glory in thunder;
Kiss my hand to the dappled-with-damson west:
Since, tho' he is under the world's splendour and wonder,
His mystery must be instressed, stressed;
For I greet him the days I meet him, and bless when I understand.

Not out of his bliss
Springs the stress felt
Not first from heaven (and few know this)

Swings the stroke dealt—
Stroke and a stress that stars and storms deliver,
That guilt is hushed by, hearts are flushed by and melt—
But it rides time like riding a river
(And here the faithful waver, the faithless fable and miss).

It dates from day
Of his going in Galilee;
Warm-laid grave of a womb-life grey;
Manger, maiden's knee;
The dense and the driven Passion, and frightful sweat:
Thence the discharge of it, there its swelling to be,
Though felt before, though in high flood yet—
What none would have known of it, only the heart, being hard at bay,

Is out with it! Oh,
We lash with the best or worst
Word last! How a lush-kept plush-capped sloe   [plum]
Will, mouthed to flesh-burst,
Gush!—flush the man, the being with it, sour or sweet,
Brim, in a flash, full!—Hither then, last or first,
To hero of Calvary, Christ's feet—
Never ask if meaning it, wanting it, warned of it—men go.

Be adored among men,
God, three-numberèd form;
Wring thy rebel, dogged in den,
Man's malice, with wrecking and storm.
Beyond saying sweet, past telling of tongue,
Thou art lightning and love, I found it, a winter and warm;
Father and fondler of heart thou hast wrung:
Hast thy dark descending and most art merciful then.

With an anvil-ding
And with fire in him forge thy will
Or rather, rather then, stealing as Spring
Through him, melt him but master him still:
Whether at once, as once at a crash Paul,
Or as Austin, a lingering-out swéet skíll,   [Augustine]
Make mercy in all of us, out of us all
Mastery, but be adored, but be adored King.

Rudyard Kipling

RUDYARD KIPLING (1865–1936) WAS BORN IN BOMBAY, INDIA, where he lived until, at age six, he was sent to England to be educated. Eleven years later, he returned to India as a journalist, which undoubtedly fostered the keen observation of people in daily circumstances that is the hallmark of his poems. After traveling extensively, Kipling settled with his wife in Vermont, where he wrote his popular storybooks for children, *The Jungle Books* and the *Just So Stories*. In 1896, Kipling returned to England to live. The shrewd, accurate, and often graphic depictions of life—whether British or Indian—in his poems are both simple and powerful. In "Eddi's Service," as in the better known "Gunga Din," we see Kipling's respect for people who perform their duty honorably, regardless of circumstances.

Eddi's Service . . . A.D. 687

Eddi, priest of St. Wilfrid
    In his chapel at Manhood End,
Ordered a midnight service
    For such as cared to attend.

But the Saxons were keeping Christmas,
    And the night was stormy as well.
Nobody came to the service
    Though Eddi rang the bell.

"Wicked weather for walking,"
    Said Eddi of Manhood End.
"But I must go on with the service
    For such as care to attend."

The altar-lamps were lighted . . .
    An old marsh-donkey came,
Bold as a guest invited,
    And stared at the guttering flame.

The storm beat on at the windows,
    The water splashed on the floor,
And a wet, yoke-weary bullock
    Pushed in through the open door.

"How do I know what is greatest,
    How do I know what is least?
That is my Father's business"
    Said Eddi, Wilfrid's priest.

"But . . . three are gathered together . . .
    Listen to me and attend.
I bring good news, my brethren!"
    Said Eddi of Manhood End.

And he told the Ox of a Manger
    And a stall in Bethlehem,
And he spoke to the Ass of a Rider
    That rode to Jerusalem.

They steamed and dripped in the chancel,
    They listened and never stirred,
While, just as though they were Bishops,
    Eddi preached them the Word,

Till the gale blew off on the marshes
    And the windows showed the day,
And the Ox and the Ass together
    Wheeled and clattered away.

And when the Saxons mocked him,
    Said Eddi of Manhood End,
"I dare not shut His chapel
    On such as care to attend."

Gilbert Keith Chesterton

G. K. CHESTERTON (1874–1936), PROLIFIC BRITISH AUTHOR of critical
studies, poetry, novels, and historical fiction, is undoubtedly best known
for his series of detective novels featuring Father Brown. Chesterton's
works are frequently polemic, ardently defending his opinions. Many of
his literary mysteries are not mere escapist literature, but are imbued with
Catholic doctrine. The first, heavily ironic carol printed below illustrates
one of Chesterton's devices—a poem written in response to a headline.

The second is more traditional, but also typical of Chesterton in its use of antithesis, the parenthetical lines in the first three stanzas contrasting the weariness of the world to the truth found in the Christ Child.

A Christmas Carol

(The Chief Constable has issued a statement declaring that carol singing in the streets by children is illegal, and morally and physically injurious. He appeals to the public to discourage the practice.—*Daily Paper.*)

God rest you merry gentlemen,
Let nothing you dismay;
The Herald Angels cannot sing,
The cops arrest them on the wing,
And warn them of the docketing
Of anything they say.

God rest you merry gentlemen,
May nothing you dismay:
On your reposeful cities lie
Deep silence, broken only by
The motor horn's melodious cry,
The hooter's happy bray.

So, when the song of children ceased
And Herod was obeyed,
In his high hall Corinthian
With purple and with peacock fan,
Rested that merry gentleman;
And nothing him dismayed.

A Christmas Carol

The Christ-child lay on Mary's lap,
His hair was like a light.
(O weary, weary were the world,
But here is all aright.)

The Christ-child lay on Mary's breast,
    His hair was like a star.
(O stern and cunning are the kings,
    But here the true hearts are.)

The Christ-child lay on Mary's heart,
    His hair was like a fire.
(O weary, weary is the world,
    But here the world's desire.)

The Christ-child stood at Mary's knee,
    His hair was like a crown,
And all the flowers looked up at Him,
    And all the stars looked down.

Jesus, Jesus, rest your head

"JESUS, JESUS, REST YOUR HEAD," A FOLKSONG COLLECTED IN KENTUCKY by John Jacob Niles, retells in simple dialect the Christmas narrative. This folksong offers a fresh viewpoint to a familiar story. The song reveals that the humble manger is preferable to luxury, because poverty is equated with virtue, and wealth with evil. The Christ Child's meager surroundings thus inspire neither awe nor pity; the babe is simply calmed and told to sleep, as in a lullaby.

Jesus, Jesus, rest your head

Jesus, Jesus, rest your head,
You has got a manger bed.
All the evil folk on earth sleep in feathers at their birth,
Jesus, Jesus, rest your head,
You has got a manger bed.

Have you heard about our Jesus?
Have you heard about his fate?
How his mammy went to the stable on that Christmas eve so late?
Winds were blowing, cows were lowing, stars were glowing.
Jesus, Jesus, rest your head,
You has got a manger bed.

All the evil folk on earth sleep in feathers at their birth,
Jesus, Jesus, rest your head,
You has got a manger bed.

To that manger came then wise men,
Bringing things from hin and yon
For the mother and the father and the blessed little son.
Milkmaids left their fields and flocks, and sat beside the ass and ox.
Jesus, Jesus, rest your head,
You has got a manger bed.
All the evil folk on earth sleep in feathers at their birth,
Jesus, Jesus, rest your head,
You has got a manger bed.

The Babe of Bethlehem

"THE BABE OF BETHLEHEM" IS A HYMN from William Walker's popular shape-note tunebook *The Southern Harmony and Musical Companion* (1835). Shape-note singing, also referred to as buckwheat harmony and Sacred Harp singing, is a type of rural American religious music. More social than liturgical, most "singings" take place outside of religious services, and most shape-note tunebooks are nondenominational. Intended to facilitate sight singing, shape-note notation uses note heads in various shapes to indicate pitch. Originally a British system referred to as "Lancashire Sol-Fa," shape-note music in America was first written in the late eighteenth century in New England. Midwestern and Southern shape-note music tunebooks compiled during the early nineteenth century added spirituals and folk hymns to the psalms, hymns, and anthems of the New England collections, thus preserving oral traditions.

The Babe of Bethlehem

Ye nations all, on you I call,
Come, hear this declaration,
And don't refuse this glorious news
Of Jesus and salvation.
To royal Jews came first the news
Of Christ the great Messiah,

Ye nations all, on you I call,
Come, hear this declaration,
And don't refuse this glorious news
Of Jesus and salvation.

As was foretold by prophets old,
Isaiah, Jeremiah.

To Abraham the promise came,
And to his seed for ever,
A light to shine in Isaac's line,
By Scripture we discover;
Hail, promised morn! the Saviour's born,
The glorious Mediator—
God's blessed Word made flesh and blood,
Assumed the human nature.

His parents poor in earthly store,
To entertain the stranger,
They found no bed to lay his head,
But in the ox's manger:
No royal things, as used by kings,
Were seen by those that found him,
But in the hay the stranger lay,
With swaddling bands around him.

On the same night a glorious light
To shepherds there appeared,
Bright angels came in shining flame,
They saw and greatly feared.
The angels said, "Be not afraid,
Although we much alarm you,
We do appear good news to bear,
As now we will inform you.

"The city's name is Bethlehem,
In which God hath appointed,
This glorious morn a Saviour's born,
For him God hath annointed;
By this you'll know, if you will go,
To see this little stranger,
His lovely charms in Mary's arms,
Both lying in a manger."

When this was said, straightway was made
A glorious sound from heaven.
Each flaming tongue an anthem sung,
"To men a Saviour's given,
In Jesus' name, the glorious theme,
We elevate our voices,
At Jesus' birth be peace on earth,
Meanwhile all heaven rejoices."

Then with delight they took their flight,
And wing'd their way to glory,
The shepherds gazed and were amazed,
To hear the pleasing story;
To Bethlehem they quickly came,
The glorious news to carry,
And in the stall they found them all,
Joseph, the Babe, and Mary.

The shepherds then return'd again
To their own habitation,
With joy of heart they did depart,
Now they have found salvation.
Glory, they cry, to God on high,
Who sent his Son to save us.
This glorious morn the Saviour's born,
His name it is Christ Jesus.

Chapter 5

The Twentieth Century

The
Age
of
Anxiety

Introduction

Twentieth-century writers express a wide range of reactions to the observance of Christmas: cynicism, nostalgia, humor, ambivalence, affirmation. After the "war to end all wars" of 1914–1918, rarely would be found the innocence regarding the human condition, or even the deliberate avoidance of unpleasantness. By 1918, a bleaker worldview had supplanted the warm Dickensian hearth-side celebration of a family Christmas. What T. S. Eliot called the "great tradition," with its common, inherited religious and cultural symbols, was replaced by a wasteland in which, as Matthew Arnold had prophesied, "ignorant armies clash by night."

Many twentieth-century works of Christmas literature are characterized by an irony that accents the discrepancy between the ideal and the actual. In some cases, the writer portrays morally ambivalent characters, as does Edward Arlington Robinson in "Karma." The bitter cynicism that engulfed many in response to the experience of two world wars is illustrated in Thomas Hardy's "Christmas: 1924" and recurs in a World War II era poem by the American Southerner James Agee entitled "Christmas 1945." Lawrence Ferlinghetti takes a deadly aim at the commercialization of Christmas in "Christ Climbed Down."

One way contemporary writers avoid despair is by turning to the past. A continuing form of Christmas literature in the twentieth century is the reminiscence, a nostalgic look at earlier, supposedly simpler times. There is something about the season that elicits remembrances of Christmas past. A Christmas in which the chief activity of the day is ice skating, as in the scene from Lee Smith's novel, *Fair and Tender Ladies*, might seem woefully inadequate from some perspectives. However, imbued with the magical glow of remembrance, the incident might be described as, to use Flannery O'Connor's term, a moment of grace.

Another response to the discrepancies between the dream and the reality is humor, a dimension of Christmas literature since the Middle Ages. The seeming relentlessness of the tragic contradictions of life can be relieved by the comic vision. Humor flourishes in natural, specific human contexts; humor acknowledges the defects, the foibles, the warts of human existence. It is in this spirit that popular American writers Grace Paley and John Irving enter the world of the ubiquitous Christmas pageant. Both pageants star a character known primarily for a remarkable voice, and both illustrate the ironic and comic discrepancy between the Nativity as performed on stage and as experienced in the heart. Stella Gibbons's "Christmas at Cold Comfort Farm" is a parody of the "olde English" rural Christmas that will make it difficult to ever again read Dickens's or Washington Irving's portrayals without mirthful comparison.

Another body of literature treats the Nativity as a matter of continuing importance, personally and culturally. Martin Bell uses a beast fable to express deep truths. Richard Wilbur, Lucille Clifton, and Rainer Maria Rilke provide fresh perspectives by reexamining biblical events with modern eyes. Such works make it clear that it is possible to take a personal look beneath the tinsel and the unlikely Santas, the cynicism and the ironies of the season, and still find the ancient magic of Christmas.

Today many writers may be able only to echo the question, posed by the twentieth-century poet John Betjeman in his poem "Christmas": Did "The Maker of the stars and sea / Become a Child on earth for me?" For some few contemporary authors, however, even in the midst of a religious and cultural wasteland it is still possible to detect the star of Bethlehem. Occasionally a writer will share a personal existential religious encounter such as that which W. H. Auden described (in *Forwards and Afterwards*, 1974) as having suddenly occurred during a casual conversation: "I felt myself invaded by a power which, though I consented to it, was irresistible and certainly not mine. For the first time in my life I knew exactly . . . what it means to love one's neighbor as oneself." Afterwards, Auden, perceiving his duty as a poet to be also that of bearing witness, appealed, in his poem "In Memory of W. B. Yeats," to his fellow poets: "With your unconstraining voice / Still persuade us to rejoice." The Bethlehem of long ago and far away may once again be recalled into the present, with more than a rumor of angels. The world has perhaps never so badly needed the words that each Christmas Eve still resound along the roads to and from Bethlehem: "Fear not: for, behold, I bring you good tidings of great

Contemporary Holy Family (Sudanese, 1992)

joy, which shall be to all people. For unto you is born this day in the city of David a Saviour, which is Christ the Lord" (Luke 2:10–11).

Stella Gibbons

STELLA GIBBONS (1902-1989), A WRITER OF POETRY AND FICTION as well as a journalist, is best known for the humorous novels and stories set at Cold Comfort Farm. When *Cold Comfort Farm* was produced on public television years ago, Americans hardly knew what to make of the strange family, the Starkadders, and the primitive English Midlands world in which they lived. The accents were also a problem—neither Oxbridge nor cockney, but an assortment of grunts and whines that sounded rather like what a linguist might call Ur-English.

Stella Gibbons's comic novel was first published in 1932. Its popularity led to a sequel in 1942 entitled *Christmas at Cold Comfort Farm and Other Stories.* The original novel and subsequent stories parody a number of aspects of early twentieth-century English life. The use of names to imply character found in melodramatic novels is satirized in the farm itself, "Cold Comfort," and in those who populate it: Ada Doom (who "saw something nasty in the woodshed" and never got over it), Adam Lambsbreath (a prototypical Earth Father), Rev. Silas Hearsay (who substitutes the word *Energy* for *God* with every utterance in the manner of the *élan vital* philosophers), and their kith and kin. "Christmas at Cold Comfort Farm" provides a memorable milieu for the holiday celebration, and a Christmas dinner the reader will long remember.

Christmas at Cold Comfort Farm

It was Christmas Eve. Dusk, a filthy mantle, lay over Sussex when the Reverend Silas Hearsay, Vicar of Howling, set out to pay his yearly visit to Cold Comfort Farm. Earlier in the afternoon he had feared he would not be Guided to go there, but then he had seen a crate of British Port-type wine go past the Vicarage on the grocer's boy's bicycle, and it could only be going, by that road, to the farmhouse. Shortly afterwards he was Guided to go, and set out upon his bicycle.

The Starkadders, of Cold Comfort Farm, had never got the hang of Christmas, somehow, and on Boxing Day there was always a run on the Howling Pharmacy for lint, bandages, and boracic powder. So the Vicar was going up there, as he did every year, to show them the ropes a bit. (It must be explained that these events took place some years before the civilizing hand of Flora Poste had softened and reformed the Farm and its rude inhabitants.)

After removing two large heaps of tussocks which blocked the lane leading to the Farm and thereby releasing a flood of muddy, icy water over his ankles, the Vicar wheeled his machine on towards the farmhouse, reflecting that those tussocks had never fallen there from the dung-cart of Nature. It was clear that someone did not want him to come to the place. He pushed his bicycle savagely up the hill, muttering.

The farmhouse was in silence and darkness. He pulled the ancient hell-bell (once used to warn excommunicated persons to stay away from Divine Service) hanging outside the front door, and waited.

For a goodish bit nothing happened. Suddenly a window far above his head was flung open and a voice wailed into the twilight—

"No! No! No!"

And the window slammed shut again.

"You're making a mistake, I'm sure," shouted the Vicar, peering up into the webby thongs of the darkness. "It's me. The Rev. Silas Hearsay."

There was a pause. Then—

"Beant you postman?" asked the voice, rather embarrassed.

"No, no, of course not; come, come!" laughed the Vicar, grinding his teeth.

"I be comin'," retorted the voice. "Thought it were postman after his Christmas Box." The window slammed again. After a very long time indeed the door suddenly opened and there stood Adam Lambsbreath, oldest of the farm servants, peering up at the Reverend Hearsay by the light of a lonely rushdip (so called because you dipped it in grease and rushed to wherever you were going before it went out).

"Is anyone at home? May I enter?" enquired the Vicar, entering, and staring scornfully round the desolate kitchen, at the dead blue ashes in the grate, the thick dust on hanch and beam, the feathers blowing about like fun everywhere. Yet even here there were signs of Christmas, for a withered branch of holly stood in a shapeless vessel on the table. And Adam himself . . . there was something even more peculiar than usual about him.

"Are you ailing, man?" asked the Vicar irritably, kicking a chair out of the way and perching himself on the edge of the table.

"Nay, Rev., I be niver better," piped the old man. *"The older the berry, The more it makes merry."*

"Then why," thundered the Vicar, sliding off the table and walking on tiptoe towards Adam with his arms held at full length above his head, "are you wearing three of Mrs. Starkadder's red shawls?"

Adam stood his ground.

"I mun have a red courtepy [cloak], master. Can't be Santa Claus wi'out a red courtepy," he said. "Iverybody knows that. Ay, the hand o' Fate lies heavy on us all, Christmas and all the year round alike, but I thought I'd bedight meself as Santa Claus, so I did, just to please me little Elfine. And this night at midnight I be goin' around fillin' the stockin's, if I'm spared."

The Vicar laughed contemptuously.

"So that were why I took three o' Mrs. Starkadder's red shawls," concluded Adam.

"I suppose you have never thought of God in terms of Energy? No, it is too much to expect." The Reverend Hearsay re-seated himself on the table and glanced at his watch. "Where in Energy's name *is* everybody? I have to be at the Assembly Rooms to read a paper on *The Future of the Father Fixation* at eight, and I've got to feed first. If nobody's coming, I'd rather go."

"Won't ee have a dram o' swede wine first?" a deep voice asked, and a tall woman stepped over the threshold, followed by a little girl of twelve or so with yellow hair and clear, beautiful features. Judith Starkadder dropped her hat on the floor and leant against the table, staring listlessly at the Vicar.

"No swede wine, I thank you," snapped the Reverend Hearsay. He glanced keenly round the kitchen in search of the British Port-type, but there was no sign of it. "I came up to discuss an article with you and yours. An article in *Home Anthropology.*"

"'Twere good of ee, Reverend," she said tiredly.

"It is called *Christmas: From Religious Festival to Shopping Orgy.* Puts the case for Peace and Good Will very sensibly. Both good for trade. What more can you want?"

"Nothing," she said, leaning her head on her hand.

"But I see," the Vicar went on furiously, in a low tone and glaring at Adam, "that here, as everywhere else, the usual childish wish-fantasies are in possession. Stars, shepherds, mangers, stockings, fir-trees, puddings. . . . Energy help you all! I wish you good night, and a prosperous Christmas."

He stamped out of the kitchen, and slammed the door after him with such violence that he brought a slate down on his back tyre and cut it open, and he had to walk home, arriving there too late for supper before setting out for Godmere.

After he had gone, Judith stared into the fire without speaking, and Adam busied himself with scraping the mould from a jar of mince-meat and picking some things which had fallen into it out of a large crock of pudding which he had made yesterday.

Elfine, meanwhile, was slowly opening a small brown paper parcel which she had been nursing, and at last revealed a small and mean-looking doll dressed in a sleazy silk dress and one under-garment that did not take off. This she gently nursed, talking to it in a low, sweet voice.

"Who gave you that, child?" asked her mother idly.

"I told you, mother. Uncle Micah and Aunt Rennett and Aunt Prue and Uncle Harkaway and Uncle Ezra."

"Treasure it. You will not get many such."

"I know, mother; I do. I love her very much, dear, dear Caroline," and Elfine gently put a kiss on the doll's face.

"Now, missus, have ee got the Year's Luck? Can't make puddens wi'out the Year's Luck," said Adam, shuffling forward.

"It's somewhere here. I forget—"

She turned her shabby handbag upside down, and there fell out on the table the following objects:

A small coffin-nail.

A menthol cone.

Three bad sixpences.

A doll's cracked looking-glass.

A small roll of sticking-plaster.

Adam collected these objects and ranged them by the pudding basin.

"Ay, them's all there," he muttered. "Him as gets the sticking-plaster'll break a limb; the menthol cone means as you'll be blind wi' headache, the bad coins means as you'll lose all yer money, and him as gets the coffin-nail will die afore the New Year. The mirror's seven years' bad luck for someone. Aie! In ye go, curse ye!" and he tossed the objects into the pudding, where they were not easily nor long distinguishable from the main mass.

"Want a stir, missus? Come, Elfine, my popelot, stir long, stir firm, your meat to earn," and he handed her the butt of an old rifle, once used by Fig Starkadder in the Gordon Riots.

Judith turned from the pudding with what is commonly described as a gesture of loathing, but Elfine took the rifle butt and stirred the mixture once or twice.

"Ay, now tes all mixed," said the old man, nodding with satisfaction. "To-morrer we'll boil un fer a good hour, and un'll be done."

"Will an hour be enough?" said Elfine. "Mrs. Hawk-Monitor up at Hautcouture Hall boils hers for eight hours, and another four on Christmas Day."

"How do ee know?" demanded Adam. "Have ee been runnin' wi' that young goosepick Mus' Richard again?"

"You shut up. He's awfully decent."

"Tisn't decent to run wi' a young popelot all over the Downs in all weathers."

"Well, it isn't any of your business, so shut up."

After an offended pause, Adam said:

"Well, niver fret about puddens. None of 'em here has iver tasted any puddens but mine, and they won't know no different."

At midnight, when the farmhouse was in darkness save for the faint flame of a nightlight burning steadily beside the bed of Harkaway, who was afraid of bears, a dim shape might have been seen moving stealthily along the corridor from bedroom to bedroom. It wore three red shawls pinned over its torn nightshirt and carried over its shoulder a nose-bag, (the property of Viper the gelding), distended with parcels. It was Adam, bent on putting into the stockings of the Starkadders the presents which he had made or bought with his savings. The presents were chiefly swedes, beetroots, mangel-wurzels and turnips, decorated with coloured ribbons and strips of silver paper from tea packets.

"Ay," muttered the old man, as he opened the door of the room where Meriam, the hired girl, was sleeping over the Christmas week. "An apple for each will make 'em retch, a couple o' nuts will warm their wits."

The next instant he stepped back in astonishment. There was a light in the room and there, sitting bolt upright in bed beside her slumbering daughter, was Mrs. Beetle.

Mrs. Beetle looked steadily at Adam, for a minute or two. Then she observed:

"Some 'opes."

"Nay, niver say that, soul," protested Adam, moving to the bedrail where hung a very fully-fashioned salmon-pink silk stocking with ladders all down it. "'Tisn't so. Ee do know well that I looks on the maidy as me own child."

Mrs. Beetle gave a short laugh and adjusted a curler.

"You better not let Agony 'ear you, 'intin' I dunno wot," said Mrs. Beetle. "'Urry up and put yer rubbish in there, I want me sleep out; I got to be up at cock-wake ter-morrer."

Adam put a swede, an apple and a small pot in the stocking and was tip-toeing away when Mrs. Beetle, raising her head from the pillow, inquired:

"Wot's that you've give 'er?"

"Eye-shadow," whispered Adam hoarsely, turning at the door.

"Wot?" hissed Mrs. Beetle, inclining her head in an effort to hear. "'Ave you gorn crackers?"

"Eye-shadow. To put on the maidy's eyes. 'Twill give that touch o' glamour as be irresistible; it do say so on pot."

"Get out of 'ere, you old trouble-maker! Don't she 'ave enough bother resistin' as it is, and then you go and give 'er. . . 'ere, wait till I—" and Mrs. Beetle was looking around for something to throw as Adam hastily retreated.

"And I'll lay you ain't got no present fer me, ter make matters worse," she called after him.

Silently he placed a bright new tin of beetle-killer on the washstand and shuffled away.

His experiences in the apartments of the other Starkadders were no more fortunate, for Seth was busy with a friend and was so furious at being interrupted that he threw his riding-boots at the old man, Luke and Mark had locked their door and could be heard inside roaring with laughter at Adam's discomfiture, and Amos was praying, and did not even get up off his knees or open his eyes as he discharged at Adam the goat-pistol which he kept ever by his bed. And everybody else had such enormous holes in their stockings that the small presents Adam put in them fell through on to the floor along with the big ones, and when the Starkadders got up in the morning and rushed round to the foot of the bed to see what Santa had brought, they stubbed their toes on the turnips and swedes and walked on the smaller presents and smashed them to smithereens.

So what with one thing and another everybody was in an even worse temper than usual when the family assembled round the long table in the kitchen for the Christmas dinner about half-past two the next afternoon. They would all have sooner been in some place else, but Mrs. Ada Doom (Grandmother Doom, known as Grummer) insisted on them all being there, and as they did not want her to go mad and bring disgrace on the House of Starkadder, there they had to be.

One by one they came in, the men from the fields with soil on their boots, the women fresh from hennery and duck filch with eggs in their bosoms that they gave to Mrs. Beetle who was just making the custard. Everybody had to work as usual on Christmas Day, and no one had troubled to put on anything handsomer than their usual workaday clouts stained with mud and plough-oil. Only Elfine wore a cherry-red jersey over her dark skirt and had pinned a spray of holly on herself. An aunt, a distant aunt named Mrs. Poste, who lived in London, had unexpectedly sent her the pretty jersey. Prue and Letty had stuck sixpenny artificial posies in their hair, but they only looked wild and queer.

At last all were seated and waiting for Ada Doom.

"Come, come, mun we stick here like jennets i' the trave?" demanded Micah at last. "Amos, Reuben, do ee carve the turkey. If so be as we wait much longer, 'twill be shent, and the sausages, too."

Even as he spoke, heavy footsteps were heard approaching the head of the stairs, and everybody at once rose to their feet and looked towards the door.

The low-ceilinged room was already half in dusk, for it was a cold, still Christmas Day, without much light in the grey sky, and the only other illumination came from the dull fire, half-buried under a tass of damp kindling.

Adam gave a last touch to the pile of presents, wrapped in hay and tied with bast, which he had put round the foot of the withered thorn-branch that was the traditional Starkadder Christmas-tree, hastily rearranged one of the tufts of sheep's-wool that decorated its branches, straightened the raven's skeleton that adorned its highest branch in place of a fairy-doll or star, and shuffled into his place just as Mrs. Doom reached the foot of the stairs, leaning on her daughter Judith's arm. Mrs. Doom struck at him with her stick in passing as she went slowly to the head of the table.

"Well, well. What are we waiting for? Are you all mishooden?" she demanded impatiently as she seated herself. "Are you all here? All? Answer me!" banging her stick.

"Ay, Grummer," rose the low, dreary drone from all sides of the table. "We be all here."

"Where's Seth?" demanded the old woman, peering sharply on either side of the long row.

"Gone out," said Harkaway briefly, shifting a straw in his mouth.

"What for?" demanded Mrs. Doom.

There was an ominous silence.

"He said he was going to fetch something, Grandmother," at last said Elfine.

"Ay. Well, well, no matter, so long as he comes soon. Amos, carve the bird. Ay, would it were a vulture, 'twere more fitting! Reuben, fling these dogs the fare my bounty provides. Sausages . . . pah! Mince-pies . . . what a black-bitter mockery it all is! Every almond, every raisin, is wrung from the dry, dying soil and paid for with sparse greasy notes grudged alike by bank and buyer. Come, Ezra, pass the ginger wine! Be gay, spawn! Laugh, stuff yourselves, gorge and forget, you rat-heaps! Rot you all!" and she fell back in her chair, gasping and keeping one eye on the British Port-type that was now coming up the table.

"Tes one of her bad days," said Judith tonelessly. "Amos, will you pull a cracker wi' me? We were lovers . . . once."

"Hush, woman." He shrank back from the proffered treat. "Tempt me not wi' motters and paper caps. Hell is paved wi' such." Judith smiled bitterly and fell silent.

Reuben, meanwhile, had seen to it that Elfine got the best bit off the turkey (which is not saying much) and had filled her glass with Port-type wine and well-water.

The turkey gave out before it got to Letty, Prue, Susan, Phoebe, Jane and Rennett, who were huddled together at the foot of the table, and they were making do with brussels-sprouts as hard as bullets drenched with weak gravy, and home-brewed braket. There was silence in the kitchen except for the sough of swallowing, the sudden suck of drinking.

"WHERE IS SETH?" suddenly screamed Mrs. Doom, flinging down her turkey-leg and glaring round.

Silence fell; everyone moved uneasily, not daring to speak in case they provoked an outburst. But at that moment the cheerful, if unpleasant, noise of a motor-cycle was heard outside, and in another moment it stopped at the kitchen door. All eyes were turned in that direction, and in another moment in came Seth.

"Well, Grummer! Happen you thought I was lost!" he cried impudently, peeling off his boots and flinging them at Meriam, the hired girl, who cowered by the fire gnawing a sausage skin.

Mrs. Doom silently pointed to his empty seat with the turkey-leg, and he sat down.

"She hev had an outhees. Ay, 'twas terrible," reproved Judith in a low tone as Seth seated himself beside her.

"Niver mind, I ha' something here as will make her chirk like a mellet," he retorted, and held up a large brown paper parcel. "I ha' been to the Post Office to get it."

"Ah, gie it me! Aie, my lost pleasurings! Tes none I get, nowadays; gie it me now!" cried the old woman eagerly.

"Nay, Grummer. Ee must wait till pudden time," and the young man fell on his turkey ravenously.

When everyone had finished, the women cleared away and poured the pudding into a large dusty dish, which they bore to the table and set before Judith.

"Amos? Pudding?" she asked listlessly. "In a glass or on a plate?"

"On plate, on plate, woman," he said feverishly bending forward with a fierce glitter in his eye. "Tes easier to see the Year's Luck so."

A stir of excitement now went through the company, for everybody looked forward to seeing everybody else drawing ill-luck from the symbols concealed in the pudding. A fierce, attentive silence fell. It was broken by a wail from Reuben—

"The coin—the coin! Wala wa!" and he broke into deep, heavy sobs. He was saving up to buy a tractor, and the coin meant, of course, that he would lose all his money during the year.

"Never mind, Reuben, dear," whispered Elfine, slipping an arm round his neck. "You can have the penny father gave me."

Shrieks from Letty and Prue now announced that they had received the menthol cone and the sticking-plaster, and a low mutter of approval greeted the discovery by Amos of the broken mirror.

Now there was only the coffin-nail, and a ghoulish silence fell on everybody as they dripped pudding from their spoons in a feverish hunt for it; Ezra was running his through a tea-strainer.

But no one seemed to have got it.

"Who has the coffin-nail? Speak, you draf-saks!" at last demanded Mrs. Doom.

"Not I." "Nay." "Niver sight not snitch of it," chorussed everybody.

"Adam!" Mrs. Doom turned to the old man. "Did you put the coffin-nail into the pudding?"

"Ay, mistress, that I did—didn't I, Mis' Judith, didn't I, Elfine, my liddle lovesight?"

"He speaks truth for once, mother."

"Yes, he did, Grandmother. I saw him."

"Then where is it?" Mrs. Doom's voice was low and terrible and her gaze moved slowly down the table, first on one side and then the other, in search of signs of guilt, while everyone cowered over their plates.

Everyone, that is, except Mrs. Beetle, who continued to eat a sandwich that she had taken out of a cellophane wrapper, with every appearance of enjoyment.

"Carrie Beetle!" shouted Mrs. Doom.

"I'm 'ere," said Mrs. Beetle.

"Did you take the coffin-nail out of the pudding?"

"Yes, I did." Mrs. Beetle leisurely finished the last crumb of sandwich and wiped her mouth with a clean handkerchief. "And will again, if I'm spared till next year."

"You . . . you . . . you . . ." choked Mrs. Doom, rising in her chair and beating the air with her clenched fists. "For two hundred years . . . Starkadders . . . coffin-nails in puddings . . . and now . . . you . . . dare. . . ."

"Well, I 'ad enough of it las' year," retorted Mrs. Beetle. "That pore old soul Earnest Dolour got it, as well you may remember—"

"That's right. Cousin Earnest," nodded Mark Dolour. "Got a job workin' on the oil-field down Henfield way. Good money, too."

"Thanks to me, if he 'as," retorted Mrs. Beetle. "If I 'adn't put it up to you, Mark Dolour, you'd 'ave let 'im die. All of you was 'angin' over the pore old soul waitin' for 'im to 'and in 'is dinner pail, and Micah (wot's old enough to know better, 'eaven only knows) askin' 'im could 'e 'ave 'is wrist-watch if anything was to 'appen to 'im . . . it fair got me down. So I says to Mark, why don't yer go down and 'ave a word with Mr. Earthdribble the undertaker in Howling and get 'im to tell Earnest it weren't a proper coffin-nail at all, it were a throw-out, so it didn't count. The bother we 'ad! Shall I ever fergit it! Never again, I says to meself. So this year there ain't no coffin-nail. I fished it out o' the pudden meself. Parss the water, please."

"Where is it?" whispered Mrs. Doom, terribly. "Where is this year's nail, woman?"

"Down the—" Mrs. Beetle checked herself, and coughed, "down the well," concluded Mrs. Beetle firmly.

"Niver fret, Grummer, I'll get it up fer ee! Me and the water voles, we can dive far and deep!" and Urk rushed from the room, laughing wildly.

"There ain't no need," called Mrs. Beetle after him. "But anything to keep you an' yer rubbishy water voles out of mischief!" And Mrs. Beetle went into a cackle of laughter, alternately slapping her knee and Caraway's arm, and muttering, "Oh, cor, wait till I tell Agony! 'Dive far and deep.' Oh, cor!" After a minute's uneasy silence—

"Grummer." Seth bent winningly towards the old woman, the large brown paper parcel in his hand. "Will you see your present now?"

"Aye, boy, aye. Let me see it. You're the only one that has thought of me, the only one."

Seth was undoing the parcel, and now revealed a large book, handsomely bound in red leather with gilt lettering.

"There, Grummer. 'Tis the year's numbers o' *The Milk Producers' Weekly Bulletin and Cowkeepers' Guide*. I collected un for ee, and had un bound. Art pleased?"

"Ay. 'Tis handsome enough. A graceful thought," muttered the old lady, turning the pages. Most of them were pretty battered, owing to her habit of rolling up the paper and hitting anyone with it who happened to be within reach. "'Tis better so. 'Tis heavier. Now I can *throw* it."

The Starkadders so seldom saw a clean and handsome object at the farmhouse (for Seth was only handsome) that they now crept round, fascinated, to examine the book with murmurs of awe. Among them came Adam, but no sooner had he bent over the book than he recoiled from it with a piercing scream.

"Aie! . . . aie! aie!"

"What's the matter, dotard?" screamed Mrs. Doom, jabbing at him with the volume. "Speak, you kaynard!"

"Tes calf! Tes bound in calf! And tes our Pointless's calf, as she had last Lammastide, as was sold at Godmere to Farmer Lust!" cried Adam, falling to the floor. At the same instant, Luke hit Micah in the stomach, Harkaway pushed Ezra into the fire, Mrs. Doom flung the bound volume of *The Milk Producers' Weekly Bulletin and Cowkeepers' Guide* at the struggling mass, and the Christmas dinner collapsed into indescribable confusion.

In the midst of the uproar, Elfine, who had climbed on to the table, glanced up at the window as though seeking help, and saw a laughing face looking at her, and a hand in a yellow string glove beckoning with a riding-crop. Swiftly she darted down from the table and across the room, and out through the half-open door, slamming it after her.

Dick Hawk-Monitor, a sturdy boy astride a handsome pony, was out in the yard.

"Hallo!" she gasped. "Oh, Dick, I am glad to see you!"

"I thought you never would see me—what on earth's the matter in there?" he asked curiously.

"Oh, never mind them, they're always like that. Dick, do tell me, what presents did you have?"

"Oh, a rifle, and a new saddle, and a fiver—lots of things. Look here, Elfine, you mustn't mind, but I brought you—"

He bent over the pony's neck and held out a sandwich box, daintily filled with slices of turkey, a piece of pudding, a tiny mince-pie and a crystallized apricot.

"Thought your dinner mightn't be very—" he ended gruffly.

"Oh, Dick, it's lovely! Darling little . . . what is it?"

"Apricot. Crystallized fruit. Look here, let's go up to the usual place, shall we?—and I'll watch you eat it."

"But you must have some, too."

"Man! I'm stoked up to the brim now! But I dare say I could manage a bit more. Here, you catch hold of Rob Roy, and he'll help you up the hill."

He touched the pony with his heels and it trotted on towards the snow-streaked Downs, Elfine's yellow hair flying out like a shower of primroses under the grey sky of winter.

Betty Smith

NOVELIST BETTY SMITH (1904–1972) BEGAN HER LITERARY CAREER as a playwright, writing mostly one-act plays for school use. The work for which she will be remembered is *A Tree Grows in Brooklyn*. The novel was made into a film, now considered a classic, in 1945. Though some critics described the story and the writing as "conventional," it appealed to American tastes and became a best-seller. The story is set in the Williamsburg section of Brooklyn during World War I. The Nolans, a struggling Irish family living in an upstairs tenement, somehow have managed to survive on dreams. It is a poignant story of the strength of human will.

A Tree Grows in Brooklyn
Book Three: Chapter XXVII
(excerpt)

Christmas was a charmed time in Brooklyn. It was in the air, long before it came. The first hint of it was Mr. Morton going around the schools teaching Christmas carols, but the first sure sign was the store windows.

You have to be a child to know how wonderful is a store window filled with dolls and sleds and other toys. And this wonder came free to Francie. It was nearly as good as actually having the toys to be permitted to look at them through the glass window.

Oh, what a thrill there was for Francie when she turned a street corner and saw another store all fixed up for Christmas! Ah, the clean shining window with cotton batting sprinkled with star dust for a carpet! There were flaxen-haired dolls and others which Francie liked better who had hair the color of good coffee with lots of cream in it. Their faces were perfectly tinted and they wore clothes the like of which Francie had never seen on earth. The dolls stood upright in flimsy cardboard boxes. They stood with the help of a bit of tape passed around the neck and ankles and through holes at the back of the box. Oh, the deep blue eyes framed by thick lashes that stared straight into a little girl's heart and the perfect miniature hands extended, appealingly asking, "Please, won't *you* be my mama?" And Francie had never had a doll except a two-inch one that cost a nickel.

And the sleds! (Or, as the Williamsburg children called them, the sleighs.) There was a child's dream of heaven come true! A new sled with a flower someone had dreamed up painted on it—a deep blue flower with bright green leaves—the ebony-black painted runners, the smooth steering bar made of hard wood and gleaming varnish over all! And the names painted on them! "Rosebud!" "Magnolia!" "Snow King!" "The Flyer!" Thought Francie, "If I could only have one of those, I'd never ask God for another thing as long as I live."

There were roller skates made of shining nickel with straps of good brown leather and silvered nervous wheels, tensed for rolling, needing but a breath to start them turning, as they lay crossed one over the other, sprinkled with mica snow on a bed of cloud-like cotton.

There were other marvelous things. Francie couldn't take them all in. Her head spun and she was dizzy with the impact of all the seeing and all the making up of stories about the toys in the shop windows.

The spruce trees began coming into the neighborhood the week before Christmas. Their branches were corded to hold back the glory of their spreading and probably to make shipping easier. Vendors rented space on the curb before a store and stretched a rope from pole to pole and leaned the trees against it. All day they walked up and down this one-sided avenue of aromatic leaning trees, blowing on stiff ungloved fingers and looking with bleak hope at those people who paused. A few ordered a tree set aside for the day; others stopped to price, inspect and conjecture. But most came just to touch the boughs and surreptitiously pinch a fingerful of spruce needles together to release the fragrance. And the air was cold and still, and full of the pine smell and the smell of tangerines which appeared in the stores only at Christmas time and the mean street was truly wonderful for a little while.

There was a cruel custom in the neighborhood. It was about the trees still unsold when midnight of Christmas Eve approached. There was a saying that if you waited until then, you wouldn't have to buy a tree; that "they'd chuck 'em at you." This was literally true.

At midnight on the Eve of our dear Saviour's birth, the kids gathered where there were unsold trees. The man threw each tree in turn, starting with the biggest. Kids volunteered to stand up against the throwing. If a boy didn't fall down under the impact, the tree was his. If he fell, he forfeited his chance at winning a tree. Only the roughest boys and some of the young men elected to be hit by the big trees. The others waited shrewdly until a tree came up that they could stand against. The little kids waited for the tiny, foot-high trees and shrieked in delight when they won one.

On the Christmas Eve when Francie was ten and Neeley nine, mama consented to let them go down and have their first try for a tree. Francie had picked out her tree earlier in the day. She had stood near it all afternoon and evening praying that no one would buy it. To her joy, it was still there at midnight. It was the biggest tree in the neighborhood and its price was so high that no one could afford to buy it. It was ten feet high. Its branches were bound with new white rope and it came to a sure pure point at the top.

The man took this tree out first. Before Francie could speak up, a neighborhood bully, a boy of eighteen known as Punky Perkins, stepped forward and ordered the man to chuck the tree at him. The man hated the way Punky was so confident. He looked around and asked;

"Anybody else wanna take a chance on it?"

Francie stepped forward. "Me, Mister."

A spurt of derisive laughter came from the tree man. The kids snickered. A few adults who had gathered to watch the fun, guffawed.

"Aw g'wan. You're too little," the tree man objected.

"Me and my brother—we're not too little together."

She pulled Neeley forward. The man looked at them—a thin girl of ten with starveling hollows in her cheeks but with the chin still baby-round. He looked at the little boy with his fair hair and round blue eyes—Neeley Nolan, all innocence and trust.

"Two ain't fair," yelped Punky.

"Shut your lousy trap," advised the man who held all power in that hour. "These here kids is got nerve. Stand back, the rest of yous. These kids is goin' to have a show at this tree."

The others made a wavering lane. Francie and Neeley stood at one end of it and the big man with the big tree at the other. It was a human funnel with Francie and her brother making the small end of it. The man flexed his great arms to throw the great tree. He noticed how tiny the children looked at the end of the short lane. For the split part of a moment, the tree thrower went through a kind of Gethsemane.

"Oh, Jesus Christ," his soul agonized, "why don't I just give 'em the tree, say Merry Christmas and let 'em go. What's the tree to me? I can't sell it no more this year and it won't keep till next year." The kids watched him solemnly as he stood there in his moment of thought. "But then," he rationalized, "if I did that, all the others would expect to get 'em handed to 'em. And next year, nobody a-tall would buy a tree off of me. They'd all wait to get 'em handed to 'em on a silver plate. I ain't a big enough man to give this tree away for nothin'. No, I ain't big enough. I ain't big enough to do a thing like that. I gotta think of myself and my own kids." He finally came to his conclusion. "Oh, what the hell! Them two kids is gotta live in this world. They *got* to get used to it. They got to learn to give and to take punishment. And by Jesus, it ain't give but *take, take, take* all the time in this God-damned world." As he threw the tree with all his strength, his heart wailed out, "It's a God-damned, rotten, lousy world!"

Francie saw the tree leave his hands. There was a split bit of being when time and space had no meaning. The whole world stood still as something dark and monstrous came through the air. The tree came towards her blotting out all memory of her ever having lived. There was nothing—nothing but pungent darkness and something that grew and grew as it rushed at her. She staggered as the tree hit them. Neeley went to his knees but she pulled him up fiercely before he could go down. There was a mighty swishing sound as the tree settled. Everything was dark, green and prickly. Then she felt a sharp pain at the side of her head where the trunk of the tree had hit her. She felt Neeley trembling.

When some of the older boys pulled the tree away, they found Francie and her brother standing upright, hand in hand. Blood was coming from scratches on Neeley's face. He looked more like a baby than ever with his bewildered blue eyes and the fairness of his skin made more noticeable because of the clear red blood. But they were smiling. Had they not won the biggest tree in the neighborhood? Some of the boys hollered "Hooray!" A few adults clapped. The tree man eulogized them by screaming,

"And now get the hell out of here with your tree, you lousy bastards."

Francie had heard swearing since she had heard words. Obscenity and profanity had no meaning as such among those people. They were emotional expressions of inarticulate people with small vocabularies; they made a kind of dialect. The phrases could mean many things according to the expression and tone used in saying them. So now, when Francie heard themselves called lousy bastards, she smiled tremulously at the kind man. She knew that he was really saying, "Goodbye—God bless you."

Grace Paley

GRACE PALEY (B. 1922), ALTHOUGH PRIMARILY A WRITER of short fiction and poetry, is also an activist in feminist and pacifist causes. The skill of Paley's fiction is evident in the deftness with which distinct characters and complex relationships emerge from dialogue; the charm of her fiction derives from her genial affection for her characters. Paley's urban background—she has lived most of her life in New York—and her Jewish and Russian heritage are reflected in the delightful story reprinted here, "The Loudest Voice." The story originally appeared in Paley's collection of short stories, *The Little Disturbances of Man* (1959). "The Loudest Voice" offers us a fresh view of the celebration of Christmas. We see the exuberance of a bright, energetic Jewish child asked to star in a Christmas pageant and the diverse, sometimes bemused, but tolerant reactions of her parents and their friends.

The Loudest Voice

There is a certain place where dumb-waiters boom, doors slam, dishes crash; every window is a mother's mouth bidding the street shut up, go skate somewhere else, come home. My voice is the loudest.

There, my own mother is still as full of breathing as me and the grocer stands up to speak to her. "Mrs. Abramowitz," he says, "people should not be afraid of their children."

"Ah, Mr. Bialik," my mother replies, "if you say to her or her father 'Ssh,' they say, 'In the grave it will be quiet.'"

"From Coney Island to the cemetery," says my papa. "It's the same subway; it's the same fare."

I am right next to the pickle barrel. My pinky is making tiny whirlpools in the brine. I stop a moment to announce: "Campbell's Tomato Soup. Campbell's Vegetable Beef Soup. Campbell's S-c-otch Broth . . . "

"Be quiet," the grocer says, "the labels are coming off."

"Please, Shirley, be a little quiet," my mother begs me.

In that place the whole street groans: Be quiet! Be quiet! but steals from the happy chorus of my inside self not a tittle or a jot.

There, too, but just around the corner, is a red brick building that has been old for many years. Every morning the children stand before it in double lines which must be straight. They are not insulted. They are waiting anyway.

I am usually among them. I am, in fact, the first, since I begin with "A."

One cold morning the monitor tapped me on the shoulder. "Go to Room 409, Shirley Abramowitz," he said. I did as I was told. I went in a hurry up a down staircase to Room 409, which contained sixth-graders. I had to wait at the desk without wiggling until Mr. Hilton, their teacher, had time to speak.

After five minutes he said, "Shirley?"

"What?" I whispered.

He said, "My! My! Shirley Abramowitz! They told me you had a particularly loud, clear voice and read with lots of expression. Could that be true?"

"Oh yes," I whispered.

"In that case, don't be silly; I might very well be your teacher someday. Speak up, speak up."

"Yes," I shouted.

"More like it," he said. "Now, Shirley, can you put a ribbon in your hair or a bobby pin? It's too messy."

"Yes!" I bawled.

"Now, now, calm down." He turned to the class. "Children, not a sound. Open at page 39. Read till 52. When you finish, start again." He looked me over once more. "Now, Shirley, you know, I suppose, that Christmas is coming. We are preparing a beautiful play. Most of the parts have been given out. But I still need a child with a strong voice, lots of stamina. Do you know what stamina is? You do? Smart kid. You know, I heard you read 'The Lord is my shepherd' in Assembly yesterday. I was very impressed. Wonderful delivery. Mrs. Jordan, your teacher, speaks highly of you. Now listen to me, Shirley Abramowitz, if you want to take the part and be in the play, repeat after me, 'I swear to work harder than I ever did before.'"

I looked to heaven and said at once, "Oh, I swear." I kissed my pinky and looked at God.

"That is an actor's life, my dear," he explained. "Like a soldier's, never tardy or disobedient to his general, the director. Everything," he said, "absolutely everything will depend on you."

That afternoon, all over the building, children scraped and scrubbed the turkeys and the sheaves of corn off the schoolroom windows. Goodbye Thanksgiving. The next morning a monitor brought red paper and green paper from the office. We made new shapes and hung them on the walls and glued them to the doors.

The teachers became happier and happier. Their heads were ringing like the bells of childhood. My best friend Evie was prone to evil, but she did not get a single demerit for whispering. We learned "Holy Night" without an error. "How wonderful!" said Miss Glacé, the student teacher. "To think that some of you don't even speak the language!" We learned "Deck the Halls" and "Hark! The Herald Angels" . . . They weren't ashamed and we weren't embarrassed.

Oh, but when my mother heard about it all, she said to my father: "Misha, you don't know what's going on there. Cramer is the head of the Tickets Committee."

"Who?" asked my father. "Cramer? Oh yes, an active woman."

"Active? Active has to have a reason. Listen," she said sadly, "I'm surprised to see my neighbors making tra-la-la for Christmas."

My father couldn't think of what to say to that. Then he decided: "You're in America! Clara, you wanted to come here. In Palestine the Arabs would be eating you alive. Europe you had pogroms. Argentina is full of Indians. Here you got Christmas. . . . Some joke, ha?"

"Very funny, Misha. What is becoming of you? If we came to a new country a long time ago to run away from tyrants, and instead we fall into a creeping pogrom, that our children learn a lot of lies, so what's the joke? Ach, Misha, your idealism is going away."

"So is your sense of humor."

"That I never had, but idealism you had a lot of."

"I'm the same Misha Abramovitch, I didn't change an iota. Ask anyone."

"Only ask me," says my mama, may she rest in peace. "I got the answer."

Meanwhile the neighbors had to think of what to say too.

Marty's father said: "You know, he has a very important part, my boy."

"Mine also," said Mr. Sauerfeld.

"Not my boy!" said Mrs. Klieg. "I said to him no. The answer is no. When I say no! I mean no!"

The rabbi's wife said, "It's disgusting!" But no one listened to her. Under the narrow sky of God's great wisdom she wore a strawberry-blond wig.

Every day was noisy and full of experience. I was Right-hand Man. Mr. Hilton said: "How could I get along without you, Shirley?"

He said: "Your mother and father ought to get down on their knees every night and thank God for giving them a child like you."

He also said: "You're absolutely a pleasure to work with, my dear, dear child."

Sometimes he said: "For God's sakes, what did I do with the script? Shirley! Shirley! Find it."

Then I answered quietly: "Here it is, Mr. Hilton."

Once in a while, when he was very tired, he would cry out: "Shirley, I'm just tired of screaming at those kids. Will you tell Ira Pushkov not to come in till Lester points to that star the second time?"

Then I roared: "Ira Pushkov, what's the matter with you? Dope! Mr. Hilton told you five times already, don't come in till Lester points to that star the second time."

"Ach, Clara," my father asked, "what does she do there till six o'clock she can't even put the plates on the table?"

"Christmas," said my mother coldly.

"Ho! Ho!" my father said. "Christmas. What's the harm? After all, history teaches everyone. We learn from reading this is a holiday from pagan times also, candles, lights, even Chanukah. So we learn it's not altogether Christian. So if they think it's a private holiday, they're only ignorant, not patriotic. What belongs to history, belongs to all men. You want to go back to the Middle Ages? Is it better to shave your head with a secondhand razor? Does it hurt Shirley to learn to speak up? It does not. So maybe someday she won't live between the kitchen and the shop. She's not a fool."

I thank you, Papa, for your kindness. It is true about me to this day. I am foolish but I am not a fool.

That night my father kissed me and said with great interest in my career, "Shirley, tomorrow's your big day. Congrats."

"Save it," my mother said. Then she shut all the windows in order to prevent tonsillitis.

In the morning it snowed. On the street corner a tree had been decorated for us by a kind city administration. In order to miss its chilly shadow our neighbors walked three blocks east to buy a loaf of bread. The butcher pulled down black window shades to keep the colored lights from shining on his chickens. Oh, not me. On the way to school, with both my hands I tossed it a kiss of tolerance. Poor thing, it was a stranger in Egypt.

I walked straight into the auditorium past the staring children. "Go ahead, Shirley!" said the monitors. Four boys, big for their age, had already started work as propmen and stagehands.

Mr. Hilton was very nervous. He was not even happy. Whatever he started to say ended in a sideward look of sadness. He sat slumped in the middle of the first row and asked me to help Miss Glacé. I did this, although she thought my voice too resonant and said, "Show-off!"

Parents began to arrive long before we were ready. They wanted to make a good impression. From among the yards of drapes I peeked out at the audience. I saw my embarrassed mother.

Ira, Lester, and Meyer were pasted to their beards by Miss Glacé. She almost forgot to thread the star on its wire, but I reminded her. I coughed a few times to clear my throat. Miss Glacé looked around and saw that everyone was in costume and on line waiting to play his part. She whispered, "All right . . . " Then:

Jackie Sauerfeld, the prettiest boy in first grade, parted the curtains with his skinny elbow and in a high voice sang out:

"Parents dear
We are here
To make a Christmas play in time.
It we give
In narrative
And illustrate with pantomime."

He disappeared.

My voice burst immediately from the wings to the great shock of Ira, Lester, and Meyer, who were waiting for it but were surprised all the same.

"I remember, I remember, the house where I was born . . . "

Miss Glacé yanked the curtain open and there it was, the house— an old hayloft, where Celia Kornbluh lay in the straw with Cindy Lou, her favorite doll. Ira, Lester, and Meyer moved slowly from the wings toward her, sometimes pointing to a moving star and sometimes ahead to Cindy Lou.

It was a long story and it was a sad story. I carefully pronounced all the words about my lonesome childhood, while little Eddie Braunstein wandered upstage and down with his shepherd's stick, looking for sheep. I brought up lonesomeness again, and not being understood at all except by some women everybody hated. Eddie was too small for that and Marty Groff took his place, wearing his father's prayer shawl. I announced twelve friends, and half the boys in the fourth grade gathered round Marty, who stood on an orange crate while my voice harangued. Sorrowful and loud, I declaimed about love and God and Man, but because of the terrible deceit of Abie Stock we came suddenly to a famous moment. Marty, whose remembering tongue I was, waited at the foot of the cross. He stared desperately at the audience. I groaned, "My God, my God, why hast thou forsaken me?" The soldiers who were sheiks grabbed poor Marty to pin him up to die, but he wrenched free, turned again to the audience, and spread his arms aloft to show despair and the end. I murmured at the top of my voice, "The rest is silence, but as everyone in this room, in this city—in this world—now knows, I shall have life eternal."

That night Mrs. Kornbluh visited our kitchen for a glass of tea.

"How's the virgin?" asked my father with a look of concern.

"For a man with a daughter, you got a fresh mouth, Abramovitch."

"Here," said my father kindly, "have some lemon, it'll sweeten your disposition."

They debated a little in Yiddish, then fell in a puddle of Russian and Polish. What I understood next was my father, who said, "Still and all, it was certainly a beautiful affair, you have to admit, introducing us to the beliefs of a different culture."

"Well, yes," said Mrs. Kornbluh. "The only thing . . . you know Charlie Turner—that cute boy in Celia's class—a couple others? They got very small parts or no part at all. In very bad taste, it seemed to me. After all, it's their religion."

"Ach," explained my mother, "what could Mr. Hilton do? They got very small voices; after all, why should they holler? The English language they know from the beginning by heart. They're blond like angels. You think it's so important they should get in the play? Christmas . . . the whole piece of goods . . . they own it."

I listened and listened until I couldn't listen any more. Too sleepy, I climbed out of bed and kneeled. I made a little church of my hands and said, "Hear, O Israel . . . " Then I called out in Yiddish, "Please, good night, good night. Ssh." My father said, "Ssh yourself," and slammed the kitchen door.

I was happy. I fell asleep at once. I had prayed for everybody: my talking family, cousins far away, passersby, and all the lonesome Christians. I expected to be heard. My voice was certainly the loudest.

Martin Bell

MARTIN BELL (B. 1937) IS AN EPISCOPAL PRIEST, singer, lecturer, story-teller, and former disc jockey. In addition to *The Way of the Wolf*, from which "Barrington Bunny" is taken, Bell has published three other collections of stories, poems, and songs. In "Barrington Bunny," Bell makes use of the device of the beast fable, a tale in which animals replace humans in order to give the reader a measure of detachment in reflecting on human behavior. "Barrington Bunny" is a story that can touch the child inside every adult. The story uses an indirect method to force us to ponder what the experience of a savior means in troubled times and situations. Readers of C. S. Lewis's *Chronicles of Narnia* will find the wolf in Bell's story reminiscent of Aslan, the lion king-protector of Narnia. The implications of the continuing presence of the divine in the midst of life—and death—is imaginatively expressed in a story that readers may find strangely moving.

Barrington Bunny

Once upon a time in a large forest there lived a very furry bunny. He had one lop ear, a tiny black nose, and unusually shiny eyes. His name was Barrington.

Barrington was not really a very handsome bunny. He was brown and speckled and his ears didn't stand up right. But he could hop, and he was, as I have said, very furry.

In a way, winter is fun for bunnies. After all, it gives them an opportunity to hop in the snow and then turn around to see where they have hopped. So, in a way, winter was fun for Barrington.

But in another way winter made Barrington sad. For, you see, winter marked the time when all of the animal families got together in their cozy homes to celebrate Christmas. He could hop, and he was very furry. But as far as Barrington knew, he was the only bunny in the forest.

When Christmas Eve finally came, Barrington did not feel like going home all by himself. So he decided that he would hop for awhile in the clearing in the center of the forest.

Hop. Hop. Hippity-hop. Barrington made tracks in the fresh snow.

Hop. Hop. Hippity-hop. Then he cocked his head and looked back at the wonderful designs he had made.

"Bunnies," he thought to himself, "can hop. And they are very warm, too, because of how furry they are."

(But Barrington didn't really know whether or not this was true of all bunnies, since he had never met another bunny.)

When it got too dark to see the tracks he was making, Barrington made up his mind to go home.

On his way, however, he passed a large oak tree. High in the branches there was a great deal of excited chattering going on. Barrington looked up. It was a squirrel family! What a marvelous time they seemed to be having.

"Hello, up there," called Barrington.

"Hello, down there," came the reply.

"Having a Christmas party?" asked Barrington.

"Oh, yes!" answered the squirrels. "It's Christmas Eve. Everybody is having a Christmas party!"

"May I come to your party?" said Barrington softly.

"Are you a squirrel?"

"No."

"What are you, then?"

"A bunny."

"A bunny?"

"Yes."

"Well, how can you come to the party if you're a bunny? Bunnies can't climb trees."

"That's true," said Barrington thoughtfully. "But I can hop and I'm very furry and warm."

"We're sorry," called the squirrels. "We don't know anything about hopping and being furry, but we do know that in order to come to our house you have to be able to climb trees."

"Oh, well," said Barrington. "Merry Christmas."

"Merry Christmas," chattered the squirrels.

And the unfortunate bunny hopped off toward his tiny house.

It was beginning to snow when Barrington reached the river. Near the river bank was a wonderfully constructed house of sticks and mud. Inside there was singing.

"It's the beavers," thought Barrington. "Maybe they will let me come to their party."

And so he knocked on the door.

"Who's out there?" called a voice.

"Barrington Bunny," he replied.

There was a long pause and then a shiny beaver head broke the water.

"Hello, Barrington," said the beaver.

"May I come to your Christmas party?" asked Barrington.

The beaver thought for awhile and then he said, "I suppose so. Do you know how to swim?"

"No," said Barrington, "but I can hop and I am very furry and warm."

"Sorry," said the beaver. "I don't know anything about hopping and being furry, but I do know that in order to come to our house you have to be able to swim."

"Oh, well," Barrington muttered, his eyes filling with tears. "I suppose that's true—Merry Christmas."

"Merry Christmas," called the beaver. And he disappeared beneath the surface of the water.

Even being as furry as he was, Barrington was beginning to get cold. And the snow was falling so hard that his tiny, bunny eyes could scarcely see what was ahead of him.

He was almost home, however, when he heard the excited squeaking of field mice beneath the ground.

"It's a party," thought Barrington. And suddenly he blurted out through his tears, "Hello, field mice. This is Barrington Bunny. May I come to your party?"

But the wind was howling so loudly and Barrington was sobbing so much that no one heard him.

And when there was no response at all, Barrington just sat down in the snow and began to cry with all his might.

"Bunnies," he thought, "aren't any good to anyone. What good is it to be furry and to be able to hop if you don't have any family on Christmas Eve?"

Barrington cried and cried. When he stopped crying he began to bite on his bunny's foot, but he did not move from where he was sitting in the snow.

Suddenly, Barrington was aware that he was not alone. He looked up and strained his shiny eyes to see who was there.

To his surprise he saw a great silver wolf. The wolf was large and strong and his eyes flashed fire. He was the most beautiful animal Barrington had ever seen.

For a long time the silver wolf didn't say anything at all. He just stood there and looked at Barrington with those terrible eyes.

Then slowly and deliberately the wolf spoke, "Barrington," he asked in a gentle voice, "why are you sitting in the snow?"

"Because it's Christmas Eve," said Barrington, "and I don't have any family, and bunnies aren't any good to anyone."

"Bunnies are, too, good," said the wolf. "Bunnies can hop and they are very warm."

"What good is that?" Barrington sniffed.

"It is very good indeed," the wolf went on, "because it is a gift that bunnies are given, a free gift with no strings attached. And every gift that is given to anyone is given for a reason. Someday you will see why it is good to hop and to be warm and furry."

"But it's Christmas," moaned Barrington, "and I'm all alone. I don't have any family at all."

"Of course you do," replied the great silver wolf. "All of the animals in the forest are your family."

And then the wolf disappeared. He simply wasn't there. Barrington had only blinked his eyes, and when he looked—the wolf was gone.

"All of the animals in the forest are my family," thought Barrington. "It's good to be a bunny. Bunnies can hop. That's a gift." And then he said it again. "A gift. A free gift."

On into the night Barrington worked. First he found the best stick that he could. (And that was difficult because of the snow.)

Then hop. Hop. Hippity-hop. To beaver's house. He left the stick just outside the door. With a note on it that read: "Here is a good stick for your house. It is a gift. A free gift. No strings attached. Signed, a member of your family."

"It is a good thing that I can hop," he thought, "because the snow is very deep."

Then Barrington dug and dug. Soon he had gathered together enough dead leaves and grass to make the squirrels' nest warmer. Hop. Hop. Hippity-hop.

He laid the grass and leaves just under the large oak tree and attached this message: "A gift. A free gift. From a member of your family."

It was late when Barrington finally started home. And what made things worse was that he knew a blizzard was beginning.

Hop. Hop. Hippity-hop.

Soon poor Barrington was lost. The wind howled furiously, and it was very, very cold. "It certainly is cold," he said out loud. "It's a good thing I'm so furry. But if I don't find my way home pretty soon even I might freeze!"

Squeak. Squeak. . . .

And then he saw it—a baby field mouse lost in the snow. And the little mouse was crying.

"Hello, little mouse," Barrington called.

"Don't cry. I'll be right there." Hippity-hop, and Barrington was beside the tiny mouse.

"I'm lost," sobbed the little fellow. "I'll never find my way home, and I know I'm going to freeze."

"You won't freeze," said Barrington. "I'm a bunny and bunnies are very furry and warm. You stay right where you are and I'll cover you up."

Barrington lay on top of the little mouse and hugged him tight. The tiny fellow felt himself surrounded by warm fur. He cried for awhile but soon, snug and warm, he fell asleep.

Barrington had only two thoughts that long, cold night. First he thought, "It's good to be a bunny. Bunnies are very furry and warm." And then, when he felt the heart of the tiny mouse beneath him beating regularly, he thought, "All of the animals in the forest are my family."

Next morning, the field mice found their little boy, asleep in the snow, warm and snug beneath the furry carcass of a dead bunny. Their relief and excitement was so great that they didn't even think to question where the bunny had come from.

And as for the beavers and the squirrels, they still wonder which member of their family left the little gifts for them that Christmas Eve.

After the field mice had left, Barrington's frozen body simply lay in the snow. There was no sound except that of the howling wind. And no one anywhere in the forest noticed the great silver wolf who came to stand beside that brown, lop-eared carcass.

> But the wolf did come.
> And he stood there.
> Without moving or saying a word.
> All Christmas Day.
> Until it was night.
> And then he disappeared into the forest.

John Irving

AMERICAN NOVELIST JOHN IRVING (B. 1942) WROTE SIX NOVELS, including the best-selling *The World According to Garp* and *The Hotel New Hampshire*, before writing *A Prayer for Owen Meany* (1989). Irving blends the ironic, the grotesque, and the comic in spellbinding plots. In *A Prayer for Owen Meany*, Owen Meany is, if not actually a contemporary Christ, certainly a figure for whom the comparison is more than coincidental. Owen is an unusually small child with an extraordinary voice, which is recorded in all capitals. In this excerpt, the novel's narrator—Owen's best friend John Wheelwright—tells how Owen becomes the pageant Christ Child in what turns out to be one of the funniest Christmas pageant rehearsal scenes in literature.

The Christmas Pageant Rehearsal Scene from *A Prayer for Owen Meany*—The Little Lord Jesus

(excerpt)

It was bad enough, Owen maintained, that he was subject to seasonal ridicule for the role he played in the Christ Church Christmas Pageant. "JUST YOU WAIT," he said darkly to me. "THE WIGGINS ARE *NOT* GOING TO MAKE ME THE STUPID ANGEL AGAIN!"

It would be my first Christmas pageant, since I was usually in Sawyer Depot for the last Sunday before Christmas; but Owen repeatedly complained that he was *always* cast as the Announcing Angel—a role forced upon him by the Rev. Captain Wiggin and his stewardess wife, Barbara, who maintained that there was "no one cuter" for the part than Owen, whose chore it was to *descend*— in a "pillar of light" (with the substantial assistance of a cranelike apparatus to which he was attached, with wires, like a puppet). Owen was supposed to *announce* the wondrous new presence that lay in the manger in Bethlehem, all the while flapping his arms (to draw attention to the giant wings glued to his choir robe, and to attempt to quiet the giggles of the congregation).

Every year, a grim group of shepherds huddled at the communion railing and displayed their cowardice to God's Holy Messenger; a motley crew, they tripped on their robes and knocked off each other's turbans and false beards with their staffs and shepherding crooks. Barb Wiggin had difficulty locating them in the "pillar of light," while simultaneously illuminating the Descending Angel, Owen Meany.

Reading from Luke, the rector said, "'And in that region there were shepherds out in the field, keeping watch over their flock by night. And an angel of the Lord appeared to them, and the glory of the Lord shone around them, and they were filled with *fear.*'" Whereupon, Mr. Wiggin paused for the full effect of the shepherds cringing at the sight of Owen struggling to get his feet on the floor—Barb Wiggin operated the creaky apparatus that *lowered* Owen, too, placing him dangerously near the lit candles that simulated the campfires around which the shepherds watched their flock.

"'BE NOT AFRAID,'" Owen announced, while still struggling in the air; "'FOR BEHOLD, I BRING YOU GOOD NEWS OF A GREAT JOY WHICH WILL COME TO ALL THE PEOPLE; FOR TO YOU IS BORN THIS DAY IN THE CITY OF DAVID A SAVIOR, WHO IS CHRIST THE LORD. AND THIS WILL BE A SIGN FOR YOU: YOU WILL FIND A BABE WRAPPED IN SWADDLING CLOTHES AND LYING IN A MANGER.'" Whereupon, the dazzling, if jerky, "pillar of light" flashed, like lightning, or perhaps Christ Church suffered an electrical surge, and Owen was raised into darkness—sometimes, *yanked* into darkness; and once, so quickly that one of his wings was torn from his back and fell among the confused shepherds.

The worst of it was that Owen had to remain in the air for the rest of the pageant—there being no method of lowering him *out* of the light. If he was to be concealed in darkness, he had to stay suspended from the wires—above the babe lying in the manger, above the clumsy, nodding donkeys, the stumbling shepherds, and the unbalanced kings staggering under the weight of their crowns.

An additional evil, Owen claimed, was that whoever played Joseph was always smirking—as if Joseph had anything to smirk about. "WHAT DOES JOSEPH HAVE TO DO WITH ANY OF IT?" Owen asked crossly. "I SUPPOSE HE HAS TO STAND AROUND THE MANGER, BUT HE SHOULDN'T *SMIRK!*" And always the prettiest girl got to play Mary. "WHAT DOES

PRETTY HAVE TO DO WITH IT?" Owen asked. "WHO SAYS MARY WAS PRETTY?"

And the individual touches that the Wiggins brought to the Christmas Pageant reduced Owen to incoherent fuming—for example, the smaller children disguised as turtledoves. The costumes were so absurd that no one knew what these children were supposed to be; they resembled science-fiction angels, spectacular life-forms from another galaxy, as if the Wiggins had decided that the Holy Nativity had been attended by beings from faraway planets (or should have been so attended). "NOBODY KNOWS WHAT THE STUPID TURTLEDOVES ARE!" Owen complained.

As for the Christ Child himself, Owen was outraged. The Wiggins insisted that the Baby Jesus not shed a tear, and in this pursuit they were relentless in gathering dozens of babies backstage; they substituted babies so freely that the Christ Child was whisked from the manger at the first unholy croak or gurgle—instantly replaced by a mute baby, or at least a stuporous one. For this chore of supplying a fresh, silent baby to the manger—in an instant—an extended line of ominous-looking grown-ups reached into the shadows beyond the pulpit, behind the purple-and-maroon curtains, under the cross. These large and sure-handed adults, deft at baby-handling, or at least certain not to drop a quickly moving Christ Child, were strangely out of place at the Nativity. Were they kings or shepherds—and why were they so much bigger than the other kings and shepherds, if not exactly larger than life? Their costumes were childish, although some of their beards were real, and they appeared less to relish the spirit of Christmas than they seemed resigned to their task—like a bucket brigade of volunteer firemen.

Backstage, the mothers fretted; the competition for the most properly behaved Christ Child was keen. Every Christmas, in addition to the Baby Jesus, the Wiggins' pageant gave birth to many new members of that most monstrous sorority: stage mothers. I told Owen that perhaps he was better off to be "above" these proceedings, but Owen hinted that I and other members of our Sunday school class were at least partially responsible for his humiliating elevation—for hadn't *we* been the first to lift Owen into the air? Mrs. Walker, Owen suggested, might have given Barb Wiggin the idea of using Owen as the airborne angel.

It's no wonder that Owen was not tickled by Dan's notion of casting him as Tiny Tim. "WHEN I SAY, 'BE NOT AFRAID; FOR BEHOLD, I BRING YOU GOOD NEWS,' ALL THE BABIES CRY AND EVERYONE ELSE LAUGHS. WHAT DO YOU THINK THEY'LL DO IF I SAY, 'GOD BLESS US, EVERY ONE!'?"

It was his voice, of course; he could have said, "HERE COMES THE END OF THE WORLD!" People still would have fallen down, laughing. It was torture to Owen that he was without much humor—he was *only* serious—while at the same time he had a chiefly comic effect on the multitude.

No wonder he commenced worrying about the Christmas Pageant as early as the end of November, for in the service bulletin of the Last Sunday After Pentecost there was already an announcement, "How to Participate in the Christmas Pageant." The first rehearsal was scheduled after the Annual Parish Meeting and the Vestry elections—almost at the beginning of our Christmas vacation. "What would you like to be?" the sappy bulletin asked. "We need kings, angels, shepherds, donkeys, turtledoves, Mary, Joseph, babies, *and more!*"

"'FATHER, FORGIVE THEM; FOR THEY KNOW NOT WHAT THEY DO,'" Owen said.

❦   ❦   ❦   ❦

It was a pity that Owen could not escape the Rev. Dudley Wiggin's Christmas Pageant. The first rehearsal, in the nave of the church, was held on the Second Sunday of Advent and followed a celebration of the Holy Eucharist. We were delayed discussing our roles because the Women's Association Report preceded us; the women wished to say that the Quiet Day they had scheduled for the beginning of Advent had been very successful—that the meditations, and the following period of quiet, for reflection, had been well received. Mrs. Walker, whose own term as a Vestry member was expiring—thus giving her even more energy for her Sunday school tyrannies—complained that attendance at the adult evening Bible study was flagging.

"Well, everyone's so busy at Christmas, you know," said Barb Wiggin, who was impatient to begin the casting of the pageant—not wanting to keep us potential donkeys and turtledoves waiting. I could sense Owen's irritation with Barb Wiggin, in advance.

Quite blind to his animosity, Barb Wiggin began—as, indeed, the holy event itself had begun—with the Announcing Angel. "Well, we all know who our Descending Angel is," she told us.

"NOT ME," Owen said.

"Why, Owen!" Barb Wiggin said.

"PUT SOMEONE ELSE UP IN THE AIR," Owen said. "MAYBE THE SHEPHERDS CAN JUST STARE AT THE 'PILLAR OF LIGHT.' THE BIBLE SAYS THE ANGEL OF THE LORD APPEARED TO THE SHEPHERDS—NOT TO THE WHOLE CONGREGATION. AND USE SOMEONE WITH A VOICE EVERYONE DOESN'T LAUGH AT," he said, pausing while everyone laughed.

"But Owen—" Barb Wiggin said.

"No, no, Barbara," Mr. Wiggin said. "If Owen's tired of being the angel, we should respect his wishes—this is a democracy," he added unconvincingly. The former stewardess glared at her ex-pilot husband as if he had been speaking, and thinking, in the absence of sufficient oxygen.

"AND ANOTHER THING," Owen said. "JOSEPH SHOULD NOT SMIRK."

"Indeed not!" the rector said heartily. "I had no idea we'd suffered a smirking Joseph all these years."

"And who do you think would be a good Joseph, Owen?" Barb Wiggin asked, without the conventional friendliness of the stewardess.

Owen pointed to me; to be singled out so silently, with Owen's customary authority, made the hairs stand up on the back of my neck—in later years, I would think I had been chosen by the Chosen One. But that Second Sunday of Advent, in the nave of Christ Church, I felt angry with Owen—once the hairs on the back of my neck relaxed. For what an uninspiring role it is; to be Joseph—that hapless follower, that stand-in, that guy along for the ride.

"We *usually* pick Mary first," Barb Wiggin said. "Then we let Mary pick her Joseph."

"Oh," the Rev. Dudley Wiggin said. "Well, this year we can let Joseph pick *his* Mary! We mustn't be afraid to change!" he added cordially, but his wife ignored him.

"We usually begin with the angel," Barb Wiggin said. "We still don't have an angel. Here we are with a Joseph before a Mary, and no angel," she said. (Stewardesses are orderly people, much comforted by following a familiar routine.)

"Well, who would like to hang in the air this year?" the rector asked. "Tell them about the view from up there, Owen."

"SOMETIMES THE CONTRAPTION THAT HOLDS YOU IN THE AIR HAS YOU FACING THE WRONG WAY," he warned the would-be angels. "SOMETIMES THE HARNESS CUTS INTO YOUR SKIN."

"I'm sure we can remedy that, Owen," the rector said.

"WHEN YOU GO UP OUT OF THE 'PILLAR OF LIGHT,' IT'S *VERY* DARK UP THERE," Owen said.

No would-be angel raised his or her hand.

"AND IT'S QUITE A LONG SPEECH THAT YOU HAVE TO MEMORIZE," Owen added. "YOU KNOW, 'BE NOT AFRAID; FOR BEHOLD, I BRING YOU GOOD NEWS OF A GREAT JOY . . . FOR TO YOU IS BORN . . . IN THE CITY OF DAVID A SAVIOR, WHO IS CHRIST THE LORD' . . . "

"We know, Owen, we know," Barb Wiggin said.

"IT'S NOT EASY," Owen said.

"Perhaps we should pick our Mary, and come back to the angel?" the Rev. Mr. Wiggin asked.

Barb Wiggin wrung her hands.

But if they thought I was enough of a fool to choose *my* Mary, they had another think coming; what a no-win situation that was—

choosing Mary. For what would everyone say about me and the girl I chose? And what would the girls I *didn't* choose think of me?

"MARY BETH BAIRD HAS NEVER BEEN MARY," Owen said. "THAT WAY, MARY WOULD BE MARY."

"*Joseph* chooses Mary!" Barb Wiggin said.

"IT WAS JUST A SUGGESTION," Owen said.

But how could the role be denied Mary Beth Baird now that it had been offered? Mary Beth Baird was a wholesome lump of a girl, shy and clumsy and plain.

"I've been a turtledove three times," she mumbled.

"THAT'S ANOTHER THING," Owen said, "NOBODY KNOWS WHAT THE TURTLEDOVES *ARE*."

"Now, now—one thing at a time," Dudley Wiggin said.

"First, *Joseph*—choose Mary!" Barb Wiggin said.

"Mary Beth Baird would be fine," I said.

"Well, so Mary is Mary!" Mr. Wiggin said. Mary Beth Baird covered her face in her hands. Barb Wiggin also covered her face.

"Now, what's this about the turtledoves, Owen?" the rector asked. "*Hold* the turtledoves!" Barb Wiggin snapped. "I want an angel."

Former kings and shepherds sat in silence; former donkeys did not come forth—and donkeys came in two parts; the hind part of the donkey never got to see the pageant. Even the former hind parts of donkeys did not volunteer to be the angel. Even former turtledoves were not stirred to grab the part.

"The angel is *so* important," the rector said. "There's a special apparatus just to raise and lower you, and—for a while—you occupy the 'pillar of light' all by yourself. All eyes are on *you!*"

The children of Christ Church did not appear enticed to play the angel by the thought of all eyes being on them. In the rear of the nave, rendered even more insignificant than usual by his proximity to the giant painting of "The Call of the Twelve," pudgy Harold Crosby sat diminished by the depiction of Jesus appointing his disciples; all eyes rarely feasted on fat Harold Crosby, who was not grotesque enough to be teased—or even noticed—but who was enough of a slob to be rejected whenever he caused the slightest attention to be drawn to himself. Therefore, Harold Crosby abstained. He sat in the back; he stood at the rear of the line; he spoke only when spoken to; he desired to be left alone, and—for the most part—he was. For several years, he had played a perfect hind part of a donkey; I'm sure it was the only role he wanted. I could see he was nervous about the silence that greeted the Rev. Mr. Wiggin's request for an angel; possibly the towering portraits of the disciples in his immediate vicinity made Harold Crosby feel inadequate, or else he feared that—in the absence of volunteers—the rector would select an angel from among the cowardly children, and (God forbid) what if Mr. Wiggin chose *him?*

Harold Crosby tipped back in his chair and shut his eyes; it was either a method of concealment borrowed from the ostrich, or else Harold imagined that if he appeared to be asleep, no one would ask him to be more than the hind part of a donkey.

"Someone *has* to be the angel," Barb Wiggin said menacingly. Then Harold Crosby fell over backward in his chair; he made it worse by attempting to catch his balance—by grabbing the frame of the huge painting of "The Call of the Twelve"; then he thought better of crushing himself under Christ's disciples and he allowed himself to fall freely. Like most things that happened to Harold Crosby, his fall was more astonishing for its awkwardness than for anything intrinsically spectacular. Regardless, only the rector was insensitive enough to mistake Harold Crosby's clumsiness for volunteering.

"Good for you, Harold!" the rector said. "There's a brave boy!"

"What?" Harold Crosby said.

"Now we have our angel," Mr. Wiggin said cheerfully. "What's next?"

"I'm afraid of heights," said Harold Crosby.

"All the braver of you!" the rector replied. "There's no time like the present for facing our fears."

"But the crane," Barb Wiggin said to her husband. "The apparatus—" she started to say, but the rector silenced her with an admonishing wave of his hand. Surely you're not going to make the poor boy feel self-conscious about his *weight*, the rector's glance toward his wife implied; surely the wires and the harness are strong enough. Barb Wiggin glowered back at her husband.

"ABOUT THE TURTLEDOVES," Owen said, and Barb Wiggin shut her eyes; she did not lean back in her chair, but she gripped the seat with both hands.

"Ah, yes, Owen, what was it about the turtledoves?" the Rev. Mr. Wiggin asked.

"THEY LOOK LIKE THEY'RE FROM OUTER SPACE," Owen said. "NO ONE KNOWS WHAT THEY'RE SUPPOSED TO BE."

"They're *doves!*" Barb Wiggin said. "Everyone knows what doves are!"

"THEY'RE *GIANT* DOVES," Owen said. "THEY'RE AS BIG AS HALF A DONKEY. WHAT KIND OF BIRD IS THAT? A BIRD FROM MARS? THEY'RE ACTUALLY KIND OF FRIGHTENING."

"Not everyone can be a king or a shepherd or a donkey, Owen," the rector said.

"BUT NOBODY'S SMALL ENOUGH TO BE A DOVE," Owen said. "AND NOBODY KNOWS WHAT ALL THOSE PAPER STREAMERS ARE SUPPOSED TO BE."

"They're *feathers!*" Barb Wiggin shouted.

"THE TURTLEDOVES LOOK LIKE *CREATURES*," Owen said. "LIKE THEY'VE BEEN ELECTROCUTED."

"Well, I suppose there were other animals in the manger," the rector said.

"Are *you* going to make the costumes?" Barb Wiggin asked him.

"Now now," Mr. Wiggin said.

"COWS GO WELL WITH DONKEYS," Owen suggested.

"Cows?" the rector said. "Well well."

"Who's going to make the cow costumes?" Barb Wiggin asked.

"*I* will!" Mary Beth Baird said. She had never volunteered for anything before; clearly her election as the Virgin Mary had energized her—had made her believe she was capable of miracles, or at least cow costumes.

"Good for you, Mary!" the rector said.

But Barb Wiggin and Harold Crosby closed their eyes; Harold did not look well—he seemed to be suppressing vomit, and his face took on the lime-green shade of the grass at the feet of Christ's disciples, who loomed over him.

"THERE'S ONE MORE THING," said Owen Meany. We gave him our attention. "THE CHRIST CHILD," he said, and we children nodded our approval.

"What's wrong with the Christ Child?" Barb Wiggin asked.

"ALL THOSE BABIES," Owen said. "JUST TO GET ONE TO LIE IN THE MANGER WITHOUT CRYING—DO WE HAVE TO HAVE ALL THOSE BABIES?"

"But it's like the song says, Owen," the rector told him. "'Little Lord Jesus, no crying he makes.'"

"OKAY, OKAY," Owen said. "BUT ALL THOSE BABIES— YOU CAN HEAR *THEM* CRYING. EVEN OFFSTAGE, YOU CAN HEAR THEM. AND ALL THOSE GROWN-UPS!" he said. "ALL THOSE BIG MEN PASSING THE BABIES IN AND OUT. THEY'RE SO *BIG*—THEY LOOK RIDICULOUS. THEY MAKE *US* LOOK RIDICULOUS."

"You know a baby who won't cry, Owen?" Barb Wiggin asked him—and, of course, she knew as soon as she spoke . . . how he had trapped her.

"I KNOW SOMEONE WHO CAN FIT IN THE CRIB," Owen said. "SOMEONE SMALL ENOUGH TO *LOOK* LIKE A BABY," he said. "SOMEONE OLD ENOUGH NOT TO CRY."

Mary Beth Baird could not contain herself! "*Owen* can be the Baby Jesus!" she yelled. Owen Meany smiled and shrugged.

"I *CAN* FIT IN THE CRIB," he said modestly.

Harold Crosby could no longer contain himself, either; he vomited. He vomited often enough for it to pass almost unnoticed, especially now that Owen had our undivided attention.

"And what's more, we can *lift* him!" Mary Beth Baird said excitedly.

"There was never any lifting of the Christ Child before!" Barb Wiggin said.

"Well, I mean, if we *have* to, if we feel like it," Mary Beth said.

"WELL, IF EVERYONE WANTS ME TO DO IT, I SUPPOSE I COULD," Owen said.

"Yes!" cried the kings and shepherds.

"Let Owen do it!" said the donkeys and the cows—the former turtledoves.

It was quite a popular decision, but Barb Wiggin looked at Owen as if she were revising her opinion of how "cute" he was, and the rector observed Owen with a detachment that was wholly out of character for an ex-pilot. The Rev. Mr. Wiggin, such a veteran of Christmas pageants, looked at Owen Meany with profound respect—as if he'd seen the Christ Child come and go, but never before had he encountered a little Lord Jesus who was so perfect for the part.

Lee Smith

LEE SMITH (B. 1944) IS UNDOUBTEDLY ONE OF THE FINEST contemporary Southern writers of fiction. Her characters and scenes have been compared to those of Flannery O'Connor and Eudora Welty. Like those authors, Smith has a fine ear for the cadences of Southern speech and an astute eye for the details of Southern life—comic, poignant, and occasionally grotesque.

Fair and Tender Ladies, an epistolary novel, consists of letters written by the spunky, vivacious Ivy Rowe. In addition to glimpsing the life and insights of an unforgettable character, we see reflected through Ivy's letters a microcosm of rural Southern mountain life. In this excerpt, the twelve-year-old Ivy describes to her teacher how Christmas was celebrated at Sugar Fork. There is an implicit ironic contrast between Ivy's enthusiastic enjoyment of a simple Christmas and the elaborate celebrations that most of us find essential to a happy holiday.

Fair and Tender Ladies
(excerpt)

Dear Mrs. Brown,

I am writing to thank you for the meal and the flour and coffee and the beans you have sent us, Green Patterson come up here with them, he says Mister Brown has payed to send them from Stoney Branhams store. We are so thankful to have them. Things is better up here now as I will relate.

To anser your questin, yes we did have Christmas it is different we do not have a tree here nor have ever seed one. Oakley Fox said you and Mister Brown have made a tree and hanged it with play-prettys I wuld admire to see it so. On December 25 they is not a thing happening as a rule but on Old Christmas Eve that is Janury 5 this is when Gaynelle and Virgie Cline comes over and tells storys all nigt with Daddy as they did it when Daddy was young, this is Christmas to us.

So to anser your questin, on December 25 they was not a thing happening up here on Sugar Fork nor even down at Home Creek but that folks drinks likker and shoots off ther guns, I do not mean us we have got no likker here now but Ethel and me shot the gun. It was fun you culd hear them bang like thunder up and down the Fork and clear down on Home Creek. Ethel and me was out in the snow I was wearing Daddys coat and his old black hat, Momma says he will never wear them agin.

It had froze all the previous nigt so when I walked out ther Mrs. Brown, it was so pretty that it like to have took my breth away. Ice just shining on each and evry limb of evry tree and isickles thick as your arm hanging down offen the house. It was like I looked out on the whole world and I culd see for miles, off down the mountain here, but it was new. The whole world was new, and it was like I was the onliest person that had ever looked upon it, and it was mine. It belonged to me.

Now it is new for me to feel this as I have not had hardly ever a thing of my own, it is handmedowns and pitching in and sharing everything up here on Sugar Fork, they is so many of us up here as you know. But I looked out over all them hills, and the land was sloped so diffrent, from the snow. And evry tree was glittering, and Sugar Fork black and singing along mostly under the ice. The snow come plum up to my knees. Nobody else had got up yet and I reckon I was the onliest one in the world. My breth hung like clouds in the air and the sun come up then, it liked to have blinded me. Well now this is the time I know Mrs. Brown when you pray, but to anser your questin if I pray, I can not. So I know I am evil but I do not feel evil.

And this is what happend next.

I heerd them guns popping all threw the hills and then I knowed it was Christmas wich I had clean forgot. All the rest of them was sleeping in the house. ETHEL I hollered, and direckly she come, wearing Daddys dead mommas old coat, she looked so funny I liked to of died. Get the gun I hollered, and whilst she was doing it I layed rigt down in the snow and made angels, I must of made a thousand angels but I never got wet, that snow was as dry as powder. Lord it was a pretty pretty day. Then I stands up and brushes off Daddys coat real good and drawed in my breth real good, it was like I was brething champane.

And I says, I am the Ice Queen, rigt out loud. I felt so good.

Then Ethel come running out with the guns and we fired them, I love that blue smoke and the way they smell. Well this woken everbody up a course and they flung open the door and all come running out hollering even Beulah who is big now and little Danny he is sick was laghing and crying at once.

And then do you know what happend next?

Our Momma tied back her hair and smiled and popped popcorn on the fire, did you ever hear the like of popping corn for breakfast? It beat all. So now that was what happend on the morning of Dec. 25, and next I will tell you of what follered which is so strange I cannot credit it yet at all.

It was along about evening and Ethel and Garnie and me was all gathered up close around the fire trying to get dryed out, we had done gone all the way down to Home Creek and slid on the ice with the neghbor people, the Conaways and the Rolettes and the Foxes, they was all out there sliding, and Delphi Rolette he was playing the fool, he brung a little old rocky chair out there and took to pushing all the littluns on the ice. One time his old woman Reva Rolette come out from there crying and twisting her hands and says oh Delphi come on back to the house, you know you are crazy drunk you are going to hell for sartin. But Mister Delphi Rolette he laghs a great big lagh and pushes little old Dreama Fox, the leastest one of them Foxes, around on the ice. I have heerd tell how Mister Delphi Rolette is so bad to drink, but you cannot tell it, I think he is nice but his old woman is touched for sure. She is crazy religios too, Oakley Fox says she talks out of her head and will swaller her tonge iffen the rest of them does not hold her down and grab it. She is a big large fleshy woman and real religios so they say. And Oakley Fox is telling me all of this. Then he says, come up to the house now, my momma says to bring you all up there afore you set off for home. Now Oakleys momma Edith Fox is real sligt and ashy-pale, her hair is as ligt as Silvaneys. Oh honey, she says to me, how are you keeping? Shes not as big as a minit, Edith Fox. And then she just up and kisses me, which set me off crying, I cant say for why thogh. It is like Oakleys momma is little and soft and sweet but my momma is hard as a rocky-clift, and her eyes burns out in her head.

Looky here younguns, Oakleys momma says, and she given us a hunk of apple stack-cake apiece it was the bestest thing I have put in my mouth so far. And Oakley and Dreama and Ray get stack-cake whenever they want it I reckon, ther daddy lives in a camp at Coeburn he has got a big job in the lumber mills ther and dont come home of a week. Ethel and me says no thank you mam after one hunk but that little old Garnie just eats and eats, I dont reckon hes ever had such as that before. Dreama and Ray is spoilt I think but Oakley is real nice in fact he is TOO nice, I gess I am like Daddy and hate to be beholden for ary a thing. Oakley has freckles and a big smile like his mommas I cannot smile back, insted I want to hit him, I can not tell why.

So we make our manners and clumb up Sugar Fork, it was coming on for dark then and all the shadders was blue. We cross Sugar Fork one, two times on the crackly ice, and then we come walking up the lastest rise, me and Ethel pulling Garnie by the hands atwixt us, and him just fussing, and then we can see the house sticking up there outen the snow with smoke rising from the chimbly and snow on the roofshakes and isickles hanging down offen the roof. The cedars looks so diffrent all bowed down with snow, and blue shadders underneath coming creepen up towards the house. Law, it looked like a picture book!

This here is Christmas, I says to Garnie and Ethel, now you all mark it.

And when we come in, my hands was too froze to work good. Did you all have a good time? Momma axed us and we said, Yesm. Her and Beulah was carding wool by the fire and Daddy was sound asleep on his pallet rigt there. You could hear his breth all around it is like a rattle way down inside him. Silvaney was looking out the winder she can look for hours and hours at the snow it is like she has never seed any such thing, she takes on so about the snow. So I go over and look out with her.

It was coming on for dark real fast then, everthing was blue and gray and white and silver, it did not look like Sugar Fork no more it looked like Fairyland out ther as nigt come on. Then the air growed as thick and as dark as the waters of that big swimming hole down on the Levisa River where Daddy taken us oncet, and when we looked out the winder it was like looking down in that swimming hole where we culd see the forms of the silver trout-fish go flashing by way down so deep in the water that you culdnt exackly see them, you just thoght you culd. Well looking out the winder was like that, I thoght I culd almost see things or the shapes of things, moving behind the dark behind the cold thick air. Silvaney and me held hands.

I know I am telling to much Mrs. Brown, it may not be approprite nether.

But this come next, you will not belive it!

We was looking out real quiet at the snow, and Momma and Beulah was carding the wool and Ethel and Garnie asleep on the floor, you culdnt hear a thing but the crackling fire and a pop ever now and then if a isickle cracked offen the roof, when all of a sudden they comes the loudest whistle you ever heerd, rigt up close to the house.

So Silvaney commences to blubbering and runs and gets down in the bed. Beulah throws down her wool and comes over ther to look out but it is dark now, you cant see nothing.

Then we hear that whistle agin, real loud and real close to the house. It dont sound like anything I ever heerd, it sounds like a screech owl but it aint a screech owl, it sounds like a shreeking hant.

Lord Lord, my momma says. I look back at her and in the fires red ligt she looks almost pretty, I swear her face is diffrent all of a sudden, she touches her hair with a hand that shakes like a moth flying.

Well that set me back some, I will tell you.

But then I looked over at Daddy, and Lord it was the biggest suprise I had seed yet. Daddy set rigt up in the bed and throwed Granny Rowes quilt rigt down on the floor and swang his legs around like he was fixing to stand up, like he was a man that culd get up outen the bed.

While now outside, this whistling has switched to a tune, they never was a bird that culd whistle as good as that.

What is it, what is it? axes Beulah and me.

Lord Lord, is all Momma says.

Then they comes a loud pounding on the door, and then Daddy turns and grins the biggest grin and I recollected all of a sudden how he used to look, how he used to be such a handsome man, and what all he used to do. He keeps on grinning.

It is Revel, is what he says.

Well let him in girls, he said then, and I run to open the door and sure enough it is our uncle Revel that we have not seed for years, not since I was a little girl and him and Daddy fell out so bad. Revel lets out a big whoop and a holler and comes rigt on in and gives Daddy a hug. John Arthur, he says, and Daddy says, Revel. Then they look at each other for a long time and then Revel goes over and says Maude, how are you? to Momma who is trying to stay mad, but she cant do no good with that. Well shut the door then Revel, your letting out all the heat, Momma says, and he done so. And all the time, uncle Revel's big black dog is wagging hisself all over the house and licking at people and jumping up. Ethel wakes up scarred to death and crying and so does Garnie.

You hush now, Momma says, this is your uncle Revel, that you have heerd tell of, and then Revel says <u>Sit</u> to his dog and it does. This dog is named Charly, we come to learn. It minds the best and is the smartest of any dog I ever seed, Ill say that. Charly goes everwhere with uncle Revel.

And now I will tell you of uncle Revel hisself and what he looks like, he wears a big black hat like a cowboy hat and black boots and a long dark coat, he has a black beard and a mustashe and kind of pale silver eyes but he is not as scarry looking as this sounds. No, but Revels eyes is just jumping, just full of fire and foolishness. When he smiles, his teeth is like a slash of white in his face. His lips is as red and full as a pretty womans. Well then he goes out, and then he comes back in with a poke, and then we see he has brung us jawbreaker candy from town, and even Silvaney comes creepen down outen the loft to get hern, and uncle Revel looks at her and says, Lovely. He has brung whisky to drink and his banjer to play, he sings like a man on the radio. Mrs. Brown, you have never heerd such-like in all your life. And Daddy is setting up now and he axes for his guitar and Momma gets it but he cant do nothing except just pluck at it a little bit, Momma lays it there alongside of him on his pallet by the fire. Uncle Revel sings a bunch of funny songs. Now I have heerd tell all my life how uncle Revel cannot keep his hands off the women nor stay outen truble but what I think is, he is just a natural antic, he gets us all to laghing so hard we cant hardly stop. We sing oh I <u>will</u> go to meeting, I <u>will</u> go to meeting, I <u>will</u> go to meeting in a old tin pan. We sing Bile Them Cabbage Down and other tunes.

One time Revel looks at Momma and jerks his head at me and says, Thats the one Maude, she takes after you shel be truble all rigt, shel be wild as a buck like you, just wait and see, but Mommas face turns as dark as a stormcloud and she says Revel, Revel, all that is past, Revel your crazy, youl never grow up.

I hope not Maude, says Revel.

We sing Skip Tum Aloo and Saro Jane. Daddy has fell asleep by now and Revel gets up and gets Daddys guitar real gentle-like and hangs it back up where it goes. He kneels down by Daddy like he is praying and tuches his face. Dont nobody say a word. Then Revel stands up and puts on his hat and pulls on his gloves and tips up the bottle and drinks the rest of that whisky down. Ho Charly, he says. Cant ye stay the nigt, Revel? axes Momma, but uncle Revel says No Maude, Ive got to get on down the road now, and then he winks at her, and I am the onliest one besides Momma that sees it. In this wink they is a woman someplace waiting on him, and all of a sudden Oakley Fox pops up in my mind, this makes me so mad I like to of died. Oakley Fox is stupid, hes too nice. I stomped on one foot with the othern, I was that mad, and Revel grinned at me, and said, Thats the one to watch Maude, to Momma. Then he picked me up and hugged me to him. His beard and mustashe is scratchy he smelled wonderful like tobaccy and whisky and out-of-doors.

Ho Charly, he said.

And then he was gone.

So uncle Revel has come to call on Christmas Day I reckon, and has gone on his way agin, he has given us all them jawbreaker candys and also money, Momma says. She says thank God.

So I am wishing you a Merry Christmas Mrs. Brown and Mister Brown too down ther, it has been a lot happening, we are fine thogh and I remane your devoted,

Ivy Rowe.

Thomas Hardy

THOMAS HARDY (1840–1928), ENGLISH NOVELIST AND POET, lived during the transitional time from the Victorian age through World War I and its aftermath. His first poems were not published until 1898. After *Jude the Obscure* (1898), poetry became Hardy's preferred genre. Hardy reflects the philosophic disillusionment of those for whom the scientific discoveries and controversies of his age proved more shattering than illuminating. Darwinian determinism, a mechanistic universe devoid of meaning—these characteristic concepts find expression in the writings of Hardy.

The two Christmas poems that follow illustrate the questioning typical of Hardy's writing. In "Christmas: 1924," the four lines are clever enough to elicit a chuckle, despite the devastating cynicism of the piece. "The Oxen," a seasonal favorite of many, has a mellower tone. The poem illustrates Hardy's fascination with rural folk and their sometimes archaic speech patterns: "lonely barton by yonder coomb." The speaker describes a gathering in which an elder relates the folk belief that animals have the power of human speech on Christmas Eve. The reader is left reflecting whether a modern person can still believe such ancient Christmas lore.

Christmas: 1924

'Peace upon earth!' was said. We sing it,
And pay a million priests to bring it.
After two thousand years of mass
We've got as far as poison-gas.

The Oxen

Christmas Eve, and twelve of the clock.
'Now they are all on their knees,'
An elder said, as we sat in a flock,
By the embers in fireside ease.

We pictured the meek mild creatures, where
They dwelt in their strawy pen,
Nor did it occur to one of us there
To doubt they were kneeling then.

So fair a fancy few would weave
In these years! Yet, I feel
If someone said, on Christmas Eve,
'Come; see the oxen kneel

'In the lonely barton by yonder coomb,
Our childhood used to know,'
I should go with him in the gloom,
Hoping it might be so.

Edwin Arlington Robinson

EDWIN ARLINGTON ROBINSON (1869–1935), A NEW ENGLAND WRITER, is best known for his short poems. Robinson's poems are often didactic, revealing—sometimes in an ironic twist—a clear moral. The language of his poems is direct and plain, with themes often revealing an obsession with failure. Many of his best-known poems, including the often anthologized "Richard Cory" and "Miniver Cheevy," are portraits of failure.

"Karma" is typical of Robinson's work in its clear depiction of a simple, realistic situation, its focus on failure, and its irony. The title refers to the Hindu and Buddhist belief that a spiritual force that emerges from human actions determines a person's destiny in the next life. We see in the unnamed character a spiritual confusion and an ambivalence about his moral responsibility. In a sudden effort to appease his conscience, he makes a feeble attempt at atonement by giving to a street-corner Santa a "dime for Jesus who had died for men."

Karma

Christmas was in the air and all was well
With him, but for a few confusing flaws
In divers of God's images. Because
A friend of his would neither buy nor sell,
Was he to answer for the axe that fell?
He pondered; and the reason for it was,
Partly, a slowly freezing Santa Claus
Upon the corner, with his beard and bell.

Acknowledging an improvident surprise,
He magnified a fancy that he wished
The friend whom he had wrecked were here again.
Not sure of that, he found a compromise;
And from the fulness of his heart he fished
A dime for Jesus who had died for men.

Rainer Maria Rilke

Rainer Maria Rilke (1875–1926) is generally considered the greatest German lyric poet since Goethe. Born in Prague, the cosmopolitan Rilke lived twelve years in Paris, a period during which he wrote prolifically. He was also strongly influenced in his writing by time spent in Russia and Germany. Rilke was especially interested in human creativity and the relationship between art and life. In some ways, his writing is reminiscent of earlier romantic poets such as Shelley and Keats.

The two poems reprinted here, "Annunciation to Mary" and "Birth of Christ," are from his collection of poems, *The Life of the Virgin Mary*. Readers find in the "Annunciation to Mary" a vivid narrative in which human and divine traits merge in a captivating version of the Annunciation. The "Birth of Christ," in which the narrator addresses the newborn Christ, offers a fresh perspective by imagining the infant's reaction.

Annunciation to Mary

Not that an angel entered (mark this)
was she startled. Little as others start
when a ray of sun or the moon by night
busies itself about their room,
would she have been disturbed by the shape
in which an angel went;
she scarcely guessed that this sojourn
is irksome for angels. (O if we knew
how pure she was. Did not a hind, that,
recumbent, once espied her in the wood,
so lose itself in looking, that in it,
quite without pairing, the unicorn begot itself,
the creature of light, the pure creature—.)
Not that he entered, but that he,
the angel, so bent close to her
a youth's face that his gaze and that
with which she looked up struck together,
as though outside it were suddenly all empty
and what millions saw, did, bore,
were crowded into them: just she and he;
seeing and what is seen, eye and eye's delight
nowhere else save at this spot—: lo,
this is startling. And they were startled both.

Then the angel sang his melody.

Birth of Christ

Hadst thou not simplicity, how should
that happen to thee which now lights up the night?
See, the God who rumbled over nations
makes himself mild and in thee comes into the world.

Hadst thou imagined him greater?

What is greatness? Right through all measures
that he crosses goes his straight destiny.

Even a star has no such path,
see thou, these kings are great,

and they drag before thy lap

treasures that they hold to be the greatest,
and thou art perhaps astonished at this gift—:
but look into the folds of thy shawl,
how even now he has exceeded all.

All amber that one ships afar,
all ornament of gold and the aromatic spice
that spreads blurringly in the senses:
all this was of rapid brevity,
and who knows but one has regretted it.

But (thou wilt see): He brings joy.

James Agee

JAMES AGEE (1909–1955) PRODUCED ONE MEMORABLE NOVEL of life in his
native Tennessee (*A Death in the Family*), a documentary on sharecroppers
in the Depression, a preparatory school novella, and a number of fine film
scripts and reviews; he also worked as a reporter for *Time* magazine. Agee
is less well known as a poet. A gifted young writer, Agee died before his
talent could be fully realized. His posthumously published *Letters of James
Agee to Father Flye* reveal a sensitive and gifted young man, aware of the
perpetual struggle between good and evil, a rural Southerner trying to
find his moral way in the urban North. Like Flannery O'Connor, he had
an inherent sense of the world as a place different from what it ought to
be, though not without redeeming characteristics.

"Christmas 1945" is set just after the Second World War. This Nativity
scene in five stanzas questions whether we have progressed morally in one
thousand, nine hundred and forty-five years. The concluding line of each
stanza serves either to accent or to counterpoint the theme of the stanza.
This poem accents an individual response to the Nativity and questions
whether the idea of the rebirth of love at Christmas still has the power to
move us.

Christmas 1945

Once more, as in the ancient morning,
The slow beasts, the fierce new-born cry;
And, in the heart the dreadful warning:
  Is it I?

All each heart holds of love, resolves
Once more, today, in angry grief,
Enduring courage; and dissolves
  In unbelief.

The Magi's gifts are subtle bribes:
The shepherds worship clock and wage:
In rattling arms, roared diatribes,
  Wakes the new Age.

And even now, at the town gate,
Welcomed by many, fought by few,
The clangor grows, of Herod's hate
  In the morning's blue.

And, in the straw, they hear; and stay.
All that is brave and innocent,
All that is love, reborn today,
  Is its time spent?

Where shall He flee, whose force is naught?
Where lies that Egypt which sufficed
Of old, now that each man is wrought
  Herod, and Christ?

[Added in pencil: "Well, he is also Mary, Joseph, the angels, the shepherds, the Magi, & the beasts—Above all he is Mary & Joseph, whose responsibility it is to protect him."]

Lawrence Ferlinghetti

LAWRENCE FERLINGHETTI (B. 1919), A VERSATILE POET, novelist, playwright, and painter, is one of America's most widely read poets. As a publisher, Ferlinghetti brought out many innovative and controversial works; he also established San Francisco's City Lights Bookstore, a center of avant-garde American literature.

"Christ Climbed Down," from the collection of poems *A Coney Island of the Mind* (1958), is typical of Ferlinghetti's work in its simple language and clear images of everyday life. The poem depicts Christ rejecting the shoddiness and emptiness of contemporary celebrations of Christmas with their "pink plastic Christmas trees" and "intrepid Bible salesmen . . . in two-tone cadillacs." Despite the shallowness of the modern Christmas celebrations portrayed here, the poem is not one of unmitigated despair: the Christ in the poem is alive, capable of action, and intending to come again.

Christ Climbed Down

Christ climbed down
from His bare Tree
this year
and ran away to where
there were no rootless Christmas trees
hung with candycanes and breakable stars

Christ climbed down
from His bare Tree
this year
and ran away to where
there were no gilded Christmas trees
and no tinsel Christmas trees
and no tinfoil Christmas trees
and no pink plastic Christmas trees
and no gold Christmas trees
and no black Christmas trees
and no powderblue Christmas trees
hung with electric candles
and encircled by tin electric trains
and clever cornball relatives

Christ climbed down
from His bare Tree
this year
and ran away to where
no intrepid Bible salesmen
covered the territory
in two-tone cadillacs
and where no Sears Roebuck creches
complete with plastic babe in manger

arrived by parcel post
the babe by special delivery
and where no televised Wise Men
praised the Lord Calvert Whiskey

Christ climbed down
from His bare Tree
this year
and ran away to where
no fat handshaking stranger
in a red flannel suit
and a fake white beard
went around passing himself off
as some sort of North Pole saint
crossing the desert to Bethlehem
Pennsylvania
in a Volkswagon sled
drawn by rollicking Adirondack reindeer
with German names
and bearing sacks of Humble Gifts
from Saks Fifth Avenue
for everybody's imagined Christ child

Christ climbed down
from His bare Tree
this year
and ran away to where
no Bing Crosby carollers
groaned of a tight Christmas
and where no Radio City angels
iceskated wingless
thru a winter wonderland
into a jinglebell heaven
daily at 8:30
with Midnight Mass matinees

Christ climbed down
from His bare Tree
this year
and softly stole away into
some anonymous Mary's womb again
where in the darkest night

of everybody's anonymous soul
He awaits again
an unimaginable
and impossibly
Immaculate Reconception
the very craziest
of Second Comings

Richard Wilbur

PULITZER PRIZE–WINNING POET RICHARD WILBUR (b. 1921) was born in
New York and has been an English professor in several major American uni-
versities. Wilbur, who uses the traditional poetic forms, has been described
as an "occasional poet," attempting no system but instead writing on a variety of subjects in a variety of modes. Readers perceive a sacramental sense in
Wilbur's work in which ordinary things can take on extraordinary meanings.

In "A World without Objects is a Sensible Emptiness," Wilbur quotes
Thomas Traherne, a seventeenth-century British cleric and author, whose
poetry both glorifies the senses and frequently catalogues loosely linked
objects. In the poem, Wilbur enjoins the "camels of the spirit" searching
for Traherne's "sensible emptiness" to turn back to search instead for that
most significant object, the "supernova," the star of Bethlehem.

"A World without Objects
is a Sensible Emptiness"

    The tall camels of the spirit
  Steer for their deserts, passing the last groves loud
With the sawmill shrill of the locust, to the whole honey of the arid
    Sun. They are slow, proud,

    And move with a stilted stride
  To the land of sheer horizon, hunting Traherne's
Sensible emptiness, there where the brain's lantern-slide
    Revels in vast returns.

    O connoisseurs of thirst,
  Beasts of my soul who long to learn to drink
Of pure mirage, those prosperous islands are accurst
    That shimmer on the brink

Of absence; auras, lustres,
   And all shinings need to be shaped and borne.
Think of those painted saints, capped by the early masters
   With bright, jauntily-worn

   Aureate plates, or even
   Merry-go-round rings. Turn, O turn
From the fine sleights of the sand, from the long empty oven
   Where flames in flamings burn

   Back to the trees arrayed
   In bursts of glare, to the halo-dialing run
Of the country creeks, and the hills' bracken tiaras made
   Gold in the sunken sun,

   Wisely watch for the sight
   Of the supernova burgeoning over the barn,
Lampshine blurred in the steam of beasts, the spirit's right
   Oasis, light incarnate.

Lucille Clifton

LUCILLE CLIFTON (B. 1936) IS BEST KNOWN FOR HER CHILDREN'S FICTION
and her poetry. Her children's books, which reflect her concern for the
African-American family, are praised for their positive view of African-
American heritage and their caring depiction of nontraditional families in
urban settings. Her poetry is spare and idiomatic, yet also evocative, con-
juring up crystal images through lean forms. The poem printed here,
from *good woman: poems and a memoir 1969–1980*, is one of several poems
describing biblical characters.

mary   mary astonished by God

mary   mary astonished by God
on a straw bed circled by beasts
and an old husband. mary marinka
holy woman split by sanctified seed
into mother and mother for ever and ever
we pray for you sister woman shook by the
awe full affection of the saints.

Index of Authors and Titles